D0037116

A TOUCH OF FIRE

The feel of a hand closing around Daisy's wrist caused her heart to leap into her throat. She looked up into Tyler's deep brown eyes about the time he took the book from her hand.

"Don't sneak up behind me," she said. "You scared me nearly half to death."

Tyler replaced the book on the shelf and pulled her away from the bookshelves. "You don't have to work for your keep."

"I don't mind."

"I'd rather you didn't."

"All right," she snapped, throwing the dustcloth on the table. "I'm sorry I touched your books, your dust, or anything else that's yours. I promise I won't do it again." She started toward her corner.

"I didn't mean for you—"

"I know. You didn't mean to hurt my feelings, but you don't want anybody to do anything for you, to thank you, even to talk to you most of the time. I don't know why you bother to go on living. You're already dead inside." Daisy couldn't decide whether her tears were from anger or disappointment. Her wrist still burned where Tyler had touched her. It seemed incredible that such a gentle touch should be a rejection. It made her furious.

It also hurt. She'd had a lot of rejection in her life. It never got easier, but this was harder than all the rest.

SEVEN BRIDES
❧ LEIGH GREENWOOD ❧

DAISY

LEISURE BOOKS ▙ **NEW YORK CITY**

A LEISURE BOOK®

Published by

Dorchester Publishing Co., Inc.
276 Fifth Avenue
New York, NY 10001

Cover Art by John Ennis

The name "Leisure Books" and the stylized "L" with design are
trademarks of Dorchester Publishing Co., Inc.

Printed in the United States of America.

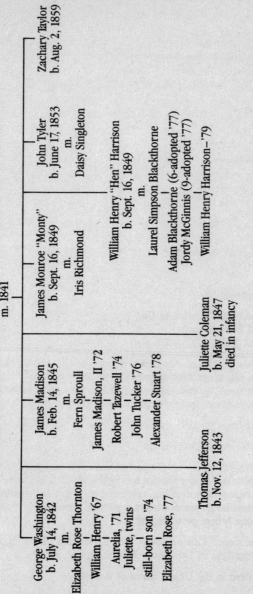

WILLIAM HENRY RANDOLPH (1816–1865) — AURELIA PINCKNEY COLEMAN (1823–1863)
m. 1841

George Washington
b. July 14, 1842
m.
Elizabeth Rose Thornton

William Henry '67
Aurelia, '71
Juliette, twins
still-born son '74
Elizabeth Rose, '77

Thomas Jefferson
b. Nov. 12, 1843

James Madison
b. Feb. 14, 1845
m.
Fern Sproull

James Madison, II '72
Robert Tazewell '74
John Tucker '76
Alexander Stuart '78

Juliette Coleman
b. May 21, 1847
died in infancy

James Monroe "Monty"
b. Sept. 16, 1849
m.
Iris Richmond

John Tyler
b. June 17, 1853
m.
Daisy Singleton

William Henry "Hen" Harrison
b. Sept. 16, 1849
m.
Laurel Simpson Blackthorne

Adam Blackthorne (6-adopted '77)
Jordy McGinnis (9-adopted '77)
William Henry Harrison—'79

Zachary Taylor
b. Aug. 2, 1859

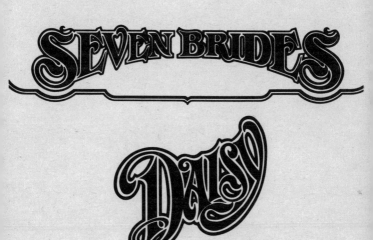

SEVEN BRIDES

DAISY

Prologue

Frank Storach was tired, cold, and mad as hell when he shoved his way into the small, crumbling adobe. He didn't take off his coat because the temperature inside was barely above freezing, but it was a welcome refuge from the blizzard raging outside. Two men looked up as he slammed the door behind him. One, a grizzled older man, stood watching the coffeepot on the stove. The second, a slim young man with a beardless face, dark blond hair, and cruel eyes, lounged on a bunk.

"What did you find?" the older man asked. His tone was nervous, anxious to please.

"I told you there was no need to go back." The younger man's manner was callous, almost challenging. "Couldn't nothing go wrong."

"The hell it couldn't!" Frank cursed, fury and exhaustion in his slate gray eyes. "I found the old man buried neatly in a grave. The girl was gone."

"What!" the older man exclaimed. "How could that be?"

The young man rolled up on his elbow, his eyes widening in surprise.

Frank grabbed the coffeepot and poured himself a cup. "Two men got her."

"If they didn't bury her with the old man, that means she's still alive," the older man said.

"You're real clever, Uncle Ed," Frank sneered. "That's what I figured, too, so I followed them."

"Did you finish her off?" the young man asked.

Frank swallowed his coffee and poured himself some more. "Some bastard started shooting at me just as I was about to plug her. I got a bullet into the other guy, though."

"Where did they go?" the young man asked. He sat up, faint interest flaring in his eyes.

"I don't know, Toby, but they're somewhere in those mountains. I tried to follow, but I lost them in the snow."

"I say we forget them," Ed said. His uneasiness had increased. "She didn't see you kill nobody."

"Somehow I think she'll be able to connect the old man's death and the bullet in her head to me," Frank replied, his voice heavy with sarcasm.

"The boss ain't going to like it," Ed said, nervously running his hand over his balding head.

"Then he shudda made sure she was away while we did the job. He didn't, and now we're in the soup."

"I ain't in nothing with nobody," Toby said. His cold eyes reminded Frank of a snake. The boy had no nerves. He would kill anybody. That was why Frank had hired him. But looking at him now, coiled, ready to strike, Frank wondered if being his cousin was enough to protect him from the boy's urge to kill.

"I was thinking about going into Bernalillo," Toby said. "I got a senorita over that way pining for me to come back."

"Nobody's going no place until that female is dead."

Chapter One

Tyler Randolph entered the cabin in a swirl of snow and blustery cold wind. He kicked the door closed behind him and dropped the armload of wood in a box against the wall. After hanging up his coat, he checked the fire in the stove. It was burning well. Wisps of steam had begun to curl on the surface of the water in a pot atop the stove. The cabin would soon be warm.

He walked over to the bed and stared down at the woman lying there. She couldn't have been more than 20. Her dark brown hair was badly scorched on one side of her head, soaked with blood on the other. Her skin had lost its color, making the freckles that dotted her cheeks all the more prominent. Her expression was blank, her jaw slack.

She moaned softly, but didn't wake. She had been unconscious for more than 24 hours.

She was the tallest woman he'd ever seen, fully six feet tall, but that appealed to him. He had never been fond of petite, fragile women. He liked a woman to be an armful. Yet despite her height, there was something childlike about her; she had a look of innocence about her that was childlike and fresh. He found it appealing. He supposed that accounted, at least in part, for his decision to bring her back to his cabin. He couldn't give himself a satisfactory reason for that decision except that a gut instinct told him she wouldn't be safe in Albuquerque. Three men had twice tried to kill her. He was certain they would try again.

Turning away from the bed, Tyler brought a table over to the bed. Then a chair. Next he poured some water into a basin, set it on the table, and got some strips of cloth and a tin of ointment from the shelf. Seating himself in the chair next to the bed, he began to clean her wounds.

She moaned again, louder this time, and rolled her head from side to side. He was afraid she might injure herself, so he held her head still. She fought him, her mouth trying to form half-syllables.

Tyler wiped some of the blood from the side of her face. It had dried hard. He cleaned her face and forehead. There was something compelling about this woman, something more than her size and innocence. Maybe it was the way she had lain lifeless under his touch, vulnerable and helpless. Maybe it was the fact that if he didn't take care of her, she could die.

She stopped trying to move her head. She kept trying to form words, but no sound came out of her mouth.

He soaked the blood from her hair until he was able to see where the bullet had grazed her skull, leaving a wound at least five inches long. It had burrowed under the skin and followed the curve of the skull before exiting. She would have a scar for the rest of her life, but she would live.

Her eyelids quivered. She seemed to be trying to form a word beginning with a *W*, Wh . . . Wh . . . Her eyelids moved, opened, then closed again.

"Everything's all right," Tyler said in a soothing voice. "You're safe. You can go back to sleep."

He covered the raw gash with a liberal coating of a whitish salve, then began wrapping the strips of cloth around her head.

She said *Daddy*. At least that was what it sounded like.

"Lie still. Don't try to talk," Tyler said. "Nothing is going to harm you now."

She tried to say something else, but he couldn't understand what it was. She seemed to tire. Her jaw grew slack. Her eyes opened wide and unseeing, then floated shut again.

She lay still.

Tyler finished bandaging her head and got to his feet. He couldn't help but wonder if he'd made a big mistake bringing her here. He didn't have time to nurse a female with a broken head, even if the snow was too deep for prospecting. He reached for his coat. He'd better cut some more wood. Once she regained consciousness, he wouldn't be able to leave her alone.

He paused. She would probably wake soon. He wouldn't tell her about her father just yet. He didn't think she was strong enough to withstand that kind of shock.

Daisy opened her eyes. She sensed she had been unconscious for a long time, yet her vision was startlingly clear. An oil lamp, the wick turned low, provided the only light in the cabin, but she could make out her surroundings with absolute certainty.

She didn't recognize anything around her. She was in a strange cabin. She had no idea where she was or how she had gotten here.

Somewhere deep in her subconscious she thought she remembered a rocking motion. She supposed that must have been a horseback ride. She couldn't explain as easily

15

the feeling of safety that kept panic at bay. Lying in a strange cabin, brought here by someone she didn't know, whose purpose she could only guess, she should have been frightened almost out of her mind.

She tried to remember where she had been, what had happened, how she got here, who brought her here and when, but her mind was blank.

The last thing she remembered was returning home. She couldn't remember where she had been, but she did know she was going home. She could see the house and all the familiar surroundings—it was cold, it was going to snow soon—but she couldn't remember anything else except a painful explosion. Something terrible must have happened, or she wouldn't be here.

Where was her father? Had he brought her here? Why wasn't he here now?

She attempted to sit up, but found she couldn't move. At first she thought she was tied, and panic flooded her mind. It took her several moments to realize she was wrapped tightly in a blanket. It kept her warm—the air in the cabin was bitterly cold—but it worried her that she couldn't move. She was completely helpless until someone came to unwrap her.

She turned her head to look around, but she couldn't see anyone. There was a bunk above her, but she couldn't tell if anyone was in it. She heard no sound of movement or breathing. She was alone in a strange cabin. Surely someone would come soon.

She tried to lift her head, but a blinding pain caused her to fall back against the pillow. The explosion she remembered must have something to do with the pain in her head, but she didn't remember falling.

She felt dizzy from thinking so hard. She felt the blackness threaten to engulf her once again. She fought it off. She would not lose consciousness again. She would lie still and wait patiently until her father returned. It must be her father. The possibility it wasn't caused her to feel faint.

She didn't have to wait long before she heard the door swing inward. She gasped in alarm when she saw the man who entered. He seemed bigger than any mortal. He had to bend down to come through the door. Covered to the knees by a snow-covered coat with a fur-lined hood, he seemed a giant. A thick growth of brown beard covered his face. Piercing brown eyes stared at her from under shaggy eyelashes dusted with snow. On his feet he wore the biggest pair of boots Daisy had ever seen.

Daisy was panic-stricken. She felt her heart beating violently in her chest.

"Who are you?" she demanded in a quavering voice. "What am I doing here? Where is my father?"

The man approached the bed. Daisy tried to draw back, but the blankets held her motionless. Her fear was so intense it was almost painful. What did he want? Why didn't he speak? What was he going to do to her? Why couldn't she move?

The man pulled off his gloves. A hand almost as large as his feet reached out toward her. Daisy felt as though her heart had stopped beating.

"What are you doing?" she asked, her voice a mere thread.

The man laid his cold hand on her forehead. "You're cool," he said. "Does your head still hurt?"

She hoped her eyes didn't show the extent of her fear. "Yes. Terribly. What happened?"

"You were shot."

Shot! That must have been the explosion she remembered, but she couldn't imagine why anybody would want to shoot her. Where was her father, and why wasn't he the one to explain all this to her? "You haven't answered my questions," Daisy reminded him. "Who are you, and why did you bring me here?"

"Lie still. You need plenty of rest. You almost died. We can talk when you're stronger."

"I'm strong enough now," Daisy insisted, but he was no longer looking at her.

"Do you feel okay?" he asked.

He wasn't talking to her. He was talking to someone in the upper bunk. It must be her father. Relief flooded through her. At least he was safe.

"I hurt like hell. If someone had to get shot because of that female, it ought to have been you. You're the one who insisted on bringing her here."

That wasn't her father's voice. Renewed tension gripped her like a vise. "Who are you talking to?" Daisy asked.

"My brother."

She was here with two men, one of them shot. The pain in her head was so intense her eyes could hardly focus. She couldn't think. She didn't understand anything. She just wished her father would come.

"What did he mean when he said he got shot because of some female?" Daisy asked. "Does he mean me?"

A young man hung his head over the edge of the bed. "Who else would I be talking about? You don't see any other females around here, do you?"

Daisy stared in disbelief. Even upside down, she could tell she was staring into the face of the most beautiful man she had ever seen, a virtual Adonis. He couldn't possibly be a brother to this man with the big feet. They were nothing alike.

"Who shot you?" Daisy asked.

"I don't know. He didn't introduce himself, but he had a gun pointed directly at you when I woke up."

"Woke up?" Daisy repeated, totally bewildered. "Where did it happen? When?" She felt the dizziness again. "I don't understand. I don't understand anything."

"Help me down," Adonis said to Big Feet. "I can't

18

talk to anybody upside down.''

"My brother and I found you with a bullet wound in your head,'' Big Feet said as he helped his brother into the chair next to the table. "We didn't know where to take you, so we brought you back with us.''

Adonis gave his brother a strange look as he pulled the blankets tight about him. "Are you crazy? We found her—''

"Wandering about the hills,'' his brother finished, cutting him off. "You couldn't answer our questions. Later you passed out.''

Daisy knew there was something the big man didn't want his brother to tell her. Some look or gesture had passed between them. A shaft of fear drove through her belly. What were they hiding from her?

Big Feet moved out of her range of vision. She could only hear his voice. It didn't sound threatening. It was very deep, very reassuring. He spoke in a slow, measured manner completely devoid of his brother's energy and animation, if Adonis was his brother. She still couldn't believe two such different men could be related.

"Where is my father?'' Daisy asked.

"We don't know,'' Big Feet answered. "We hoped you'd be able to tell us.''

Pain exploded in Daisy's head, and she remembered. She had been returning home when she heard a shot. She assumed it was hunters. They had been all over the hills this winter, even on her father's land. She had been surprised to see three horses at the house. Her father hated visitors and discouraged them from staying long. Still, she hadn't been alarmed when she rounded the corner to find herself face-to-face with a man she didn't know coming out of their house. That was when the pain exploded in her head.

She had been shot.

She could hardly take it in. It seemed incomprehensible.

Were the men merely robbers she had surprised? What had happened to her father? Had he been gone when the men came? If not, what had they done with him?

"Why didn't you take me home?" she asked. "I couldn't have wandered very far."

"We found you in the hills," the bearded man repeated. "We didn't know who you were."

"I'm Daisy Singleton. My father owns a ranch between Bernalillo and Albuquerque. Anybody could tell you that."

"We didn't see anybody to ask."

"You could have asked in town. Why did you bring me here?" Daisy heard her voice rising, tinged with hysteria. She struggled to remain as calm as possible.

Big Feet came back into view. His brown eyes looked at her with the intensity of an eagle picking out its prey. "I don't know who tried to kill you. I didn't know where I could safely leave you."

"Who are you? Where am I?" she asked again. She felt desperate for answers, for some reason for this terrifying nightmare.

"I'm Tyler Randolph," the man answered as he turned away. He went over to some shelves and began taking down various containers.

"I'm his brother, Zac," Adonis said. "We're on top of some damned mountain practically buried alive in snow."

She found the whole thing too fantastic to believe. But her head ached too abominably to try to make sense of it. Her father would be worried. He couldn't get along without her. Still, there was nothing she could do. Not until she was strong enough to go home. She refused to believe anything had happened to him. He was harsh, often unlovable, but he was all she had.

"You've got to send a message to my father. He'll be worried sick."

"We can't go anywhere," Tyler said, still focusing his

attention on his work. "There's a blizzard outside."

"That's absurd. We never have blizzards here."

"You're nine thousand feet up," Tyler explained. "There's more than three feet of snow outside the cabin, and it's coming down harder than ever."

"Was it snowing when you found me?"

"No, but it started soon after. We couldn't wander about looking for people we didn't know. With that gash in your head, you'd have been dead before morning."

Daisy started to lift her hand to her scalp, but the blankets kept her hands at her side.

"Let me out of these blankets," she said. "Is it a bad gash? Did I bleed a lot?"

"Like a stuck pig," Zac informed her. "Your hair was full of blood. At least the part that wasn't burned off."

"Burned off!" Daisy cried. "What do you mean my hair is burned off!" Instinctively she tried to touch her hair, to see for herself if this calamity were true, but her arms were pinned to her sides. She struggled to get out of the blankets, but she succeeded only in causing the pain to become so intense she nearly fainted.

"You needn't get yourself all worked up," Zac said. "It's already gone. You can't get it back."

"Let me loose," Daisy begged. "Please!"

"You need to stay wrapped up until the cabin is completely warm," Tyler said. He watched her from his position at the stove. Concern filled his eyes. His beard hid the rest of whatever he might be feeling.

"You might as well lie back," Zac advised. "Tyler's fixing dinner. You ought to be starved by now. We tried to feed you, but you slobbered it down your chin. Tyler had to wipe your face I don't know how many times."

Daisy didn't know why she'd ever thought Zac was good-looking. He was the most heartless and thoughtless man she'd ever met.

He subjected her to a speculative look. "If I were you,

21

I wouldn't be in a rush to look at myself. It's bound to throw you into a depression. I shouldn't think that would be good for anybody trying to get over being shot in the head.''

Daisy groaned.

"Your hair will grow back," Zac said encouragingly. "In a few years nobody will ever know."

Daisy thought she might die of mortification. But first she wanted to smash her fist into the face of this heartless young man who talked about her disfigurement as though it were of no consequence.

"Let me up," she moaned. "I've got to get up."

"She can have her arms out," Tyler said to Zac, "but she has to stay in bed."

"You can talk to me," Daisy said, practically shouting at him. "They're my arms."

"You're not in your right mind," Zac said. "You wouldn't know what to do with them."

"I could punch you in the face."

"See, I said you weren't in your right mind. Why should you want to hit me after I slept with you last night?"

Chapter Two

"You did what?" Daisy's voice was weak from shock.

"Tyler slept with you, too."

Daisy prayed the darkness would descend and swallow her again, but she remained agonizingly alert. She had heard every word and misunderstood none.

"I was afraid you might freeze to death," Tyler explained.

Daisy experienced a wave of relief that was dizzying, but at the moment she wasn't sure a nice quiet death wouldn't have been preferable to the madness that seemed to surround her. She knew her head wasn't working right, but surely a bullet wound couldn't account for all of this.

"Help me get my arms free," she said to Zac. Maybe if she could sit up, she wouldn't feel so overwhelmed.

"You got to promise not to get up. Tyler gets real ugly when people don't do like he wants."

"I just want to prop myself up a little so I can see. I feel helpless lying here trussed up like a mummy."

23

"Help her up," Tyler said.

Daisy didn't know why Tyler should be acting as if he were God, but a perfectly divine aroma had begun to drift into her part of the cabin. Her stomach started to rumble and saliva filled her mouth. She was starved.

Zac tugged at the blankets, but they wouldn't come loose. "Roll over. I can't get to the end."

"If I could roll over, I wouldn't need you," she replied, her mind still on the smell of the stew.

Zac acted as though he had never taken care of anyone in his entire life, but he finally managed to unwrap the blankets enough for Daisy to free her arms. She pulled herself up against the wall until she could sit up. Her head ached cruelly, but she was determined. She felt too much at a disadvantage lying flat on her back.

Tyler handed her a cup of coffee. It was hot, black, and loaded with sugar and dried milk. She nearly choked on it. Without saying a word, Tyler took the cup from her hands, diluted it with some hot water, and handed it back. He was treating her like a baby, but she swallowed her pride and accepted the coffee. It warmed her insides. Even with the blanket, she was aware of the cold.

"How long do you mean to keep me here?" she asked.

"Keep you here!" Zac echoed. "We haul you I don't know how many miles up a mountain through the worst blizzard I've ever seen, I get a bullet in my side that was supposed to go in your head, and you want to know how long we're going to keep you here. You can go right now for all I care."

Daisy decided she'd better rephrase her question. Bearded Big Feet at the stove wasn't going to talk, and Adonis seemed ready to take umbrage at half the things she said. She didn't think they would hurt her, but they were strangers. Despite being six feet tall, a cruel twist of fate she had suffered from her whole life, both men were even taller.

"How long do you think it will be before I'm able to travel?" she asked. "My father will be worried sick."

"I don't know," Zac said. He sounded slightly mollified. "You were out about twenty-four hours. You can't expect to be jaunting over a mountain in five minutes."

"But my father—"

"Your father will just have to worry," Tyler told her. "You're not well enough to travel."

He turned back. Clearly he had said all he intended to say. That infuriated Daisy. He was just like her father, passing out orders, expecting her to obey them without question. Well, she had to take it from her father, but not from him. A wave of dizziness washed over her, robbing her of the little strength she had. She'd tell him later, when she felt up to it.

She was sorry he had to be the one to find her. She was even more sorry he had had to carry her across a mountain and put her in his bed, but it wasn't her fault. There were dozens of people in Albuquerque he could have left her with. Anyone could have told him her best friend was Adora Cochrane, daughter of the richest man in Albuquerque. They'd have been happy to take care of her. They would have notified her father at once so he wouldn't worry.

"Where did you get shot?" she asked Zac.

"In the side."

"Is it bad?"

"It's bad enough."

She held out her cup. "Do you feel you can get me some more coffee?"

"I guess I could." Zac made a face when he got to his feet. He made an elaborate production of limping across the room and returning with her coffee. Daisy told herself he might not be shamming, but she couldn't quite believe it. It was impossible to tell how much was due to real

25

pain, how much was for her benefit. She decided Zac liked to be appreciated.

"Let me see your wound," Daisy said when Zac handed her the coffee. "I'm very good at taking care of cuts."

Zac recoiled. "No female is getting her hands on me."

"I just want to help. After all, you said it was my fault you got hurt."

"Time to eat," Tyler announced. "Zac, you come get your own. You," he said, clearly indicating Daisy, "stay where you are. I'll feed you."

Daisy threw back the blankets that had been covering her. "I feel much better now. I—"

"Stay where you are!"

The command pinned her to the bed as effectively as if he had used a hammer and nails. Daisy felt almost literally frozen in place. She couldn't help but draw back when he pulled up a chair and sat down next to the bed.

"You don't have to shout," she said.

"I didn't shout."

"Yes, you did." He hadn't, but it felt like it.

"You don't have to crawl into the corner. I'm not in the habit of violating girls."

"I'm not a girl," Daisy retorted, regaining some of her spunk. "I'm a woman. I turned twenty several months ago."

"It's the freckles that misled you," Zac observed helpfully. "They make her look like a gamine even if she is as tall as a giraffe."

Daisy decided it was a good thing Zac was so handsome. Otherwise someone would probably have throttled him years ago. She hated her freckles. Her mother had tried everything she could to get rid of them. All she succeeded in doing was to make Daisy even more sensitive.

"How long do I have to stay in bed?" she asked.

"Maybe you can get up for a little while tomorrow," Tyler said.

Daisy swallowed the contents of the spoon Tyler held out to her. She felt foolish being fed, but she was hungry, and the food was delicious.

"Can't I even feed myself?"

"No."

"I promise not to dribble or drool." Okay, so it wasn't very funny, but he didn't have to look at her as though she were a schoolgirl who had misbehaved. Didn't the man ever smile? He looked as if he'd taken something for constipation that hadn't worked.

He leaned closer, and she had to brace herself to keep from backing away. She felt uncomfortable being this close. She didn't fully trust him, and she resented his constantly telling her what to do. Besides, she hated his beard. It made him look like some kind of animal.

She expected him to smell. Every mountain man she'd ever met smelled worse than a refuse pile, but Tyler didn't. All she could smell was the wonderful aroma coming from the bowl in his hands. She noticed his hands. He had very big hands. He also had immaculately clean fingernails. He was, in fact, very well groomed. His clothes didn't look new, but they were clean.

Why would a man who lived by himself go to so much trouble to keep clean and neat?

A man who could cook anything that smelled as good as this stew would be unusual enough to do anything. She opened her mouth to accept the next bite. It was still too hot to really savor, but it was the best food she'd ever tasted.

"What is that?" she asked as soon as she had swallowed.

"Venison. I was looking to kill another deer when we found you."

It didn't taste like venison. It tasted much better.

27

"Wait until you taste the rest of his cooking," Zac said, his own stew now completely finished. "It's gruesome to watch. He dumps all kinds of stuff into the pot, but it tastes great."

Daisy accepted another spoonful. She didn't know about the seasonings, but it was good.

"You'll have to tell me how you do it," she said.

"Tyler never tells anybody about his recipes," Zac said. "Most of the time he won't even allow anybody around him when he's cooking."

"I hate having people in the kitchen, too," Daisy said. "It destroys my concentration."

"It doesn't bother Tyler's concentration," Zac informed her. "He just doesn't like people. He's been trying to get rid of me ever since I got here."

"Eat more and talk less," Tyler said.

Zac did, but Daisy decided it was because he was hungry, not because he was intimidated by Tyler.

She ate in silence. She spent most of the time trying to figure out these two brothers, if they were brothers. As far as she could see, all they had in common was height. Zac was more personable, but it was Tyler who aroused her curiosity. She wondered if he really did hate people. A lot of mountain men did.

She noticed he didn't look at her. She had just started to speculate on the reason why when she remembered Zac had said half her hair was gone, the rest matted with blood. Her hand went to her head. Her fingertips encountered the thick bandage. She felt mortified. He probably didn't look at her because he couldn't stand the sight. Just the thought of what she must look like almost killed her appetite, but Tyler kept spooning the rich stew into her mouth.

She was miserable. She'd never been a beauty. Her freckles and her size had ruined any hopes of that, but she'd always been attractive. She hated looking ugly in front of this man. He obviously begrudged the effort it had taken to save her and take care of her. She'd never seen a woman with singed hair, but the picture her imagination conjured up was pretty grim. She probably looked worse than a half-drowned buffalo calf.

Daisy consoled herself with the knowledge that she didn't find him attractive either. He had nice eyes and a noble forehead, but the beard ruined everything.

"Do you have a mirror?"

"You don't need one."

"I want to see what I look like."

He didn't answer, just fed her more stew. She tried again.

"I need to change my bandage. It's too tight."

"I'll do it."

"I can. I feel much better now."

"No."

He got up. She was so stunned at his point-blank refusal she almost failed to notice he was taking away the delicious stew. "I'm still hungry," she said.

"You've had enough."

Daisy could hardly believe her ears. Nobody had ever refused her food or told her she had had enough to eat.

"You only gave me a small bowl. I'm practically starved."

"You haven't eaten in more than twenty-four hours. You shouldn't eat too much at once."

"I should think I'm the best judge of when I've eaten too much."

He didn't turn back. He wasn't even going to discuss it with her. Obviously her opinion didn't matter. He was worse than her father. At least he'd never tried to starve her. She wanted to yell at this man, to give him a piece of her mind.

But even as Daisy opened her mouth, it struck her that while Tyler did expect her to do exactly what he wanted, he *was* taking care of her. He didn't expect her to do any work. He wouldn't let her when she tried. She'd never met a man who didn't expect a woman to do everything for him. He even took care of Zac.

This was new to Daisy. She'd have to think about it, but the hot food had made her feel sleepy. The thought of a nap was very inviting. She was very quickly losing the energy to do anything but let Tyler do what he was going to do anyway.

"What time is it?"

"About five in the afternoon," Tyler said. He poured some clear liquid from a little bottle into a pan of warm water. He reached for some long strips of cloth. "Lie very still," he said as he sat back down next to her. "This may hurt a little."

"What did you put in the water?" Daisy asked.

"Disinfectant."

Tyler held her head off the pillow as he unwound the bandage. Zac practically stuck his face in hers to get a look at her wound. "It doesn't look too bad to me," he observed. "It looked a whole lot worse yesterday."

It did hurt. Whatever he used as a disinfectant had a painful sting, but he seemed to be trying to be gentle. She wondered if he had ever been around a woman for more than five minutes. He certainly acted like a man unfamiliar with their ways.

She wondered if he cared to learn.

"Is it going to leave a scar?"

"Yes."

"A bad one?"

"You can cover it with your hair."

In two or three years when it grew back! She could imagine herself with half her hair singed to the scalp, the other part of her head covered with a huge, red scar. She almost burst into tears. She'd probably scare little children. No man would want to talk to her, much less marry her.

"I want to go home," she said, weighed down by all the calamities that seemed to be descending on her. Things would somehow be better if she could just get home, away from Adonis and his perfection, from Big Feet and his absolute certainty he knew what was right for her. She wasn't strong enough to stand up to them. At least not now.

"You can't go anywhere," Tyler informed her. "You're so weak you'd fall out of the saddle."

"Tyler had to ride with his arms around you all the way up the mountain or you'd be in some ravine right now," Zac told her.

"He had his arms around me?"

"How else was he supposed to keep you in the saddle? Tie you to the pommel?"

Daisy felt the color rise in her cheeks. She didn't know why, but knowing she had ridden in Tyler's arms, their bodies in prolonged intimate contact, caused her more embarrassment than Zac's remark about sleeping with her. That had shocked her, but she didn't quite believe it. This stunned her because it was the most obvious explanation of how they brought her to the cabin. She closed her eyes. She couldn't bear to look Tyler in the face.

"Somebody ought to sew your mouth shut," Tyler said to Zac.

"I don't understand—"

"Just get me that tin of ointment."

Daisy kept her eyes closed. She listened to Zac's halting footsteps as he crossed the room and came back.

The ointment was cool and soothing. It didn't smell very good, but she didn't care. She just hoped Tyler would finish quickly. She wanted to turn to the wall and never look him in the face again.

She didn't know why she should care what this man

thought of her. He was taciturn to the point of being rude. He acted as though taking care of her was a duty his conscience wouldn't let him shirk. The sooner she left, the better for both of them.

"Keep still. I need to rebandage your head."

Daisy opened her eyes and glared at him. "What are you going to do if I don't? Tie me to the bed?"

"If I have to."

Daisy decided he meant it. She sat still while he began to wind the fresh strips of cloth around her head. He kept on doing it until she felt certain she must look like a mummy.

"That's probably too thick, but I wanted to make sure it was thick enough to protect the wound," he said. "I'm not good at this. I don't get hurt much."

"He never gets hurt at all," Zac remarked, a slightly peevish tone to his voice. "I've been shot, fallen down a mountain, and barely escaped a rock slide getting here. He's never had so much as a skinned knuckle."

"Then why does he have a bandage on his hand?"

"He got it—"

"I got it when the killer came after you the second time," Tyler said.

Just when she was able to get angry at him, he made her feel guilty. "I'm sorry. I'll lie as still as a mouse."

"If you think mice are still, you ought to see this little critter that lives in the woodpile," Zac said. "He—"

"I don't think Miss Singleton wants to hear about mice," Tyler said. "Hike up that shirt so I can get a look at your side."

Blocking Zac's facile chatter and Tyler's gruff responses from her mind, Daisy wiggled down in the bed until she lay flat. Imagining what she looked like with yards of bandage wrapped around her head made her want to crawl under the covers and stay there. Besides, her head hurt, her body felt as if it weighed a ton, and she was tired and sleepy. She was also worried about her father and depressed about her hair. On top of that, she was obviously going to have to spend several days locked up in this cabin with Bearded Big Feet and his court jester. She thought she might go crazy.

The sound of the wind as it whistled through the trees, around the corner of the cabin, and under the eves told her she couldn't possibly leave. But surely the snow would melt quickly. It hardly ever snowed in the Rio Grande valley, even in the Sandia Mountains. When it did, it didn't stay long.

But one glance at the ice-encrusted windows told her that whatever it usually did, it was snowing hard outside with no sign of letting up.

Daisy closed her eyes. She was too tired to fight sleep anymore. She wanted to escape. Maybe this was all a bad dream. Maybe she'd wake up and find herself in her own bed in her own home, Bearded Big Feet just a nightmare.

But even as she slipped into the welcoming arms of sleep, she couldn't help wondering what he looked like behind that awful beard.

"You think she's playing possum?" Zac asked.

"She's asleep," Tyler replied, "even if she doesn't snore like you."

"I don't snore."

"Not when you're awake." Tyler put disinfectant on Zac's side. The boy winced.

"Take it easy. I'm not one of your damned mules."

"Daisy didn't complain, and her wound is worse than yours."

"Some brother you are, making me out to be worse than a girl."

Tyler turned his gaze toward the bed where Daisy slept. "Woman," he corrected. No girl could have aroused feelings of such intense physical desire in him. Not even freckles and a bandage could make him forget the softness of the body he held close to him all the way up the mountain. Even now the mere thought of it caused his body to harden.

"I suppose she is," Zac agreed, "especially if she's twenty like she says, but she's nothing like Laurel."

"Laurel has been a mother since she was seventeen. That ages a woman."

"Being Jordy's mother would age anyone," Zac said. "I don't know how Hen talked her into adopting him."

Tyler grinned. "He is a handful."

"A terror's what he is. You finished torturing me?"

Tyler chuckled softly. "I'd like to torture you, just for a few minutes, to see if you have any real guts behind all your foolishness."

"I've got as much guts as any of the rest of you," Zac retorted. "Just because I don't like cows, wandering about in the wilderness, or having crazy gunmen shoot me in the ribs doesn't mean I'm a coward. I just like cities better than the country."

"There's more danger there than in the country."

"What city has blizzards and mountains and people who shoot you and try to burn your house down over your head?"

"I don't get along well with people."

"That's because you don't know how to handle them. I do."

Tyler had to admit that was true. He'd never known how to get along with his own family. He didn't even try with strangers. Though it seemed a contradiction—one his brothers hadn't failed to point out more than once—he would happily give up wandering through the wilderness for his dream of owning his own hotels and running them exactly the way he wanted.

Tyler didn't hold it against Madison and Jeff that they had voted against selling some of the family's holdings to give him the money. Nobody could think of him as the right kind of person to manage a hotel. But neither did he intend to change his mind. He wanted the hotels for himself. As far as he was concerned, his family need not have anything to do with them.

With an inward sigh, Tyler took one last look at Zac's wound. "You might as well go to bed, too. It's going to hurt for a while, but it's fine."

"That's easy for you to say," Zac said, "but you don't have to climb into that bunk with your side hurting like sin every time you move."

Tyler took Zac by the collar and the seat of the pants and lifted him into the bunk with one powerful thrust.

"Good God!" Zac exclaimed. "Are you trying to kill me?"

"This way the hurt's over quickly."

"Jesus," Zac grumbled. "Being by yourself has made you crazy."

"Go to sleep before I throw you on the woodpile with your mouse."

Tyler picked up the basin and bandages and went over to the stove to clean up. The rest of the deer would be thawed soon. He needed to cut some more. But as he cleaned up, he was thinking more about Daisy than the task before him.

He hadn't told her about her father because he didn't think she was strong enough to take such a shock. The longer he waited, the harder it was going to be on her. He didn't know what to do with a grieving female, and it was certain Zac wouldn't be any help.

He never had known what to do with grief. He didn't feel any, ever. He could remember how much Hen suffered when their mother died. To Tyler it meant he had to take over the cooking. The news of his father's death had been a relief more than anything else.

Ever since that one day Tyler had hated his father.

He dreaded having to listen to her cry. It wasn't the crying so much as the feeling of helplessness. He wondered if she would become hysterical and scream and rant, or if she would sit in the corner and whimper quietly hour after hour. He almost preferred the screaming. At least that would be over soon.

Ever since that day he couldn't stand to hear anybody cry.

He remembered how Rose grieved when her baby was born dead. He wasn't sure she had ever really gotten over it, not even after Elizabeth Rose was born. Even George had had a rough time, and George could handle anything.

He couldn't ask Zac to tell her, though he was tempted. That rascal could do it without turning a hair. Maybe he would take Daisy to Laurel. She would know what to say. No, that was cowardly. As much as he dreaded doing it, it was his responsibility.

He was reaching for his coat to go out and bring in more wood when a scream turned him rigid.

Chapter Three

Daisy was sitting straight up in her bed, her hands clutching at her bandage, emitting scream after scream. Her head bumped against the slats of the bed above her.

"Hellfire!" Zac exclaimed, rising out of his bed. "It sounds like somebody's killing her."

Tyler crossed the room in less than a second. He pulled Daisy's hands down, but the screams continued without interruption. Acting on instinct alone, he pulled her to him, pressed her mouth against his chest, and closed his arms tightly around her.

The screams stopped immediately.

"Thank God!" Zac said, relief throbbing in his voice. "What do you think set her off?"

"He's dead!" Daisy moaned into Tyler's chest. "My father's dead."

Zac fell back on his bed. "She remembers."

Daisy began to cry in great, gusty sobs. She threw her arms around Tyler and held on tight. He had no idea what to do. He'd never held a woman in his arms except in moments of physical release.

This was nothing like that.

"What are you going to do with her?" Zac asked.

"I don't know. You got any suggestions?"

"Yeah, but it's too cold to run away."

That was the first thought that had come into Tyler's mind. The blizzard made that impossible, of course, not that he would have run anyway. The only decent thing to do was help her get over the worst of the shock.

He remembered the afternoon his own body shook with sobs. He also remembered the beating his father gave him because of it.

Daisy's body trembled as the heartrending sobs tore through her. Tyler felt warm tears soak through his shirt, and felt guilty he couldn't do anything but sit there holding her, waiting for her to cry herself out, waiting for her to tell him what to do.

Gradually he felt less awkward. His arms relaxed around her, and he actually held her rather than merely encircling her body with his arms like an iron hoop encircling barrel staves. It was a strange sensation.

After a minute he actually liked the warmth of her body in his arms, the feel of her bones through the coarse material of her dress. He didn't mind the roughness of the bandage against his cheek. For such a tall woman, she was surprisingly slender. The smell of the salve stung his nostrils, but he didn't mind that so much either.

"How long is she going to go on?" Zac asked.

"Ssshhh!" Tyler hissed. Just because he and Zac hadn't had any reason to mourn their parents was no reason other people shouldn't. From all he'd heard, that sort of thing affected females the most.

"Well, she doesn't look like she's going to stop."

"I'm going to stop right now," Daisy muttered into

Tyler's chest, her voice a tremulous thread. "I promise I won't cry another minute."

"I didn't mean you couldn't cry," Zac said, apparently not quite so insensitive that he didn't know when he had been callous. "I just wondered how long you were going to be too upset to sleep. Rose always says sleep's the best medicine."

"I don't know if I can sleep, but I won't keep you awake," Daisy promised. She started to cry again, then stopped abruptly. She wiped her eyes with her fists. She tried to sit up, her gaze questioning, when Tyler didn't release his hold on her. Flushing, Tyler immediately relaxed his arms. Much to his surprise he had felt more comfortable holding her. His arms felt empty now, and he was acutely aware of her nearness. Looking into her eyes made him nervous. He felt as if he ought to say something, do something, but he had no notion what.

"What happened?" she asked Tyler. "I only remember looking through the door and seeing my father lying on the floor." She nearly broke down again, but after a brief struggle, she seemed finally to have regained her composure.

"We don't know," he said, trying not to let her gaze unsettle him. No woman had ever been so close, had ever looked at him with large brown eyes swimming with unshed tears. He knew her weakness was only temporary, but that didn't lessen her need now. She had no one else to depend on, and he had failed. He had never felt so inadequate. "We heard the shots, but I thought it was hunters. We only went to investigate when I realized it was a gunshot, not rifle fire."

"Tell me what you saw," Daisy said, her voice stronger now.

"There wasn't much to see. The house was on fire, and both of you were inside. We pulled you both out, but your father was already dead."

39

"Is that all?"

"We saw hoofprints of three horses in the snow."

"You didn't go after them?"

"We had to take care of you. Besides, our mules could never overtake their horses. Do you have any idea who might have wanted to kill you and your father?"

"No. He didn't have an enemy in the world. We were too poor to have anything to steal."

"Did your father keep money in the house?"

"Daddy could never keep money anywhere. If he didn't spend it staying in hotels, he spent it looking for his lost gold mines." After she'd said it, she seemed to wish she hadn't. She was angry.

Zac opened his mouth to speak, but Tyler gave him a look that caused him to shut it again.

"Did he ever find any gold?" Tyler asked.

"A little now and then, but never enough to make it worthwhile. He wouldn't tell anybody where he went, but nobody wanted to know."

"I thought you said you had cattle."

"We do, but Daddy never had many cows to sell. Anything he got he could drink up in fine brandy in less than a month."

Rustlers, maybe, but Walter Singleton's operation was so small Tyler doubted any rustler would have a reason to kill him. Certainly not enough to corner him in his house and burn it over him.

"If rustlers keep stealing your cows, maybe you can get Tyler to look for your mine," Zac suggested.

"Only a fool would spend his life looking for lost gold mines," Daisy said with a vehemence that startled Tyler. "It ruined my father's life. He was always so sure he was on the verge of making a fabulous strike. He couldn't think of anything else, unless it was drinking brandy and telling people what he was going to do when he struck it rich.

40

"It killed my mother. She hated the desert. She hated the heat and the loneliness and the scorpions. She was raised pampered and spoiled, but she worked herself into an early grave for Daddy. She wouldn't hear a word against his gold mine." Daisy glared at Tyler. "Have you ever heard anything so ridiculous?"

Zac's gaze found Tyler during the awkward silence that followed, but neither of them responded to her question.

"Is your family from Bernalillo or Albuquerque?" Tyler asked.

"Neither. I don't have any relatives."

"Everybody has relatives," Zac said. "We've got loads of them all over back East."

"Well, I've probably got loads of them all over back East, too," Daisy mimicked, "but I wouldn't spend one minute under any of their roofs."

"Why?"

"None of your business."

"You don't have to get huffy. I don't want to know. I was just asking to be polite."

"You can take me to the Cochranes in Albuquerque," Daisy said. "Adora Cochrane is my very best friend."

"Good," Zac said, his feelings still hurt. "We'll see about getting you there as soon as there's a break in the snow."

"You needn't bother to accompany me. Just lend me one of your mules. Mr. Cochrane will see it's returned."

"Give you a mule!" Zac exclaimed. "We might as well give it to the first rustler who happens by."

Tyler stood up and pushed Zac back down on the bed. "You need your rest. All this talking has given you a fever."

"I don't have a fever."

"You'll have a broken head if you don't shut your mouth."

"Why are you such a sorehead?"

"It comes from being around you." Tyler turned to Daisy. "My brother and his wife are in Albuquerque just now. I'll take you to them."

"I don't want to go to your brother," Daisy objected. "I want to go to the Cochranes."

"I'll leave it up to Hen to decide if that's a good idea."

"You'll do what?"

"He's a much better judge of people than I am. He—"

"I'm perfectly capable of judging for myself," Daisy declared. "I insist you take me to the Cochranes."

"We're not going anywhere at the moment. There are a couple of problems—"

"Such as?"

"We'll talk about them later," Tyler said. "You've just had a terrible shock. You need to rest. Do you think you can sleep?"

"Not until you promise to take me to the Cochranes."

"Try."

"You're not going to promise, are you?"

"You're tired. We'll talk about it later."

She lay back, but Tyler suspected she wouldn't sleep, not now anyway. He didn't want to leave her, but she did need to rest. He could see the exhaustion in her eyes. Besides, he had to take care of the livestock and cut the meat. If he didn't get started, he'd be late with dinner.

"I've got some work to do outside," he told her. "If you need anything, ask Zac."

"I'd rather not."

"Yell if you want me."

"I'd rather not."

So she wanted to sulk. That was okay with him. He sat down to put on his heavy shoes. When he had laced them up, he put on some gloves with the fingertips cut out and his heavy sheepskin jacket with the hood. "I should be back in an hour. Try to get some sleep."

42

He opened the door and stepped out into the howling blizzard.

Try to get some sleep!

She had just remembered her father was dead and he wanted her to sleep. All she wanted to do was to go to the Cochranes. Yet he insisted upon taking her to more strangers who couldn't possibly understand her grief. She didn't exactly want people to pity her or shower her with sympathy, but a little understanding would help. Didn't these men have parents? Didn't they have any idea what it was like for her to lose the last of her family?

Her mind drifted to the many evenings when, as a little girl, she had sat in her father's lap as he read to her. Long after she could read for herself, she would sit entranced while he read, adding any details that struck his fancy. He had a way of making her forget the long weeks and months when he wasn't around.

Even after she grew up and he changed toward her, she tried to love him. She felt guilty when she couldn't. He was as unaware of the pain he caused her as he was incapable of changing.

She missed her mother even more. Harriet Singleton had been reared to expect comfort and servants, but she accepted the life her husband gave her because she loved him passionately. Daisy could remember the hours they had spent working together in the kitchen or trying to coax food from their rocky garden patch, the years of sharing dreams for her future. More than once she had watched her mother stare at her cracked and bleeding hands, tears pouring down her face. She had sworn that someday, somehow . . .

But it was too late now. They were both gone.

The tears started to roll again. She made no attempt to stop them. There was nobody to see her. She was alone. That thought only made her cry harder. She searched in her pockets for something to wipe her eyes but found nothing. She wiped them on the sheet. More tears poured forth. She let them roll down her cheeks. She leaned back against the pillow and propped herself up in the angle formed by the bedpost and the wall. A soft sob escaped her. She froze momentarily, fearful that Zac would hear her.

But no more sobs came. She sat in silence, the tears the only sign of her broken heart.

Tyler entered the cabin in a shower of snow. The wind tried to force its way in, but he closed it out with a negligent push of one shoulder. The sound of the slamming door wasn't very loud, but it reminded him he was no longer alone in the cabin. His gaze cut to the beds where Zac and Daisy slept.

Daisy sat propped up in the corner, sound asleep. As he drew closer, he could see the trails of tears that had dried on her cheeks.

She had cried herself to sleep.

He didn't know why that should make him feel so awful. She needed to cry. It would only be worse in the end if she didn't. But there was something about the loneliness of it that bothered him. He never minded being alone, but he sensed she did, that she would always prefer people and cities to isolation and wide-open spaces.

Yet she had been forced to mourn the loss of her only family in solitude, in virtual silence. Worse, neither he nor Zac understood. Worse still, they hadn't tried very hard.

He stood looking at her. She didn't look unattractive, just woebegone, but he doubted she'd appreciate the difference. Women put a lot of stock in looks, too much to his way of thinking. Hell, some of the best people he knew were ugly as sin. Besides, they were all going to get old and wrinkled in the end. It would be hardest on those who looked the prettiest when they were young.

He doubted Daisy felt that way, but she was lucky to be an only child. He'd suffered his whole life from having six brothers who were all better-looking than he was— Madison who'd steal your shirt and cut your heart out for a dollar; Zac who didn't care about anyone but himself; the twins who were so stunning they only had to walk down the street together to have women feel faint; Jeff whose sullen moods seemed to attract more women than they repelled; George who was everybody's idea of a perfect son. Rose had once told Tyler he had grown the beard so nobody could compare him to his brothers.

Rose always did see too much.

He wondered if Daisy thought he was ugly. Of course she did. She couldn't think otherwise with Zac around.

Tyler told himself to stop being foolish. Daisy disliked him too much to care what he looked like. She was even less interested in whether he was hiding behind his beard to escape comparison with his brothers. She'd probably forget him within a week after she left.

But he wouldn't forget her. He had never held any woman in his arms while she cried out her grief. He knew that had changed a part of him forever.

He took off his coat and gloves, unlaced his boots, poured a little hot water in a basin and diluted it with cold. On stocking feet, taking care to avoid any board he remembered squeaked, he tiptoed over to the bed. Kneeling down, he dipped a handkerchief in the water. Being as gentle as he could, he washed the tearstains from her cheeks.

She didn't move.

When he had finished, he slid her down until she lay flat in the bed. For a moment he thought she would wake, but she merely sighed and rolled into a ball. He pulled the covers over her and stepped back.

He felt guilty for having wanted to be rid of her. But

he and Zac were strangers, and there was nothing they could do for her. She probably wanted to get away from them. She had no reason to like them or to feel she could depend on them. When it came right down to it, she had no reason to trust them except that she was alone and vulnerable. She must be terrified.

Tyler decided he would have to think of some way to relieve her anxiety. It must be terrible to live in fear. He had never felt like that, but he imagined it must be terrible.

He wondered if she would be safe at the Cochranes'. He was not without his weakness for women, and he had no reason to believe Zac was a saint, but neither of them would consider taking advantage of a helpless female. He had heard of the Cochranes, but he didn't know them.

As he started to prepare dinner, he couldn't help but wonder what would happen to Daisy when he took her to town. She wouldn't want to depend on the hospitality of friends for long, and she had already said she wouldn't return to her relatives back East. Neither could she run that ranch by herself.

The only other solution was marriage.

But she couldn't find a decent husband looking like she did now. He didn't mean the freckles. They didn't bother him. In fact, they intrigued him. They were like snow-flakes: every one was different. They had a friendly look about them, as if they were announcing she was a woman with a sense of humor.

No, it was the scar, the singed hair, and her size that worried him. The only men who would marry her now were men who made virtual slaves out of their wives. He had seen such women during his wanderings over the Southwest, women worn out, overworked, and colorless, women who had given up on life.

Daisy deserved better than that. Not that it was his business to worry about who she married, but he couldn't help thinking about it. She was a gutsy woman. She had taken a tremendous shock without hysterics. He imagined she realized what she faced in the months ahead. Still, all she had done was cry silently so she wouldn't disturb Zac.

Daisy woke to the sound of hushed conversation and the muted clink and rattle of dinner preparations. She started to turn over when one of Zac's sentences emerged from the hush with startling clarity.

"Do you like her?"

"Why do you ask?" Tyler questioned.

"You're falling all over yourself to please her."

"I'm just trying to do the best I can for her while she's hurt. What else did you expect me to do? Once she goes to Albuquerque, I doubt I'll ever see her again."

Daisy heard the soft scraping of spoon against pot.

"Dinner's ready. Is she awake?"

"No. Want me to wake her?"

"No. Let her sleep."

He doesn't want to be bothered with me, Daisy thought. He'll be glad when I'm gone. That was okay. She'd be glad when she left. But somehow that didn't make her feel better, certainly not good enough to get up to eat. Giving in to the exhaustion that weighed her down, she drifted back to sleep.

Daisy came half awake. A comforting sense of warmth pervaded her whole being. She snuggled closer, her entire body luxuriating in the warmth. She turned over. But just as she was about to slip over the edge into oblivion, she realized the heat was coming from a virtual wall next to her. Still more than half asleep, Daisy became aware the wall was neither flat nor straight. It curved as her own body curved.

She froze. Zac was in the bed with her.

But even as the thought flashed through her mind, she

heard soft snoring coming from the bunk above her.

Tyler! It had to be.

What could she do? She couldn't lie here nestled against his back. Neither could she start screaming. Gradually the panic receded. He was only sleeping with her to keep her warm. That had to be it.

Daisy eased away from Tyler until her body was pressed hard against the log wall of the cabin. She kept telling herself he wouldn't do anything to harm her. But no matter how much she reassured herself, she couldn't sleep. It was all she could do to stay in the bed.

Daisy felt the cold gradually settle around her. That didn't bother her as much as the realization that something in her wanted to stay close to Tyler. His presence made her feel warm and loved, like when she was a little girl and her father let her sit on his lap. She had felt beautiful then.

But that wasn't all. Her body responded to Tyler's presence in a way that startled her. She detected a kind of warmth, or heat, that caused her muscles to become taut, her skin to feel extra sensitive, her stomach to flutter nervously. Her lips felt dry. She moistened them with the end of her tongue. Even her breasts felt funny, a kind of tingle running through them. She felt cold and hot at the same time.

All in all, she felt quite unlike herself.

It shouldn't have happened. She didn't want it to. Several minutes passed before the prickly sensations began to fade and die away. She made up her mind she wouldn't let it happen again.

Daisy woke up starving. She sat up in the bed, and pain shot through her head. She sank back to the pillow wondering what could have happened to make her head ache so. She put her hand to her head and encountered the heavy bandage.

Everything came rushing back.

For a moment, the shock of her father's death nearly overwhelmed her. It seemed unreal. But she remembered the shot, seeing him lying on the floor.

Once again tears welled up in her eyes and rolled down her cheeks. Once again she felt bereft, alone, abandoned. But she couldn't afford to give in to her grief. She was alone now. There was no one to take care of her but herself.

But she was not alone. Tyler was in her bed.

She turned her head, but Tyler wasn't there. Surely she couldn't have dreamed it. Nothing else in this horrible nightmare had been a dream. But there was no question about it, Tyler was not in her bed.

Taking care not to move too quickly, Daisy sat up. The fire had gone out, and the room was bitterly cold. She pulled the blankets tightly about her. Her head hurt, and the room spun before her eyes, but she could see Tyler asleep on the floor between the stove and the door. His feet hung off the thin mattress from the knees down. She was sleeping in his bed, and he was sleeping on her mattress.

She felt a pang of guilt. Tyler was silent, bossy, and taciturn, but he had taken care of her. He had held her while she cried. Despite what he said to Zac, she didn't believe he had done it just because she was sick. She wasn't experienced with men, but for a moment she had felt truly cared for. She thought she had sensed a reluctance to let her go. Maybe he didn't like her, but he wasn't as devoid of human compassion as he pretended.

Without warning, Tyler rolled into a sitting position, and Daisy found herself looking directly into his eyes.

Chapter Four

Daisy turned away almost immediately. His gaze was too direct, too disconcerting. Besides, she was convinced he had spent at least part of the night in her bed. The implied intimacy embarrassed her. It also had the same startling effect on her body she remembered from last night. She recognized the warmth of embarrassment as it flowed upward and threatened to flame in her face.

"When can I go home?" she asked. It wasn't what she meant to say. Those warm, brown eyes in that shaggy face raised conflicting emotions in her. She wanted to flee, yet she wanted to stay, to find out what he was really like behind that beard.

She had to do something. She couldn't just lie there with him looking at her. Tyler moved first. He threw back the covers and sat up. Daisy was relieved to discover he had slept fully clothed.

"You're too weak to travel."

"I don't feel weak."

Tyler folded his blankets with quick, practiced moves. "You may be able to walk around the cabin or even go a short way down the mountain, but you'd never survive a two-day trip in freezing temperatures."

"I can't stay here forever."

"You'll stay for the time being."

Her temper flared. Why must he always be telling her what to do? She felt stronger today, and he irritated her more.

Tyler folded the mattress and stacked blankets and mattress in the corner. He put a match to the fire he had laid in the stove and put a pot of water on to boil. He began slicing bacon and putting the thick slices into a heavy black pan.

"I ought to cook breakfast," she said.

"Stay where you are."

She did, but she felt guilty. Cooking was considered almost as much a part of being a woman as breasts and babies.

"You don't mind cooking?"

"He's crazy about it."

The sound of Zac's sleepy voice from the upper bunk helped ease the tension inside Daisy. As long as there was someone else awake in the cabin, she didn't feel the weight of their intimacy. She might not know either man well enough to trust him completely, but she trusted two more than one. Besides, she didn't have this startling reaction to Zac. The fire had taken the chill off the air in the cabin, but she snuggled deeper under the blankets.

"He's studied cooking all over the place," Zac continued, sounding bored with the subject. "Who else would have enough stuff in a prospector's cabin to stock a hotel restaurant?"

So he was a prospector, Daisy thought with mingled surprise and disgust. He seemed the type—beard, old clothes, and long silences. She didn't understand why a man who liked to cook would hide out in the mountains.

"My mother would have liked your kitchen," Daisy volunteered. "She was a good cook. She always complained she couldn't make anything taste as good as the cook they had when she was growing up."

"If your ma's family had a cook, what was she doing living in this godforsaken place?" Zac asked.

"I've often admired the Turkish practice of cutting the tongues out of their servants," Tyler remarked, giving Zac a threatening glare.

"I'm just asking what you're wondering," Zac said, clearly unperturbed.

"My mother was raised in very different circumstances," Daisy explained. "My father, too. It's just he was never good at handling money." Daisy resented having to admit her father's shortcomings, but defending him was pointless.

"You don't have to explain anything to Zac," Tyler said without turning away from his stove. "He's always been plagued by a rude tongue, no sense of decency, and a curiosity to know what's none of his business."

"If we're going to be locked up in this place, we've got to talk about something," Zac said. "Besides, it might explain why somebody wanted to kill her."

"I don't mind answering your questions," Daisy said, telling a bald lie. "You're kind to have taken so much trouble with me."

"That doesn't entitle us to be nosy."

"It damned well does," Zac contradicted. "Suppose that blasted killer is still after her? Our necks are in the same noose now."

"I'd be happy to put your neck in a noose," Tyler said. "It's probably the only way to still your tongue."

"Do you think they are? After me, I mean?" Daisy asked.

"Why not?" Zac said. "He's already come back once."

"It's impossible for anybody to have followed us," Tyler said. "It's been snowing for two days."

Daisy didn't feel that confident. The killer might not know where she was now, but he could be waiting for her to come out of the mountains. "Is that one of the problems about my going back to Albuquerque?"

Tyler nodded.

"What can your brother do?"

"Nobody will touch you if Hen's around," Zac said proudly. "He can shoot the eyes out of a snake and is twice as mean."

"Hen used to be a sheriff," Tyler explained. "He'll know what you ought to do. Now unless nobody's hungry, it's time to eat." He tossed some clothes onto Zac's bunk. "Get dressed before you come down. I doubt Miss Singleton wants her breakfast ruined by the sight of your skinny body."

"You're not such a wonderful sight yourself."

"People don't notice me much. But to hear you tell it, you're so gorgeous they can't stop gaping at you."

Daisy smiled at the banter between the two brothers. They apparently meant the awful things they said, but it didn't seem to bother either of them. Her father would have had apoplexy if she or her mother had ever spoken to him like that. He expected no criticism, only blind and instant obedience. She didn't understand the brothers' relationship, but she was drawn to it. It must take a special kind of bond, a special kind of belonging, to feel that free.

All her life she'd felt hemmed in by her father's domination and her mother's efforts to make her pretty enough to attract a husband. She was filled with things she was dying to say but had never had the courage. She listened to Tyler and Zac with envy. To feel this uninhibited must be heaven.

The smell of bacon scattered her thoughts and caused her mouth to water. It was unnerving to realize hunger of the body could be sharper than hunger of the soul. It could make her forget her thoughts of freedom.

It couldn't make her forget Tyler had slept with her to keep her warm, but had left her bed before dawn so she wouldn't know and be afraid of him. That completely changed the way she felt about him. True, Zac was unbelievably handsome, even mussed from sleep and unshaved. But time and time again she found her gaze wandering back to Tyler.

It wasn't his conversation. He hardly spoke. It wasn't his eyes or his broad forehead. His eyes were an ordinary brown, and he was careful to keep them devoid of emotion. His forehead was nice, but it was practically lost in a sea of rich brown hair. Her father's hair had been about the same shade, but he had no hair on his body. She could remember him sitting in the tub, his body white and soft.

She wondered if Tyler had hair on his chest. She wondered what it would look like, what it would feel like to touch. Would it be long and silky or did it form a thick, curly mat?

Daisy felt heat in her face. Involuntarily, her gaze cut to Tyler. He was looking at her. The heat in her cheeks became more intense. He couldn't know what she was thinking, but her blushes had to tell him she was thinking about him.

Tyler's gaze didn't alter. "You'd better put on your shoes," Tyler said. He walked over to the shelf by the door and picked up her shoes. They looked so small next to his boots. "You'll get splinters if you walk around barefooted."

"And I'll have to take them out," Zac said. "Tyler can't see anything that small without his glasses. That's why he's looking for gold-bearing rock. He can't see anything as small as gold dust."

Whipped between two emotional extremes, Daisy's gaze flew to Tyler. "You're prospecting for gold!"

"I have been for three years," he replied.

"The lost Indian mines?"

He nodded.

Daisy felt as if she'd had the breath knocked out of her. Here she was on the verge of becoming rhapsodic because Tyler had endangered his life for her, and he was a victim of gold fever just like her father.

She actually felt unwell. She dropped her gaze to the blanket covering her. She hadn't realized until now how much she had counted on his being a sensible, dependable man.

"If you don't feel like getting up, you can eat your breakfast in bed," Tyler offered.

"No, I'm all right," Daisy said, throwing off the covers. The cool air was a relief from the scorching heat of embarrassment and shock. She wouldn't have minded splinters. Anything to take her mind off her thoughts.

Daisy stared out the window at the huge snowflakes floating down to earth like pieces of heavenly confetti. The whole world seemed to be white—the ground, the trees, the mountains in the distance, even the air itself. The wind had finally stopped. Nothing moved now. She heard no sound, not even the snap and pop of pines and firs as they adjusted to the bitter cold. Only Tyler's footsteps in the snow showed evidence of any living creature outside the cabin.

Tyler was the reason she was staring out the window. She was trying to understand why learning he was searching for gold had devastated her so. She didn't know him well enough to be so strongly affected.

He was the first man who had ever made her feel she was special, not just someone to do the cooking and cleaning. He seemed unaffected by her size, her freckles, the dreadful bandage, or the danger that surrounded her. He had taken everything in stride, even her crying.

He had risked his life for her, continued to risk it, without expecting anything in return. That made her feel important. She had placed a great value on that importance. It made her feel worthy in a way nothing else ever had.

Only now it wasn't worth anything at all. She couldn't value the opinion of a man who would waste his life looking for gold. But even as she told herself to put Tyler out of her mind, that she didn't want to know anything more about him, have any more to do with him, doubts began to appear.

He had rescued her. He had taken her to his cabin knowing the killers were still after her, that they were likely to be after him as well. Maybe he wasn't as consumed by the search for gold as her father had been.

She told herself not to be a fool. She was probably reading too much into his acts of kindness. Any decent man would have done what he did. She'd better get herself down this mountain before her imagination got her into trouble.

She sighed deeply. "The weather's clearing," she said to Zac. "The sun might come out. Maybe I can leave tomorrow."

Tyler had left her alone with Zac for most of the morning. He was avoiding her. She was tempted to tell him he was jumping at shadows. She had no desire to live on this mountaintop with a taciturn, bearded prospector who had no money and did his best to appear unlikable.

"Why are you so anxious to leave?" Zac asked. "You'd think you were afraid of us."

"I'm not afraid, not anymore, but I'm sure your brother would like his bed back. And quite frankly, I'd feel better at home."

"But you don't have a home. It burned."

Stupid of her to forget. She still couldn't get used to it.

"I meant at my friend's home." The lump in her throat made the words difficult. "Besides, he can't be used to having a female about."

"He's not used to having anybody about."

Zac had been dealing cards all morning. Daisy wondered what a nearly grown man could find in cards to interest him so much.

"He was fit to be tied when I showed up."

"You don't stay here with him?"

"Good God, no. I've been at school, but I ran away."

"Why?" Daisy had always wanted to go to school. Her father had told her of the colleges for women that had begun to appear after the end of the War Between the States, but she had always known there was no chance she might actually go to one. Zac had been given that wonderful opportunity and he had thrown it away.

"It's boring. I hated it. I like action and excitement."

"Then why did you come here?"

"Because I'm hiding from George."

"Who's George?"

"My oldest brother. He fancies himself the head of the family," Zac said, aggrieved. "He let everybody else do what they wanted, but he sent me to college."

"Everybody else?"

"Yeah, I've got six brothers."

"Six!"

"Not a one of them went to college except Madison. You couldn't get Monty or Hen inside one with a gun. Maybe Jeff, but nobody else."

"Well, I think you're a great fool to run away. Just think of all you're missing."

"I know what I'm missing. That's why I left." Zac stopped dealing his cards and glared at her. "Why do you care?"

"I don't care, exactly, but I think you should have stayed at school."

Daisy turned back to the window to escape Zac's indignant gaze. She considered going for a walk just to get a few minutes to herself. She needed some privacy. She missed her own room. It was hard always being in the presence of someone else, especially when that someone wasn't the least bit pleased about it.

She looked out the window again. The sun hadn't come out, but it had stopped snowing. It was clear enough for her to see the snow was far too deep to even consider trying to make it home.

She turned and surveyed the cabin. It was smaller than her home had been. It had a wood floor but no loft and was dominated by the most elaborate cooking stove she had ever seen.

It was obvious the cabin was very well made. The doors and windows fitted without cracks. Everything looked smooth and square. Even the logs in the walls had been planed, the mud between them worked smooth until it gave the walls a finished look. The floorboards fitted without cracks, splits, or warping.

The cabin was surprisingly well furnished. In addition to the bed, there was a table with four chairs, a chest of drawers, and a large trunk. A double row of pegs lined the wall on either side of the door for coats, slickers, and hats. Shelves below that for shoes. The shelves covering the far side of the cabin contained books, a wide selection of tools, and the largest collection of ingredients, seasonings, and cooking utensils Daisy had ever seen.

She looked around, but she could see no sign a woman had ever lived in the cabin. It was without decoration.

There was plenty of room for her to mark off a small corner for herself.

"Does your brother have any cord or rope?"

Zac's reply was surly. "What do you want it for?"

"To put a curtain across that corner," she said, pointing to the window she had just left. "I need some privacy."

"I don't see why."

"I'll need it when I take a bath."

Zac's eyes widened. "I don't think Tyler will let you."

"Why not? He takes baths himself."

"How do you know?"

"Every prospector I ever met smelled worse than a cow yard. Your brother doesn't."

"Look for yourself," Zac said, pointing to the shelves on the wall between the door and the fireplace.

Daisy found several coils of rope. They were all too thick for her purposes, but she found nothing else. "Will you put some nails in the wall for me?"

"Not on your life. I don't want Tyler breaking my head."

"You think he won't like it?"

"Tyler never likes anybody messing with his things. I used to think he'd rather wear dirty clothes than have Rose get her hands on them."

"You keep talking about so many people," Daisy said, "that I hardly know what you're talking about."

"Rose is George's wife. She practically brought me up."

Daisy was of the opinion Rose hadn't done a very good job of it, but she thought it better not to say so.

"Where's your brother? Since you think he might disapprove, I'd better ask him."

"Stick your head out the door and yell," Zac said. "He shouldn't be too far away."

"He's probably busy," Daisy said. "I'll wait."

"If you wait for Tyler to stop working, you'll be a year older."

Daisy felt like telling Zac that working too much was better than wasting his morning playing with a deck of cards, but she didn't say so. She decided he wasn't used to being taken to task by a female, especially one he didn't know very well.

Frank entered the adobe. The wind whistled through cracks around the ill-fitted door. There were at least a dozen small piles of snow under the eves where the wind had driven the powdery flakes through the cracks.

"It's slacked off," Frank said. "I expect we can get up into those hills now."

"Hell, Frank," Ed cursed, "it's cold as a bear's butt out there." Ed wore all his clothes, yet he hovered next to the stove for warmth.

"No colder than it'll be in your grave if that female makes it to Albuquerque."

"Maybe they died in that blizzard," Toby said. He lay in his bunk, the covers up to his nose. "The whole damned mountain is covered in at least six feet of snow."

"I ain't taking no chances," Frank said. "She wasn't supposed to be alive after I shot her. Nobody was supposed to see the house before it burned. Then that man came back just as I was about to plug her. That female is shot full of luck."

"What are you going to do when you find her?" Ed asked.

"Kill her, dammit. What did you think?"

"And the two men?"

"They're mine," Toby said, the dullness leaving his eyes.

"Sure," Frank said. It made him nervous when Toby's eyes glowed. It usually meant he was itching to kill somebody.

"I don't like all this killing," Ed said uneasily.

"We don't got no choice," Frank said. "If we do this job right, people like that damned Regis Cochrane will start respecting us. If we don't, we're just some two-bit cowhands nobody wants anymore."

Daisy

*   *   *

Tyler returned along the high ridge. He paused to study the landscape through powerful binoculars, but he could detect no sign of human life. He had spent the morning looking for any indication the killers had followed them into the mountains. He hadn't found any, but he was still uneasy. A gut feeling told him any man who'd tried twice wasn't going to give up easily.

Now that the blizzard had stopped and the killers could travel, he would have to check again tomorrow. They could move quickly. They didn't have a wounded woman to worry about. He had to take Daisy to Albuquerque as soon as possible. If they were caught in the cabin, they'd be like sitting ducks.

His steps lagged as he approached the cabin. He'd stayed outside because he was uneasy around Daisy. If her blushes and hiding in the corner were any indication, she was just as uncomfortable around him.

Tyler paused to look back at the spectacular view before him, a series of mountain peaks covered with snow-laden trees. Against the stark white of the snow, the green of the firs and pines seemed even deeper and richer. There was a hazy look to the air, as though it might snow again any minute.

He looked up at the crest. The high pass was the only way down to Albuquerque for miles in either direction. It must be under a dozen feet of snow. It would be impossible to cross for days. The trip would be twice as long if they had to go around the mountain. If the snow melted all at once, every stream would be out of its banks. Like it or not, the wisest choice would be for Daisy to stay here until all danger of snow, cold, and flooding was past.

Tyler felt the tension in his chest tighten another notch. Every day the snow stayed on the ground brought him a day closer to the seventeenth of June, his twenty-sixth birthday. He had promised George he'd quit if he hadn't made a substantial strike by then. Just thinking about giving up caused the tension to twist a little tighter. He had to get back into the hills. He was close. He knew it. But there was no point in blaming Daisy or Zac for tying him down. He couldn't go prospecting now even if he were here by himself.

He had stayed outside for another reason. He wanted to escape the way Daisy looked at him ever since she heard about the gold. He had seen the shock and disgust in her eyes. He shouldn't have expected anything else. Nearly everybody reacted that way.

For as long as he could remember, he had been indifferent to people's opinions. That was the way he survived being the ugly Randolph, the one his father said was too tall and skinny to be a natural athlete like his brothers. It hadn't bothered him that his brothers thought his search for gold was crazy, so he couldn't understand why he should care what Daisy thought. But he did.

Well, he might as well stop. It was a waste of time. She would be gone in a few days. She didn't want anything to do with a man like him, and he had no desire for a permanent relationship with any woman. He might as well begin putting her out of his mind right now. But that was more easily said than done. Cursing his luck, he picked up a load of wood and headed for the cabin.

The wind blew the door out of his grasp. Daisy and Zac jumped like two people caught doing something they shouldn't.

Chapter Five

"She wants to put a lot of nails in the wall," Zac announced without preamble. "She's gotten modest all of a sudden."

Tyler closed the door and put his wood down before turning to Daisy. She looked upset. Not surprising, since nearly every word out of Zac's mouth seemed calculated to distress her.

"I just need two nails," she said.

"What for?"

"To hang a bunch of sheets," Zac explained.

"Concentrate on your cards and let me talk to Daisy," Tyler said, his temper beginning to rise.

Zac hunched a shoulder.

"Now what is this about hanging sheets?" Tyler asked.

Daisy blushed. Tyler hadn't realized how endearing a blush could be on a female with a handful of freckles scattered across her nose and cheeks. Not even the bandage could lessen its effect. He felt some of his irritation drain away and sympathy take its place. The closest he'd ever come to being in a similar situation was when Rose came to live with them on the ranch in Texas. He could still remember how out of place he felt even though Rose and George had done everything they could to make him feel it was his home as much as theirs.

This must be ten times as hard for Daisy.

"I need some privacy," she finally managed to blurt out. "I thought if I could hang some sheets across that corner . . ."

Tyler didn't know why he hadn't thought of it himself. It was ridiculous to expect a woman to feel comfortable with two strange men staring at her all the time. He guessed he'd have known that if he'd ever had a sister. Rose had a parlor just to get away from the family she loved. She said it didn't matter everybody invaded it all the time as long as she knew she could close the door when she needed to.

Tyler went to the shelf, picked up a hammer and two nails. "I'll hang a line across the end of the room. Do you think that'll be enough?"

"I don't need that much. Just enough space for a mattress."

"We can move the bunk to the back wall," Tyler said. He pushed the chest of drawers up against the shelves, then picked up the trunk and moved it across the room next to the chest of drawers. "Give me a hand with the bunk," he said to Zac.

"I'll break open my wound."

"Not if you bend at the knees rather than the waist."

"I can help," Daisy offered.

"You ought to be sitting down instead of standing up," Tyler said.

"But it's okay for me to be dragging furniture about the cabin," Zac complained.

Tyler was tempted to lock Zac outside. Nearly every

word out of the brat's mouth made Daisy feel worse about being here. He hadn't done a lot better himself, but he was trying. He lifted the bunk and practically dragged Zac across the floor behind it.

"If I'd known you wanted to race, I'd have told you to harness one of the mules," Zac said, staggering back to his chair, his hand clutched dramatically to his side.

"You're stubborn as one. I guess I got confused."

"I've a good mind to leave as soon as the snow melts."

"I'm counting on it," Tyler said. Choosing a spot behind the door, he drove a nail into the log wall. It would leave a hole, but he could fix that later. He drove a second nail across the room to match. "How many sheets do you think you'll need?"

"I'm sure two will be enough."

Tyler measured the distance in his mind. "Make it three." He pulled three sheets from a pile on one of the top shelves.

Daisy stooped down to pick up the mattress. Almost immediately Tyler saw her stagger and reach out to steady herself. He caught her before she fell. The effect of holding her was everything he'd spent the morning outside trying to avoid.

Daisy fit his arms perfectly, as if she'd been made just for him. She looked up at him with startled eyes, a little fear mingled with surprise, chagrin, and some of the hot excitement that rushed through him like a flash flood down a narrow canyon. He couldn't move.

Holding her didn't feel strange or uncomfortable anymore. It seemed natural, as natural as wanting to kiss her. He'd never really noticed her mouth before. Most likely it was like many other mouths, but it seemed special to him. Her lips were slightly apart, her expression one of tense expectation. Her eyes were open wide, their deep brown almost a mirror of his own.

Tyler felt himself lean forward, his arms drawing Daisy

closer. She watched him with a look of disbelief. As their lips grew closer, he felt her body tense.

"You going to lay her down or stand her up?" Zac asked. The sound of his voice broke the spell.

"I said you were too weak to be up," Tyler said as he helped Daisy to her feet. He felt a little shaken. When he tried to steer her toward the bed, she balked.

"It was just bending down so suddenly," she insisted. "I'll know better next time."

"Next time you need something, tell me or Zac." Acutely conscious that his arms were still around Daisy, Tyler guided her over to a chair at the table and made her sit down. For a change she didn't argue with him.

"I'm sorry to be so much trouble."

"It's not that. It's just Zac and I aren't used to taking care of a woman. We don't mind doing things. We just don't know what we ought to do."

And he didn't. At first he had looked on her as something to keep him from his work, but she had added a new dimension to his feeling for women. He recognized he would never again be satisfied with his old ways of thinking about them. He picked up the mattress and laid it in the corner. "Is that where you want it?"

"Yes."

He looked at the thin mattress. She couldn't possibly be comfortable on that. He got his own mattress from the bunk and put it beneath her mattress.

She looked at the bare boards that were all that was left of his bed. "What will you sleep on?"

"I'll fold up some blankets."

"But that will be hard."

"Not nearly as hard as sleeping on the ground. How do you want me to hang these sheets?"

Tyler knew Daisy didn't want him to do everything for her, so he let her help. She got to her feet slowly. He watched closely, but the dizziness didn't return. She picked up the top sheet from the pile on the table and unfolded it. He helped her adjust it so the hem barely brushed the floor. The other two sheets went into place just as easily.

He watched her breathe a sigh of relief. With a smile of satisfaction, she stepped behind the sheets and pulled the barrier closed. He knew she must feel better. The smile told him she did.

He felt cut off.

"You're not done yet," Zac said. "She wants a bath now."

Daisy decided then and there that one day Zac would die by torture.

She expected Tyler to refuse, but he didn't say a word. He simply opened the stove door and put in more wood. He was going to heat water for her bath!

"The creek's frozen. Where are you going to get that much water?" Zac asked.

"There's snow. Give me a hand."

"I don't want a bath."

"You will. Get moving."

He went outside and came back with a metal pot full of snow. He placed it on the stove and went out again. He was back in a moment with another. He didn't stop until he had six.

Daisy would have preferred to hide behind the curtain. It would have given her time to consider if Tyler's capitulation had anything to do with what had happened between them when she had her dizzy spell. But she couldn't let him prepare her bath and not lift a finger, not after all the work she had caused him.

"What can I do?" she asked when he came in carrying snow in a blanket.

"Help me get this in the pots," he said.

Daisy was amazed at the amount of snow it took to make water. She scooped load after load into the pots and almost immediately it melted into nothingness.

"I'm sorry. I didn't know a bath would be this much trouble."

"There's plenty of snow," Tyler said, and he disappeared outside.

Zac wasn't nearly so sanguine. "I hope you're not planning to do this every day."

She'd never been able to have a bath every day, not even when her father had taken her and her mother to stay in a hotel while he drank up his money.

The pots and tubs were finally full, the cabin hot from the heat required to warm so much water. Tyler brought in a large bathtub. "This is the only one I have."

The bath was twice as large as any Daisy had ever seen. No wonder Tyler had heated so much water. He pulled back the curtain and pushed the tub into Daisy's corner. He took down soap and a towel from the shelves.

"The water will be ready soon. Don't take off the bandage," he warned as he handed them to her.

"But my hair feels awful." It was the main reason she wanted a bath.

"You might reopen the wound."

"I'll be very careful."

"If you must wash it, I'll do it for you."

Daisy was immobilized in her tracks. The strange feelings that had teased her earlier assaulted every part of her body in a furious barrage of hot and cold flashes. Her stomach seemed to be trying to learn how to fly. Her tongue fluttered uselessly in her mouth, and her brain seemed to be spinning faster than a top.

"Zac can wash it if you'd prefer."

"I don't need to wash it today," Daisy said. She retreated behind her curtain.

But she had no sooner pulled the sheets together when Tyler said, "I think your water's hot."

Curls of steam had begun to swirl on the surface. It

reminded her of a thermal spring her father had once shown her. She dipped her finger into the water. It was a little too warm, but she knew it would cool rapidly. Tyler poured it into the tub for her.

"Thanks," she said. "Both of you are welcome to use my corner whenever you want a bath."

"I plan to wait until my side gets better," Zac said.

"I'll be happy to accept your offer," Tyler said. The look he gave her was innocent enough, but once again fireworks exploded inside her. She decided she would have to keep her distance until she figured out what was happening to her.

She pulled the sheets across the line and overlapped them to make certain there were no gaps. She started to unbutton her dress. Tyler was far too bossy, but he wasn't as bad as her father had been. He might even shape up if some woman were to take the time to work on him, but she wouldn't be that woman. After what she had endured, she wasn't about to marry a domineering man, especially one who was looking for gold.

Daisy stepped out of her dress and began to unbutton her chemise.

Of course now that she had a scar on one side of her head and burned hair on the other, she couldn't really expect anybody to marry her.

Daisy slipped the chemise over her shoulders and let it drop on top of the dress. The chill of the air in the cabin made her teeth chatter. She stepped into the bath.

The water was almost too hot. She eased one foot in, then gradually lowered the rest of her body into the tub. The water rose almost to the tops of her breasts.

For the first time in two days, she was able to relax. The men had been good to her—really they had, even if they hadn't been terribly gracious about it—but she needed the privacy of her little sanctuary. After all, when everything was said and done, Tyler and Zac were strangers—and men.

She sank down in the tub until her knees protruded and the water came up to her chin. For once she was thankful for Zac's big mouth. She doubted she could have summoned the courage to ask Tyler to let her have a bath. But now she knew he was willing, she intended to take one as often as possible.

"Psst!"

Zac's squeaking chair broke Tyler's concentration. "Sit still," he said without looking up. "I can't concentrate with you wiggling about."

"Psst!"

"Go back to your cards."

Zac got up and tiptoed across the room. Tyler opened his mouth to speak, but Zac's finger over his mouth silenced him. With his other finger, Zac pointed excitedly in the direction of Daisy's corner.

The sun had come out, its golden rays pouring through the window in Daisy's corner. Daisy was standing upright in the bath, her body cast into perfect silhouette. Tyler didn't pretend to be a connoisseur of the female form, but he had never seen a woman as perfectly shaped as Daisy.

The shock was like a fist to Tyler's solar plexus. He felt air enter his body in a gasp and leave in a long, shuddering moan.

The curve of Daisy's breasts, the line of her slender waist, the slope of her rounded bottom were as clear as if drawn in charcoal on a stark white background. He could almost see the color of her lips, feel the softness of her skin. He could see the triangle where her legs joined her body. Even her nipples were agonizingly clear. He felt as if he could reach out and touch them.

Tyler's body hardened painfully.

No woman had ever affected him like Daisy. He reminded himself he'd never had a woman in his cabin, certainly not one who was taking a bath, whose modesty was protected by nothing more than three sheets hanging on a rope.

He could sweep them aside with one flick of his hand.

Simultaneously he was assailed by a feeling of deep chagrin that he would even think of doing such a thing and by intense physical arousal at the thought of what Daisy must look like in the bath. He was helpless. He had been on this mountain too long.

As soon as he handed Daisy over to Hen, he had to find himself a woman.

He took several deep breaths, but it didn't help. Daisy turned in the light as she ran a cloth over her body to absorb the drops of water that clung to her skin. She might as well have been torturing Tyler. His entire body ached. His muscles bunched in rebellion.

Jerking himself up short, Tyler signaled for Zac to avert his gaze, but the boy continued to gape. Tyler grabbed his arm and spun him around.

"Bastard!" Zac exclaimed.

Tyler positioned himself between Zac and Daisy, but the wretched boy simply moved to one side. Infuriated, Tyler grabbed Zac by his shirtfront and jerked him off his feet. Walking across the room, he opened the door and threw him out into the snow.

"You damned crazy son of a bitch!" Zac shouted. "What's gotten into you?" Zac rose, covered from head to foot with snow.

Tyler stepped outside and closed the door behind him. The freezing air did nothing to cool his senses or his anger. "Who taught you to spy on a decent woman in her bath?"

"I wasn't spying. She was standing right in front of me."

"I suppose there was nothing to keep you from turning your head."

"I noticed you got a eyeful, too."

Tyler couldn't explain that he had felt paralyzed, incapable of moving. Zac wouldn't understand. He wasn't certain he did himself.

Zac brushed himself off and attempted to walk by Tyler.

"You're going to stay outside until she finishes taking her bath."

"Are you crazy? I'll freeze to death."

"Not with your blood as hot as it is." Tyler pushed Zac away from the door.

"What's gotten into you?" Zac demanded. He tried to pass Tyler and was repulsed again. "You're acting like she's your wife. You hardly know the woman."

"Even if she were a perfect stranger, she has the right to take a bath without being stared at. You might have been brought up in the brush country of south Texas, but you know that much."

"All right," Zac said, trying and failing to get around Tyler once more. "I'll sit with my nose in the corner and not look at anything but my toes until she's done."

"You'll stay out here," Tyler said. "I don't trust you."

"Go to hell! I'm not freezing my butt off to please your puritanical soul."

"You can wrap up in one of the horse blankets."

"You're crazy if you think I'll wrap up in anything worn by a mule."

When Tyler continued to block Zac's path, Zac swung at him. Tyler avoided the blow. Zac's spoiled behavior belied the fact he was as strong and physically capable as the rest of the Randolph brothers. Seconds later they were rolling in the snow, locked in fierce combat. It took several minutes, but Tyler finally subdued his younger brother.

"You wouldn't have pinned me if you weren't so much heavier," Zac managed to mutter between gasps for breath. Zac gave a heave, and he and Tyler were rolling in the snow once again.

"What on earth are you two doing?"

Neither man stopped until Tyler managed to pin Zac once more. Then Tyler looked up to see Daisy standing in the doorway of the cabin, her incredulous gaze on both of them.

"You'll both die of pneumonia."

Tyler felt like an idiot. All the heat that had fueled his lust and his anger evaporated, leaving him feeling cold and foolish.

"Just a friendly tussle," he said. "A man could go stir crazy sitting in that cabin day after day."

"I'll be damned if that's true," Zac said. "It's all because this pious bastard didn't want me—"

Tyler slammed Zac's head into the snow. "You agree with every word I say, or I'll turn your head into mush," he hissed.

"You're not strong enough," Zac grunted, struggling to break Tyler's hold.

"Promise," Tyler whispered, knowing that once Zac gave his word, he wouldn't break it.

"Okay, okay, I promise! Just let me up before you break my ribs. I'm already bleeding."

"It's your own fault," Tyler hissed.

"Hypocritical son of a bitch," Zac muttered rudely. "My turn will come. Just remember that."

"Your shirt's bloody," Daisy said when Zac entered the cabin.

"Thanks to my thoughtful brother," Zac said, casting Tyler a furious look.

"Sit down," Tyler ordered. "I'll take care of it."

"The hell you will!" Zac snapped. "I'll do it myself."

"I'll do it if you'll let me," Daisy said. "You'll never

be able to reach it yourself."

Tyler could see Zac start to refuse, think about it, then change his mind. "I'd be ever so grateful if you would," he said in that sweet, syrupy voice Tyler knew meant he was feeling diabolical. "Tyler's so rough."

"Here, sit down and take your shirt off."

"I don't think you ought," Tyler said.

"Why?" Daisy asked.

"Tyler thinks seeing me without my shirt might offend your modesty," Zac said. "Sorry, but I hadn't thought of that."

Tyler itched to get his fingers around Zac's throat. There was nobody on earth who could pull the wool over people's eyes like Zac when he really wanted to. Those big, dark brown eyes, that youthful, handsome face, that incredible smile would have charmed the devil.

Poor Daisy didn't have a chance.

Chapter Six

Tyler itched to toss Zac back into the snow. It didn't matter that Daisy wouldn't understand. At least she'd be safe. But he couldn't do that. The little beast was his brother. And when it came right down to it, he had been responsible for his wound.

Tyler gritted his teeth and put some water on to heat. Maybe he'd get it so hot it would scald the little weasel. He laid out some lint and strips of cloth for bandages. He glanced up as Zac removed his shirt. They really had made a mess of the wound. Blood was smeared all over his side.

"Does it hurt?" Daisy asked.

"Not much," Zac replied, looking as though the pain was just about to kill him.

"I'll try to be very careful," Daisy said, "but it's bound to hurt some."

Tyler decided Zac had a real future on the stage. His look of martyrdom was perfect. In fact, if he hadn't known his brother so well, he'd have sworn the rascal was the bravest man he knew.

"It's not as bad as I thought," Daisy said. "You smeared the blood all over when you were tussling."

Zac winced. It was a scarcely noticeable movement, an almost imperceptible sound. It was masterful.

Daisy looked stricken to have caused him so much pain. "I'm sorry. Are you sure you don't want Tyler to do it?"

"Please," Zac said to Daisy, his eyes huge and pleading, "I want you to do it."

Tyler itched to take the bandages from Daisy and wrap Zac from head to foot. "As soon as you've finished, I'll put him to bed," he said to Daisy.

"I don't want to go to bed," Zac protested.

"I think it'll be enough if he sits quietly and plays with his cards," Daisy said.

Zac looked at Tyler with a triumphant grin.

Tyler unclenched his fists, rinsed the bloody clothes, and threw out the dirty water.

"How's that?" Daisy asked when she had finished the bandages.

"Perfect," Zac said, smiling up at her.

"Good. Now I suggest you both take a nap," Tyler said. "Neither one of you is fully recovered. You'll need plenty of rest if you expect to ride out of here in a couple of days."

"You think the snow will have gone by then?" Daisy asked.

"It can either be gone, or it can snow several more feet. I don't know which," Tyler admitted. "But you can't leave if you're not strong enough. It's a long ride over the mountain. It's even longer if we have to go around. And you've been up too long. You may feel stronger, but you can never be too careful with a head wound."

Daisy didn't argue, but Zac showed all the signs of not being nearly so agreeable.

"If you have a good nap, you might feel up to a nice roast for dinner," he said, hoping to bribe Zac into being more cooperative. "And maybe something rich for dessert." He paused. "If not, I'm afraid it'll be clear soup again." Tyler knew if Zac had one weakness, it was for sweets.

"Chocolate?" Zac asked.

Tyler nodded.

Zac climbed up into the bunk without a protest.

"Can you really cook all that up here?" Daisy asked.

"Sure," Zac said. "He gets someone to bring him milk, eggs, and butter once a week. That's in addition to everything else he gets. He wouldn't stay up here if he didn't."

"I thought you were a prospector," Daisy said.

Tyler couldn't tell whether she was merely surprised or whether she thought he was crazy. Many people did. "Prospectors have to eat."

"I never knew one who made desserts."

"Go to sleep before he changes his mind," Zac said.

"Would you cook a special dish for me if I asked?"

"If I know how. What is it?"

"I'm not sure. If I only get one, I want to make sure it's what I want most."

"You can have more than one."

"I can't go to sleep with all this talking," Zac announced.

"I'll tell you tonight," Daisy said, then disappeared behind her curtain.

Tyler felt unaccountably weak. He sat down, but that didn't correct the feeling. Maybe he was coming down with a fever. It was just the thing to happen with him going in and out of the cabin in all this cold. Wrestling in the snow hadn't helped matters either. He probably ought to lie down as well, but he knew he couldn't sleep.

Daisy couldn't be falling for Zac, could she?

Tyler felt ashamed of himself for even thinking such a thing. It was none of his business what Daisy did. Besides, Zac was too much in love with himself to love anybody else. Tyler had thought Daisy knew that, but the way she acted made him wonder. He knew it was unwise to underestimate the power of physical beauty. He had seen intelligent men ruin themselves over beautiful women. There was no reason to think a woman wouldn't do the same for a beautiful man.

And Zac was beautiful.

Tyler wasn't. He had felt that difference his whole life. His father had once introduced him to some guests by saying, "This is my ugly son. He doesn't look like his brothers." There were times when Tyler didn't even feel like a Randolph. From birth he'd been lanky and angular. His brown hair and brown eyes lacked the dramatic impact of his brothers' blond fairness or black swarthiness. Even though he was the tallest, he seemed to slip a little farther into the background with every passing year.

Tyler hated to see Daisy blinded by physical beauty, but what could he do? He couldn't say, *You can't fall in love with my brother because he's not in love with you*, or *You can't fall in love with Zac because he'll hurt you.*

If Daisy had to fall in love with anybody, she ought to fall in love with him. At least he liked her. Tyler nearly dropped the egg he had just picked up. What was wrong with him? He was jealous of his own brother over a female he hadn't even set eyes on until two days ago. He must have cabin fever. Some kind of fever. Never had he been so obsessed with a woman.

Tyler cracked the egg. He probably ought to leave Zac and Daisy to take care of themselves. They really weren't sick anymore. He could come back when the snow melted. He didn't need to be locked up with Daisy, unable to think of anything except her body silhouetted against the sheets.

He nearly dropped another egg.

Damn, he really was coming apart. First chance he got, he'd go hunting, even if there wasn't a deer between here and Colorado. He had to get out of the cabin. It was beginning to seem like his life depended on it.

Daisy didn't sleep long. "Do you have any clothes I could wear?" she asked Tyler less than 30 minutes later.

He didn't know what she was talking about.

"I need to wash my clothes," she explained, "and I don't have anything to wear while they dry."

He smiled at the picture in his mind of her in his clothes. "Nothing that'll fit."

"I know, but I don't plan to parade through the streets of Albuquerque."

He thought of offering her some of Zac's clothes, but they wouldn't fit much better. Besides, if she had to wear anybody's clothes, he wanted them to be his.

He didn't understand that. He didn't even want to try.

He found a shirt and an old pair of pants that were too small for him. "You'll need something to keep them up," he said.

Daisy held the shirt up in front of her. It fell to her knees. "I could use it for a nightgown."

He hadn't thought about that. She shouldn't sleep in her clothes. He'd offer her one of the white linen shirts he wore when he went to town.

He could hear her as she moved about behind the curtain. The sun was still out. He could see her outline. She would be changing her clothes any minute now. He glanced over at Zac, but the boy was asleep with his face to the wall. But Tyler wasn't certain he could make himself turn away.

Glancing over the shelves, his gaze fell on two thin

blankets he used in the warmer months. He took them down.

"I've been thinking you need something heavier than sheets," he said to Daisy.

She stuck her head out. "Why?"

"It'll help block out some of the noise of us moving about."

"You don't keep me awake."

"Just in case," Tyler said as he hung the first blanket.

"Won't you need them?"

"No." He hung the second and stepped back. Perfect. Daisy came to stand next to him. She looked first at the curtain, then at him. It was obvious she didn't believe his explanation. When she pulled the curtain back, her gaze was immediately drawn to the sunlight streaming in the window. She blushed crimson. She knew.

"Thank you."

"You'd better get started on your clothes if they're going to be dry by dinner," Tyler said. "I've never sat down to the table with a lady in pants." He turned back to the stove, but he couldn't keep his mind on his work. He kept thinking about Daisy—nude, wearing his clothes.

The thought sent chills of excitement racing through his body. They were his clothes. Her body would be brushing up against material that had brushed against his body. Her legs would be in trousers that had encased his legs. He thought of the rough material about to be pressed against the triangle between her legs, and his body exploded with lust.

He could almost feel the silky smoothness of her body as she removed her own clothes. They were soft, supple, clinging, worn thin with use. For the second time in the same day, he imagined the dress slipping from her body to fall into a pool at her feet.

Now she was unbuttoning the chemise. The material was so thin it was almost transparent. Her fingers traveled slowly down the middle of her body, across her breasts, down her stomach to her abdomen. One side of the chemise would fall open, exposing a small, round, perfect breast. It stood out from her body, young and firm, the nipple in a circle of rosy flesh, soft and pliant to the touch.

Warm to the touch.

Sweet to the taste.

She would slip the chemise off her shoulders, one at a time. Ivory-colored, silky smooth shoulders. He could imagine how it would feel to run his fingers over the gentle curve, to rest his head in the hollow. He could hear her soft breathing, feel the slight rise and fall of her chest, of her breasts.

She had slipped the chemise over her second shoulder, down to her waist, fully revealing her breasts. The silhouette of hours before was clear in his mind, only now it was drawn in vibrant color. He imagined Daisy's flawless female form, her perfect breasts lifted and separated in their youthful perfection, their roundness accentuated by the circle of her nipples. He could almost reach out and touch her slim body as it tapered at her waist, then flared in rounded hips.

Shivers caused his entire body to tremble. He tried to refocus his thoughts on the meal he was preparing, but it was useless. He might have imagined the almost inaudible whisper of her chemise as it glided over her skin or the soft sound as it fell to the floor, but he knew she was naked. His entire body trembled with a hunger that shook him like an aspen in the wind.

Gripping the spoon, Tyler stirred vigorously. He refused to think of her naked beauty. He refused to think of the white softness of her thighs, of the seductive depression of her navel. He refused to let himself think of losing himself in her softness or of the ecstasy to be found in her arms.

He beat the thick chocolate mixture until his arm ached.

But his need was more powerful than his good intentions. As the speed of his beating slowed, the power and vividness of his imagination increased.

He imagined Daisy lying next to him, her body receptive. Lovingly he explored every inch of her. From head to toe, he tasted, touched, and smelled until his vision became misty with passion. Yielding to the desire that had built from a tiny kernel of want to a thundering crescendo of need, he sank into her, releasing the pent-up desire that had turned his body into an inferno.

He took a deep, slow breath to calm himself. He poured the batter into pans, put them into the oven. Satisfied the heat would hold for the next 30 minutes, Tyler grabbed his coat and headed outside. It didn't matter that he had nothing to do. Just standing around watching the snow melt was safer than remaining inside the cabin. Maybe the frigid air would cool him off.

He laughed to himself, a humorless chuckle. He could take Daisy home right now. All he had to do was lie down and roll. He was hot enough to melt every flake of snow between here and Albuquerque.

Tyler couldn't sleep, and it had nothing to do with the bare boards that were his bed. The blankets muffled the sound, but he was positive he heard Daisy crying. He heard it again. A tiny sob choked off before it could grow to its natural fullness. He got out of bed and padded across the floor on silent feet. He slept in all his clothes except for his shoes. "Are you all right?" he whispered, hoping not to wake Zac.

She didn't answer.

"I know you're awake. Is there anything I can do?"

"No."

The word seemed choked, as if it were all she could do to get out the single syllable. He waited. The corner was her refuge. She probably wouldn't want him invading it, but he couldn't ignore her. He hesitated on the verge of pulling back the curtain. What could he do? He felt her sadness, her sense of isolation. That he did understand. He had felt alone all his life.

Then he heard it again, only there was no mistake this time. She was crying in earnest.

"I'm coming in," he said, then paused to give her a minute to cover herself if necessary. But he heard no rustling of covers, no scrambling about in the bed, just the steady sound of brokenhearted sobbing. He couldn't wait any longer. He pulled back the curtain.

Bright moonlight from the unshuttered window illuminated the bare cabin floor. Daisy sat in the center of her bed, just out of the aura of moonlight, her pale face streaked with tears. She wore the shirt he had given her. Somehow it made her look even younger and more vulnerable, like a child playing dress-up. Only she had to grow up now because she had no one but herself.

"Is it your father?" Tyler asked.

She nodded.

What could he do? He couldn't bring the man back. He couldn't make her miss him less. He couldn't even tell her she wasn't alone in the world. He knelt down in front of her. He was intruding. She must want him to leave. He would feel uncomfortable if anyone were to see him crying.

Yet she didn't draw away. She twisted her hands in her lap, then put them to her mouth as though to stop the sound of her sobs. To no avail. She brushed away some tears. Not knowing what else to do, Tyler sat down on the mattress next to her and put his arm around her.

Daisy sat rigid in the curve of his arms. He half expected her to pull away at any moment. He remembered that George used to hold Rose when she was upset. After she lost the baby, he sometimes held her for hours, not talking, not doing anything but holding her.

So he put his other arm around Daisy and sat still, just holding her. He felt her muscles quiver. Then the rigidity collapsed, and she leaned against him. Her sobs had become less noisy. She seemed to be more calm. She put her arms around him and rested all of her weight against him.

Tyler had the oddest feeling he was going to explode. Then just as oddly, the feeling went away, leaving him more relaxed than he had been at any time since he pulled Daisy from the burning house. He felt his arms tighten ever so slightly around her, and an odd kind of peacefulness came over him.

He found it hard to believe this was happening to him. Here he was in an isolated cabin on the backside of a mountain covered with ten feet of snow, sitting on a woman's bed, holding her in his arms while she cried her heart out.

Yet he was content to remain exactly where he was. A sense of comfort, of well-being flowed through him. It couldn't have come from Daisy. She still whimpered softly, sniffed occasionally. It couldn't have come from him. His entire equilibrium had been destroyed. Yet there it was. And God bless his soul, he was enjoying it.

Maybe he was going crazy. It happened to prospectors sometimes. People said it was all the solitude, the obsession with gold. You started liking your animals better than people. You liked talking to yourself better than to other folks. You found rocks and gnarled trees more beautiful than the ordered streets of towns and cities. You felt more comfortable in a rickety cabin than a well-furnished home.

He didn't think he had progressed that far, but everything in his life was out of kilter. Besides, it was well known that crazy people insisted they weren't crazy, that it was everybody else who was behaving in a peculiar fashion.

Maybe that was a good sign. He was behaving oddly, and he knew it.

Daisy gave a rather loud sniff and pulled away. "I'm better now," she said.

"You sure?" He was reluctant to release her. Crazy felt pretty good. He wasn't sure he wanted to return to sanity. As he recalled, he'd been pretty miserable the last couple of days.

"Yes. It just gets to me sometimes. My father and I didn't get along very well, but that seems unimportant now." She sniffed, wiped her eyes, and sat up. She didn't seem the least bit uncomfortable with his nearness. She seemed to take it for granted.

But Tyler could sense a difference in her sadness this time. She wasn't crying from shock, hurt, or pain, but from a deep sense of loss. "This afternoon you cried for your father," he said. "You're crying for yourself now. Why?"

"You're wrong."

"No, I'm not." He'd only cried for himself once, but he remembered what it was like. He leaned back far enough from Daisy to look into her eyes. "You didn't like your father, did you?"

"Of course I liked him."

He pulled her close again. "I hated my pa."

"Why?" She pushed him away so she could look him in the eye.

"Because he was a cruel, vicious man. Now tell me why you disliked your father."

Chapter Seven

Daisy felt a lifetime of pretense collapse. For the first time, she felt able to face her feelings for her father squarely and honestly. She hadn't liked him at all. It was a great relief to finally feel free to admit it. She felt sadness but no guilt. He had deserved her dislike.

Daisy snuggled into the crook of his arm. "Daddy was wonderful when I was a child, but when I grew up, he changed. I went from being his precious little girl to an overgrown frump who couldn't find a husband. I was to do what I was told, never argue or talk back. I didn't understand. The more I tried to stay close to him, the harder he pushed me away.

"It was worse after Mama died. If I expressed any opinion contrary to his, he told me I was stupid. If I argued with him, he shouted at me, complained about how ungrateful I was, threatened to beat me. I think that's why he gave me so many books to read. He didn't care if I learned anything just as long as I left him alone. After a while I stopped talking to him at all. I couldn't wait for him to go to his mines. It was the only time I felt free.

"But I wasn't free. I was stranded on that ranch twenty miles from anywhere. I only went to town when he got money from his investments. We would stay in a hotel until it ran out. That's how I met Adora. That's how I knew not everybody treated their daughters the way he did. That's when I started saving money to run away."

"Where did you intend to go?"

"I don't know. It doesn't matter now. I'm sure my money burned in the fire."

"I wouldn't give your father another thought. He wasn't worth it."

"But I can't just forget he was killed."

"What do you want to do?"

"Find out who killed him. But I don't know where to start. It doesn't make sense."

"The killers could have been vagrants. Some people are just mean."

But Tyler knew those men hadn't wandered up by accident. They came to kill. Their reason was so strong they followed Daisy to finish the job. "Try not to think about it too much right now. When you're better—"

"I can't stop."

"It won't bring your father back."

"I know that, but I can't forget about it. What if it had been your father?"

What if it had? He couldn't walk away without finding out who had done it. Neither could his brothers. Even though they had hated their father, they would have felt a driving obsession to find the killers and even the score. They were not a forgiving family.

"I'd feel the same way you do. Probably more so."

"Then you'll help me find who did it?"

Tyler stiffened. "You need to talk to the U.S. marshal in Albuquerque or the sheriff of Bernalillo County. I don't know a thing about looking for killers.''

"It probably wouldn't take long, not for a person as smart as you.''

Tyler was not about to let himself be lured into something like this by a few flattering words. Even if he had been willing, he didn't have the time. He had lost too many days because of the snow. He couldn't afford to lose any more.

"I know nothing about your father's affairs, your neighbors, the people in town.''

"You could learn. There aren't many people to consider, and I could tell you about everything you need to know.''

"Then you already know the name of the killer and why he did it.''

"You're not going to help me, are you?''

"I can't.''

"You mean you won't.''

"I mean I can't.''

It was obvious she didn't believe him. Tyler felt her pull away. That tiny movement made him feel self-conscious, made him aware of the compromising nature of where he was. He got to his feet. "Try to get some sleep. It won't change anything, but it'll help you feel a little better.''

Daisy's scathing glance told him she didn't believe a word from a yellowbelly like him. Reality had returned with a bang, and it was just as miserable as he remembered.

By the next morning Daisy had decided to escape.

She had lain awake most of the night adding up Tyler's transgressions. His refusal to help her find her father's killer was the final straw.

She was tired of being told what to do. She was tired of having her opinions ignored. He treated her like a prisoner. Most of all, she resented his determination to take her to another member of his family rather than the Cochranes. Adora's father would help. He had been her father's friend. He wouldn't stop until the killers were brought to justice.

For a brief moment she considered asking Zac to help her, but she doubted he would do anything to endanger his own hide.

"I'm going hunting," Tyler announced after breakfast.

"See if you can find something besides venison," Zac said.

"I'll be lucky if I can find any game at all," Tyler replied.

"Which way are you going?" Daisy asked.

"Why do you want to know?"

She could see suspicion in his eyes. "I was just curious. You said you couldn't go anywhere because of the snow."

"I can't go to Albuquerque. The pass is snowed in."

"There must be other paths if you can go hunting."

"There are always paths along ridges or in the lee of a cliff. But you have to go where they take you. That's seldom where you want to go."

"Won't there be less snow farther down the mountain?"

"Yes."

"So if you could get down far enough, you could go just about anywhere you wanted."

She could tell he wasn't fooled. His eyes bored into her until she wanted to squirm.

"I doubt it, but in any case, you can't make it down the mountain. I'm not sure I can get more than a few hundred yards myself, and I'm using makeshift snowshoes."

"Just wondering," she said.

"You still don't believe me when I say it's too dangerous. You think if you keep asking, I'll give in and take you back now."

He didn't know why she was asking. Daisy found it difficult not to breathe a sigh of relief.

"I just want to go home," she said, trying to sound pathetic. Apparently she succeeded. Zac jumped up like a prairie dog escaping a burrow invaded by a snake. "I can look for rabbits," he said, grabbing for his shoes. "It's not much, but it'll be a change."

"Stay within sight of the cabin," Tyler warned. "You're not one hundred percent well yet."

"I'm just a little stiff."

Tyler looked at Daisy. "I hope you don't mind being left alone for a while."

"No."

"Don't go outside."

"Why would I do that?"

Tyler gave her a hard look. "Try to get some rest."

"I'll take good care of myself," Daisy promised.

"There's plenty of stew on the stove. All you have to do is heat it."

"She'll be just fine," Zac said impatiently. He grabbed his coat. "How much trouble can she get into by herself?"

"I'm not in the habit of getting into trouble," Daisy said.

"Maybe not," Zac said, "but you've sure done a bang-up job so far."

Tyler handed Zac a shotgun and pushed him out the door. "Keep the door locked and don't let anybody in," he said to Daisy.

"I won't." She doubted she'd see a new face if she stayed here a month.

The minute the brothers were out of sight, Daisy began gathering enough food to last her two days. She warmed the stew and ate as much as she could hold. That was one less meal she would have to fix.

She chose a coat with a hood and searched until she found a pair of gloves that didn't entirely swamp her hands. She put on the pants Tyler had lent her and the smallest pair of boots she could find.

Outside she saddled the first mule she came to. Then tying everything to the saddle, she headed down the mountain.

She felt a little guilty about taking Tyler's food and clothing. She also felt guilty about running away the minute his back was turned. It made it look as if she didn't appreciate what he'd done. She did, but she'd never make him understand why she had to get away.

Most surprising of all, she discovered she was a little reluctant to leave. She had the vague feeling she was leaving something important behind. But that couldn't be true. Tyler had tried to be kind and thoughtful, but he hadn't been very successful. She doubted he would ever learn. Besides, the last thing she needed was to be even vaguely interested in a man eaten up with gold fever. There would be no room in his life for anything else. Gold would be his mistress, his wife.

Daisy wanted to stay as far away from the routes taken by Tyler and Zac as possible, so she decided to go around the mountain rather than straight down as she wanted. One look at snow deep enough to cover trees to their upper branches convinced her it would be impossible to go over the crest.

She headed due north, or what she thought was north. An hour later she knew she'd made a serious mistake. The snow was deeper than Daisy had anticipated. Even under the trees, it came up to the mule's belly. Where it drifted, it was too deep to allow passage. In places it was over her head.

She had hoped travel would be easier in the open, but she had never been on the eastern slopes of the Sandia

Mountains. She expected them to be covered with rocks and small stunted trees like the west side.

They weren't. Tall pines, spruce, even aspen covered the mountainside. They kept the snow from drifting so badly, but the shade of their branches also kept it from melting or blowing away. The recent thaw-and-freeze cycle had formed a crust too fragile to hold her weight but strong enough to rub the mule's legs raw. Daisy was afraid if she didn't find some softer going his legs would start to bleed. If that happened, it would be impossible for the animal to continue.

She worked her way through a stand of fir only to find her path blocked by a wall of snow that towered well above her head. The mule refused to attempt to break through. She suspected his instincts told him the snow concealed some dangerous terrain such as a canyon or a ravine. After several minutes spent in a futile attempt to find a way around, Daisy turned back to look for another path. She didn't find one. As much as she hated to admit it, Tyler was right. It was impossible to reach Albuquerque until the snow melted.

She would have to go back to the cabin. She cringed at the prospect of having to face Tyler and admit what she had done, of having to acknowledge her failure. He had been remarkably patient with her. After this, he'd probably tie her to the bed. Maybe if she hurried, she could get back before he did.

But retracing her steps wasn't as easy as she had expected. Even though they had broken a path through the snow, fighting his way through the deep drifts had tired the mule. Going up the mountain was much more difficult than going down.

Daisy was miserably cold.

It was stupid to have gotten mad at Tyler. Catching her father's killers wasn't his responsibility. She had no reason to think Tyler was a gunman or that he'd ever hunted murderers. She'd just assumed he could do anything he wanted. He somehow gave her that feeling.

Maybe he wasn't good with a gun. He hadn't killed the man who came back that second time. He'd have to face three men who had twice tried to kill her and probably wouldn't hesitate to kill him. She had already endangered him and Zac by just being here. She was an ungrateful female, and if she lived long enough to get back to the cabin, she'd apologize to him.

Suddenly, for no reason she could see, the mule let out a squeal and plunged through a drift, running her into snow-covered branches, nearly knocking her into the snow. Clutching desperately for a secure hold on the mule's mane, she righted herself. Frantically, she looked around her for the cause of his wild behavior.

At first she saw nothing. Then she caught a glimpse of a tawny streak. Struggling to stay in the saddle, she craned her neck. A moment later she detected the top of a small, elegant, furry head with white and black markings. Just then the animal seemed to leap straight into the air. The mule brayed in panic and plunged into the center of a huge drift.

They were being followed by the largest cougar Daisy had ever seen. It was struggling through snow almost over its head. Daisy didn't know if it could catch them, but she did know there was nothing she could do to stop it if it did.

She had failed to bring a rifle.

"She's run away," Zac announced when Tyler walked into the clearing around the cabin.

"What are you talking about?" Tyler hadn't found any game, and he was irritable.

"Daisy. She's run away. She's not here. She took one of the mules."

It had started to snow again.

"Where did she go? When did she leave?"

"She went that way," Zac said, pointing to a trail through the snow. "I expect she left soon after we did."

"She'll never get through."

"I know that. You know that. Apparently she doesn't."

She was angry at him. Tyler had seen it in her eyes at breakfast, but he hadn't expected her to do anything as crazy as this. He'd told her over and over again she was too weak to travel. She could easily pass out and freeze to death in the snow.

Tyler had run away once. George had found him and brought him back.

"There's a crust on the snow," Zac pointed out. "If it cuts the mule's legs enough for them to bleed, it'll attract wolves or cougars."

Tyler didn't need to be reminded. He knew wild animals could smell blood from amazing distances. Their senses would be all the more acute if they were starving. He didn't relish the idea of being stalked by a wolf pack.

He saddled the second mule. "Don't leave the cabin. It'll probably be dark before I get back."

"If you don't find her in a hurry, her trail might be drifted over," Zac said, pointing to snow falling fast enough to make it hard to see. "I don't imagine she has any idea how to get back to the cabin."

Tyler decided if Zac had been a female, he would have been named Cassandra. No one he knew could deliver so many gloomy predictions in such a short time.

"You'd better pack something to eat in case you get caught in the storm," Zac said.

"I don't have time. Besides, if we get caught, food won't do us any good."

The look of Zac's features altered subtly. He looked so much like George it was unnerving.

"If you're not back in two hours, I'm coming after you," he said.

"Stay here."

Zac looked like himself again.

"I may be selfish, spoiled, and self-centered, but there's no way I'm going to face the family and say I stayed here and let you die."

Zac's reaction surprised and pleased Tyler. The brat was full of nonsense, but there might be some good in him yet. "No point in both of us snuffing it. There's got to be somebody to tell George what happened."

"It sure as hell won't be me!"

But as Tyler mounted up and headed after Daisy, he had another cause for worry. Two miles down the mountain, along an exposed shelf where the snow was hardly more than a foot deep, he had found the trail of three horses. The big horse carrying the heavy rider was one of them.

The killers were still after Daisy.

They were going in the wrong direction and the snow now falling would make it even more difficult for them to find the cabin, but Tyler had to face the fact that those men meant to find her. He couldn't go on depending on the snow to protect them. Sooner or later he was going to have to do something about her pursuers.

He wouldn't tell Daisy just yet, assuming he found her safe. He wouldn't put it past her to head out after the killers. All he had to do to get her to do something was tell her to do the opposite. He admired her determination, but worried she didn't seem to have any understanding of danger.

Tyler heard the cat scream a long way off. It made the hair on the back of his neck stand up. Daisy could be around the next ridge, or she could be a mile away. It was impossible to tell. He drove his mule forward at a faster pace, but his mount had also heard the cougar; he might have caught its scent as well. The animal was reluctant to head toward what instinct told him was a mortal enemy.

Tyler cursed the swirling snow, which nearly blinded him and was already filling the trail left by Daisy's mule. A mule brayed somewhere ahead, and he felt a little reassured. If the animal was still on its feet and capable of fighting, Daisy would be okay until he could reach her. But when he rounded a grove of snow-covered pines, the sight ahead caused the breath to catch in his throat.

Daisy was on the ground, up to her waist in snow. She had the plunging mule's rein caught in the crook of her arm while she used a spruce branch in her other hand to hold off the cougar. The cat, confused by the branch as well as the sight of a human being, the one member of the animal kingdom it feared, circled warily.

Tyler drew his rifle from the scabbard and fired a bullet into the snow close to the cougar. The cat whirled and snarled.

Daisy whirled, too, her expression a mixture of fear, surprise, and relief.

Tyler put another bullet into the snow. He didn't want to kill the cougar, but he didn't want it stalking them all the way back to the cabin. The cat still seemed unwilling to abandon its prey. Tyler slammed the rifle back into its scabbard. He jammed his heels into the mule's side, and, letting out a yell, he charged forward in a shower of snow.

The cat held its ground for a moment. Then favoring them with a parting snarl that showed four gleaming white five-inch fangs, the beast bounded away through the snow and was soon lost from sight.

Daisy turned to face Tyler.

Chapter Eight

Tyler had expected to be furious at her. And he was. He hadn't expected to feel so relieved he felt weak in the knees. But he did. Yet even as his body sagged with relief, he felt anger rise up in him that she could do such an incredibly foolish thing.

"What in hell did you think you were doing coming out here after I told you to stay in the cabin?" he demanded as he dismounted, rage pouring out like custard boiling out of a pot.

"I wanted to go home," she said.

"I told you I'd take you as soon as the snow melted." He took her by the shoulders and spun her around. "Does this look like melted snow?" he asked, forcing her to look at the world of white that surrounded them.

Daisy shrugged out of his grip. "You got through," she said, turning back to face him. "I thought I could."

"How? Do you see any wings on that mule?"

Daisy didn't answer.

"You could have ended up dinner for that cat. Why didn't you leave the mule and climb a tree? Cougars prefer mule meat."

"I didn't know that."

"I suppose you didn't know you could have gotten lost or fallen and frozen to death, either."

She had scared him half to death. Even now, knowing she was safe, his heart beat too loud and too fast. He couldn't put into words the horror he had felt when he saw Daisy fighting off the lion with a pine branch. He refused to allow himself to consider what might have happened if he'd arrived a few minutes later. It would have been a guilt he wouldn't have been able to shake for the rest of his life. She had no right to do that to him.

"I didn't risk my neck pulling you out of that fire so you could die in a snowdrift. Neither do I like giving up my bed and half my cabin to have you run away the first time my back is turned."

"I'm sorry," Daisy stammered. "I just wanted to go home."

"So you steal my mule and head off into a blizzard." The snow was coming down harder.

"I didn't mean—"

"You may not have any consideration for your own life, but you ought to think of the mule. He hasn't done anything to you. He doesn't deserve to die."

"I'm sorry, I'm sorry, I'm sorry!" Daisy shouted at him, her balled-up fists pressed to her temples.

"If you're so damned sorry, why did you do it?"

"To get away from you!" Daisy flung at him. Her mule took exception to her tone of voice. He half reared, pulling her backward by the rein caught over her arm.

Tyler couldn't have been any more shocked if she'd made a snowball and hit him in the face. "To get away from me!" he repeated, incredulous.

"I appreciate your taking care of me, but I can't stand

your bossing me around all the time,'' Daisy said, able to turn around only after she had convinced the mule she wasn't mad at him.

"My what?'' Tyler decided the bullet must have given her a concussion after all.

"Your telling me what to do.''

"I never tell you what to do. I—''

"Yes, you do,'' Daisy contradicted. "All day long. I feel like a prisoner. You tell me when to go to bed, when to get up, how long I can stay up, what to eat, how fast to eat it, and how much. You hedge me in until I could scream.''

"I only did what I thought was best.''

"Then you decided to take me to your brother instead of Adora's family,'' she said, ignoring his interruption. "He'll probably dislike me as much as Zac. Then George will show up and blame me for Zac's not going back to school.''

With a defiant toss of her head, Daisy started back along the trail, her mule following behind her. Tyler had to follow if he wanted to talk to her.

"George would never do that. He is a sensible man.''

"That's not the point,'' Daisy said over her shoulder. "I'm not a child, and I'm no longer sick.'' She pulled at her bandage, but it wouldn't come off.

"I never realized—'' Tyler began.

"You never listen. You go around doing exactly what you want, and you're so big nobody can stop you.''

Tyler was furious at how she saw what he'd done. He knew women could be blind, but he never expected Daisy to be so perversely ungrateful.

"I can make my own decisions,'' Daisy informed him.

"I suppose you're used to bullet wounds in your head, being snowed in by a blizzard, and being tracked by murderers,'' Tyler said, sarcasm dripping from his voice.

"No, but—''

"I gather it's no concern to you that the killers are still after you or that they probably mean to kill Zac and me as well."

Daisy turned back, her face drained of color. "What do you mean?"

Damn! He hadn't meant to mention the tracks, but she made him so mad he couldn't think straight.

"I found their tracks a couple of miles down the mountain," he said, trying to make it sound like he didn't attach much importance to the discovery. "They are going away from us, but it means they're still looking for you. If you had gotten down the mountain, you could have run into them."

She looked directly into his eyes. "I shouldn't have left. I shouldn't have taken your mule. I'm sorry."

"There'll be time to talk about that later," he said, his voice gruff. His temper had cooled. "Here, let me help you into the saddle."

Daisy resisted, but he mounted her on his mule anyway.

"See what I mean?"

"What?" He didn't have time to play Daisy's games.

"I didn't think you did."

"Hold on while I climb up," he said.

"I can ride by myself."

"I'm riding behind you. Your mule is exhausted." Tyler caught up the reins of her mule, then climbed up into the saddle. "I'm not taking any more chances. You've caused enough trouble for one day."

That was unfair, and he hadn't meant to say it, but he wouldn't retract a word. They were safe words. She would know he was angry. She wouldn't know it was because he had been so scared for her.

And he was angry.

He was furious she had so foolishly risked her life. He was enraged she would take his every attempt at kindness and turn it back as heartless determination to have his own way in everything. At the same time he was upset that, despite everything he'd done, she felt unwelcome in his cabin.

He didn't know whether it was more her fault or his, but it just went to show he wasn't suited to have anything to do with women. And she still hadn't forgiven him for not helping her find her father's killers. Well, she'd get that one wish, at least. He would have to do something about the killers. He couldn't wait until they found her again.

Daisy rode in silence, her mind and body prey to conflicting emotions. Tyler rode with his arms around her, his legs on either side of her, his body practically encompassing hers. It set her body at war with her mind and heart.

She was so angry at Tyler she couldn't trust herself to speak. He had no right to treat her like a rebellious child any more than he had a right to take her to his brother against her will. It was cruel of him to accuse her of willfully endangering his and Zac's lives. How was she supposed to know the killers were still after her?

A chill raced down her spine. She found herself wanting to draw closer to Tyler. That made her even madder. After what he'd said to her, she wanted to hate him.

But she couldn't. All she could think of were the powerful arms that held her in the saddle. She wanted to stay with him, to accept his protection. Not even her anger could block out the feeling that she was safe as long as she was with him.

But she felt something more than safety. As his legs ground against her legs, as his arms and chest rubbed against her arms and back, she felt a slow fire begin to build deep in her belly. She had never felt anything like it before, but she knew immediately it had to do with Tyler's nearness. Trying to remind herself she was angry

101

with him did nothing to stem the flow of heat that seemed to penetrate every part of her body. Intimate contact with a man was new to her. Even a simple touching would have set off fireworks in her body. His embrace had created a conflagration.

Especially in her breasts. She was acutely aware of a tingling sensation heightened by Tyler's arms rubbing against the sides of her breasts. She tried to move away, but it was impossible. His arms held her tight against him. This was no simple embrace. She felt engulfed by his body. She felt assaulted. She strove to concentrate on the landscape, the rocking of the horse, his anger. It only seemed to make her more aware of his nearness

She reminded herself it wasn't a friendly embrace. It might as well be a cage. But somehow it didn't feel like that.

Zac was waiting outside the cabin when they returned. "I see you found her," he said to Tyler. "Where was she?"

Daisy knew he'd find out about the cougar sooner or later. She preferred he find out now.

"I was in a snowdrift about to be eaten by a mountain lion. It was stupid of me to try to escape, worse to take Tyler's mule."

Zac wasn't about to be taken in by a confession that didn't sound in the least bit contrite. "You don't have to sound so proud of yourself."

"I'm not."

"You act like it."

"Put the mules up," Tyler said. "Be sure to rub them down well."

"I'll see to the mules, but I mean to find out why she took off. She can kill herself if she wants, but she's got no business trying to get you killed, too."

"Get moving," Tyler said, a sharp edge to his voice.

"You knew he'd come after you, didn't you? Even if it meant he might die in a snowstorm." Zac snatched the reins of the two mules from Tyler and stalked off. "You're not only selfish and stubborn as hell, you're stupid."

Zac's censure forced Daisy to face the enormity of what she had done. She supposed she had known Tyler would follow her, but it hadn't occurred to her that anything would happen to him. He seemed much too big to be in danger. She resented being called stupid, but she suspected she had been.

"Don't pay any attention to Zac," Tyler said as he started toward the cabin. "He was just afraid he was going to have to cook his own dinner."

Daisy didn't smile. She preceded Tyler inside, painfully aware she was going to have to find some way to apologize. She wanted to retreat to her corner, to hide behind the curtain until she felt able to face him again, but she knew she had to do it now if she was ever to do it at all.

She looked at Tyler out of the corner of her eye. He was taking off his heavy clothes, putting up his rifle.

"Did you find a deer?"

"No."

"Why not?"

"Too cold, I guess."

He wasn't going to help her. Okay, she could do it on her own. "I didn't mean for you to follow me. I didn't mean to put you in danger."

"I know."

"I thought I could get through. I wanted to go home."

"I know."

"Don't keep saying that in that calm, tolerant voice. Yell at me or something."

"I already did." Tyler looked at her out of veiled eyes. "You don't have to feel guilty."

"Yes, I do."

103

"Okay, if you want to."

Daisy stomped her foot. "I don't *want* to. I want to hit you for making me so mad. I have to apologize, and you're making it virtually impossible."

"I don't want your apology," he said.

"Then you can go on being angry at me."

"Do you want me to be angry with you?"

"You ought to be. Zac is."

"He's just afraid he'll—"

"I know, afraid he'll have to cook his own dinner."

"I was going to say he was afraid he'd have to rescue both of us."

Daisy stopped. "Would he?"

"Of course."

"Why? You two say terrible things to each other. You practically buried him in the snow yesterday."

"He's my brother."

Daisy thought about that for a moment. "Then I endangered two people besides myself." She sat down at the table and didn't speak again until Zac returned.

"I want to apologize to both of you," she said before Zac could open his mouth. "It was stupid of me to attempt to escape. I wouldn't have done it if I had known it would put either of you in danger."

Zac's gaze cut to Tyler, then back to Daisy. "Why did you run away?"

"I was angry."

"You headed out into a blizzard because you were angry?" Zac asked, incredulous.

"Tyler refused to help me find out who killed my father."

"I told you I couldn't do it as well as the sheriff."

"It's not that. You made it sound so unimportant, like it didn't matter."

"There's another reason, isn't there?" Tyler asked.

Daisy looked surprised at his question, but she didn't reply.

"What else is she mad about?" Zac asked.

"What is it?" Tyler asked. "You don't have to be afraid to tell us."

"I don't feel comfortable here," Daisy confessed after some hesitation. "You don't want me."

"Is that all?" Zac asked, disgusted.

"I'm a lot of trouble," Daisy interrupted. "I've taken your bed, half your room. You wouldn't have to go hunting for more food if it weren't for me."

"I didn't mean to make you feel like that," Tyler said. "It's just that I don't know how to make people feel welcome."

"You've tried," Daisy said, "but I don't belong here."

"It was a little awkward at first," Tyler agreed. "Zac and I don't have any sisters, so we don't know how to treat females, but we're glad of the company."

Zac looked at his brother as if Tyler had suddenly lost his mind. "I'm going to be sick if I listen to much more of this." He grabbed his coat. "When you're in your right mind again, let me know."

"Zac doesn't like me," Daisy said after Zac slammed the door behind him.

"Zac can't stop thinking of himself long enough to feel strongly about anybody else."

"But he was prepared to go after you if you got lost."

"We're a strange family, but we look after each other."

"Is that the reason you're looking after me?"

He had thought so. Randolph men always protected women. Any man would. But her presence had caused him to experience so many new feelings, he couldn't be sure why he did anything. From his fascination with her freckles to his never-flagging lust, she had rocked him right down to his foundations.

He could still feel a lingering tension from riding double. He could remember every curve of her body; he could still feel her warmth and softness. It had been all he could do to remember he was rescuing her from a blizzard. There were times when he wasn't even aware it was snowing.

"I'm looking after you because you needed help, and I was the one to find you."

She turned away, displeased with his answer. No more than he. The words didn't begin to touch on the welter of feelings that kept erupting unbidden within him. She had touched something inside him, something he had buried more than 20 years ago. It upset his balance in a way he couldn't explain. All his life he had refused to feel. Now that he did, he didn't know what to do about it.

He watched her disappear behind her curtain. He used to think she was only mildly pretty. Now even the bandage couldn't dim her loveliness in his eyes. He could see some hard case, some shiftless skunk, gazing into those brown eyes and promising anything just to be able to look into them every day. He didn't think Daisy would be taken in, but he couldn't be sure.

He'd have to make sure she was in good hands when he took her to Albuquerque. That shouldn't take long. Then he could go back to prospecting. June seventeenth loomed over his head.

Toby lifted his coat and turned his backside to the fire. "I say we forget about them until all this snow melts," he said. The three men had taken refuge in a miner's cabin. The miner, unwilling or unable to give them the information they wanted, was tied up in the shed.

"At least we ought to wait here until it stops snowing," Ed said. He held his hands out to the fire, which was just beginning to thaw out his nearly frozen limbs.

"We can't afford to wait," Frank said as he paced the cramped, untidy interior of the cabin. "What if they decide to go down to Albuquerque?''

"What if they do?'' Toby countered.

"They'll notify the sheriff.''

"So what. Nobody's coming up here in weather like this.''

"She can describe me. The sheriff'll be on the lookout when I come down.''

Toby climbed into the prospector's bunk, pulled the covers up to his chin. "If you got to worry about something, worry about what we're gonna eat. I ain't seen no game in three days.''

"There's some stuff in here,'' Ed said, rummaging around on the shelves.

"It won't last long.''

"I ain't got time to worry about your stomach.''

"You'd better,'' Toby said, comfortably settled. "It was your idea to get us up here. If it was up to me, I'd be snug in Bernalillo. A couple of times I thought it'd be our bodies that was bleached bones come spring.''

"Don't worry,'' Ed said when he saw Frank was unhappy. "If we can't get out of these mountains, she can't neither. We'll get her yet.''

But Frank had a bad feeling about this. He had missed twice when it was easy. Now they were caught at 10,000 feet in a killer snowstorm. Like always, things just seemed to keep going wrong. And his damned uncle and cousin weren't helping. Trouble was they had no ambition. They didn't see anything wrong with being a cowhand.

But Frank had bigger ideas for himself. And this job was his first step up. He didn't mean to let it slip away.

The next day dawned bright and sunny. But the cabin was blocked in by an extra foot of snow.

"If it stays like this all day, it'll melt a few inches,'' Tyler announced after coming in from taking care of the mules.

Zac shuffled a deck of cards. "Yeah, but it might snow again."

"Not for a day or two."

"Then can I go home?" Daisy asked.

"When that snow melts, every stream between here and the Rio Grande will be a boiling cataract. It'll be another day or two after that before you can leave."

Daisy was feeling the strain of confinement. She was also feeling overpowered by her sense of guilt. It all had to do with Tyler, but she wasn't going to admit her feelings for him were so strong they had caused her to do something that crazy. She didn't want to admit she had run away to escape his disapproval. Nor would she admit she didn't mind so much being here anymore. That raised too many questions she couldn't answer.

She longed to see Adora, to ask if she had ever felt this way. But after living such a sheltered and uneventful life, Adora would never understand the conflicting feelings which raged in Daisy's breast. She knew Adora's brother wouldn't. Guy Cochrane had always admired Daisy for her calm, levelheaded approach to life. He would never be able to understand the feelings that had driven her to flee into a snowstorm.

Neither could Daisy, but she couldn't concentrate enough to figure them out, not with Tyler and Zac almost within arm's reach. She needed more privacy than she could find behind her blanket. She needed to be safe in Adora's bedroom, miles from Tyler's disconcerting presence.

She was also bored by the long hours of inactivity. She was so restless she couldn't sit still to read. She had to do something or go crazy. "I have an idea," she announced. "Let's tell our secret dreams."

"Our what?" Zac asked.

"Our secret dreams. It's one of the things Mother and I used to do on dull days."

"I don't have any."

"Sure you do. Everybody does."

"They're not secret because he's told everybody," Tyler explained.

"He hasn't told me."

"Why would I want to?"

"Because you're bored. You've dealt yourself a top hand and you didn't even notice."

Zac looked at his cards, shrugged, laid them down. "I want to go to New Orleans and be a gambler on a riverboat," he said.

Daisy's smile disappeared. "I'm not going to do this if you're going to make fun of me."

"I'm not making fun."

"Yes, you are. Nobody wants to do anything as stupid as that."

"I tried to tell him that," Tyler said from across the cabin. "So did George."

"It's not stupid," Zac protested, irritated. "Prospecting for gold you'll never find or staying in this godforsaken territory, marrying a dirt-poor rancher and raising a dozen kids—now that's stupid."

"Okay," Daisy said, willing to placate Zac, "you want to be a riverboat gambler. What then?"

"What do you mean *what then*?"

"There's got to be something else. You can't want to do nothing but gamble."

"What else should I want to do?"

Daisy couldn't believe Zac was serious. Instinctively she looked at Tyler.

"He's telling the truth," Tyler confirmed. "His only ambition is to become a successful parasite."

"A spectacularly successful one," Zac amended, not the least abashed.

"What about you?" Daisy asked Tyler.

"I don't want anything."

"Yes, you do," Zac said.

"What?" Daisy asked, but Tyler wouldn't speak.

"He wants to build fancy hotels," Zac informed her. "He's up here looking for gold to pay for them."

Chapter Nine

Tyler closed his book with a snap, an involuntary action he immediately regretted. He would have preferred for Daisy not to know how much Zac's words irritated him. Neither did he want to explain his dream to her. He wondered how, in such a short space of time, she had come to expect to be allowed into the private world of his mind. He wondered how he had come to consider letting her in.

Daisy was watching him, waiting expectantly. He remained silent.

"Aren't you going to say anything?"

"What do you want to know?"

"Where you're going to build your hotels. What they'll be like. I love hotels."

Tyler knew what he wanted right down to the last detail, yet he was reluctant to tell Daisy. If he did, it wouldn't be his dream anymore. Yet it was pointless to remain silent. Nothing short of strangulation would prevent Zac from telling everything he knew. "I want to build hotels in Denver and San Francisco every bit as luxurious as anything in New York.''

Daisy looked shocked. ''I imagine a plain, clean room is all most people would want.''

''Tyler doesn't care about most people,'' Zac explained. ''He means to please himself.''

''But what if nobody else wants the same thing?'' Daisy asked, apparently unable to believe anyone would build an entire hotel just to satisfy himself.

''They can stay somewhere else,'' Tyler said.

''But that's crazy,'' Daisy exclaimed. ''You'll go broke in a month.''

Tyler felt as if he'd been dashed with a bucket of ice water.

''Uh oh, now you've made him mad,'' Zac said.

''Have I?'' Daisy asked.

''No,'' Tyler replied, but he was afraid he gave the lie to his denial by asking, ''How does living in the Centennial or Post's Exchange Hotel a few days a year make you an expert on what people in Denver and San Francisco might want?''

Now it was Daisy's turn to get angry. ''I may not know anything about rich people in big cities,'' she replied, cheeks flaming with embarrassment, ''but I know a great deal about people who build castles in the air. My father did that, and he never made a cent. The same thing will happen to you.''

Tyler wanted to get up and walk out of the cabin. He wanted to be as far from Zac's wide-eyed expectation and Daisy's scornful earnestness as possible. He had tried to explain to George why he wanted the hotels, why he needed to earn his place in the family. He guessed he hadn't done a good job. He hadn't been able to make George understand that after being described by his father as being unworthy of the family, being born a Randolph wasn't enough to make him feel he deserved his share of the family fortune. Besides, the others had done something to earn their portion.

George had voted to give him the money, but the others had refused. Tyler didn't need to be rejected by Daisy as well.

"What would you do?" he asked Daisy.

"Me!"

"You seem to think you know how hotels ought to be run."

"I never said that, but I do know people want hot baths, good food, and comfortable beds. If you want them to have anything else, you'll have to convince them it's worth paying for."

"What would you suggest I do?"

"I don't know," Daisy admitted. "I doubt I've seen half the things you're talking about."

"Then I suggest you not criticize until you have."

Daisy looked so shocked Tyler was sorry he'd spoken, but she had no right to judge him. It was obvious she wasn't rejecting his idea of a hotel, just the kind he wanted. She was rejecting him. That hurt even more because he liked Daisy and wanted her to like him.

"We've both told you what we want," he said, forcing a weak smile to his lips. "Now it's your turn."

Tyler noticed Daisy's hesitation. He wondered if she was reluctant to tell him what she really wanted or if she was simply reluctant to tell him anything after the way he'd acted.

"Come on," Zac urged. "This whole thing was your idea."

Daisy still looked uncertain when she said, "I want to live in a house like my mother grew up in."

"Is that all?" Zac asked, disgusted.

"When Mama used to fall into a melancholy, she would tell me about it. She made it sound wonderful."

113

"What could be so wonderful about a house?" Zac wanted to know.

"She lived in a big house in Philadelphia with trees and grass and flowers everywhere. Granddaddy worked for a bank. They were important people and had lots of friends. Summer evenings they'd sit on the porch. People would stop and talk until late at night. Mama had a room to herself and never had to clean or wash or cook. Granddaddy used to take them to all kinds of wonderful places in the summer. Mama had dozens of young men who came courting, wanting to take her places, to buy her things." She sighed. "My mother was extremely beautiful. Lots of men wanted to marry her."

"Then why did she marry your pa?"

"Because she fell in love with him," Daisy said, her eyes flashing angrily.

"That was a mistake."

"What was?"

"Falling in love."

"Why do you say that?"

"She left all that to come to New Mexico, didn't she?"

"You'll have to excuse Zac," Tyler said. "He's never loved anybody but himself, so he wouldn't understand."

"You're no different," Zac snapped. "You don't even like your own family."

"You still haven't told us your most secret dream," Tyler said to Daisy.

She flushed. "W-why do you s-say that?"

"You hesitated a minute ago. Just now you stammered and turned pink. What do you really want?"

"I just told you," Daisy insisted.

"But that's not what you want most of all. That was the game you asked us to play, wasn't it?"

Daisy threw Tyler a resentful look.

"What else could a woman want besides money, position, and some rich man to fall in love with her?'' Zac asked.

"Freedom," Daisy said. The word burst out like a balloon held underwater. "The right to run my own life."

Zac acted as though he thought she was crazy, but that didn't matter. Tyler didn't look as if she'd just given the wrong answer to an important question, and she was really talking to him.

"All my life my father made every decision for me— what I wore, what I did, even what I fixed for dinner. Mama always said he was very smart—he graduated from Yale. I swore if I ever got the chance, I'd show him I was just as smart as he was."

"How were you going to do that?" Tyler asked.

"By getting married and having my own home."

"Why get married?"

"I want to. Mother said every woman needs a husband to protect her and do things for her."

"Make up your mind," Zac said. "First you want to be your own boss; then you want to get married."

"If you get married with that attitude, you're giving up on yourself," Tyler said.

"What else can I do?"

"You have a ranch and a gold mine."

"They're both worthless. Besides, I don't know how to run a ranch."

"You can learn. My family did."

"It's easier for a man," Daisy said.

"Maybe, but you're smarter than most men."

Tyler's answer stunned Daisy. No one had ever considered her intelligence an advantage. Even Guy Cochrane, the least domineering man she knew, considered it no more than something to be tolerated. No one had ever suggested she actually put her mind to use, especially not to learn how to run her own ranch.

On days when her father was away at his mines, she

would sometimes spend hours imagining what she would do when she had her own home. The more tyrannical and unkind he got, the greater her need to escape him, to learn to feel some self-worth.

But since she was poor, she never expected to have any real control of her life. She saw marriage as only a partial escape, but the only route open to her. Now her father's death had freed her from his domination, but it hadn't provided her with an income. It had possibly given her the means of making her own living, but now that she was faced with the opportunity for total freedom, the idea frightened her. She was ignorant of just about everything she needed to know to survive. Marriage to a kind and understanding man seemed safer.

But Tyler seemed to think she could learn. She wondered if he could be right.

He was asking her to look at herself in a whole different way. She didn't know if she had the courage. She had never liked having someone else control her life, but it terrified her to think of being completely on her own.

Yet a tiny sliver of excitement danced wildly in the pit of her stomach.

Tyler believed she could do it. Maybe she could.

But Tyler was a dreamer. She knew from bitter experience some men built their dreams out of the tissue of impossibility. She was afraid Tyler was one of those men. If so, his faith in her was as meaningless as her father's certainty that someday, somehow, he would find gold.

"I'll think about it." She knew she would think of little else for days to come.

Tyler and Zac were cutting firewood. Zac sawed the logs into one-foot lengths and Tyler split them into pieces small enough to fit into the stove.

"Do you think she's a fortune hunter?" Zac asked.

The same question had teased Tyler all morning. He

hoped Daisy was just like most women, wanting a little beauty and romance in her life. But he couldn't ignore the possibility that she was concerned only with money, clothes, fancy trips, and a big house. This didn't match the image of her in his mind. Not at all.

"I wouldn't take everything she says literally."

"Why would she say it if she didn't mean it?"

"Maybe because she's afraid of being poor again."

He remembered their first years in Texas well enough to know what it meant to worry about your next meal. But his family hadn't given up. They hadn't compromised. They had stuck together and fought until they had won.

But there had been seven of them.

"Maybe because she's alone," Tyler said as he cleaved an oak log in two with a single swing of the ax. "If she decides to go back to her ranch, she'll need help."

"You could do that."

"I don't have time."

"You wouldn't have to stay with her, just look in on her now and then."

But he wouldn't. He didn't trust himself to spend time alone with Daisy. He didn't think he'd lose his head, but he couldn't be certain. He hadn't been acting like himself these past few days. No telling what he would do if they were together for weeks at a time.

He was petrified at the thought of being caught in marriage by a woman who wanted him for his money. He intended to live on what he could make. Which so far was nothing. It was okay for him to live in poverty because of principle and pride, but he couldn't ask a woman to do that. And if they started a family, he'd be forced to accept the inheritance he didn't want.

He had already made up his mind that if he hadn't found gold by his deadline, he would disappear. He could never live on his family's charity. On that there could be no compromise. He was already considering places to go. Australia figured high on his list.

But he didn't want to disappear. He might not get along well with his family, but he liked them. Tyler tossed aside several split pieces and settled a new log in place.

"She'd need somebody around the ranch all the time," he said, then split the log in half. "And unless we find out who's trying to kill her, it won't matter. She'll have to stay in Albuquerque." He methodically reduced the half log to four wedge-shaped pieces.

"If you're not willing to look after her, you'd better stop encouraging her to go off on her own."

"I'm not encouraging her," Tyler said, tossing the split pieces aside and positioning the second half of the log. "I just don't think she ought to marry somebody just to have a husband."

"Why not if that's what she wants?"

Why not indeed? What gave him the right to think he could order other people's lives? No one approved of what he'd done. They said he was a fool to refuse his inheritance. They'd probably say Daisy was wise to make a sensible marriage.

But he believed she was too capable to sell herself short. If she compromised, it would be out of fear. He wanted to tell her she didn't have to be afraid, but he couldn't, not if he didn't intend to be around to pick her up when she stumbled. He wasn't willing to give up his dream to help her gain hers. It sounded awful, even to him, but that was the way it was. His whole future depended on the next few months.

So did hers.

But she wasn't his responsibility. Besides, she didn't want his help. She disapproved of him so much she had tried to run away. She'd ridiculed his plan for the hotels. The best thing was to take her to Albuquerque as soon as possible. If he didn't know what she was doing, he wouldn't worry about her. He needed to keep his mind on his work if he wanted to find gold before his deadline. He really didn't want to go to Australia.

Tyler finished splitting the last log and started gathering an armload to take inside. "It probably won't matter what I say," he said to Zac. "I'm sure the Cochranes will be happy to give her any advice she needs." Knowing that should have been a relief to him, but instead it was an irritation.

Daisy sat down so Tyler could change her bandage. So far he had refused to let her do it. She hadn't minded so much at first, but she felt better with each passing day. And as she grew stronger, she became more irritated by his restrictions.

"I don't suppose you'll let me change it myself today," she said. The question was purely rhetorical.

"You can't see as well as I can."

"I can't see you at all," she snapped. "Your beard covers your face so completely I wouldn't know you if I were to see you without it." She hadn't meant to mention his beard, but it was a constant source of irritation to her.

"You aren't likely to get the chance," Zac said. "He hasn't shaved in years. Or cut his hair, from the looks of it."

"I always think people with a beard have something to hide," Daisy said.

She felt Tyler's hand still for a fraction of a second before it resumed its work.

"Why do you say that?" he asked.

She was glad she didn't have to look into his eyes. He could be rather intimidating.

"A beard is like a mask. You can't see the face behind it. You can't tell if a man means what he says."

"You can see his eyes, hear the tone of his voice, observe his behavior."

119

"But the face is the only true means of expression," Daisy insisted. "He who covers his face, covers the window to his soul."

"Sounds like something you read in a book," Zac said with a shudder.

"Not everybody wants people looking inside them," Tyler said.

"I wouldn't like to have a beard," Zac said, "but it's nobody's business what I'm thinking."

"They wouldn't have to wonder long," Daisy said. "You'd tell them soon enough." Daisy was startled by her own words, but neither Zac nor Tyler seemed to take offense.

"Your wound is healing nicely," Tyler said. "I doubt you'll have much of a scar."

He covered it with salve and began bandaging it again.

"Now all I have to do is hide in a closet for three years until my hair grows out." She didn't mean to keep harping on the same complaint, but after suffering with freckles and being six feet tall, a scar and a singed head added stinging insult to grievous injury.

"What you need is a wig," Zac said. "You'd be amazed what they can do nowadays. I had a marvelous one for a play we did at school a couple of years ago. I wonder if I still have it? You're welcome to borrow it if I do."

"I'm sure Daisy's friends will be happy to have her safe and sound no matter the length of her hair," Tyler said.

"It's not my friends I'm worried about," Daisy said.

"It should be. No one else matters."

Daisy didn't reply. Only a man could be so right and so completely wrong at the same time. And never understand why.

* * *

Daisy was even more bored the next day. Rain had been falling since dawn. The sky was a dull gray, and the clouds showed no sign of breaking up. The steady drip from the roof was getting on her nerves, but Tyler said it was still impossible to start for Albuquerque.

"It'll freeze tonight and turn into a sheet of ice. That'll make it even more dangerous."

"I've never been cooped up so long. I need to do something. Let me fix dinner tonight."

Zac lifted his gaze from the cards.

"Thanks," Tyler said. "It's no trouble."

"I want to," Daisy said. "It's about the only thing I can do for you. I feel utterly useless."

"I'd get over that soon if I were you," Zac advised.

"Get over what?" Daisy asked.

"Needing to feel useful. People will take advantage of it. Before you know it, they'll be expecting you to do things for them all the time."

Daisy smiled. "I gather you've managed to control the impulse."

"Never had it."

Daisy looked back at Tyler. "I mean it," she said.

"I'd rather do it myself."

"I promise to put everything back in its place." She couldn't disguise the annoyance in her voice.

"Tyler doesn't like anybody cooking for him," Zac said.

"I'm a good cook," Daisy said.

"Tyler's better."

"I'll have to spend the rest of my life cooking, so why don't you teach me some of your tricks?" she asked.

"I'm not very patient," Tyler confessed. "Besides, I make up a lot of things as I go."

Daisy didn't have to be hit over the head to figure out Tyler was trying to tell her to leave him alone. "Okay, suppose I wash your clothes?"

One look at Zac's expression told her she'd stumbled into another forbidden area.

"I don't know how you can stand living in a place without curtains on the windows," she said, frustration making her petulant. "Do you mind if I make some?"

"What are you going to use?" Zac asked. "Your petticoat?"

"It would be better than bare walls," Daisy said.

She was frustrated, hurt, and thoroughly miffed. Tyler was the most self-contained man she had ever met. He could do everything better than she could. What he couldn't do, he didn't want done. He didn't need a woman. He didn't even want one. She was just in the way.

She didn't understand why she should care about Tyler when she didn't care what Zac felt. It must be because Tyler was the one who took care of her, who seemed to be genuinely concerned about her.

"You ought to buy some curtains next time you're in Albuquerque," she said. "It would make the place look nicer and give you some privacy."

"There's nobody to be private from," Tyler pointed out.

"You could use some pictures, too," she said, persevering. "This place looks like a cabin in the woods."

"It is a cabin in the woods."

"I know, but it shouldn't look like it."

She didn't know why she bothered. He clearly wasn't going to take her suggestions. Maybe he had lived by himself so long he didn't know how to include other people in his life, even let them know he wanted to include them. Feeling excluded annoyed her.

She guessed she liked him.

That didn't really surprise her. She had thought for some time he was rather nice even though he was domineering and uncommunicative to the point of rudeness.

What did surprise her was discovering it was important he like her back.

Frustrated and confused, she started pulling books off the shelf and dusting them. The cabin was very neat, but this was one area Tyler had forgotten. She found herself imagining what she would do if she lived here, how she would rearrange the furniture, decorate the walls, the things she would buy if she had the money. It was really a remarkable cabin. Most homes in Albuquerque weren't built half so well.

The feel of a hand closing around her wrist caused her heart to leap into her throat. She looked up into Tyler's deep brown eyes about the time he took the book from her hand.

"Don't sneak up behind me," she said. "You scared me nearly half to death."

Tyler replaced the book on the shelf and pulled her away from the bookshelves. "You don't have to work for your keep."

"I don't mind."

"I'd rather you didn't."

"All right," she snapped, throwing the dustcloth on the table. "I'm sorry I touched your books, your dust, or anything else that's yours. I promise I won't do it again." She started toward her corner.

"I didn't mean for you—"

"I know. You didn't mean to hurt my feelings, but you don't want anybody to do anything for you, to thank you, even to talk to you most of the time. I don't know why you bother to go on living. You're already dead inside."

She retreated to her corner and drew the curtains behind her.

"I see you haven't lost your charm," Zac remarked dryly.

"Go to hell!" Tyler said and slammed out the door.

Daisy couldn't decide whether her tears were from anger or disappointment. Her wrist still burned where Tyler had touched her. It seemed incredible that such a gentle touch should be a rejection. It made her furious.

It also hurt. She'd had a lot of rejection in her life. It never got easier, but this was harder than all the rest.

Tyler turned back toward the cabin. It was getting dark. The rain had stopped and the temperature had plummeted, but he was hardly aware of the cold. He couldn't stop thinking about what Daisy had said.

He had closed her out just as effectively as if he'd slammed a door in her face. He hadn't meant to. He hadn't even wanted to, but when she'd started to mess with his things, he'd experienced a moment of panic. He knew she was trying to help, but she was stirring up new feelings. He couldn't handle the ones he had.

He stepped across the stream that ran near his cabin. The snow melt gurgled noisily around the rocks, but a lacy network of ice trimmed the banks. If it got cold enough, the spray would freeze into a kind of ice foam.

He'd been self-contained for so long he didn't think about it. Until today. Until he realized he didn't want to close Daisy out. He had spent so many years keeping to himself, denying any emotion, he didn't know how to express feelings, to let anybody into his life. He certainly didn't know what to do once they were there. He didn't know how he wanted Daisy to fit, how long he wanted her to stay, how much he wanted her to mean. None of his feelings toward her were familiar or comfortable.

He did know he was not going to forget her easily, if at all.

He found himself wishing he could talk to George, but he knew nobody could figure this out for him. He would have to do it himself. But how should he begin?

Begin with what you want. If you know that, all the rest will follow.

He decided to check on the animals before he went inside. There was something peaceful about being around the mules, and right now he was experiencing more than his share of turmoil.

The next morning Tyler was taking boiling water to melt the ice in the water troughs when he caught sight of Willie Mozel stumbling along the ridge. The temperature had dropped below freezing overnight, turning everything to ice. Six inches of sleet and snow had fallen on top of that. The day was overcast, bitterly cold. Nothing would melt today.

Tyler intended to send the crusty old prospector on his way the minute he made it to the cabin, but by the time Willie staggered into the yard, Tyler knew something was wrong. Willie looked half dead.

"What happened to you?" Tyler asked.

"Damned thieving bastards!" Willie managed to say before he sagged against the shed.

"What are you talking about?" Tyler asked. He took Willie by the arm and started toward the cabin.

"Three men came to my cabin yesterday. They wanted to know about all the prospectors in these mountains."

Tyler stopped in his tracks. "Why?"

"They wouldn't say." Willie was clearly anxious to get inside the cabin, but Tyler didn't move.

"What did they say?"

"Just wanted to know who lived in the cabins and where they were. They kept asking about their ages. Seemed a damned fool thing to do to me. Ain't nobody under fifty except you."

"True," Tyler said, half to himself.

"Seemed to think there was a pair of young fools up here. I couldn't make them understand a prospector don't want nobody else hanging around, especially if he's got a claim worth having. Never know when a partner might

125

conk you over the head and drop your body into some ravine.''

''What are you doing here?''

''They tied me up with some grass ropes, left me in the shed,'' Willie said, still angry at the abuse of his hospitality. ''I'd still be there now if my burro hadn't chewed through the ropes. The fools didn't know that crazy burro will eat anything that ain't rawhide.''

''Did you walk here through that storm last night?''

''Couldn't have got here any other way,'' Willie said. ''Now stop making me talk until I'm blue in the face and help me inside. I could use some of that fancy chow you're always cooking up.''

''I don't want you to say anything about those men when we get inside,'' Tyler said.

''Why?''

''My brother's here.''

Willie's brow cleared. ''So you're the two young men. Why should they be after you?''

''You'll see in a minute.''

Chapter Ten

"What happened to him?" Zac demanded the minute Willie stepped into the cabin.

"He got caught in the storm last night."

"Why did you leave your cabin?"

"He was trying to get back from Albuquerque," Tyler said, filling in with his own invention before Willie could speak.

"You should have stayed in town," Zac said, inspecting Willie with a disapproving eye. "You look like you spent the night in a snowdrift."

"Never did like Albuquerque," Willie said, sinking into a chair. "Too many scalawags ready to take everything you got."

Tyler took some of the stew he kept on the back of the stove, put a generous helping in a tin plate, and handed it to Willie. The old prospector dug in as though he hadn't eaten in days.

"Hey, take it easy," Zac said. "Tyler hasn't been able to find another deer."

"He won't until this weather breaks," Willie said through a mouthful of stew. "They can stay holed up longer than you or me."

Willie ate in silence for a few moments. Tyler opened the stove and ran a poker through the coals to stir them up, but Willie drank the coffee without waiting for it to get hot.

Willie swallowed the last mouthful of stew and allowed a look of satisfaction to lift the deep lines on his face. "I think I'll live now," he said.

"You don't look like it," Zac observed.

"I'll look a lot better for some sleep." Willie got up and started toward the portion of the cabin set off by the barrier of sheets and blankets.

"You can't go in there!" Tyler said.

"Why?" Willie asked.

"Because I'm back here," Daisy announced. Before Willie could demand an explanation, she stepped from behind the curtain.

Willie looked from Daisy to Tyler then back again. "Two young men," he muttered, suddenly understanding. "So that's why—"

"Why you can't go behind the curtain," Tyler finished for him. "You can sleep in my bunk if you want."

Willie dragged himself back to his chair and sank down. "I'm not as sleepy as I thought."

"This is Daisy Singleton," Tyler said. "We found her in the snow a couple of days ago. She had injured her head. Daisy, this flea-bitten old crookshanks calls himself Willie Mozel. He claims he's a prospector, but I figure he's just looking for a claim to jump."

Daisy cast Tyler a questioning glance, but his expression gave nothing away. She looked at Zac, but his face was equally uninformative. It was clear they didn't mean to let Willie in on the true state of things. She wondered why.

"What were you doing so far from your cabin?" Willie asked.

"Her father was dying, and she was trying to reach a doctor."

Daisy marveled at Tyler's ability to invent a tale on the spur of the moment.

"What happened?"

"He died, so we buried him and brought her here so she could get better."

Willie looked skeptical. "Well, you're going to have to find someplace to take her."

"I'm going to the Cochranes' in Albuquerque as soon as the snow melts," Daisy announced. "Adora Cochrane is my best friend."

"That's as may be, but they're in Santa Fe," Willie told her. "They won't be able to get back until the snow melts."

"How do you know that?" Zac demanded.

"Like Tyler said, I'd been to town when I got caught in the storm," Willie said, tying into Tyler's story.

Daisy hoped her surprise didn't show. All along she had depended on being able to go to the Cochranes'. It was a shock to realize that option was cut off. She would have to stay here for several days more.

But that wasn't the worst. Daisy realized the news hadn't upset her very badly because she didn't really want to leave. That was more than she could understand.

Because for the first time in your life, somebody is taking care of you, not the other way around.

Her father had always been the center of their household. But now she was the focal point of Tyler's day. He might spend hours fussing with his mules, reading his books, or taking longer than necessary with the meals, but nearly everything he did had to do with her comfort and well-being.

But there was more to it than that. She could feel it

sometimes. She could see it in his eyes once in a while when she caught him off guard. He liked her. He wouldn't say so. He wouldn't do anything to indicate it, but she could tell he liked her. She found this as hard to believe as the understanding that sprang up between Tyler and Zac the moment Willie Mozel came into the cabin. They hadn't said a word. It was just there.

It was a bond meant to protect her.

It was an experience so new, so unexpected, she was tempted to question her judgment at first. But it only took a moment to realize she was right. That was when Daisy decided she didn't care how long the snow lasted.

"I guess that means I'll have to go hunting again," Tyler said. "We're getting low on meat. You can come with me, Willie."

"Me!" Willie exclaimed. "I can't go tramping through that snow. I'm worn to a nub."

"I'll let you rest up an hour or so," Tyler said. "You ought to be recovered by then."

Willie looked as though he was going to argue but changed his mind after a glance at Tyler's expression. "I guess I'd better get what sack time I can," he said, getting up and hobbling over to the bunk. "Probably a good thing if I do go with you. You'd never find so much as a rabbit by yourself."

Toby stared into the malevolent eyes of Willie's burro. "Where do you think the old fool got to?" he asked Frank.

"How the hell should I know!" Frank barked. "I can't find a single footprint in all this damned snow." They had come out expecting the old prospector to be ready to talk after a miserably cold night spent in the shed with the burro. Frank was stunned to find him gone.

"Shouldn't have tied him up," Ed said. "Made him jumpy."

"Shut up!" Frank growled. He looked all around the shed and down both trails from the cabin, but the snow had covered all trace of the old prospector's escape.

"You think he knows where the girl is?" Toby asked.

"I don't know," Frank said. "These old codgers stay as far away from each other as possible. There could be a dozen females living up here and none of them know it."

"I think he knows," Toby said.

"More likely he knows the men," Frank said. "And if he knows them, so do others."

"What are you going to do?" Ed asked.

"We're going to saddle up and go from one cabin to another until we've hit every one of them," Frank said. "They've got to be up here. With her hurt and all this damned snow, they can't have gone anywhere. We'll find them."

Frank's temper was on edge. His instinct told him to cut and run. The plan was doomed. Too many people knew. But the longer it took him to catch up with the girl, the more chance others would find out.

He intended to kill the old bastard for sneaking out during the night. No one would miss him. Probably nobody would even know he was dead for several months.

He also meant to kill the two men with the girl. Nobody made a fool of Frank Storach.

"You're both to stay inside," Tyler told Zac and Daisy as he and Willie prepared to go hunting. "Neither one of you is completely well, and it's a lot colder out there than it seems."

"I'm sick of staying in this cabin," Daisy said.

"Me, too," Zac agreed.

"You'll get plenty of chance to get away soon enough," Tyler said.

As soon as the trees screened them from the cabin,

Willie stopped and turned to Tyler. "Now tell me what's going on in there, or I'll not go another step."

"Those men are after Daisy. They killed her father and twice tried to kill her."

Willie whistled between his teeth. "You think they came up here looking for her?"

"What other reason would they have to go around asking about two young prospectors?"

"Aren't you worried about leaving her alone?"

"They won't find us today. The wind blew the snow into your tracks. Besides, I warned Zac not to let anybody come near the cabin."

"That useless piece of fluff!" Willie scoffed. "He'd probably hide behind her."

Tyler chuckled. "Zac may not look like much, but he's the most cold-blooded cuss you'll ever meet. And he can shoot the spines off a cactus."

"You can't be talking about that slicked-up kid back in your cabin."

"The same," Tyler assured him. "Now stop worrying about Daisy and show me where the deer are hiding. We'll soon be out of meat."

But Tyler wasn't so sanguine as he tried to appear. If it hadn't been necessary to find more food, he wouldn't have left Daisy. The killers had shown greater speed, persistence, and intelligence than he had expected. He still believed someone else was behind them, a sharp, devious, cruel mind. That really frightened him. It might not be as easy to protect Daisy as he first believed.

And he knew he had to protect her. She might consider herself practical, but she had no more idea how to survive in this country than an easterner.

"I said I'm surprised you didn't lay in extra supplies," Willie repeated when Tyler didn't answer him. "It ain't like you to be short."

"I wasn't expecting Zac," Tyler said, refocusing his

attention. "He eats enough for two."

"How about the girl?"

"I wasn't expecting her either."

"You could have left her with some farmer."

"I couldn't, could I, when I didn't know who'd tried to kill her?"

"That's what I figured."

"You didn't figure any such thing," Tyler said. "You figured I got her up here for some nefarious purpose."

"I don't know what you mean by nefarious—I don't strain my brain reading all them books like you do—but if it means what I think it means, no, I don't. I don't think you're worth a damn as a prospector, but you got enough of the gentleman in you to get yourself killed over some female." Willie halted when they came upon a set of footprints. "I see you got a cat hanging around."

"He's got his eye on my mules."

"I'd shoot him first chance I got. Otherwise he'll get 'em sooner or later. Them cats are determined critters."

While Willie busied himself studying the cat's tracks, Tyler's mind wandered back to Daisy. He wasn't anxious for the snow to melt just yet. He needed to understand his attraction to this woman. Was it just lust? He couldn't be sure. It didn't take much to excite his body. Just touching Daisy was enough. He'd lain awake half the night remembering the feel of her in his arms, the warmth and softness of her body as it pressed against his, the stiffness in his groin that made every step the mule took a misery.

But there was something more than lust working inside him. He recognized that. He didn't identify the feeling that took hold of him whenever he looked at her. It tugged at something inside him, its pull gentle but insistent. Something forgotten or never known. Tyler couldn't decide which. He wasn't sure it mattered. Whatever it might be, thoughts of her were in his mind, waking and sleeping.

Maybe his interest stemmed from the fact that she had

been hurt and he wanted to protect her. That was a natural instinct with all the Randolphs, even Zac. If so, once he had taken her to the Cochranes, he'd be able to forget about her.

He could be interested in her because she was a gutsy young woman who had a poor opinion of herself and had been left with no way to survive except to marry the first man who asked her.

"That cat's probably got a den somewhere around here," Willie decided. "From the looks of his tracks, it's been a long time since he's had much to eat."

Tyler was afraid the cat's presence meant they wouldn't find any game within two miles of the cabin. "Maybe he'll eat one of those killers if they show up," Tyler said.

"You think they will?"

"I'm certain of it."

Tyler couldn't understand why a woman who thought so little of herself, who expected even less of the world, should be of such importance to the killers. The world rarely took notice of any but the most beautiful women.

Tyler understood all about not being beautiful. He couldn't count the times he'd been unfavorably compared to his brothers, and not just by his father. He'd even heard one woman commiserating with George about being burdened with such a brother. George had defended him— George always did—but that didn't change things.

For a long time, Tyler pretended not to care, not even to be aware of people's opinions of him. The most immediate result was that, believing he truly didn't care what they said, they spoke more freely around him. It drove him to silence. Finally it drove him into a solitary existence.

Never once did anyone imagine he took with him a terrible feeling of unworthiness. He'd even refused to admit it to himself. Seeing it in Daisy had forced him to recognize it. He couldn't help her until he figured out how to help himself.

But he couldn't go prospecting for the gold he needed to build his hotels, the hotels he needed to feel worthy of his family, without deserting Daisy. He couldn't take her with him, and he couldn't leave her behind. Even if she were safe from the killers, leaving her would only reinforce her poor opinion of herself.

"If I'm going to have to keep speaking to you two or three times before I get your attention, I might as well be out here by myself," Willie complained.

"Sorry. I was thinking."

"If you don't get your mind off that gal, you're not going to find a deer, even if it's right in front of you."

"What makes you think I'm thinking about Daisy?"

"Nothing but a female can make a man stumble along like he's blind as a bat. If you're not careful, that cat's going to have you for dinner."

Tyler stopped in his tracks. "I'm going back."

"What for?"

"If those men do find the cabin, Daisy would be safer outside than pinned down inside. Zac knows that, but he doesn't know these mountains like I do. He could get lost."

"You sure you aren't afraid of something else?"

Tyler smiled. "Zac doesn't like Daisy well enough to try to seduce her. Come on, I'll let you take Zac with you. You can feed him to the cougar if he gives you any trouble."

Daisy paced the cabin impatiently. She was supposed to be trying to figure out who killed her father, but thoughts of Tyler kept intruding. He and the cougar were after the same thing—a deer. She couldn't think of that animal without a cold shiver. What if he were stalking Tyler?

135

"Sit down," Zac ordered. "All this charging about is making me too nervous to concentrate on my cards. If it's Tyler you're worried about, don't."

"I can't sit still," Daisy said, refusing to admit to Zac she was thinking of Tyler. "I'm about to go crazy locked up in this cabin."

"Up in Wyoming, people stay in cabins for months at a time and are perfectly all right."

"But they're not locked up with you, are they?"

Zac's gaze snapped up from his cards. His dark eyes glistened brightly. "Watch it. Another crack like that, and I'll—"

"You'll do what? Lock me in my corner? Pitch me out into the snow?" Shock at her own words brought Daisy's outburst to an abrupt halt. "I'm sorry," she apologized. "I don't know what's gotten into me." It was more than confinement. It was Tyler, but she didn't know what to do about it.

"It's the snow," Zac said, the glitter in his eyes becoming less intense. "Tyler says people out here aren't used to it."

"No, we're not," Daisy admitted, happy to let him blame it on the snow. She couldn't explain about Tyler. She couldn't even explain him to herself.

She figured she had to be losing her mind. There was no reason for her to be thinking about him so much, especially not the way she had been thinking about him. She had been thinking it would be mighty nice to have him around all the time.

She couldn't like him that way. It didn't make sense. Outside of the fact he had shown no interest in her except as a casualty to be cared for, he was exactly the kind of person she had sworn never to marry. He was a dreamer, an impractical spinner of fantasies.

Luxury hotels! What a fantastic scheme!

She was too impatient with the idea to give it any serious consideration. Even if he found his mine, he'd lose his money and end up living in a cabin for the rest of his life, hunting for his food, reading his books. She picked one up and read the spine. *The Lost Indian Mines of New Mexico.* She put it down and picked up another. More lost mines.

She snorted in disgust. Thousands of men had wasted their lives looking for these mines. Tyler was a fool to think he'd be the one to find them.

But that was how dreamers were. They were convinced the rules didn't apply to them, that they'd be the exception, that somehow fortune would favor them above all others. That was what her father had thought. But instead of doing something to realize his dreams, he had sat around reading, talking, and wasting the money he did have.

"Why don't you sit down and read one of those books?" Zac suggested.

Daisy's gaze focused on the title. She had forgotten she was still holding the book on mines. "I'm not interested in lost mines," she said, shoving it back in its place.

"He's got plenty more."

"I don't want to read."

"If you don't stop pacing, I'm going to tie you to a chair."

Daisy walked over to the window and looked out. Her spirits rose. "It's getting lighter outside."

"Good. Maybe Tyler will find something besides a deer. I don't like venison."

"Then why didn't you bring something when you came?"

"I don't go shopping," Zac replied, shocked. "I wouldn't know where to begin."

"You go in the store and ask for what you want," Daisy said sarcastically. "They find it and give it to you." Zac was more useless than she was, yet he didn't seem the slightest bit apologetic. In fact, he seemed to think it was other people's obligation to take care of him. Why couldn't she feel that way?

"If the sun comes out, maybe we can go out for a few minutes," Daisy said.

"Tyler said to stay inside."

"I didn't mean to go far. Just walk about the yard a bit."

"Tyler said stay inside," Zac repeated. "He gets real irritated when people don't do what he wants."

"I get irritated when people tell me what to do," Daisy snapped. She was startled at her second outburst in the same morning. Her father made her furious all the time, but she had always kept a tight rein on her tongue. Yet she hadn't hesitated to speak her mind to Tyler or Zac. More surprisingly, they always seemed to take her objections in stride. At times she wondered if they even heard her. Her father would have had a fit.

She walked back to the bookcase and began to take out one book after another, but she didn't pay any attention to them. She kept wondering why Tyler didn't mind anything she did. More than that, she wondered why he thought she would be able to learn to manage her own ranch.

She was terribly afraid she could never succeed, but the possibility kept her mind spinning out of control, kept her nerves on edge.

"I'm going outside," she announced. "I can't stand being cooped up in here one more minute."

"Damn!" Zac exclaimed as he slammed his cards down on the table and got to his feet. "Why can't females ever do what they're told?"

Chapter Eleven

Weak sunlight shone through the thin layer of clouds. After so many gloomy days, it almost seemed sunny. Daisy hugged her coat under her chin to keep out the bitter cold. Beneath the snow, ice crunched with each step she took.

"It's miserably cold out here," Zac said, picking his way across the snow.

"Then stay inside."

"I don't trust you not to get into trouble."

"That's no skin off your nose."

"Tyler will make it skin off my hide," Zac complained. "He has the mistaken notion I can keep you from doing exactly what he's told you not to do."

"He'd pick me up and carry me back inside," Daisy taunted. She didn't understand why that thought should excite her.

"I wouldn't carry any female across this ice."

Daisy abandoned her attempt to goad Zac. He wasn't a

bit like Tyler. She didn't want Zac to pick her up, but she practically skipped through the snow imagining herself being carried in Tyler's powerful arms.

"You promised to stay in the clearing," Zac reminded her.

"I just want to walk a little way along the ridge," Daisy said. "Somebody's already made a path."

The clouds suddenly parted and the sun shone brightly. The warmth seeped into Daisy's bones, radiated throughout her body. It made her feel so good, so full of energy, she couldn't possibly consider returning to the cabin. She had never seen the mountains from this vantage point. They were magnificent.

She trudged along, drinking in every sight and sound, ignoring Zac's litany of complaints interspersed between warnings. The tree branches hung low with their weight of snow and ice. She broke off an icicle she found on a sapling bare of leaves; she put it in her mouth and sucked on it like candy. Birds huddled on tree branches, feathers puffed out to twice their normal size in an effort to insulate themselves against the cold. A squirrel dashed along a tree limb, causing a chunk of ice to hit the ground with a thump. Daisy didn't know whether its rapid chatter was a greeting or a complaint about the weather.

She looked back, but Zac no longer followed. She laughed and hurried on. In a short while the cabin was out of sight, but she didn't stop. She knew she would be locked inside the cabin as soon as Tyler returned.

She hadn't gone much farther when she noticed movement up ahead. Memory of the cougar flashed in her head, and she stopped. She glanced behind her, but a stand of snow-covered firs blocked Zac from view. Even as she turned to go back, she realized the animal wasn't the right color for a cat. It was much too dark. Besides, it appeared to be hiding behind a fallen tree.

After studying the animal for a few moments, Daisy

decided it was struggling, not hiding. Drawing closer, she found herself looking into the deep brown eyes of a small doe. It had somehow become trapped under a fallen tree limb. Its struggles had brought it to the point of exhaustion. As Daisy came close, the animal made one last feeble effort to get to its feet, then lay still.

"You poor thing," she murmured. "I'll help you."

But the tree limb was six inches in diameter and partly frozen into the snow. Try as she might, she couldn't lift it. She was relieved when she thought she heard Zac come up, stunned when she turned and saw Tyler advancing toward her with a rapid and purposeful stride. She couldn't see his expression because of his beard, but if his eyes were any indication, he was furious.

Involuntarily she backed away. She hadn't ventured out to defy him, but it would probably look like it.

"What do you mean by running away every time I turn my back?"

He grabbed her by the shoulders. Even through the thick layers of clothing, she could feel his fingers dig deep into her flesh. She felt helpless in his grip.

"I just wanted to get a breath of fresh air."

"Couldn't you find any air closer to the cabin to suit you?"

In spite of his anger, Daisy had to laugh. "No, I could still hear Zac's complaints. What did you do with him?"

Tyler shook her. "Is it worth getting killed to escape Zac? Those men are still out there."

"I didn't mean to come this far, but I saw where you'd made a path. And the sun felt so good—" A second shake wiped the smile from her face.

"It felt so good you thought you wouldn't mind getting shot."

"I admit I forgot about the killers. You said they couldn't follow us with all this snow."

"They wouldn't have to follow you. You keep along

this ridge, and you'll soon be exposed. A man with glasses could see you from five miles away.''

Daisy glanced around her, but her view was cut off by stands of fir, pine, and aspen.

''What can I do to convince you to stop running away?'' Tyler didn't seem so very angry now, just disheartened. ''If I thought you'd be safe, I'd take Zac and move to another cabin.''

''I wasn't running away. And don't you dare leave. I'd be scared to death.''

''Are you sure? You're not lying to get me off my guard?''

Daisy hated for Tyler to think she was so desperate to escape from him, but she couldn't think of anything to say that would change his mind. Only completely different behavior could do that, and the best time to start was now.

''I'm not afraid of you, and I'm not mad at you. I just wanted to get out of the cabin for a few minutes. I thought Zac was following. What happened to him?''

''I sent him off with Willie.''

''Why did you come back?''

''I had a feeling you might not stay put.'' He didn't look upset now, just resigned.

''Did you find a deer?''

''No, but Willie's still looking.''

''I did. Right here.''

Tyler's gaze followed where she pointed. Catching sight of the deer, he climbed through the branches until he reached the trapped animal.

''Are you going to kill it?'' she asked.

''No.''

''You said we were almost out of food.''

''I don't kill helpless animals. Let's see what's wrong with it.''

Daisy didn't understand Tyler, didn't suppose she ever

would, but she was too relieved to care just now. She marveled at how gently he handled the deer. The animal seemed to know he didn't mean it any harm.

"It's got a gash where the limb hit it, but I don't think anything's broken," he said. "I won't be able to tell until I move this limb."

Daisy hadn't been able to budge the limb. Tyler lifted it without seeming to try hard. Daisy couldn't deny the thrill that shot through her. She'd never met a man she felt was big and strong enough for her. Tyler was big enough with room to spare. She never felt overgrown or unfeminine around him.

She vividly recalled the feel of his arms around her, the pressure of his thigh against her leg, the shivers that lanced through her when his arms brushed the sides of her breasts. Despite the cold, liquid heat warmed her entire body. Why couldn't he have been the man for her?

Daisy told herself it was useless to dwell on what couldn't be changed. She would do better to think about the deer. The animal struggled to rise, then fell back. "Poor thing, it can't stand up."

"It's mostly just tired. It'll be fine after some rest." Tyler bent down and gathered the struggling doe into his arms.

"What are you going to do?"

"I hope it doesn't mind sharing the shed with the mules."

The deer made one final attempt to escape, then gave itself up to its fate.

"Is the shed strong enough to keep the cougar out?"

"It's kept him away from the mules."

Daisy couldn't stand the thought of the cougar getting the little doe. She didn't know why it should bother her so much. Maybe it was the doe's helplessness. Maybe it was because she felt the same way.

"We'll have to give it something to eat."

143

"I've got hay and oats in the shed."

"Wait until Zac sees it."

Tyler laughed. "He's likely to want to eat it."

"But he doesn't like venison. I heard him say so."

"He likes it better than nothing."

"Are we out of food?"

"We're close."

Daisy jumped in front of Tyler. "Promise me you won't let Zac hurt it."

"He won't slaughter it, if that's what you mean. He's more likely to get Willie to do it for him."

"Nobody can hurt this deer. Promise."

Tyler smiled, and Daisy's heart turned a flip. His eyes were so warm, so inviting, she hardly noticed his beard.

"While we have it in the shed, nobody will touch it," Tyler said. "But I can't promise you it won't end up on somebody's table after we let it go."

Tyler started toward the cabin again, and Daisy followed, still feeling a little giddy. "Maybe we can keep it."

"No."

"I don't mean in the shed. You can make a corral for it."

"It wouldn't stay in a corral. If it did, the cougar would surely get it. Wild animals are meant to be free. If you're going to lock them up, you might as well kill them. It would be a greater kindness."

Daisy walked behind Tyler, knowing what he said was true, angry because it was.

"Not all deer get eaten by cougars or men," Tyler said. "I saw a magnificent twelve-point buck this past fall."

"Did you shoot it?"

"No. I let it stay with its harem. This doe might be one of his offspring."

Daisy felt a little better. Tyler wouldn't let anybody harm the deer.

144

She wasn't too sure the mules and the burro felt the same way. They didn't seem pleased to be sharing their home.

"I'll need water and bandages," Tyler said. "There's warm water on the stove, bandages on the shelf."

By the time Daisy returned, Tyler was bending over the deer, his knee on its neck.

"Now that it's safe, it doesn't want to lie still," Tyler explained.

As she watched Tyler work with the deer, Daisy tried, and failed, to make sense of the last half hour.

She had found the deer, but she had only meant to let it go. Tyler, who would have killed it for food if it had been running free, had carried it back to the shed, cleaned its wound, and bandaged it for protection. He even put some poles across the end of the shed to protect it from the mules and burro. It didn't seem like it was her deer anymore. It was Tyler's. He was always protecting the vulnerable or weak. First her, now the deer. She suspected he was protecting Zac as well.

Daisy leaned over and patted the doe. Its coat was coarse and rough. It lay still, its big eyes watching. "Why doesn't it eat?" she asked.

"It's too tired now. It'll be time enough to worry if it hasn't eaten anything by morning."

Daisy wanted to stay to assure herself the deer would be okay, but Tyler clearly meant for her to leave with him.

"Let's hope Willie and Zac found a deer," he said as they returned to the cabin. "If not, I'm going to have a hard time explaining why I'm keeping one in the shed."

A hard time hardly covered it. Zac and Willie came back empty-handed after a long, cold afternoon.

"Of course we didn't get anything," Willie said. "I couldn't surprise a deaf coyote with your brother talking his head off and floundering about making more noise than a bull moose in rut.''

Willie received the news about the deer in shocked silence. Zac's reaction was more vocal.

"You got *what* in the shed?" he asked.

"A young, female mule deer," Tyler said, his brown eyes glittering with amusement. "It's at the end of the shed, behind the poles, if you want to go take a look at it. Daisy will show you. She'll even let you pet it if you promise to be gentle."

Zac stared at his brother, his mouth open. "Here we are about to starve, and you got a deer in the shed eating its head off."

"It's too tired to eat," Daisy explained.

"I'm surprised you're not feeding it by hand," Zac snapped.

"You should have cut its throat while it was down," Willie said. "It can be right tricky once it gets on its feet."

"Nobody's going to cut its throat," Daisy said. "It's hurt. We're going to keep it until it gets well."

"Next you'll be taking in badgers and coyotes," Zac said, turning unbelieving eyes on Tyler.

"He already took in one coyote," Daisy said.

"Of all the ungrateful brats!" Zac exploded. "After everything I did for you."

"What did you do for me?"

"Take a bullet for one thing," Zac reminded her.

"I told you I was sorry about that, but that's no reason to want to kill Tyler's deer."

"It's not his deer. It's—"

"There's no point in discussing this," Tyler interrupted. "The deer will stay in the shed until it's able to survive on its own. In the meantime, we'll eat the rest of the venison, then the bacon. If we must, we'll boil some of the harness leather. But nobody is eating that deer."

Daisy hoped Tyler still felt that way when the food ran out. She didn't think Zac would defy him, but she wasn't sure about Willie Mozel.

The huge cat circled Daisy, its fangs dripping with saliva, its breath billowing out in thick, white clouds of moisture that almost reached her cheek. Daisy tried to run away, but her feet seemed too heavy to move. Each step was more difficult than the last. The snow seemed to become deeper with each step.

The cougar circled in an ever-tightening ring. Daisy tried to scream, but no sound came from her throat. She searched for some weapon, something to fend off the beast, but there was nothing around her except an endless expanse of pure white snow. The beast crouched, bared its fangs, and launched itself at Daisy.

Daisy woke up with a pounding heart and heaving lungs. Inside her nightshirt her skin was damp. It was a dream. A horrible nightmare of a dream, but a dream nonetheless. She fell back on her bed, but over the pounding of her heart she detected the sound of crunching snow and claws on wood.

Her body stiffened. The cougar.

She jumped out of bed and ran to her window. She used her warm palm to melt the frost that covered the pane in a lacy pattern. Weak moonlight left most of the yard in shadow, but Daisy had no trouble seeing the cougar.

He was trying to get into the shed. She could see claw marks all over the boards. The mules and burro brayed their fear.

Daisy gasped in shock when Tyler came around the corner of the cabin, yelling and swinging a long club. She couldn't believe he would attack the cougar without a gun, but he charged the animal as if he were bigger, stronger, and had nothing to fear.

147

The big cat whirled to face Tyler, but rather than attack, he started to give ground. He uttered bloodcurdling snarls, his enormous fangs snapping at the club, claws capable of eviscerating a full-grown deer swiping at Tyler. Tyler kicked a spray of snow in the cougar's face and jabbed at it with the club. The animal whirled and bounded away. It screamed, and then disappeared into the pines down the trail.

"You awake?" Zac called out.

"Yes," Daisy answered, still staring out the window, wondering if the cougar would come back.

"There's nothing to worry about. You might as well go back to bed. Tyler has to chase that damned cat off about once a week. It's practically a game by now."

Daisy took a last look before she crawled back into bed. She snuggled deep in her blankets. She'd forgotten how cold it was in the cabin after the fire went out. The Randolphs were crazy. There could be no other explanation as to why a supposedly sane man would attack a cougar with a stick.

Willie left at dawn the next morning. "I gotta see what those creeps have done to my cabin," he said.

"What creeps?" Daisy asked.

"Some prospectors who couldn't get through to their own cabin," Tyler said. He left with Willie, a rifle under his arm.

"You gotta stop telling that girl lies," Willie told Tyler when they were out of earshot. "You're gonna tell so many, you'll forget one and get all tangled up."

"I don't want her to know those men are so close," Tyler said. "It wouldn't serve any purpose, and it would worry her."

"It might keep her from going out looking for deer to adopt." Willie looked at the sky. "Looks like it might clear up, but it's still mighty cold. Ice can be more trouble than snow.''

''Let's hope it is for them. Will you come back and tell me where they're headed?''

''Sure,'' Willie said as he headed along the ridge Daisy had followed the day before. ''I got a score to settle with that bunch.''

Tyler paused. An idea had just taken hold of his imagination. He smiled. ''Want to have a little fun?''

''What did you have in mind?'' Willie asked, giving him an appraising glance.

''I'll show you when we get to the cabin.''

Two hours later the men crouched behind a rocky outcropping about a hundred feet from Willie's cabin. ''I guess they're still there,'' Willie said, disgusted. ''Looks like they're trying to burn up all my wood at once.''

''You think you can get their horses away without them noticing?'' Tyler asked.

''I could get a herd of buffalo through here and that lazy bunch wouldn't know nothing,'' Willie said scornfully.

''Get them as far away as you can. I want those men to still be looking for them when I take Daisy to Albuquerque.''

''Wouldn't it be easier for me to draw them out so you can shoot them?''

''It's probably what they deserve,'' Tyler said.

''But you ain't going to do it?''

Tyler shook his head.

''I didn't think so. I always said you were too much of a gentleman for your own good.''

''Just hide the horses.''

''I can do better than that. I'll move 'em every day until the snow melts. That way they'll be too busy to go after you.''

"You sure? It could be dangerous. They're not as harmless as you think."

"Nothing to it. Besides, I owe that bunch. They tore up my place something awful."

Tyler cursed as he watched Willie, careless of keeping under cover, make his way to the shed. Moments later he emerged astride his burro and leading three horses. Willie led them right in front of the cabin. The fool was intentionally trying to draw the killers out. Cursing, Tyler raised the rifle to his shoulder. He had barely put his finger on the trigger when a man ran through the door, shouting to the men inside.

Tyler squeezed off a shot. The bullet hit the corner of Willie's cabin, sending a shower of splinters through the air. The man hit the ground. A second man had just emerged from the cabin. He disappeared inside again. Tyler got off two quick shots, one clipping the corner of the man's boot.

With a yell of triumph, Willie and the horses disappeared into the trees. Someone inside knocked out a window. Tyler placed a shot through the open space. A yell from inside told him he'd hit someone. He cursed. He hadn't intended to start an all-out fight. He changed his hiding place. By now they could have located him by the flash from his rifle.

He fired a shot at the man on the ground. He dived through the door headfirst, an audible curse on his lips. Tyler shifted location again and waited. He wanted to give Willie at least five minutes' head start. Then he'd use the horse tracks to cover his own trail back to the cabin.

A rifle showed through the window. Tyler took careful aim and fired. Luck was with him. His bullet hit the rifle barrel, knocking the rifle from the man's hands and sending shards of metal ricocheting inside the cabin.

Somebody yelled. Someone else shouted, "Son of a bitch!"

Tyler smiled and changed location. He could almost enjoy this. He waited five minutes. A hat appeared at the window, a boot at the door. In quick succession, Tyler nicked them both. More cussing inside the cabin, but no more targets.

Convinced the killers would stay put for a while, Tyler slipped into the woods and headed back toward the cabin.

Tyler returned in time to see Daisy, almost swallowed up in one of his coats, coming outside.

"Did Willie get home safely?"

"Yes. You shouldn't be out. It's too cold."

"I want to see how the deer is doing."

Tyler didn't understand what could be so endearing about a female swallowed up by a coat too big for her, but he felt a sudden rush of warmth all through him at the sight of Daisy slogging through the snow, her face peeping out of the fur-lined hood. Protective feelings he didn't know existed welled up inside him. He was probably the least violent of all the Randolphs, but some things he just couldn't tolerate. No one was going to hurt Daisy while she was with him.

"Do you think it was too cold last night?" Daisy asked as they headed toward the shed.

"The heat from the mules and the burro would have kept it warm."

"The icicles are hard as rocks."

"This deer has survived blizzards. I'm sure it's okay."

There wasn't much room inside the shed. The mules had apparently accustomed themselves to their strange companion, but the burro had not. The deer scrambled to its feet when they entered. The burro immediately swung its head around, teeth bared.

"It hasn't eaten anything," she said, pointing to the oats and hay. The deer didn't seem to have touched the food.

151

"It's probably still tired. Now that it's rested up, its appetite is bound to come back."

"Are you sure?"

Tyler had no idea. He didn't know a damned thing about deer, but he didn't figure that would be the best thing to tell Daisy. "Sure. It's just not used to people," he said, grasping for any explanation as to why this blasted animal wouldn't behave the way Daisy expected. "It's used to running away when it sees people."

"Oh." Daisy looked thoughtful.

"Let's leave it alone for a while. Maybe it'll eat."

"And if it doesn't?"

"I'll have to find something it will eat."

The sun was up over the trees when they left the shed. "It's going to be a pretty day," Tyler said.

"But cold. It doesn't look like much of the snow will melt."

"No, but it'll be pretty."

"Do you think I'll have to stay here much longer?"

"I wish you didn't think of it that way."

"What way?" she asked. She pushed the hood back from her face so she could see him better.

"Like you *had* to stay."

She lifted her hand to shield her eyes from the glare of the sun. Her gaze became intense. "I thought you did."

"Not anymore."

"Me neither."

They stared at each other for a long moment. Daisy was the first to move away.

Daisy started to walk back to the cabin. "I thought you didn't like having people around. Zac says you're the loner of the family."

Tyler fell in beside her. "I don't mind people. It's just I don't find I need them much."

"Not at all if you mean to live here," Daisy said, swinging her arm in an arc that took in the cabin, the shed, and the snow-covered mountains.

"There are some needs within a man other people can't satisfy."

"I know, but to stay up here alone for months at a time . . ."

"Let me show you something." He extended his hand toward her.

Daisy stood still. "What?" she asked.

"You'll have to see for yourself."

Daisy felt reluctant to follow him. She sensed going with him would be making some kind of admission, lowering a barrier, taking a step forward from which she might later find it impossible to retreat. Yet there was something irresistible about the smile that curved his lips, the light that danced in his eyes. He was usually so unemotional, so unmoved by any kind of feeling, it was impossible to refuse to discover what could have caused the light within him.

"It's not very far," he said. "It won't take long."

It wasn't time or distance that bothered her. She didn't trust the feeling that made her smile, reach out to take his hand, and answer, "Okay." Some unknown emotion stirred, some restless unbridled spirit she had thought long since bludgeoned into stillness. She was afraid of the uprush of excitement, the expectation that something special was at hand, something good, something wonderful.

She knew it wasn't true. She had learned her lessons long ago. She didn't want to forget them now. They had cost her too much.

For a time, Daisy wondered if they were actually going to be able to reach the spot Tyler had in mind. The snow was deep and the crust hard enough for her to walk on. But not too deep or too hard for Tyler. He powered though the snow with amazing strength, leaving a path in his wake Daisy could follow. She wondered if anything could stand in the way of such a man. If anybody could make his dreams come true, it was Tyler.

She told herself not to be foolish. Physical power didn't translate into control of one's fate or command of the forces pitted against anyone who tried to succeed against fantastic odds. Tyler would never manage to turn his dream into reality by looking for lost gold mines. That took something more, something dreamers didn't have.

That was before he picked her up and carried her through a particularly deep drift.

He didn't ask. He didn't give her any warning. He simply turned around, scooped her up, and headed into a waist-high snowdrift as if he were walking through whipped cream. Nothing like this had ever happened to Daisy, and the sensation was breathtaking. She felt weightless, like the merest wisp of a female. At the same time it felt wonderfully exhilarating. It was as though being swept off her feet, as though not being responsible for the movement or direction of her own body, relieved her of the weight of responsibility for everything else.

She felt feminine, fragile, and petite.

The optimism with which Tyler faced life invaded her mind and soul. For a few brief seconds her spirit felt free of the pressure that had always kept it weighed down. Things she had never considered possible seemed within her grasp if she would only reach out.

Then he set her on the ground, and her merry-go-round came to a halt.

"It's not much farther," he said, taking her by the hand and pulling her forward. "It's just around those rocks."

Dazed by the whiplash effect of her abrupt mood swings, Daisy followed. The fact that she was climbing over rocks covered with ice and snow hardly registered. When she finally reached the top and stood up, a blast of frigid air nearly knocked her off her feet. Tyler took her hand to steady her and then put his arm around her shoulders and drew her close.

"This is what I wanted you to see."

Chapter Twelve

They stood atop a saddle between two high peaks. The face of the mountain fell away in a sheer drop of several thousand feet, giving Daisy an unobstructed view of the Rio Grande valley more than 9,000 feet below.

For a moment she was too stunned to breathe. She felt as if she were perched on the spine of the world. Looking up at the peaks on either side made her feel dizzy. Looking down at the valley, the Rio Grande a thin line winding its way among the brown and green, she felt terribly small. She could see the mesa 75 miles across the valley as clearly as if it were only 75 feet away.

"I come here whenever I feel discouraged," Tyler said. "Sometimes I come just because I like being here."

"Why?"

"My family thinks I'm crazy to keep looking for gold. After so many years, so many failures, it's sometimes hard to keep going."

Daisy was surprised he would make such a confession

to her. She was certain he'd never said anything like that to Zac. She didn't know why he had brought her here, or why he was holding her so close.

"But each time I stand here and look out, each time I see an eagle floating on the updraft or a mountain sheep climbing what looks like a sheer cliff, I realize anything is possible. Compared to this, finding gold is nothing."

Daisy tried to feel what Tyler felt. She thought she caught a fragment of the exultation that transformed him from the quiet, phlegmatic prospector into a beaming visionary, but it slipped through her fingers with the softness of a sigh.

"You can't see it when you're down there," Tyler said, pointing to the town below and its tiny, almost invisible buildings. "People and passions get in the way. But up here, you can see the world as God sees it."

Then Daisy felt it, too. She felt the shackles of her own fears fall away as though turned to dust. The restraints she had always accepted seemed to have lost their unbreakable hold. The limits, the rules, the conventions that dashed every hope as it was born lost the poison in their bite.

A paroxysm of joy seemed to lift her literally off her feet. She held tight to Tyler and turned her face to the wind. It wasn't cold now. It was bracing, invigorating, filled with energy that flowed into her limbs. For the first time in her life, possibilities felt as limitless as the extraordinary panorama that stretched before her.

She felt so happy, she wanted to dance across the rocks and laugh aloud. Wanting to share this moment, she looked up at Tyler. His expression was so intense it scared her.

Then he kissed her.

No man had ever kissed Daisy. Even shared confidences with Adora Cochrane were insufficient to have prepared her for the impact of Tyler's embrace. She felt

156

her strength drain away, leaving her weak and helpless. Yet even as she thought she must slip from his grasp and fall to the ground, energy flooded her with a power that left her breathless.

She found herself kissing Tyler back, something she'd never imagined doing with him or any other man. She knew nothing of the art of kissing or of the pleasures it promised. Her body responded instinctively to Tyler's embrace just as it hinted at something even more marvelous.

Daisy wasn't prepared for Tyler's tongue to invade her mouth, but she felt no desire to resist. Like a key turning in a lock, Tyler's probing tongue unleashed such a flood of passion within her that Daisy broke away, more shocked at herself than at Tyler's boldness.

"Why did you do that?" she asked, breathless.

"I've been wanting to do it for days."

"But why?"

"Do I have to have a reason?"

In that instant, Daisy realized that though Tyler might not need a reason, she did. In her need, she had read reason into his actions. In that golden moment between the time his lips first touched hers and the instant they broke apart, her mind had built up a whole host of reasons and expectations. Even though she hadn't had time to put them into words, not even into conscious thought, she knew her reasons were quite different from Tyler's. Hers spoke of a future as endless as the vista before them.

His spoke of passion of the moment.

Knowing that cooled the magic warmth that had flooded her body.

The vista before her lost its enchantment. It was no more than rocks and snow. The wind bit into her skin and whipped her skirts about her ankles. Her foot slipped, and she was fearful of falling. Holding on to Tyler's hand long enough to climb down from the rocks, Daisy started back toward the cabin.

"What's wrong?" he asked, following.

She didn't answer. He caught up with her when she floundered in a snowdrift.

"I didn't mean to upset you," he said as he helped her to her feet.

Daisy held his hand only as long as it took to steady herself. Then she started running.

"Slow down. You'll hurt yourself," Tyler called.

She didn't stop.

Suddenly he was in front of her, blocking her path.

"What's wrong?"

"Nothing."

"There has to be something. You were all right one minute, running from me the next."

"I don't like heights."

She knew he didn't believe her, but she couldn't explain how his kiss had promised her everything one moment and his words snatched it away the next. He wouldn't understand what she was talking about. For one moment she had believed there was more to her future than marriage to the first man to ask her. For a moment, she had hoped for everything a young woman dreams of when she first realizes she's a woman.

"Are you sure that's all?" Tyler asked.

"Yes. I want to go back to the cabin. It's cold up here."

He hesitated, but Daisy didn't give him time to ask more questions. Following the path he had made through the snow, she hurried down the mountain.

It was all her fault. She shouldn't have gone with him. Neither should she have allowed the view to cause her to forget the experiences of a lifetime. Looking over the edge of a mountain couldn't change anything. It didn't matter if people were too small to be seen from so high up. They were still there. They would always be there.

Daisy pushed past a limb laden with snow and heard it

thwack against Tyler. She turned in time to see him snap the limb from the tree with one angry flick of his wrist. That frightened her a little.

He was so much like her father, always ready to command, to expect others to follow. He displayed just enough common sense to make you think he was sensible and responsible, but underneath there was nothing substantial. He planned his whole life around the possibility he would find his fortune in the ground. When common sense caused him to doubt, he rekindled his folly by standing on a mountaintop.

She knew better. Being around Tyler confused her. His kiss had rocked her off her foundation. She had used her disapproval of him to deny that she liked him, that her reaction was anything more than a physical response. She knew better now, and she wouldn't let that happen again. She stumbled into the yard, relieved to be anchored once more to reality by the solid presence of the cabin.

"You sure you won't tell me what's wrong?" Tyler asked.

"You'd better see about your deer," Daisy said. She brushed some of the snow off the skirt of her dress.

"I'm more worried about you."

She forced a smile to her lips. "It was nothing more than a moment of panic. I've never stood at the top of a mountain before. All of a sudden it was too much."

"I shouldn't have kissed you," Tyler said, "but I thought you trusted me."

"I do," Daisy said, upset Tyler would interpret her reaction as fear. "Nobody could have taken better care of me."

"Until now."

"Even now," Daisy said. "There was nothing improper about that kiss. I wasn't afraid of you. I enjoyed it."

Tyler's disbelief was obvious, but she wasn't willing to

take him any deeper into her confidence. He had penetrated too far as it was.

"Go see about your deer. I'm going to see if Zac's awake."

He was up, dressed, and poring over his cards when she entered. "Is Tyler back?" he asked.

"Yes."

"Did he find a way down the mountain?"

"The snow's still too deep."

"You were gone a long time," Zac said, eyeing her suspiciously.

"Tyler took me up to the top of the ridge. He wanted to show me the view."

"On a day like today!" Zac exclaimed, looking out the window at a huge icicle which hadn't started to melt.

"It was a spectacular view."

"You must be as crazy as he is. It's nine thousand feet straight down." Zac shuddered. "As far as I'm concerned, I'd just as soon never climb another mountain."

"You don't feel excited when you look out over the edge?"

"Not unless you call wanting to throw up excitement."

Daisy walked over to the pegs along the wall. She unbuttoned the coat and slipped out of it. She felt better knowing Zac wasn't affected by the mountaintop view the way Tyler was. She didn't admire Zac, but as long as she didn't ask him anything about cards, he did show a certain amount of common sense. It comforted her that his reaction should be so close to her own.

Yet she could not forget that moment. It was unlike anything she'd ever experienced. It was probably nothing but a dizzy spell—more likely wishful thinking, the same kind of groundless optimism that had supported her father all his life—but she couldn't erase it from her memory. It had happened, and for a moment she'd felt better than she ever had in her life.

That is probably how a drunk feels, she thought, when the first rush of alcohol reaches his brain. The first moments are sheer euphoria. But soon everything crashes and you're left feeling miserable. Daisy had no intention of crashing or of feeling miserable. She might not be able to forget the experience—she couldn't always control her mind—but she refused to give it any credence. It was a mirage, wonderful but unsubstantial.

The door opened to admit Tyler. "The deer hasn't eaten. I'm going to look for something else."

"What do they usually eat?" Daisy asked.

"Leaves, twigs, small tree limbs, bark, moss."

"Ugh!" Zac said. "No wonder I don't like venison."

"Want to come with me?" Tyler asked Zac.

"I'm not going tramping around the mountains stripping bark off trees to feed a deer."

"I'll go," Daisy offered.

"You ought to take a nap," Tyler said. "Climbing that ridge was more exercise than you've had in a long time."

She didn't know whether he really didn't need help or if he just didn't want her company. After the way she had acted, she couldn't blame him.

"How about fixing some breakfast before you go?" Zac asked.

"I'll do it," Daisy offered. "I'm not as good as Tyler, but I can cook."

"I don't suppose you can ruin breakfast," Zac murmured.

"I can, but I won't."

"I'd let him starve," Tyler said. He waited a moment, as though for Daisy to say something; then he closed the door and was gone.

Daisy walked to the window and watched Tyler cross to the trees. She hugged her arms around herself. That kiss had changed something. Not just the relationship between them, but something deep inside her. She was glad

161

of the time alone. She needed to look within herself. Only there would she find the key to everything else.

Daisy paced back and forth.

"I thought you were going to cook breakfast," Zac said.

"I changed my mind," Daisy said. It felt wonderful to say that. She'd never refused to cook before. She paused, almost certain he would do something to her for this defiance.

"Do you always go back on your word?"

"No."

"Why did you this time?"

"I just don't feel like cooking."

Zac watched her in silence. Daisy didn't like that. He saw too much.

"What happened out there?"

"Nothing."

"Liar."

"Nothing important." She flushed. "I don't want to tell you about it."

"I didn't think you would."

"Then why did you ask?"

"You got Tyler upset."

"Me? Isn't it possible he got me upset?"

"You're always in a taking, but Tyler never gets upset over women. What did you do to him?"

"Nothing!" Daisy nearly shouted.

"I don't believe you."

"Fine. Don't!"

She retreated to her corner, but she could almost feel Zac's eyes boring through the blankets. She picked up one of the books she had stacked against the wall. But try as she might, she couldn't concentrate.

Zac said Tyler never got upset over women. He should know his own brother. Maybe she *had* upset him. Maybe he did like her. Maybe he'd meant the kiss to be something more than just a spur of the moment reaction.

No, she was simply indulging in wishful thinking, the kind of thing she had sworn to avoid ever since she could remember. If Tyler had been interested in her, she would know it.

What if he was so self-contained he didn't know how to communicate with other people?

Daisy couldn't endure the numberless questions that bombarded her mind. She tossed her book aside and got up.

"Where are you going?" Zac asked when she crossed the room and took the coat down again.

"I'm too jumpy to stay inside."

"A guilty conscience?"

"No!"

"Tyler doesn't want you outside."

"I just want some air."

"There's plenty of air in here."

"I feel cooped up."

"He's going to be mad."

"According to you, I've already made him mad. A little bit more won't make any difference."

"It will with Tyler."

Daisy made an impatient noise and rushed outside.

The sun was brighter, but the cold was just as intense. She had to put her hand over her eyes to shield them from the glare. The intense white was almost unbearable.

She looked around for someplace to go, something to do, but there was nothing unless she wanted to split wood or go feed the animals. And Tyler had already done both of those.

She gazed down the mountain through the trees. It was hard to believe Albuquerque was only some 20 miles away. It seemed like a world apart. She looked up toward the ridge where Tyler had taken her such a short time ago,

163

where he had kissed her and thrown everything out of balance.

Turning away, she started toward the shed. She wasn't really interested in the deer at the moment, but it would give her something to do.

When she reached the shed, she found the door ajar. She stepped inside. The mules and burro were there, but the deer was gone. Tyler must have failed to secure the latch when he left. She ran to the cabin. "The deer's gone!" she shouted inside to Zac.

"So?" he said.

"Tyler has done everything he could to make it better. We've got to find it and get it back."

"I'm not chasing after a deer."

Daisy stalked inside the cabin. "You are the laziest, most good-for-nothing boy I've ever seen in my whole life. I don't know what your brother sees in you, but if it were up to me, I'd trade you for a deer any day." She walked over to the wall where Tyler kept his rifles.

"Hey, what are you doing?" Zac demanded.

"Getting a rifle."

"Put that back," he said, getting up from the table.

Daisy paid him no attention. She grabbed a handful of shells and put them in her pocket.

"Do you know how to load that?" Zac asked.

"No, but I'll figure it out."

"Hellfire!" Zac exclaimed, wresting the rifle from her grasp. "Let me have this. You're liable to shoot yourself."

"Are you coming?"

"You don't leave me much choice, do you?"

"Hurry. No telling what might have happened to the deer."

It was hard to follow the doe. It was so light it could run on top of the icy crust.

"It would serve the stupid beast right if I shot it," Zac complained.

"You do and I'll use that rifle on you."

Zac eyed her unhappily. "You're crazy enough to do it. Why do you care about that deer? The cougar will probably get it."

"It's Tyler's deer."

She knew that sounded dumb. She couldn't explain why it was Tyler's deer or why it was so important, but that deer stood for something in Tyler she didn't understand, but something she wanted very badly to be able to share. She felt it was a secret that made his life better than hers.

"If we don't find it, it won't be anybody's deer."

"Look!" Daisy said, pointing to a paw print in the snow.

"The cougar," Zac said. "That deer's a goner. We might as well go back."

Daisy should have been frightened. But she had defied the beast once. For some crazy reason, she felt certain she could do it again. "We can't just leave it."

"You plan to tell that cougar he can't have it?"

"You've got a rifle. Shoot him. Now stop talking and hurry up."

"I'm just as crazy as you," Zac muttered. "That damned cat is liable to decide it would like some young, tender Randolph flesh better than a stringy deer."

"You may be young and tender," Daisy snapped, "but you're bound to taste sour."

"For a country girl, you sure have got a nasty tongue."

"Hush!" Daisy hissed. "There's the cat."

The cougar was perched on the lowest limb of a Douglas fir. He was watching something. As they watched, he gathered his muscles under him, ready to spring.

"Shoot him!" Daisy urged Zac. "Hurry up."

"Be quiet, you silly female. I can't aim with you screeching like an Indian."

"Shoot!" Daisy shouted. She grabbed for the rifle. It exploded into the silence.

"Dammit to hell!" Zac cursed as they both tumbled into the snow.

Tyler muttered under his breath as he tramped through the woods, ripping branches from trees as he went.

"You fool! You big, stupid, horny fool! Why couldn't you keep your hands to yourself? The least you could have done was work up to it gradually. How did you expect her to react when you grabbed her like some sex-starved lunatic who hasn't seen a woman in six months?"

He cut a limb from the sapling, tossed it into a pile to be picked up on his way back, and moved on.

"You had no business putting your hands on her. You asked her up to the ridge to look at the view. You said you wanted to show her something more beautiful than anything man could create. And what did you do? You attacked her like a bull in rut."

He swung down around a large boulder and stopped where a trickle of water had melted a path through the snow. Listening intently, he could hear the sound of water falling over rocks. The snow was melting. If it stayed clear, Daisy would be able to leave before long.

"You'll be lucky if she doesn't take off while you're gone."

He was mad at himself for losing control. It was stupid, especially after he'd been so careful for so long. Until today she'd had no idea of the need burning inside him. Now she wouldn't feel safe. She would only have to look at him to be reminded of what he had done.

"She'll probably hide behind Zac."

That would hurt. It would be bad enough if she kept

her distance—he deserved that—but he didn't know if he could stand it if she turned to Zac for protection.

It was time Tyler admitted he liked Daisy. A lot. The lust was still there, but it was all mixed up with something else now. He wanted to kiss her because he wanted to touch her, to feel her in his arms, to feel her close to him. He was haunted by the memory of her in the bath. Last night he had dreamed of making love to her again. He had lingered lovingly over every inch of her body until he lost himself in a release so exquisitely powerful it woke him. That was probably what sent him over the edge. He'd been able to hold himself together when he put his arms around her and drew her to him, but he'd lost all restraint when she threw her arms around him.

He found a grove of oak trees and proceeded to cut several supple branches. He didn't know why he was being so particular. Any animal that could strip the bark from a tree could eat any kind of limb. He had just started to collect the branches when he heard a shout followed closely by a rifle shot.

The killers! How could they have found the cabin so quickly? He had been a fool to get so caught up in his own thoughts that he forgot about them. Cursing himself, he started for the cabin at a run.

Chapter Thirteen

"Did you hit him?" Daisy asked, scrambling to her feet.

"Not likely with you throwing my aim off," Zac grumbled. He picked up the rifle and held it out of Daisy's reach. "At least he's gone," he said, pointing at the limb.

"He's after the deer." Daisy started in the direction of the tree at a run. "Hurry!"

"Stop! You can't go running after a cougar," Zac called as he started after Daisy. "You might catch him."

Daisy didn't slow down. She stumbled through the snow, making as much noise as possible. She wanted to scare the cougar, but she hoped she wouldn't scare the deer so badly it would run too far for her to find it. Zac followed, making almost as much noise, only he was shouting at Daisy, not the cougar. She didn't pay him any attention, just kept plowing through the snow until a bloodcurdling snarl brought her to an abrupt stop.

The cougar was a short distance ahead. But instead of running after the deer, he was facing her. Only then did

168

she notice the splotches of red in the snow. Zac had wounded the cougar, not enough to kill him, but enough to make him mad. And he was intent upon taking out his anger on Daisy.

Daisy turned and headed back, but a glance over her shoulder told her that despite a badly wounded hip, the cougar was gaining on her. She couldn't see Zac. If he wasn't going to keep up, he should have given her the rifle.

After climbing to the crest, worrying over Tyler's kiss, and trailing the deer, Daisy wasn't sure she had enough energy to make it to the safety of the cabin. She stumbled, and then scrambled to her feet immediately. She was surprised to see blood on her hands. She had cut them on the ice when she fell.

Ignoring the blood, she struggled on. She considered climbing a tree. Her skirts would be a serious handicap, but maybe the cougar couldn't climb with a wounded hip. She stumbled again. She tried to get to her feet, but she slipped on the ice and fell flat. She looked over her shoulder, fearful the cat would already be upon her.

A rifle shot rang out. The cat let out a heart-stopping snarl that nearly caused Daisy to faint. A second shot cut the snarl short.

Daisy looked up to see Tyler standing over her, a rifle in his hands. The look on his face was balm to her soul. He was too frightened to be mad, but that wouldn't last long. She knew now there had been a reason for the kiss on the ridge.

Tyler helped her to her feet. "Are you all right?"

"Yes," she said, brushing some of the snow from her. "I just slipped."

"You cut yourself."

"Not badly. Just some scratches."

"You sure?"

"Yes."

Tyler looked to where the cougar lay still in the snow. "He was close."

"Zac wounded him."

"Where's the deer?" Zac asked, coming up behind his brother.

"I don't know," Daisy answered. "Gone, I guess."

"Why did you let it out?" Tyler demanded, his temper flaring out of control.

"You must have left the door unlatched," Daisy said. "It was gone when I came out."

"And you went after it?"

"I had to. It was hurt."

"It wasn't hurt so much as tired. It's probably halfway to Colorado by now." He turned to Zac. "You should have had better sense than to let her go after it."

"Me!" Zac exclaimed.

"You know more about living in the wild than she does."

"She's the one who grew up in this miserable place," Zac pointed out. "I've been in Boston, remember. We don't have stupid deer and rampaging cougars there."

"You still knew better," Tyler said, really angry now. "I ought to wring your neck." Tyler took Daisy by the elbow and started for the cabin. "She could have gotten killed or seriously hurt. I hold you responsible."

Zac gaped at his brother. "You try stopping her from doing any addlebrained thing she takes into her head. I told her not to go. You ought to be thankful I took the rifle from her. She'd probably have shot herself."

Zac protested all the way back, but Tyler refused to speak to him. When they reached the cabin, he ushered Daisy inside. Zac followed close on his footsteps, but Tyler blocked the doorway. "You can stay outside until you get some sense."

With that he closed the door on his brother and bolted it. Zac banged on the door with his fists and shouted

170

curses at both of them, but Tyler ignored him.

"You can't leave him outside," Daisy said. "It was my fault. He told me not to go."

"He could have stopped you."

"I wouldn't have listened to him."

"He could have made you stay."

"How?"

"Like this," Tyler said and grabbed her by the shoulders. "Do you think I would have let you go?" he asked in a tight voice.

"No."

Zac had started kicking the door with his boots, but the door showed no sign of breaking. Daisy found the banging very distracting, but Tyler seemed oblivious to it.

"You had no business out there, not even in the yard."

"I had to find the deer."

"That deer is a wild animal. It knows how to live outside. You don't."

"But he was your deer."

"What difference does that make?"

"I don't know. It just did."

Tyler stared at her hard for a moment. "You faced the cougar because of me?"

"I didn't know it was there. I'm not sure I'd have gone if I had," she confessed.

Now Zac was banging on the window. Daisy was sure he'd break the panes any minute.

"You went after that deer because of me?"

"I thought it was important to you," she answered, distracted. "You went to all that trouble to take care of it and find it something to eat. I thought you'd be upset if it got away."

Zac left the window and started hitting the door with something like an ax handle or a log. Daisy couldn't keep her mind on Tyler with all that racket.

Without warning, Tyler pulled her close and kissed her

with such fierce intensity Daisy thought her legs would buckle under her. There was nothing tender or loving or gentle about it. It was a hot, fierce kiss born of tightly held passion. When Tyler released her, she simply stood there, unable to move, unable to account for what had just happened.

She would probably have remained in a state of shock for some time longer if she hadn't heard footsteps on the roof. Next thing she knew, the sound of sizzling and popping came from the stove.

"Zac's putting snow down the stovepipe," Tyler explained.

"Don't you think you ought to let him in?"

"Not until he starts to tear off the roof. I figure he'll start in about five minutes. Either that or break the windows."

Daisy had the distinct feeling she was in a dream. None of this made sense: not the deer, the cougar, Tyler's kiss, or Zac on the roof. It couldn't be happening. If she wasn't already as crazy as the Randolphs, she soon would be.

"You've got to let him in," Daisy said, starting for the door. "It was all my fault. I can't let you lock him out or tear up your cabin. You'll freeze without windows."

"I've more glass and shingles," Tyler said.

Daisy wasn't capable of dealing with anything more just then. She opened the door. "Zac," she shouted. "Come on in."

About three seconds later Zac and an avalanche of snow landed at her feet. Delivering himself of a string of curses that caused Daisy's eyes to widen, he stalked inside. Much to her surprise, he didn't say a word, though he was clearly enraged. He stomped over to the table, sat down, picked up his cards, and began to deal. Daisy glanced at Tyler, but he showed no visible reaction to his brother's silence. He merely put his coat up, sat down, and began cleaning the rifle.

Daisy felt incapable of dealing with the whole situation and retreated to the privacy of her corner.

Tyler had kissed her again. Once could have been a fluke. Twice was no accident.

He had been afraid for her. She saw it in his face. But there was more than anxiety for her safety. It was fear of irreparable loss. Daisy could not believe she could have been the reason for such a look.

It was hard to know what he meant by that kiss. It was so hard and fierce and short. It couldn't have been much else, not with Zac banging over their heads. But he wouldn't have kissed her like that if he didn't like her.

Maybe he liked her a lot. Zac said he never gave women much attention. He hadn't paid her much attention in the beginning. He had lately. Did the second kiss mean he was in love with her?

More important, was she in love with him?

The question nearly threw Daisy into a state of shock because she didn't know the answer. Her feelings for Tyler had changed in the last couple of days. She had finally figured out that, underneath that unemotional exterior, he was a kind, thoughtful, gentle person. She had come to like him very much.

Then there was the effect his nearness had on her body. He aroused some primal instincts that were beyond her brain's control. She distrusted these feelings, yet she couldn't wait to experience them again.

Daisy fell back on her bed. This was insane. She was trying her best to fall in love with precisely the kind of man she had sworn to avoid. Worse still, he might be falling in love with her. She groaned. That was the kind of thing *he* might do, but she was too sensible.

But even as she told herself she could never do anything so stupid as waste her few hopes on empty dreams, she thought of the kiss, the strength of his embrace, the feeling of security she felt when she was around him.

173

She told herself it was false security. He could protect her from cougars and killers, but he'd never provide a decent life for her unless she wanted to live in a mountain cabin and eat venison.

Tyler stared at the book with unseeing eyes. He could deny it no longer. His attraction to Daisy was more than physical. He had suspected it, but until this morning he had kept coming up with reasons why it couldn't be so. Terror such as he'd never known before had filled his heart when he saw the cougar running her down. Even now the thought of what might have happened had the power to cause his stomach to bunch and cramp.

Was he in love with her?

No, but he'd been a stranger to emotion of any kind for so long he didn't know what it would feel like to be in love. If what he had experienced so far was any example, he didn't like it. He remembered Rose's glowing happiness, George walking around like somebody had just given him a million cows.

He didn't feel like that. He felt miserable. He wanted to throttle Zac, take Daisy to the Cochranes, all the way to Santa Fe if necessary, bury himself in the hills, and pretend these last few days had never happened.

Willie would say he'd been in the mountains too long. He said prospecting was for old men who'd forgotten what to do with a woman. He believed Tyler would never find gold because he couldn't get his mind off the women who waited for him in town. Tyler could never convince Willie he didn't think of those women until he was actually in their presence. He forgot about them as quickly.

It wasn't like that with Daisy. He couldn't get her out of his mind. He looked at the curtain stretched across the end of the room and wondered if she was thinking of him. Had the kiss affected her as it had him? She hadn't said anything. He was afraid she'd paid more attention to the noise Zac was making on the roof.

But it hadn't left her completely unaffected. She'd looked stunned. Maybe she hadn't known what to say.

What would he have wanted her to say?

Knowing she had gone after the deer because of him had thrown him off his feet as neatly as a calf roped for branding. An unexpected feeling of warmth and happiness had flooded through him, all directed toward Daisy. He felt like laughing at himself. How did you tell a woman you'd kissed her before you'd had time to think and didn't know why you'd done it? She'd probably slap him.

What was he going to do when she came from behind the curtain? He couldn't go on acting like nothing had happened. Something had changed. But he wasn't ready to deal with it. He had to have time to figure out just what it was, then decide what he wanted to do about it.

He sighed. This wasn't a good time to have something like this happen. It looked as if the weather was going to stay clear. With the snow melting steadily, he would be able to take Daisy down the mountain in a couple of days, then get back to his prospecting. That would leave a whole lot of questions unanswered.

Daisy eyed Tyler across the table. He met her gaze, but his eyes were empty of any message. He looked away, and she sighed and settled back in her chair. Zac was equally silent. This was the way things had been since Tyler locked Zac out yesterday morning, since he had kissed her.

She knew there was a lot that ought to be said, but she didn't know where to begin. The tension was so great she hesitated to break the silence. Something had to give soon.

"I'm going hunting," Tyler announced, getting up from the table. "We're out of meat."

Daisy looked up but said nothing. Zac didn't look up.

"You're both to stay inside," Tyler said.

175

"But the cougar's dead," Daisy said.

"The killers are still out there."

Daisy decided to stay inside. Something happened every time she went out. "I'll clean up," she offered, glad to do anything she could to ease the tension.

Tyler didn't say anything until he was ready to go out. "I may be gone all day."

Zac made no response. Daisy decided to do the same.

The cabin felt empty without Tyler. There was a vitality about him Zac lacked. He sat hunched over his cards while Daisy started clearing away.

Daisy wondered if it was because Tyler was older. He was definitely the one in control. She glanced out the window and caught a glimpse of him as he disappeared into the trees.

She picked up Zac's plate. He gave no sign he noticed.

She knew the snow would soon melt enough for Tyler to take her down the mountain. She would be glad to leave. She needed to get her emotions under control. She couldn't go on feeling this way about him. She didn't want to. But she was afraid she couldn't do anything about it as long as they were in the same cabin. Thank goodness Zac was here. Even sulking, he was a buffer between them.

"I have stood his mistreatment long enough!" Zac announced suddenly. "And I'm fed up with sitting on this mountain, freezing and eating deer meat." He got to his feet and walked over to the shelves. He took down a canister, opened it, and took out a wad of bills.

"What are you doing?" Daisy asked.

"I'm leaving. I've been bossed around long enough."

"I mean what are you doing with that money? Isn't it Tyler's?" She didn't know how Tyler could have so much money, but it made sense it would belong to him rather than Zac.

"He won't need it," Zac answered.

"What are you going to do?"

"I'm going to New Orleans. I've wanted to go there all my life. I don't see any reason why I should wait any longer."

"But you can't do it by stealing Tyler's money."

"It was bad enough when he blamed me for everything that went wrong around here, but he had no business locking me outside."

"He was upset about the cougar. He was planning to let you in."

"It doesn't matter. I don't care anymore," Zac said. He laid the money on the table and started to gather up his belongings.

He was really planning to leave. And he was planning to take all of Tyler's money.

"You won't need that much money to get to New Orleans," Daisy said. She continued cleaning up, but she was waiting for Zac to turn his back. "How will Tyler buy his supplies?"

"George will give him more."

"Why don't you ask George for money?"

Zac turned his back and Daisy edged closer to the table.

"George wouldn't give me a red dime."

"Why not?"

"Because I left school. He'll be angry with me, but he'll feel sorry for Tyler."

Zac turned just in time to snatch the money before Daisy's fingers could close around it.

"It's not yours," Daisy said. "You have no right to it." She made a grab for it, but Zac stuffed it in his pocket.

"I'll pay it back."

"You still have no right to take it."

"You can tell Tyler it's his own fault for the way he treated me."

"It's not," Daisy contradicted. "It's because you have no character." She didn't like the look in Zac's eyes, but she didn't back down. "What kind of person would take his brother's money? Don't think you can scare me by glaring at me like that," she said, hoping she wasn't going too far. "You may be a thief and a brat, but you're not a woman beater."

For a moment Daisy was afraid the question hung in the balance. Then Zac suddenly smiled.

"I have a better punishment for you."

"What?" Daisy asked nervously.

"Leaving you two here alone together. You deserve each other."

"What do you mean?"

"You're crazy about Tyler. I've known it for days. And he's goofy over you."

"He's not."

"He doesn't know it yet, but he is," Zac said, gathering up the last of his belongings. "I make you a present of each other." With that he slammed out the door.

Daisy watched helplessly as Zac went into the shed and reappeared moments later leading one of the mules. She ought to stop him, but short of using a gun, she didn't know how she could.

She sank into a chair. Could what he'd said be true? Could she really love Tyler?

But she already knew the answer. She had come upon it sometime during the night. It didn't matter that it was stupid or that she was so mad at herself she didn't know what to do. She loved Tyler, and that was that.

She didn't know if he loved her—she doubted it—but that wasn't her problem. She had to figure out how to teach herself not to love Tyler. Loving him would ruin her life.

She was still sitting at the table when Tyler returned with a deer. She looked up and knew instantly Zac was right.

"Zac stole your money and left for New Orleans," she said, wondering what else could go wrong with her life. "He took one of the mules, too."

Chapter Fourteen

Tyler had shown no discernible reaction to her news. "Did you get anything to eat?" he had asked. She had shaken her head. Without saying anything more, he had started dinner. They ate in silence that remained unbroken until they cleared away the dishes.

"I want to take this bandage off my head," she said once they'd finished.

"I don't think—"

"I'm tired of looking like a freak. I want to wash my hair. I feel like my scalp is crawling." She paused. "I'll probably have to cut it, too." She wondered if he remembered he had said he'd wash it for her.

"I'll heat the water," Tyler said. In minutes he had the stove covered with pots.

"I just want to wash my hair," Daisy said.

"You'll need a bath afterward."

She hadn't wanted to ask him, but she wanted a bath very badly. She helped fill the buckets. It was easier this

179

time since they were able to get water from the stream.

"Sit down," Tyler said when he was ready to remove the bandage.

Daisy had been having nightmares about her looks. At the same time she was glad he had no mirror to show her what she looked like.

Tyler removed the bandage. "It's still a little red," he said, "but I think it's safe to wash your hair. I'll cut it."

Daisy wasn't sure about this. No one had cut her hair except to trim the ends, but it was probably best to let Tyler do it while she couldn't see the results.

"Don't cut any more than you have to."

"I won't."

Daisy was relieved when the first singed ends hit the floor. She had had an uncomfortable feeling Tyler was cutting too high on her head, but the pieces that fell were short.

When a foot-long strand hit the floor, she leapt out of the chair. "I'll look like a boy," she cried, staring at the lock of hair.

"Your hair will still be down to your shoulders," Tyler assured her.

"But that's too short."

Tyler took her by the shoulders and gently guided her back to the chair. "It'll grow out. In the meantime, you can wear it in a knot."

"Unmarried women don't wear buns," Daisy said.

"Then you can wear a bonnet."

"That's for old women."

"Well, you can't go around with a hole burned in your hair."

With that prosaic comment he continued to cut off huge amounts of her hair. Each hank of hair that hit the floor seemed to carry a part of her with it. By the time Tyler had finished, she felt like a shorn sheep.

"I'll wash it, then trim any ends I've missed," he said.

She waited listlessly as he brought a shallow pan to the table and poured some water into it. He tested it. Apparently satisfied, he fetched soap and a towel from the shelves in the corner.

"Let me do the work," he told Daisy as he positioned her head over the pan. "You just keep your head still and your eyes closed."

As Daisy waited, she tried to imagine what she would look like with short hair. Horrified by every picture that came to mind, she tried to think of ways to dress it; she fabricated excuses for its length. But it was pointless. Not even saloon girls wore their hair short.

It was a strange sensation to feel the warm water poured over her head, but it was even more disconcerting to feel Tyler's strong fingers gently working the soap into her scalp. It had been years since her mother had washed her hair. She had forgotten how pleasant it could be.

But this was more than pleasant. There was an intimacy in allowing Tyler to wash her hair, an unspoken admission that they shared something special. As his callused hands gathered and twisted her hair, she felt ripples run from her head to her toes. She hadn't realized how tense she was until Tyler began to massage her neck at the base of her skull. She could feel the gentle pressure of his thumb and forefinger gradually loosen the tension in her scalp. It felt wonderful. She realized he wasn't just washing her hair. He was as aware of the tension between them as she was.

She suddenly realized he had been washing her hair too long. She was enjoying this too much, but she didn't want him to stop.

Tyler rinsed her hair by pouring water over her head. That broke the spell. He threw away the first pan of water and rinsed her hair again.

"What do I look like?" she wanted to know.

"I won't be able to tell until it's dry." He combed her

hair, being careful to avoid the scar. Then he trimmed a few uneven ends. He dried it by rubbing it in a towel between his hands. Daisy felt the damp tendrils against her cheeks as Tyler combed it once more. He stood back a little when he finished.

"I like it like this," he said. "It frames your face." He took a strand between his fingers. "You've got some curl, too."

He was just trying to make her feel better. No man could find a woman with short, curly hair attractive.

"You can take your bath now," he said.

Daisy waited patiently as Tyler emptied all the buckets of water into the tub.

"I'm going to get more," he announced. "I want a bath, too."

Daisy felt something tighten in her chest. She was relieved to have Tyler leave the cabin. She was even more relieved to be able to retreat behind the curtain.

She was acutely aware she would be alone with Tyler tonight.

As she unbuttoned her dress, she was very sensitive to the feel and pressure of her fingers against her skin. She imagined they were Tyler's fingers, and her body became warm and quivered from involuntary muscle spasms that raced from one end of her to the other.

She wanted Tyler to make love to her.

That thought was even more shocking than knowing she was in love with him. What could she be thinking? All her life her parents had drummed it into her head that her only possession of any real value was her virginity. Here she was wanting to give it away to a bearded mountain man she had no chance of marrying. If she didn't know better, she'd swear the bullet had affected her brain.

Daisy had stepped into the tub and settled down into the water before Tyler returned. She felt completely vulnerable, as though the curtain was transparent. She found herself sitting with her arms across her chest, her hands hugging her shoulders. She felt foolish, but couldn't drive the feeling away. Every time she touched herself, she imagined it was Tyler doing it.

Her skin was ultrasensitive. Even the lapping water sent shivers through her body. Her nipples hardened until they were achingly sensitive. A feeling of nervous excitement had settled in her belly. She began to experience a feeling in her feminine parts she had never felt before. In a matter of minutes Daisy felt she was about to jump out of her skin.

Resolutely pushing aside every thought of Tyler, Daisy stood up to dry her body. She was intentionally rough, pummeling her flesh, rubbing her skin until it glowed pink, anything to destroy the feelings that were threatening to destroy her control.

She dressed quickly and stepped back into the room. Tyler sat reading a book. He put it aside.

"I want you to cut my hair," he said.

His request floored her. "I don't know how."

"It's not difficult. Just keep cutting until it's about the same length as Zac's."

Tyler's brown, wavy hair fell to his shoulders. She would have to cut nearly as much off his head as he had off hers. She felt a shiver of satisfaction, but thrust it aside, ashamed of it. Tyler had cut her hair because it was necessary.

"How long has it been since anybody cut your hair?" she asked.

"Years."

"Why do you want me to cut it now?"

"It's time."

Typical answer from Tyler. She figured it was just as well he didn't know she'd fallen in love with him. That would probably dry up his conversation entirely.

Tyler seated himself in the same chair she had occupied

and handed her the scissors. Daisy was reluctant to take them, but Tyler continued to hold them out to her.

"Okay, but you'll have nobody to blame but yourself if it turns out a mess."

She wasn't totally without experience. She had cut her father's hair, but his hair was nothing like Tyler's luxuriant growth. She hesitated to start.

"Hurry up. The water will soon be hot."

Grasping a handful of hair, Daisy held it straight out from Tyler's head and cut it off. She set to work trimming all around until the hair was off his collar. Then with painstaking care, she proceeded to cut it short all over his head.

Daisy found it exciting to see Tyler's ears appear from under the mass of hair. Strange, but she'd thought of him as an older man. She found that once some of the hair was removed, he looked much more youthful.

She was amazed to discover he had a long, slim neck, surprisingly elegant for a man of his size. His shoulders were just as powerful as she had imagined. And he was so big.

"You'll have to bend over for me to get the top," she said.

Tyler inclined his head. She wondered at his trust. He didn't know she wouldn't make a comical mess of his hair. Maybe he didn't care. She wished she had his lack of concern, but it wasn't the same for women. Too much depended on their looks.

For the hundredth time, she wondered what he would look like without that beard. Some women liked bearded men, but she never would, not even if he trimmed it quite short. It was brown. A beard had to be black to look decent.

Oddly enough, she found the shape of his head appealing. In fact, the more of him she uncovered, the more appealing he became. She found herself almost shivering from the intense desire that kept shooting through her body, causing her muscles to quiver uncontrollably, causing her legs to feel as though they might fall out from under her.

"I'd better stop before I cut off too much," she said, stepping back. She took a deep breath and forced a smile. She had no intention of letting Tyler guess any of what she'd been thinking.

Tyler ran his hand over his head. "It feels about right," he said. "You sure you don't mind my using your corner?"

"Of course not," she said, trying to sound as normal as possible. "It's your cabin."

Daisy stood by, tense and stiff, while Tyler dragged the tub to the door and emptied her bathwater. Then he filled it with fresh water, gathered some clothes and fresh towels, and disappeared behind the barrier.

Daisy collapsed into a chair, but her trial wasn't over. Her imagination reached new heights in picturing what must be taking place behind the screen. Tyler was so tall his head and shoulders were visible over the top of the blankets as he stood behind them disrobing. His shoulders were as smooth and free of hair as she had imagined. They were also as powerfully muscled.

She shivered when she heard the soft rustle of his clothes on the floor, the sloshing of the water as he stepped into the bath and sank down in it. She couldn't imagine how he did it. It was a tight fit for her. It would be impossible for him to fit his long limbs into the tub.

She tried to imagine how he would situate himself. She imagined his legs out of the tub, long powerful legs that had enabled him to run so swiftly to her rescue. Most of his torso must also be above water level. She remembered the powerful arms and shoulders that had lifted and carried her so easily. She had been able to feel the shape and strength of his muscles even through the heavy shirt and coat he wore.

If she could only touch him now, feel the muscles, feel the power under her fingers.

Her hand opened and closed. She couldn't imagine why she was so preoccupied with Tyler's body. No man had ever affected her like this, not even Guy Cochrane. And he was more handsome than Tyler.

She heard the sloshing of water, and Tyler stood and began to dry himself. He had washed his hair. As he dried it vigorously, it curled into ringlets like the hair of the Greeks in her father's books. It gave him an entirely different appearance. It made him look young and virile. She thought of his beautiful brown eyes and broad, clear forehead. There must be something wrong with his face for him to hide it behind a beard. It was a shame.

She told herself she was no prize. Now she had no hair, she'd be lucky if she didn't become a laughingstock. She was thinking about her dismal future when Tyler pulled back the curtain and stepped out, naked to the waist.

Daisy stopped breathing.

Even with the beard, he was the most overwhelming man she'd ever met. The sight of him from the waist up rendered her speechless as well as breathless. Rising from a slim waist and a flat abdomen was the most fantastic chest and pair of shoulders Daisy had ever seen. They were even better than she had imagined. He wore black pants that fitted his body like a glove. After the baggy clothes he had worn before, they were a revelation. Long slim legs, powerful thighs, and a beautifully rounded behind.

Not in her wildest dreams had she imagined such a perfect body was concealed in the shapeless clothes Tyler wore.

"Do you mind if I shave?" Tyler asked.

"No," Daisy managed to murmur.

Tyler extracted a mirror from inside a small cabinet.

"You said you didn't have a mirror," Daisy said.

"I didn't want you to see yourself until you were better."

"Can I see now?"

"After I finish. It'll give your hair time to dry."

Daisy tried to be angry at him, but it was impossible when she couldn't take her eyes off his naked torso. Except for a dusting of hairs at the center of his chest, he was perfectly smooth. His broad shoulders seemed almost too large for the slim waist. She watched, fascinated, as he gathered his shaving implements. The powerful muscles of his chest bunched and quivered. The muscles in his arms and forearms rippled smoothly under his skin.

He sat down at the table next to her. She practically had to sit on her hands to stifle the impulse to reach out and touch him. She could. He was that close.

Her breath came slowly and with great effort. Gathering all her willpower, Daisy concentrated on his shaving.

She had watched her father shave so many times she had stopped noticing, but she watched, fascinated, as Tyler worked lather into his still wet beard. Before long he looked as though he'd fallen face first into a bowl of whipped cream. Daisy's resulting smile helped a little to relax some of the tension, which seemed about to break her bones.

It struck her all at once. Tyler wouldn't have lathered his beard if he only intended to trim it. He was going to shave it off!

She watched his first pass with the razor in stunned surprise. It cleared only a small spot high on his cheek, but an amazing amount of beard fell to the table. Gradually, clearing a small spot at a time, one side of Tyler's face emerged. Much to Daisy's shock, she realized it looked a lot like Zac's face.

Could Tyler be as handsome as Zac? She wanted to see

his mouth. She had to know what his mouth and chin looked like.

But Tyler turned his head and started to shave the other side of his face. His mouth and chin remained buried under an obscuring growth of brown hair soaked with shaving lather. What an incongruous sight.

Daisy waited with growing impatience. It seemed Tyler took longer to shave the other side of his face. When he at last raised the razor to his upper lip, she almost held her breath.

In a matter of a few moments, the most kissable mouth she'd ever seen emerged. A few minutes more, and an adorable chin followed. He was gorgeous. He wasn't as handsome as Zac, but he was gorgeous. Common sense told her it was the contrast from the beard, that once she got used to his face, she wouldn't think it all that special, but common sense wasn't very popular with her right now. She'd spent her life at the beck and call of common sense. And once she reached Albuquerque, she'd have to go back to being sensible. For now she felt a reckless desire to forget common sense, to let her senses run wild.

"Are you satisfied?" Tyler asked.

"You shaved it off for me?"

"You said I was hiding something." He ran his hand over his smooth face. "I'm not hiding now."

"You shouldn't. You are a good-looking man."

"How can you say that after seeing Zac?"

"You're handsome, too. In fact, I think I like your looks better."

"Why?"

"Your face has character."

Tyler's smile was wry. "When a man says a woman's face has character, he means she's ugly as sin."

"When a woman says it, she means she admires the man behind the face."

She could tell he wanted to believe her. She could also tell he didn't.

"Sit," he said. "I need to brush your hair before you see yourself." He had no brush, so he used a comb. When he finished, he handed her the mirror.

She was afraid. She had been able to live with her fears up to now because they were unconfirmed. But if she looked in the mirror, she would no longer be able to tell herself Zac had exaggerated. Daisy took the mirror, closed her eyes, and held it up to her scar.

"You can hardly see it," Tyler said. "Your hair practically covers it already."

Daisy opened her eyes and felt some of the tension ease. The scar truly was almost hidden by her hair. Once it was completely healed, it would probably be invisible. She would know it was there, but nobody else would. Her hair was a darker brown than Tyler's. His was closer to chestnut, hers more light mahogany, a nice contrast with her fair skin.

Gradually she lowered the mirror. The freckles had not disappeared, but they didn't seem so numerous or so dark. Her father had always said his sister's freckles disappeared. Daisy hoped hers were about to follow suit.

But she could indulge no hope for her hair.

She held the mirror out from her until she could get a full picture of her head and shoulders. It took a few seconds for the full enormity of the disaster to sink in. Her hair barely touched her shoulders. It billowed about her head in a riot of curls like a bunch of tumbleweed.

She was ruined! She might as well go to work in a dance hall. It didn't seem important that she looked younger and more innocent or that her face seemed less angular. She ignored the fact that her eyes looked less prominent or her neck ivory smooth. She only saw her hopes for a decent marriage cast on the floor with her hair.

The mirror slipped from her loosened grasp and shattered on the floor. The only thing that penetrated the nightmare was the realization that Tyler had taken her in his arms and was holding her close.

"Nobody will want to marry me now," she said.

"Lots of people will want to marry you."

"I saw what I look like."

"If I were wanting to get married, I'd want you."

"You're just being kind," Daisy said, not raising her head from his chest. "You know I'm homely. Now I look worse than ever."

Tyler pulled her arms from around him and held her away from him. He raised her chin when she refused to look up. "You'll find somebody who loves you," he said.

"Not now." She twisted her chin from his grasp and brushed aside some of the hated hair that got in her face. That would never have happened before he cut it.

"Daisy, men don't choose a wife because of her hair."

"You've never been a woman. You don't know how men think."

"Tell me."

"As far as men are concerned, women come in types. There are the soiled doves, the women who're so beautiful they're worshiped for their looks no matter whether they're good or bad, the women who are saintly, and all the rest. I come with all the rest."

"That's absurd."

"I have no money, I'm not pretty, and I have no family. Now I've lost my hair. I'm worthless."

"That's ridiculous. You—"

"I'll probably end up marrying some ignorant man without an idea in his head. He'll expect me to cook his meals, wash his clothes, keep his house, and let him father any number of children on me. He won't listen to what I say, care what I want, or think I have any right to be

190

treated decently. He'll beat me when he's angry and rape me when he's drunk.''

''No, he won't.''

''You don't know anything about it. My father was like that. Except he wasn't violent unless his will was crossed, and even then he didn't strike us. But it never occurred to him we might want something else or be able to provide an answer when he couldn't.

''You don't understand,'' she told him, trying to control herself. ''Your entire existence doesn't depend on the whim of some man. You can do as you please.''

''Even men have limits.''

''Not like women. It would be impossible for me to live up here like you do. Nobody would think I was an honest woman.''

''I think you are.''

''That's just like you,'' she said, exasperated. ''You never can face reality. People won't take something like that on faith.''

''I defy anybody to insult you.''

He really was adorable. It was a shame he was such an idiot. ''There you go again, ignoring reality. You'd be the last person to be able to establish my innocence.''

''I'm the only one who really knows.''

Daisy became aware she was being clasped to Tyler's naked chest. She tried to pull away, but he wouldn't let her. She couldn't tell whether it was her hair or the hair on his chest, but something tickled her nose. Moving her head only made her more aware her cheek was against his soft, warm skin.

Swiftly her entire mood changed, and she found it quite easy to forget the tragedy of her hair. In fact, there was no room in her mind for anything but the man who held her in his embrace. She wanted to run and hide, to pretend he'd never seen her at her worst. But she clung to him because having seen her at her worst, he had not rejected her.

All the love she had for him welled up in her heart, and she clung to him more tightly. He was the dearest man she knew. No one else would have cared for her, put up with her demands, endured her complaining and criticism, and still tell her she was pretty.

It was impossible not to love him. It was also impossible not to want him to kiss her, not to want him to hold her, to comfort her.

"You've got to learn to have more faith in the goodness and fairness of human nature," Tyler told her. "Most people are willing to believe the best if you only give them the chance."

Daisy didn't think they would, but Tyler did, and for that she would be forever grateful. Holding on to him, she was imbued with his optimism. As long as he held her, she really was the woman he thought her to be.

Daisy held on tighter. It would soon be time to let go, but not now, not yet. Maybe if she stayed here long enough, she could come to believe in herself the way Tyler did.

Tyler tipped her head up and placed a gentle kiss on her lips. That definitely helped. Guy had kissed her on the cheek once, but his kiss made her feel like his sister.

There was nothing brotherly about Tyler's attitude toward her, or about his kisses. He was making it plain he found Daisy desirable.

Daisy was wholly lacking experience in love, but she could tell when a man was aroused. The proof of Tyler's desire burned against her abdomen. Yet he didn't desire her merely for physical release. He said he found her pretty. He said he thought she was an admirable woman capable of doing just about anything she set her mind to. He said she was a woman whose company he enjoyed, whose presence was exciting.

Daisy's resistance collapsed. Pushed up against his chest, her breasts had become full and sensitive. Even the slightest movement sent enervating tongues of desire spiraling through her body. The last bit of resistance fled, and holding on to him with all the fervor of her newfound passion, she sank into his arms.

Without warning, Tyler scooped her up and carried her over to her bed. He set her down, then dropped down beside her. He pulled her to him once more, kissed her forehead and eyelids. His hands seemed to roam all over her shoulders and back, setting her body into a frenzy of spiraling sensations.

Once more Tyler took her lips in a deep kiss. His hungry tongue forced its way into her mouth. The intimacy of it, the opening of herself to him, there were so many new things she couldn't absorb at once. But she didn't want to hold back, didn't want to miss any part of this wonderful experience. Her tongue joined his in a sinuous dance that had Daisy nearly melting with the heat.

Tyler's hand cupped her right breast. The shock caused Daisy to gasp, but Tyler did not release her lips. She knew she should tell him to stop. She knew she had already gone far enough, but he was tracing circles around her nipple through her clothes. The sensation was enough to dissolve her willpower. It was more than enough to unleash a powerful desire from some well deep inside her. She wanted more.

She yielded to temptation.

Daisy let her head fall back so Tyler could kiss her neck and throat. The feel of his mouth on her skin curled her toes. She made no objection when he unbuttoned her dress and slipped his hand inside. She was beyond objection when he unbuttoned her chemise and cupped her breast with his naked hand.

She felt helpless, unable to resist.

Tyler laid her back on the bed, caressed the tops of

her breasts with his hot lips. No one had never touched her body. She had no idea that a mere touch could overwhelm all resistance, all caution, all reserve. Neither had she suspected the pleasure of his touch. It was so intense she thought she might faint. She didn't care that he was opening her dress and slipping it and her chemise off her shoulders. Every part of her consciousness focused on his other hand as it moved down her side, along her thigh, cupped her bottom, pulled her against him.

His body was so hot, so swollen with desire, she felt molten, on the verge of bursting into flame.

Tyler bent down and took one of her nipples into his mouth. Nothing could compare to this. Every nerve in her body flamed with aching sensitivity. Her body arched off the bed, pressed against him. When his hand covered her other breast and began to tease her nipple, she thought she would lose control completely.

But even as she felt herself on the verge of sinking into a mindless pool of pleasure, Daisy knew she must stop. She fought to regain control, but each time she slipped a little further into passionate release. Try as she might, she couldn't summon the willpower to pull clear.

Until she felt Tyler's hand move across her leg to the inside of her thigh. It was clear he intended to open every part of her body to his hunger.

Desperately reining in her numbed and scattered wits, Daisy realized she had allowed him to go too far. She had to stop him. If she didn't, she'd never forgive herself. Once he found out, he'd never speak to her again.

"We've got to stop," she whispered, her voice a trembling thread. She tried to pull her dress back up.

"You're driving me crazy," Tyler murmured into her shoulder as he tugged her dress farther down her body.

"Please, you must stop."

"There's no reason," Tyler said. "You want me as much as I want you."

Daisy captured both of his hands in hers. "Yes, there is. I'm engaged."

Chapter Fifteen

Tyler froze. "You're what?" he demanded, his face only inches from her own.

Daisy knew she should have told him sooner. There had been any number of opportunities. It just never seemed to be the right thing to say.

"I'm engaged to marry Guy Cochrane." She hated the look in Tyler's eyes.

"The brother of your best friend?"

She nodded.

"And you let me kiss you," he said, stunned. "You almost let me—"

"I didn't mean to do more than let you hold me," Daisy said. "I didn't think that would be so terrible. But I liked it so much I didn't stop you when I should have."

"Stop me when you should!" Tyler echoed, fury turning his eyes dark and hard. He backed away from her. "An honorable woman wouldn't have even let me kiss her. She'd have slapped me for just thinking what I did."

That hurt more than the rest. "I'm sorry, I guess I don't come up to your standards," Daisy said, close to tears. "It doesn't matter. No one else seems to think I do either."

"Obviously Mr. Cochrane does, or he wouldn't have asked you to marry him."

"I don't know why he did," Daisy confessed, too distraught to be thinking of what she said. "I'm sure he doesn't love me."

"Then why did you accept him?"

She couldn't tell him she'd accepted Guy because she was certain she'd never get another offer. "Not all marriages are based on love," Daisy replied. "As a matter of fact, a feeling of affection is more than most women ever get. Many actually spend their entire lives married to men they despise."

"That's absurd. No woman should do that."

"It's clear you don't know anything about being a woman. I was more fortunate than most."

"But not so fortunate you were willing to turn down a little fun before the vows were said."

"That's not fair," Daisy cried. "I told you I didn't mean to let things go so far. I was foolish." She struggled to keep the tears from her eyes. "Anyway, it doesn't really matter. Guy won't marry me looking like this. We-'ve both gotten upset over nothing."

"That's not the point," Tyler said. "As long as you're engaged, you shouldn't allow another man to touch you."

"Considering both you and your brother have spent the night in my bed, I doubt anyone would consider me untouched. I mean to release Guy from his promise the minute I see him."

"Why should you do that?"

"For the very reason you got so angry at me. I've spent a week locked away in a cabin with two men and no woman present to vouch for my virtue.''

''It need never be known. We can think of something.''

''I might as well have let you ruin me. Now go do something, cook or hunt or take care of your mules. I need to be alone.''

She pushed him out of her corner and pulled the curtains closed. Then the tears started. She sank down on the bed. Why had she let Tyler go so far? She had never been the victim of her physical appetites. She hadn't even known she had such appetites. Yet she had wanted him to make love to her.

Why?

Because she loved him. She might think him the most impractical man on the face of the earth, but she had fallen in love with him precisely because he wouldn't let his dreams be bounded by the limits of common sense. He had the guts to want, the courage to go after what he wanted despite what anybody else might think.

He had no doubts about himself. He was confident he would be able to do anything he put his mind to. He was everything she wanted to be and wasn't. He had the strength she wished she had, the determination she lacked. He was not afraid to dream.

He would never have accepted Guy Cochrane's offer.

But she hadn't felt this way six months ago when Guy proposed. She had been relieved someone had finally offered to free her from her father's tyranny. She might not be able to live in Philadelphia like her mother, but she would have a nice house, decent clothes, and a chance to go to parties. After the years of poverty and empty evenings, she had been looking forward to it.

And she liked Guy. He was very attractive and a gentleman. She expected they would have a pleasant life together. She hadn't worried that his attentions were few and perfunctory. Her mother had taught her that proper men and women were careful to restrain their feelings for each other before marriage and afterward in public. The kind of kisses she had shared with Tyler would have been enjoyed only in the privacy of their bedchamber, or not at all if she behaved according to conventional rules.

But then someone had killed her father, she had ended up with Tyler, and everything had come unraveled. Her reputation was ruined. She hadn't let herself think about it before, but after what had almost happened tonight, she had to face facts. Guy would break off their engagement. She couldn't expect him to do anything else.

But it hardly mattered. Tyler had made her thoroughly dissatisfied with any relationship she and Guy might have been able to forge. She felt the tears run down her cheeks. The only logical thing left for her to do was marry Zac or Tyler, but she wouldn't marry either. She didn't love Zac, and even though she did love Tyler, she refused to spend the rest of her life in a mountain cabin waiting for him to find gold that wasn't there.

She didn't know what she was going to do, but there had to be some other way. Tyler had said she could do anything she wanted, but she didn't know how to do anything except cook, take care of a house, and read books. Maybe she'd get a job as a housekeeper. She wouldn't starve, and she wouldn't have to marry some man she didn't care for.

The tears flowed faster.

It didn't do any good to hope Tyler might change, that he might settle down and get a real job. He didn't love her. He had never pretended he did. He might say he liked her. He might say he thought she was attractive, but he would feel differently when he got back to town and there were other women available.

"The snow has melted over much of the mountain," Tyler announced at dinner that evening. "I think we'll be able to get through tomorrow."

"Good." She didn't feel like saying anything else. She felt empty. He was getting rid of her.

"My brother and his wife are in Albuquerque awaiting the birth of their first child. I plan to take you to stay with them. That way nobody need ever know that you haven't been with them the whole time."

"Will your brother agree?"

"Of course."

"And his wife?"

"She'll do anything she can to help."

Anything they can to help get Tyler off the hook. She would be the one to suffer the consequences of these last few days, not he.

"You will be able to stay with Hen and his wife until your friends return from Santa Fe."

"I don't have any money." She hated making that confession.

"Hen will see to anything you need."

He and Zac were certainly free with their brothers' money.

"I want to thank you for all you've done," she said after a long pause. "I know I've been a lot of trouble, and now with everything going wrong . . ."

"Don't worry about it. Everything will be right as rain in a few days."

She thought of her hair, the scar on her head, the scar in her heart. Things would never be right again.

They said little more for the rest of the evening. Daisy retired to her corner. She had become rather fond of the little space. It gave her more privacy than she had enjoyed in her own home. But then things here were different from her home. Her father could never stand for her or her mother to be out of his sight for more than a short time. Since he didn't like other people, that meant they had no social life.

Here Zac and Tyler had organized everything around

her. That didn't happen even in Adora's home. Mr. Cochrane ruled just as absolutely as her father. Adora had never heard her mother or Guy question anything he said. Even though Guy was easygoing, he showed signs of expecting his home to be much the same. Daisy would have accepted that if she had married him before she met Tyler. Now she didn't know what she would do.

Any man she did marry, if she could find one to marry her now, would probably be even more demanding. She had noticed the poorer the man, the more he expected of his wife. She didn't know enough of society yet to understand that, but she did know what she had seen.

Poverty made a slave of women. She decided if she were going to be poor, she would be poor by herself. She wasn't going to be a slave to anybody.

But that brought back the frightening thought of having to make it alone, and she didn't know a thing about surviving on her own.

Tyler tossed and turned in his bed. Despite trying all day to put it out of his mind, he was still furious at Daisy for what he felt was a betrayal. The engagement stuck in his craw. Without that, what they had almost done would simply have been a decision made between two adults. With the engagement, it made him look like a lecher.

He had never in his life made an improper suggestion to a woman whose feelings were attached. He might not want to be married himself, but wedding vows were as sacred to him as they were to his married brothers. He felt like a heel. No decent man went around trying to make love to an engaged woman.

Make love! That wasn't what he had been meaning to do. He had been intent on making lust, and he couldn't glorify it by any other name.

It was this weakness that worried him as much as anything else. He never would have been tempted before. What was it about Daisy that caused him to lose control?

She was damned attractive. He couldn't call her cute or beautiful, but there was something about her that he found irresistible. He had found her attractive even when her head was bandaged. That should have told him something.

He guessed part of it was her courage. She never lost heart or went to pieces. And she wasn't a pest. She went out of her way to be as little trouble as possible. She even tried to help with the work. She had gone after that deer because of him. He couldn't explain to her he had no interest in it except to please her, not after she had dragged Zac out to help her fight off the cougar.

He had to laugh at that. After her first encounter with the beast, he would have thought she'd never want to go near one again. Yet she charged out into the snow to protect his deer.

His deer!

He was glad to see the last of the creature. She had no idea how difficult it was to tear limbs from oak trees in winter. The trees seemed particularly determined to hold on to them.

He ought to feel guilty sitting here feeling sorry for himself when Daisy was hiding behind the curtain because her whole life had fallen apart. It wasn't often a poor woman got the chance to marry the only son of the richest man in town. It was exactly what her mother had taught her to want. It was the only role her father had prepared her to take on.

Tyler had helped take it from her.

He absolved himself from most of the blame because he hadn't known she was engaged. But even as he tried to assuage his conscience, he was angry she would agree to marry a man she didn't love. There was more to life than that. She must have dreams. Surely she wanted to find someone she could love with a great and lasting passion.

Why should she? He didn't. If someone told him he had to marry tomorrow, he would look for a sensible woman who would perform her duties efficiently and cause him the least trouble and worry. He had no right to criticize Daisy for doing basically the same thing.

He guessed he was used to thinking of women in terms of Rose and Iris. Two less compliant females would be hard to find. But he wondered what compromises they might have been willing to make if they hadn't married George and Monty. In all likelihood they had considered a marriage of convenience at one time or another, yet nobody held it against them now.

In the end, he wasn't able to reach any conclusion that satisfactorily explained why he should suddenly be behaving in a fashion completely unlike himself.

But one thing he did know. He would have to start for Albuquerque tomorrow. He didn't dare trust himself in the cabin with Daisy another night.

Daisy woke up to find Tyler standing over her.

"We need to get started early. It's a long trip, and I don't want to spend more than one night on the road."

Daisy opened her eyes, but she could barely make out Tyler's features. "It's still dark," she said.

"It'll be dawn by the time we start."

Daisy groaned. She didn't think she had slept as much as two hours. But she got up. There was nothing to pack. Everything she had was on her back.

"We'll take the mattress and blankets," Tyler said. "You won't like sleeping on the ground."

"You do."

"I'm used to it."

"I can get used to it, too."

203

"There's no need. You'll be sleeping in a bed tomorrow night."

She wanted to prove something to him—she needed to—but it seemed pointless to argue. She rolled up the mattress and folded the blankets.

"Can I help you pack?" she asked. He was fixing their breakfast. The least she could do was gather up his things in the meantime.

"I packed everything before I woke you. Sit down and eat. I'll tie your things on the burro."

"You sit down and eat as well," Daisy said, angry he had done everything himself. The perfect man who didn't need anybody. She realized he thought he was better off this way.

Maybe he was. She wished she didn't need people.

But she did. It was essential to her to feel wanted, needed, loved. There were times she thought she would do anything just to feel that way. When she was little she thought her father wanted, needed, and loved her. Later she discovered he loved no one but himself.

"I guess it's time to go."

Tyler did let her take care of the dishes while he tied the mattress and blankets on the burro.

"I'd let you have a mule, but—"

"Don't apologize. The poor burro would never stand up to your weight."

As she waited for him to help her into the saddle, she looked back at the cabin and felt a pang. It would be some time before she knew the full consequences of her time here, but in some ways these last nine days had been the best of her life. None of the old equations worked, but then none of the old constraints bound her. It had been a halcyon time, a time of simplicity, of restfulness, of a happiness of a kind she would never experience again. It had been a time for seeking new horizons, of pushing limits, of discarding old ideas.

Now she was about to return to the world where the old constraints bound until they pinched, where new ideas were frowned on, where new horizons were avoided. She felt afraid.

She was wearing one of Tyler's heavy coats with the fur-lined cape over her head. She wondered if he would let her keep it. He'd probably offer to buy her a new one, but she'd rather keep this one. It would be a mute reminder of their time together.

Tyler lifted Daisy into the saddle and was just mounting up himself when they saw Willie Mozel coming through the forest at a trot.

"They're coming," he managed to gasp.

"Who?" Tyler asked.

"The three men who tied me up. Old Man Carver told me they were at his place last night. They plan to work their way along the ridge until they hit every cabin. They ought to be here before tonight."

"Thanks," Tyler said. "You take care of yourself." He took hold of the reins to the burro and started out at a trot.

"Who's coming?" Daisy asked. She didn't like riding at a trot. The burro had a rough stride. She didn't think she could stand the pain of being bounced in the saddle for long.

"The men who tried to kill you," Tyler replied.

"How do you know it's the same men?" Daisy managed to call forward to Tyler despite the bouncing. Fear of these men clutched at her throat and made it hard for her to speak.

"They stopped by Willie's a few days ago asking about two young men," he answered over his shoulder. "They tied him up when they didn't like his answers. He got away and came here."

"Why didn't you tell me?"

He slowed down to let her come alongside. "You

would have worried. There was no need. They couldn't follow him. The snow covered his tracks.''

"But they could have come anytime since.'' She thought of the time she had spent outside the cabin, her thoughtless comings and goings, never looking over her shoulder, never checking to see if anyone were around.

"I told Zac. He was on the lookout.''

She turned her gaze away from overhanging limbs to glare at him. "You told Zac, but you wouldn't tell me!'' She was so mad she didn't feel the bouncing. He was the one person who had been telling her she could do anything she put her mind to, yet he didn't tell her three bloodthirsty killers were hot on her trail. What did he think she'd do, fall into a dead faint?

"What could you do?'' Tyler asked. "Besides, you were still recovering.''

"It's my life we're talking about here, Tyler Randolph. I think I have a right to know when it's in jeopardy.''

"Well, you know now, so I don't see why you're so upset.''

"I know because I overheard Willie talking to you, not because you thought to tell me. That's why I'm upset.''

The trail had become so steep they had to slow down to a fast walk. Deep snow still remained in some places under the trees. The crust was hard, the footing icy. It would be all too easy for one of the animals to fall and break a leg.

"Willie didn't mean for you to hear. You shouldn't have been listening.''

"You're just like my father,'' Daisy snapped. "If it's men's talk, then women should be deaf, dumb, and blind. But when it comes to work, we're supposed to be smart enough to figure it out for ourselves.'' She jerked on the burro's reins. The animal brayed its objection when she nearly bent his neck double to make him turn around on the narrow trail. He backed her into a pine tree, which retaliated by showering her with snow and ice.

"What are you doing?" Tyler asked.

"I'm going back," Daisy said, digging her heels into the burro's flanks. "You've been wanting to find these men for days."

Tyler was at her side in a flash. He leaned out of the saddle and grabbed the reins of the burro. "We can't go back up there. We'd be sitting ducks."

"Why?" She yanked on the reins, but he wouldn't let go. "We could hide in the cabin. You've got plenty of ammunition."

"But we don't have plenty of food," Tyler pointed out. "They could starve us out. Or burn us out. There are three of them against one of me."

"You forgot about me."

"Can you shoot?"

Her gaze became less defiant. "My father wouldn't let me learn."

"One of me," Tyler repeated. "I can't take that risk with your life."

"Can't we wait to get a look at them?" Her tone was more conciliatory.

"No. They're better mounted than we are. Our only hope is to be so far ahead they can't catch us before we reach Albuquerque."

Daisy still didn't move. She looked unconvinced.

"If we stop them now, we may never find the man behind them. You'll never be safe until we know who he is and why he wants you dead."

The thought sent chills up and down Daisy's spine. She might not have to worry about Guy jilting her. She could be dead before he got the chance.

"You won't be safe either," Daisy said. "Your life is as much in danger as mine."

"But I can take care of myself. Now let's get moving.

We can't afford to lose any more time." Still holding the reins, Tyler turned the burro and started down the mountain.

"You've made your point," he said without turning around to face her. "I promise I won't keep anything from you."

Daisy hadn't anticipated the satisfaction that surged through her upon having gained that victory. She realized it was only a small thing, but she felt as if she had achieved something momentous. For the first time, she had stood up for herself against a man and won a point. She liked the feeling and decided she was going to try it again as soon as she found the opportunity.

"What are they like?" Daisy asked.

"I never saw them," Tyler replied, "but they're plenty determined. They came back to check on the fire, and they found us in the mountains quicker than I thought possible. Somebody wants you dead real bad."

Daisy wished she hadn't asked. She felt helpless to defend herself. "The only person I can think of who might want to kill me is Bob Greene."

"Why?"

"He wanted my father's land."

"Enough to kill for it?"

"That's what doesn't make sense. It's not worth much, even as grazing land."

"How much does he have?"

"I don't know. Our . . . *my* land runs from the river to the base of the mountains."

Tyler whistled.

"Is that a lot?"

"Your father ought to have been a wealthy man."

"He never was. It seemed we had just enough cows to pay for the expense of rounding them up. Daddy said it was rustlers. Greene is the only man I can figure who might be doing it."

"But that's no reason to want to kill you. If he's been rustling your cows, he could just keep on doing it."

"I can't think of anybody else."

They slowed down as they allowed the animals to pick their way across a sparkling stream engorged with the runoff from the melting snow. The deep green of spruce and pine formed a sharp contrast to the white snow. Here and there the browns and yellows of the rocky mountain soil showed through, muting the effect of the sunlight on the snow's pristine surface. The call of an occasional bird broke the silence, but Daisy saw no animals. It was almost as though she and Tyler were alone in this winter wonderland. It was almost impossible to believe that somewhere out there three men were following them, determined to kill her.

She kicked the burro in the flanks, encouraging him to keep close to Tyler. He might be a dreamer more concerned with fabulous hotels and lost gold mines than a decent future for himself, but he was the only thing standing between her and those crazy killers. Despite his tendency to concern himself with the fanciful, she was confident he was fully capable of dealing with them.

After they left the mountains, Tyler and Daisy rode through an area of low hills and shallow, flat canyons covered with a sparse growth of buffalo and grama grasses and stunted pines, juniper, and serviceberry. From any one of a dozen ridges, in almost any direction, an unbroken vista of up to 70 miles stretched before them. Thirty miles away, across the Rio Grande, a flat-topped mesa rose like a black wall, cutting off the fertile valley from the dry plains beyond. The expanse of sky overhead was a dull blue-gray.

A thousand feet below, the Rio Grande wound its leisurely course through a narrow valley that had never entirely lost its green. Cottonwoods, willows, and a few maples, oaks, and alders hugged its shore, their leaves shivering noisily in the cold wind that wafted down from the snow-covered peaks. A dozen rivulets of snowmelt glistened in the bright sun.

It was on a slight rise in this pastoral setting that, late in the afternoon, they reached Daisy's ranch.

Chapter Sixteen

Daisy hadn't expected the sight of the charred remains of her home to affect her so strongly. She knew the house had burned, but seeing it was a shock. The charred spot on the desert floor bore no resemblance to the home she remembered.

"It's almost as if it was never here," she said to Tyler. She couldn't explain the feeling of loneliness that assailed her. Not only was her family gone, almost all trace of her life had disappeared. It was almost as if she had never existed.

"We buried your father next to your mother." Tyler looked over the charred remains of her home but found nothing worth salvaging. "I wonder why your father didn't build closer to the river. The soil would have been better for a garden."

Her mother had asked her father to move several times, but he wouldn't. For him the difficulty of finding water to irrigate the garden didn't outweigh the view of the mountains above and the river valley below. Daisy slipped from the saddle and reluctantly approached the graves. She had been here so many times before, times when talking to her mother was all that kept her sane. Her father had never understood. Now he lay here as well. She wondered if he would be glad of her visits now.

"I know it's not much, but the ground was frozen."

"It's okay." If she managed to find the money, she would have a nice stone marker made. Her mother would like that. She would hate having nothing but her name carved on a piece of board. In a few years, there would be nothing to show she had lived or died in this place.

Daisy found that unutterably sad.

"Let's go," she said, turning away from the graves. "I imagine the killers know we've left the cabin by now. I won't feel safe until I'm in Albuquerque."

"Son of a bitch!" Toby cursed when he slammed through the cabin door. "There ain't nobody here." The whole left side of his head was badly swollen from a nasty-looking wound to his cheek.

"Looks like they ain't been gone long," Frank said.

Ed dismounted with painful slowness. He hobbled inside and dropped into a chair to take his weight off a heavily bandaged leg. "This can't be the place," he said. "Looks like a woman's been living here. I never seen so much kitchen stuff in all my life."

"If it's a woman, why do they have bunks?" Toby asked.

Frank threw back the curtain to Daisy's corner. "They got a bed back here," he said. "Now why would a man keep a woman and let her sleep in the corner?"

"Maybe there's two of them and they take turns at her," Toby said with a lewd snigger.

"You ain't never seen that kind of woman keep a place like this," Ed said.

"You two stop jawing and let me think," Frank ordered.

He didn't understand. Three animals had occupied that shed, but he could find the tracks of only two leading down the mountain. The cabin sure looked like a woman lived here regular, but mountain men didn't go to any trouble to hide it if they were keeping a woman. None of the dried-up pieces of leather he'd talked to these last few days had said anything about a woman. If the Singleton woman was brought into the mountains, this had to be the cabin. They had been everywhere else.

"We'll stay the night," Frank said. "The answer is here somewhere."

"You'd better catch up with that son of a bitch soon," Toby said, making himself comfortable in Tyler's bunk. "I mean to fill him full of lead for this cut across the cheek."

"And my leg," Ed reminded him.

"You just find him," Toby said to Frank. "Then you leave the rest to me."

"I wouldn't be too anxious to tangle with that hombre if I was you," Frank said. "Any man who can hit a rifle barrel at a hundred yards can kill you before you got within pistol range."

"This ought to do for tonight," Tyler said as he pulled up his mule in a cottonwood grove on a wedge of land between a noisy stream and the Rio Grande. He dismounted and tied the mule to a willow. Daisy slid from the saddle, her body stiff, her legs sore. She stumbled when she tried to take a step. Tyler caught her. The electricity was still there. Even his touch was sufficient to send her pulse racing.

She had to put some distance between them. After tonight she wouldn't have to worry about her desire to be in his arms, but just now it was nearly overpowering.

"I'm not used to riding," she said, reaching out to lean against the trunk of a massive cottonwood. "Papa thought women should ride in a buggy. Only we didn't have a buggy, so we stayed home or walked."

Tyler waited, but Daisy didn't release her hold on the tree. "You ought to meet Iris. She wouldn't allow Monty to go anywhere without her. She rode down the outlaw trail once in little more than a week."

Daisy didn't know a thing about the outlaw trail, but she gathered Iris's accomplishment was something out of the ordinary.

"Who's Iris?"

"My sister-in-law."

"You've got so many relatives, I lose track."

Tyler began to unsaddle the animals. "You wouldn't forget her if you ever saw her. She's enough to knock your eyes out."

Not only could she ride better than Daisy, she was ten times as pretty. No wonder Tyler wasn't interested in her. He'd seen far better.

Tyler spread out Daisy's mattress and blanket. "Here, sit down for a few minutes."

"I'd better walk around a bit to loosen my muscles." She hobbled away from him. Anything to keep her mind off her desire to be near him.

She told herself Tyler wasn't the kind of man she wanted for a husband, that if he asked her to marry him, she'd refuse. But would she? Her heart leapt at the thought, and she realized with a sinking feeling she did want to marry him. She sighed aloud as she hobbled back and forth. It was silly enough she should fall in love with him. It was inexcusable she should consider marrying him.

She walked around a second huge cottonwood, letting her fingers trail over its rough bark. A mat of damp leaves squished under her feet.

She tried to tell herself Tyler was exactly like her father, but she knew that wasn't true. He might be a dreamer, might never make anything of himself, but he was thoughtful and kind and handsome and so big that for the first time in her life she felt small and feminine. She could marry him for that alone. Feeling a little better, she walked toward him. He was arranging stones for a fire.

"I can help," she offered, determined to put such thoughts out of her mind.

"No need. I can handle it."

She stopped. She was so close she practically stood over him. "Why won't you ever let anybody help you?"

Tyler looked up, surprised. "It only takes one person to make coffee."

"There's water to fetch, wood to find, the fire to build, the food to dig out of the saddlebags, and everything to get ready for eating. That's more than enough work for two people. Sometimes I think you'd eat for me if you could. That way you wouldn't have to be bothered with me at all."

"It isn't that." He broke some dry sticks and lit them with a match.

"I know. You don't even think about it. You did the same thing to Zac. You only let him take care of the animals when you wanted to get rid of him."

"I don't need help." Tyler arranged some larger sticks over the tiny flame.

"That's just it," Daisy said, waving her hands about in frustration. "You don't need anything. Don't you think that's strange? It's not normal for a person to go through life not needing other human beings, not wanting their company, never depending on them for anything."

"I've always been this way." Tyler dipped some water from the stream and put it on to boil for coffee.

Daisy knew she ought to stop right there. It was none

215

of her business how Tyler chose to live his life, but this was her last chance. It was inconceivable she should disappear tomorrow and leave no trace in his life.

"Look where it's got you. You live in the mountains by yourself, avoiding the company of every living soul but your mules. You spend all your time searching for lost gold mines that don't exist. You seem to have a large family, but you never see them. Twenty years from now you'll still be there, and what will you have to show for it?"

Tyler dropped some coffee beans into the steaming water. "I've got less than six months."

His response dried up the stream of words she was about to utter. "What do you mean?"

"I've given myself a deadline. If I don't find anything by June seventeenth, I'll quit."

Daisy felt a surge of hope. "What would you do?"

Tyler opened the pack where he'd put the meat. "My family would find me a job in Denver, probably in a bank."

Daisy spoke before she thought. "But you'd hate that."

"Yes, I would, but I promised George I wouldn't play in the woods for the rest of my life. Like you, he finds it an inappropriate pastime for a grown man."

"It might not be as bad as you think," she said hopefully. "You'd have a regular income. You could have a house and everything."

"I don't want a house." He opened another pack and took out a pan.

"Well, you can't expect your wife to want to live in a cabin in the mountains. It's no place to bring up children."

Tyler looked up at Daisy, a faintly baffled expression on his face. "Whatever made you think I want a wife and children?" He put some venison steaks in the pan.

"I j-just assumed y-you did," Daisy stammered. "I thought every man did."

"I don't."

Daisy felt hope die. It wasn't a terrible death because it had only been a faint hope, but it was a sad death nonetheless. It was the only hope she had.

"Don't you ever get lonely?"

"No." He carefully seasoned the meat.

"Don't you want to like people and have them like you?"

"I've got family."

"You might as well not. You never see them. I can't imagine wanting to hide in the mountains from my family."

"I'm not hiding."

"Yes, you are."

"I'm there because that's where the gold is."

"You mean you'll like living in Denver?"

"It doesn't matter where I live." He unwrapped some bread he'd cooked at the cabin.

Daisy gave up. She didn't believe Tyler knew what he was talking about. He had probably convinced himself that as long as he had his hotels he could live anywhere. She imagined he was in for a big surprise. She had to confess she didn't know anything about big hotels or big cities, but she didn't think a man who liked living alone in the mountains would feel comfortable there.

Tyler poured some coffee into a cup and handed it to Daisy. Then he put the steaks on to cook.

Daisy took her coffee and settled on her blanket. If Tyler wanted to do everything himself, he could. She wasn't going to offer anymore. She wasn't going to do anything except work at putting him out of her mind.

Tyler leaned against the trunk of a cottonwood, standing watch. He didn't think he needed to. He doubted the killers would have followed this far today, but he couldn't afford to be wrong.

Anyway, he couldn't sleep. Daisy's accusations had raised questions in his mind he couldn't answer. Everything he'd told her was true. At least, it had been until now. Now he didn't know. He only knew he didn't feel comfortable leaving Daisy.

It wasn't just because of her safety. He was concerned about what she was going to do for her future. He believed she could do anything she wanted. But she didn't.

He was concerned about her marrying Guy Cochrane. He didn't know the man, but he couldn't be worth much. Daisy had never mentioned him. No woman kept quiet about her fiance if she thought he was the greatest guy to wear pants.

Then there was the fact she had almost let him make love to her. If she loved this Cochrane fella, she'd never have done something like that. She might have let him kiss her in a casual, brotherly fashion, but she wouldn't have let him kiss her like he did. Or allow him to repeat it.

He didn't know why she had agreed to marry Guy Cochrane, but she didn't love him.

No. He did know. She had told him. Cochrane's father was the richest man in Albuquerque, and her mother had spent her whole life telling Daisy never to marry a poor man.

Hell, the Randolphs were probably richer than the Cochranes. He wondered if she'd marry him for his money?

He knew that wasn't fair, but the thought wouldn't leave his mind. She'd never missed an opportunity to tell him how little she thought of his notion of finding gold. Clearly she had no intention of linking her future with anyone she considered a dreamer.

Then why had she almost let him make love to her?

Everything in Tyler's head was a muddled mass of questions and fragmented ideas mixed up with a few hopes and a lot of fears. Most confusing of all, he couldn't figure out why this was all happening to him.

He didn't love Daisy. He didn't want to marry her. He did want to make love to her, but he had wanted to make love to other women as well. No. He had wanted to find sexual relief with a lot of other women, but what he looked for with Daisy was something entirely different.

That unsettled him. What was he looking for? Why should he be looking for it with Daisy? All he could say for sure was that he liked her and enjoyed having her around. He found her attractive and wanted to make love to her. He hoped she wouldn't marry Guy Cochrane.

What did it all add up to? He'd be damned if he knew, except it had given him a headache and was keeping him awake.

The color drained from Ed Peck's face as he stared at the stack of letters in his hand. "Do you know who this place belongs to?" he asked. His voice sounded hoarse.

"A dead man," Toby promised from the bunk.

"What you got there?" Frank asked.

"Letters," Ed replied, "all of 'em addressed to Tyler Randolph."

Toby's cigarette paused on the way to his mouth. "You sure?"

"Yeah," his father replied.

"Who the hell is Tyler Randolph?" Frank demanded.

"If you'd ever worked cows in Texas, you wouldn't have to ask such a dumb question," Ed said.

"Well, I didn't work no damned cows in Texas, and I'm damned glad of it. And I ain't heard of no Tyler Randolph."

"There's seven of them," Ed said.

"Seven men named Tyler Randolph?" Frank asked in disbelief.

"No, seven brothers, you fool," Toby said.

"Then I guess the Randolph in town must be his kin."

"There's a Randolph in town?" Toby asked. He sat up so fast he hit his head on the slats.

"Yeah. He has a stupid name, I can't remember it just now."

"Hen?" Toby asked.

"Yeah, that's it. Arrived with enough wagons to start his own train." Frank paused. "That's it! This Randolph fella did find that woman. And he's taken her into Albuquerque to his brother's wife." He grinned, pleased to have solved the puzzle. "All we have to do is follow him and kill her."

"You'll do it without me," Toby said, getting up from the bunk. "Don't you know who Hen Randolph is?"

"No, and I ain't interested."

"You damned well better be. He's the fastest gunfighter you'll ever see," Ed said. "Ain't nobody else can come close."

"I'm not planning on going up against him," Frank said. "We can get her and this Tyler fella from cover."

"You touch one of them Randolphs, and you'll have the rest down on you faster'n you can spit," Toby said.

"I ain't going with you, either," Ed said. "I didn't agree to killing that gal in the first place. I sure ain't having nothing to do with killing no Randolph. You should have knocked her over the head. It's about all you did anyway."

"What the hell are you going to do?"

"Head south, probably to Mexico."

"Okay, run out on me, but you ain't getting no more money."

"You go around shooting at Randolphs, and you won't live to spend it," Toby said.

"Go on, get out," Frank shouted.

Toby looked defiant. "I think I'll stay a few more days," he said. "No need for Pa and me to rush off. This Randolph won't be back for a week or so. It'll be a lot easier traveling after the snow melts some more."

"Where are you going?" Frank asked.

"I don't know exactly," Toby replied, "but I don't want to be anywhere near here when you tangle with those Randolphs. Besides, it's too damned cold here, and Pa needs to rest up while that leg heals. What are you doing?" he asked when Frank started to collect his gear.

"I'm leaving tonight. I'll kill them on the trail, and beat you to Mexico."

Frank smiled to himself. This was exactly what he needed to make his reputation. If he could kill a Randolph on top of the other work he'd done for Regis Cochrane, his reputation would be secure.

"I didn't know the Parrishes had sold up and left," Tyler said as they turned from the ranch road back onto the route to town. "I was planning on getting some horses here."

"That's the third rancher to sell out within the last year," Daisy said. "I wonder why none of them said anything before they left?"

Tyler took the time to scan their back trail with his binoculars.

"That's the fourth time you've done that today," Daisy said.

"Somebody's following us."

"This is the road to Albuquerque. I imagine we'll see lots of people."

"I'm just being careful."

But Tyler had a bad feeling. Three men followed them, and one of them was riding a big horse. He knew the killers could easily identify them. No other travelers would be riding a mule and a burro, certainly not a man and a woman. The coincidence would be too great.

"You think they're the killers, don't you?" Daisy said after he stopped twice more to study the horsemen through the binoculars.

"Yes," Tyler said.

She looked anxious but calm. She expected him to know exactly what to do.

"Here. You look through the glasses," Tyler said.

"I can't tell. They're still too far away," Daisy said. Fifteen minutes later Daisy still couldn't be sure. "I only saw one of them. What are you going to do?"

"Nothing until I know they're the men I'm after. We'll wait in those cedars and hope you recognize one of them when he passes."

"That's not the man," Daisy said a short while later. "I'm sure of it."

Tyler was relieved these men weren't the killers, but he was certain they were somewhere behind them.

"I think we'll take the trail down by the river," Tyler said. "We'll be late reaching town, but a man and woman traveling on a mule and a burro are too easily noticed and remembered."

The town of Albuquerque was irregularly laid out around a plaza of some two or three acres into which all the principal streets led. Adobe buildings were grouped without order, giving the town a tumbledown look. A white picket fence surrounded the plaza, which contained a low adobe building used as a barbershop, its flagpole 121 feet high on top, the tallest west of the Mississippi. The twin towers of San Felipe de Neri Church dominated the north side of the square, its yard also enclosed by a picket fence. Businesses and private homes crowded the other three sides of the plaza. Some fronted immediately on the street. Others had the luxury of covered walks.

Some of the roofs were made of wood, others of sod.

Albuquerque was not a large town. Even late at night, it wasn't difficult to locate the hotel. Tyler led Daisy down a narrow alley just off the plaza. They stopped at the back of a two-story building; he dismounted and helped her down. She was just as stiff as she had been the night before.

"We're going in the back," he told her. "I don't want anyone to see you enter. That way nobody will be able to say for certain when you arrived."

"But how can you manage that?"

"There's a stairway at the back. While I find out where Hen and Laurel are staying, you can sneak up the stairs when nobody's looking."

"Are you certain they won't mind helping me?" Daisy asked. She had been worrying about that the entire way.

"All you have to do is volunteer to look after Jordy and Adam, and they'll welcome you with open arms."

"Zac mentioned Jordy. Is he truly a terror?"

"That's his reputation. I stay out of the way. It was Hen's idea to adopt him."

Daisy wondered if anything would ever penetrate Tyler's heart. She was beginning to wonder if he even had one. There were times when he didn't seem to have any of the feelings ordinary people had. She wondered what the rest of his family was like. With Zac and him for examples, she had no idea what to expect.

Daisy felt abandoned when Tyler left her on the back stairs. The building was dark and quiet, the three-foot-thick adobe walls rough and cold. She forced herself to mount the stairs despite her uneasiness. The abrasive scrape of her shoes on the steps was loud in the confined space. She was relieved to reach the upper floor and feel a straw mat under her feet. The dim glow from a lamp below pierced the gloom of the upper hallway. She felt her muscles unclench when she saw Tyler emerge from the stairwell.

"He's reserved the whole top floor," Tyler said when he reached her. "He ought to have plenty of room for both of us."

A tall blond man opened the door in response to Tyler's knock. Daisy knew it had to be Hen. There was a strong resemblance between the brothers.

"What brings you out of the hills?" Hen asked, not moving aside to invite his brother in. "I was sure you'd have dug through half the Sandia range by now."

"I need your help."

Only then did Hen notice Daisy standing in the shadows behind Tyler. He moved aside.

"You'd better come in."

Chapter Seventeen

Daisy looked into the most intensely blue eyes she'd ever seen. She could find nothing there to let her know what Hen might feel toward his brother or toward her. Fortunately, before she could get cold feet, a lovely woman with cascades of black hair falling down her back raised herself out of a chair and came forward. She moved with the awkwardness of a woman in the last stages of pregnancy.

"Come in. You look like you've been traveling all day."

"Two days," Tyler said.

"You must be exhausted. Here, take my chair."

"No," Daisy said, horrified at the thought of taking the seat of a pregnant woman. "I'd just as soon stand for a while." She glanced at Tyler. "I feel like I've almost forgotten how."

Hen brought a chair from another room. "You can use this when you feel ready."

"I'm Laurel Randolph," the lady said as she reseated herself. "And this is my husband, Hen." Laurel smiled warmly. Hen's expression didn't seem to change. "Now tell us how we can help you."

"It's Daisy really," Tyler began.

Daisy watched Laurel's face as Tyler chronicled the events of the last week. She was relieved to see Laurel show sympathy, shock, and anger as the story unfolded. She relaxed a little. This woman might not be able to help, but at least she was sympathetic.

"Of course she can stay with us," Laurel said when Tyler finished. "I wish you'd brought her to us right away."

"Looking back, so do I," Tyler said.

Daisy wondered what he meant by that, but she didn't have time to search his face for clues. Laurel was talking to her. "Do you have a room?"

"No," Tyler answered for her, "but since Hen reserved the whole floor, I figured we could use one of yours."

"We do have an extra bedroom," Laurel said. "You and Hen can sleep there. Daisy will stay with me."

Daisy turned quickly to see how Hen would react to his wife's banishing him from her bed, but she could see no change in his expression. The man made her nervous. She had thought Tyler was hard to read. This man was impossible.

"I can't do that," Daisy protested.

Laurel looked at Hen and held out her hand. He immediately took it. "Hen won't like it, but I can't have you sharing a room with Tyler."

"Why? I've done it for a week."

"As far as everybody in Albuquerque is concerned, your father was killed today. Tyler brought you here right away."

Daisy looked helplessly at Tyler.

"Thanks," Tyler said. "I know this is a terrible imposition at such a time, but I didn't know what else to do."

"You did the right thing," Laurel assured him. "Are you sure you're not hungry?" she asked Daisy.

"No." Daisy was, but she was too nervous to eat. She doubted she'd be able to sleep a wink.

"Don't you want to sit down now?"

Daisy sat.

"Tyler can bring in your things, and we can think about getting you settled."

"This is all I have," Daisy said. "Everything else was destroyed in the fire."

Laurel looked dismayed. "I see. Well, it won't be easy to replenish your wardrobe. You're built along generous lines."

Daisy managed a weak smile. "I've never heard it put so beautifully. I'm much too tall for a woman. I was relieved when your husband opened the door and I had to look up to him."

"You'll like the Randolphs," Laurel said with a comforting smile. "All seven of them are taller than you. George's son, William Henry, is only twelve, and he's nearly six feet."

Daisy thought of how wonderful it would be to wander among this forest of towering men. She pushed that thought from her mind. No use teasing herself with the impossible.

"You must be tired," Laurel said, getting to her feet. "I know I am."

It had been a long evening. Over dinner they had worked out the story they planned to present to the public. Now the hot food and fatigue were telling on Daisy. Though she was extremely nervous, she was also very tired.

"I think we should retire for the night," Laurel said. She walked over to Hen. He kissed her gently.

"You sure you're going to be all right?" he asked.

That was the first softening Daisy had seen in the man. Clearly he doted on his wife.

"I'll be just fine. I have been fine all along. You and Tyler can talk over what to do about Daisy's future. I'll worry about how to find her some decent clothes."

"You don't have to do that," Daisy protested. "I can wear this dress for a while longer."

"No, you can't," Laurel stated emphatically. "It looks ready to fall apart." She gave Daisy an appraising look. "I think we can find something to fit you. If the skirts aren't long enough, we can stitch on a border."

She led Daisy into a comfortable bedroom. "It'll do the men good to share tonight. They won't talk to each other unless you force them."

"Zac talks enough for both of them."

Laurel laughed. "I'm sorry you had to put up with him. He'll be the death of George yet."

With Daisy's help, Laurel quickly changed into her nightgown. "Here, take one of mine," Laurel said with a grin. "It may not be long enough, but it's big enough for two of you." Daisy laughed when she put on the gown. It hardly came down to her calves, but she was too happy to be out of the dress and shift to care. She would have preferred to wear Tyler's nightshirt, but she didn't think Laurel would understand.

Laurel got into bed and propped herself up on several pillows. She patted the bed next to her. "Now tell me what really happened between you and Tyler. Of course, you're in love with him."

Looking at Tyler across the table, Hen regarded him with a jaundiced eye. "Still sticking your nose into what doesn't concern you, I see."

"What was I supposed to do? Leave her there to burn?"

"Of course not, but you have to admit you've got a problem on your hands."

"Look, I'm sorry to move you out of your bedroom, but it never occurred to me Laurel would do anything like that."

"What did you expect her to do? Have the girl sleep with you?"

"I suppose I thought she'd sleep on the couch or something."

"While you and I slept in comfortable beds? You don't know much about women."

"Nothing at all, if the last few days are any example."

Hen cast his brother a quizzical look.

"I'm not telling you anything."

"Your love life interests me only slightly more than Zac's, which is to say not at all."

"Thanks."

"You're welcome."

"How is the prospecting going?" Hen asked as reached for the coffeepot. It was empty. Only the muted drumming of an index finger indicated his irritation.

"Can't do any with all this snow."

"Making any progress?"

"I think so."

"You don't have to do this, you know."

"Yes, I do."

"You're just like Monty."

"How?" Tyler asked, surprised at the comparison to Hen's twin.

"Trying to prove something that doesn't need proving."

"It does to me."

Hen sighed. "What happens if you don't find any gold?"

"I'll worry about that bridge when I come to it." He didn't intend to tell anyone he was leaving. He'd just disappear.

"Working for Jeff or Madison won't solve anything, will it?"

"No."

"Then don't do it."

Tyler stared at his brother. "You think I should spend the rest of my life looking for gold?"

"I don't think you ought to spend five minutes looking for it, but if you think you need to make a place for yourself, keep trying until you're satisfied you've done it."

"What would you do?"

"I wouldn't work for Madison, and especially not for Jeff, even if it meant I had to be the sheriff of Sycamore Flats for the rest of my life."

Tyler laughed. A knock sounded at the door. When Hen opened it, a man handed him a tray containing a fresh pot of coffee. Hen poured a cup, laced it generously with cream, and carried it to the bedroom door. Laurel answered his knock. She took the coffee, gave him a kiss, and promptly closed the door on him. Hen returned to his seat and poured himself a cup, which he drank black.

"You could always cook," Hen said. "There must be places in New York that would pay a king's ransom to have somebody like you."

"I don't want to work for anybody. I want to be my own boss."

"Do what you have to do," Hen said, apparently losing interest in the subject. "Now, tell me how you got mixed up with this woman."

"I'm not mixed up with her."

"You brought her here. You spent the last week with her. You're mixed up with her."

"It couldn't be helped."

"This sort of thing never can."

"If you're going to be sarcastic, there's no point talking."

"I'm not being sarcastic. I'm speaking from experience."

"Yeah, you had so much experience before Laurel."

"I had enough."

"I had some, too, and I'm not mixed up with her. I feel sorry for her. She's had a rough time, but she's got a fiance. As soon as they get back from Santa Fe, she's going to stay with his family. I won't be responsible for her after that."

"So what do you want us to do?"

"Take care of her until they get back. It can't be more than a few days, a week at the most. The snow's melting fast."

"And what are you going to be doing?"

"Heading for the hills. I've lost too much time already."

"So you really aren't involved with her?"

"No. She's not interested in impractical dreamers like me. What she said about my hotels made Madison's and Jeff's comments sound kind in comparison."

"She seems like a nice girl."

"She is."

Hen finished his coffee and set the cup aside. "What's her fiance like?"

"I don't know."

"Is he taller than she is?"

"No."

"It'll never work."

"He's rich."

"She may have been after his money before, but she's changed her mind."

"How do you know?"

"She came here with you."

"She had no place else to go."

"Every woman has someplace else to go. She chose to come here." Hen stood. "I'd better check on the boys. They never sleep when they share the same room."

Absently, Tyler poured himself a cup of coffee. As he sipped the strong, hot liquid, he wondered if Hen could possibly be right. He hoped not.

A fire burned in the grate of Regis Cochrane's luxurious sitting room. His entire suite in the expensive Santa Fe hotel was furnished with bad Louis XV upholstered in wine-colored velvet. He chewed a one-inch cigar stub while he studied a large map which gave the boundaries of every piece of land from the river to the mountains between Bernalillo and Albuquerque. Dressed in a three-piece black wool suit, white shirt, and bow tie, he looked exactly what he was, a very wealthy banker and the richest man in Albuquerque. A less prosperous man sat across from him.

Cochrane impatiently brushed aside an ash that fell on the map. "Are you certain this is the route the railroad will take?" he asked.

"It might swing a mile or two either way but—"

"Where will it cross the river? That's the important thing."

"Somewhere below Albuquerque."

"Are you positive?"

"Not where exactly, just that it will be below Albuquerque."

"They can't change the route to the west side of the river?"

"It'll cost them twice as much to do that."

A slow smile spread over Regis's features. He leaned back, put down the cigar, and took a swallow of his brandy. "Then I've got every last one of the damned bastards who tried to close me out of the deal."

"Who?" the other man asked.

232

"The five richest men in Albuquerque after me. I don't look much like it, but I got mixed blood in me. They don't like that, so they tried to squeeze me out and keep all the profits for themselves. They bought up all the land around the proposed depot. They plan to sell it for a fortune once the railroad arrives."

"But how is buying up more ranches going to hurt them? They'll still own the land in town."

Regis's fist slammed down on the table. "If I own every piece of land between Bernalillo and Albuquerque, not one damned train can enter that town until I say so. And I won't say so until they hand over half that deal."

"Suppose they hold out against you?"

Regis's face hardened into cruel lines. "There's no man alive who's done that."

Next morning Tyler found it hard to say good-bye. His feeling of awkwardness wasn't helped by the formal atmosphere of the sitting room. Hen and Laurel had remained in their bedrooms, but he still felt they were looking over his shoulder. Laurel had pinned Daisy's hair up in a tight bun. Tyler liked it better in loose curls.

Tyler knew Daisy was in better hands with Laurel, but he felt he was abandoning her. Daisy looked as if she felt the same.

"I'd better be getting back," he said. "The snow's melting, and it doesn't look like we're going to have any more storms."

"I hope you find the biggest gold deposit in New Mexico," Daisy said with a lost-puppy look.

"A medium-size one will do," Tyler said, trying not to feel like a heel. "I'll come by to see you when I'm in town again." That was a stupid thing to say. She'd probably be married by then, and her husband wouldn't want him about.

"That would be nice. I'd like for you to meet the Cochranes."

Hen and Laurel came out of the bedroom. "You'd better get going if you're going," Laurel said, giving each of them a rather penetrating glance. "You have a long way to go, and Daisy and I have lots of shopping to do." Hen helped Laurel into her coat.

"I'll walk down to the livery stable with you," Hen offered.

Tyler hadn't expected that—wasn't sure he welcomed it—but it was impossible to get rid of Hen when he made up his mind to do something.

"Will you see Zac?" Daisy asked.

"I doubt it."

"If you do, wish him luck for me. It's stupid to want to be a gambler, but tell him I hope he wins enough money to buy his own riverboat."

"I imagine George will have something to say about that," Laurel said as she pulled on her gloves.

"I hope he won't try to stop him," Daisy said. "Zac may change his mind later on, but he'll never do it if his brother tries to make him."

"That's a lesson he learned with the rest of us," Hen said.

Tyler wondered if Hen included him in that, but he didn't much care. He was caught between a strong desire to escape to the mountains as fast as possible and an equally strong desire to stay. Despite her engagement, he would like to know for himself that Daisy was going to be all right.

Be honest. You want to check out her fiance. What are you going to do if you don't like him, tell Daisy she can't marry him?

He'd better get himself out of town before he did something disgraceful. Daisy wasn't his responsibility. He'd probably be something of an embarrassment to her, something she would have to explain, and right now he couldn't think of any explanation her fiance was likely to find acceptable.

"You sure you'll be all right?" he asked once more.

"Of course she will," Laurel assured him. "Now go." She pushed him toward the door.

There was nothing left for Tyler to do but leave. He and Hen walked together in silence until they reached the boardwalk.

The church, blazing white in the sun, dominated the plaza. The streets overflowed with wagons, carriages, horses, burros, and pedestrians. Men wore sombreros with tall crowns and draped their bodies with brightly colored serapes. Ladies wore full dresses and enveloping shawls.

The plaza was the place of rendezvous for every public purpose, housing markets, religious processions, and a camping place for travelers. Peddlers were everywhere, hawking wares in the center of the plaza and occupying porches in front of the business houses where they spread piles of fruit, vegetables, cheese, pinon nuts, and leaf tobacco. Vendors took over the hitching racks, using them to hang meat carcasses—both wild game and mutton. It was hard to find a place to tie a horse or mule. Gamblers roamed about with cards in hand, hoping to entice someone into a fast game of three-card monte. Almost every store, whether it specialized in dry goods or bakery goods, sold liquor by the bottle over the counter.

"Did Zac head for New Orleans?" Hen asked as they headed west along James Street.

"That's what he told Daisy."

There was a taut silence.

"I hope you find the gold."

"Thanks."

There was another long silence until they reached the stable. Tyler paid a man to fetch his mule and burro. "You don't have to stay," Tyler told Hen. "It won't take

235

but a few minutes to saddle up.''

"I think you're making a mistake leaving," Hen said.

"I'm not."

"You're just going to have to come back to finish it."

"There's nothing to finish."

Hen flashed a rare smile. "It's a shame we're such a stubborn family. If we weren't, maybe we could learn something from each other's mistakes."

"It would be a mistake to stay."

"See you in a week or so."

"I can't possibly find . . ." Tyler stopped, realizing Hen was referring to Daisy, not the gold. "I hope everything goes well with Laurel," he said and turned to go inside the livery.

Tyler was angry at Hen. He was having enough trouble without his brother making things worse. But Hen never considered anybody but himself. Sometimes Monty. He never seemed to think what he said to his brothers might actually do more harm than good.

Be honest, Tyler thought to himself, you're just as bad. The fact that you're upset about it just goes to show what a sad state you're in.

Determined to put this last week and all its questions and uncertainties behind him, Tyler saddled the mule, strapped the pack on the burro, and headed out of town. But he couldn't shake the feeling that Hen had been right. He would have to come back. He had unfinished business to settle.

Daisy and Laurel returned to the hotel from a full morning of shopping. Daisy wore a hat specifically chosen to hide her lack of hair. She carried several packages under each arm. Several more had already been delivered to the hotel. Still more were to come. A porter relieved Laurel of her packages at the door.

"I'll never be able to repay you for all of this," Daisy

said for the hundredth time as she entered the parlor and gratefully set her packages down.

"Don't worry about it," Laurel said as she slipped the porter a few pesos. "Hen needs to find ways to spend his money."

"I wish he would give some of it to Tyler so he could build his hotels. He doesn't want to work in a bank. I'm not even sure he likes living in that cabin." Daisy helped Laurel out of her coat.

Laurel settled down on the sofa with a tired sigh. "Tyler has plenty of money. All the brothers do."

Daisy stared uncomprehendingly at Laurel. "But he said he didn't have any money. Zac stole what little he had to pay his way to New Orleans." She draped Laurel's coat over the back of a chair and sat down herself. She was worn out.

Laurel laughed. "Zac never could stay within his allowance."

"Allowance?"

Laurel poured cocoa from a pot on the table next to her. She handed a cup to Daisy. "All the Randolph property is held jointly," Laurel explained, "ranches, banks, companies, stock—everything. The brothers draw an equal share from the income. I believe Zac's is being held in trust until he's twenty-five, but he and Tyler have just as much as anybody else. Except Madison. He's got several business ventures of his own that seem to make money faster than the national mint."

Tyler was rich, and he hadn't told her.

"Tyler has this bee in his bonnet about being worthy of his place in the family." Laurel poured herself a cup and settled back. "When his brothers wouldn't sell some of the family holdings to give him the money for his hotels, he broke with his family. I could hardly believe it when Hen opened the door and there Tyler stood. We haven't seen him in more than a year."

Daisy's head was spinning. Tyler had told her none of this. After her babbling about Philadelphia and her rich grandfather, he must think she was a fortune hunter. Beyond that, she had ridiculed his ideas. She hadn't meant it the way he had apparently taken it, but it was too late now. He wouldn't come back to Albuquerque.

She knew it was best—she'd decided that long ago—but she regretted she couldn't see him just one more time to make him understand.

Make him understand what? You try to make him believe you don't care for money just when you've found out he's terribly rich, and he'll never believe anything you say ever again.

They became aware of shouts and running feet outside. A door down the hall slammed.

"Jordy and Adam," Laurel informed her. "At the ranch they'd be on their horses. Here they have no way to work off their excess energy except on each other. Hen tried to get me to leave them at the ranch, but there's nobody who can control them except Hen or me. Hen, actually. They do what I ask because they know Hen will take the skin off their hides if they don't. They walk in awe of him."

Daisy could understand that. She was a little in awe of him herself.

"I'm going to lie down for a while. We'll tackle those dresses when I get up."

Daisy had taken over the bedroom Tyler and Hen had shared the night before. She was grateful for the chance to be alone before her thoughts overwhelmed her.

Chapter Eighteen

"You don't like the dress?" Laurel asked. It was the middle of the afternoon, and she was on her knees in the sitting room pinning a wide border to the hem.

Daisy snapped out of her reverie. "It's beautiful. Of course I like it." They had found only one made-up dress in the whole of Albuquerque that, with the addition of a border, fit Daisy. Material for two simple dresses had been sent out to be made up by the next day. Three dresses of more complex design were promised within five days.

"You don't look like it."

"I'm sorry. I was thinking."

"And not about your father."

Daisy reacted guiltily. "How can you tell?"

"I once despaired of Hen loving me or wanting to marry me." Laurel smiled. "I felt like you looked just now."

"I don't suppose it'll do any good to deny it, but it's so foolish. He's not at all the kind of man I want for a husband."

Laurel laughed heartily. "I swore up and down Hen Randolph was the last man on earth I'd marry. I told him to stay away. I tried to drive him off. I even tried to run away from him. None of it made any difference. When you love somebody like you love Tyler, nothing else matters."

"He doesn't love me."

"Turn. Are you sure?"

Daisy rotated about 45 degrees. "He never said he did, and he couldn't wait to get back to his mountains."

"You mean he's running away. All the Randolphs do that."

"Why?"

"They believe they're constitutionally unsuited to marriage. They practically have to be hog-tied and dragged to the preacher. Turn."

Daisy rotated again. "I wouldn't marry anybody who had to be forced into it."

"I exaggerated, of course," Laurel admitted, sobering. "But they do resist beyond what's reasonable. But once they're convinced, you're stuck with them for life."

She smiled in a manner that made Daisy feel wildly jealous that Tyler didn't feel about her the way Hen obviously felt about Laurel.

"Hen says it's their family history. I think it's the responsibility. My first husband was quick to marry, but he got himself killed and left me to bring up my son alone. Hen was so aware of his responsibility he tried to hide. Rose and Iris said their husbands were the same way. Now help me up. You'd never believe I climbed a mountain canyon every day while I was carrying Adam. Turn around slowly so I can see if I got it even."

"I don't think Tyler will ever marry," Daisy said, circling slowly. "He doesn't need anybody."

"I think you're being too hard on him. He was the first

240

brother to show up when he thought Hen might be in trouble.''

''But you said you hadn't seen him in a year.''

''That's true,'' Laurel admitted. ''Take off the dress.''

As soon as Laurel unbuttoned the dress, Daisy pushed it off her shoulders, let it fall to the floor, and stepped out of it. She picked up her old dress and put it on.

''I thought he liked me at one time, but now I believe it was only because we were locked up together. He would have felt the same for any other woman.'' Daisy did up her buttons.

''I'm not trying to say Tyler knows he's in love with you, but I will say I've never seen him so unsettled by a woman as he is by you. It's going to take him a while to accept it. If you think he's worth the wait, don't give up on him.''

Daisy picked up the new dress and turned it inside out. She settled on the sofa next to Laurel, accepted a threaded needle, and began to sew the border onto the dress. Laurel threaded a second needle and started on the other side.

Daisy didn't know if Tyler was worth the wait. There was so much about him that frightened her. At the same time, there was so much that drew her to him. It was as if there were two people inside him. He wasn't enough of either one for her to be able to make up her mind.

''I don't think we have much in common,'' Daisy finally said. ''The things he wants frighten me. The things I want don't appeal to him at all.''

''In that case, you ought to put him out of your head as fast as you can. It'll be nothing but heartache if you don't.''

Daisy agreed. Only it would be nothing but heartache if she did.

Daisy had been in Albuquerque four days when she emerged from a store and practically ran into Adora Cochrane and her mother.

With an exclamation of pleasure, Adora embraced her friend. "I never thought your father would let you go long enough to come to town."

The joy in their reunion fled. "My father is dead. He was killed last . . . a few days ago." There was no chance Guy would still want to marry her, not looking the way she did, but she needed to stick to her story. There was no reason to ruin Tyler's reputation.

"What are you doing here?" Mrs. Cochrane asked as soon as she had offered her condolences.

"They burned our house. A prospector found me and brought me here to stay with his sister-in-law."

Daisy noticed the frown produced by the word "prospector" eased at the word "sister-in-law." Laurel was right. Everything would be all right as long as no one knew about that week in the cabin.

"What are you going to do?" Adora asked.

"I don't know," Daisy said.

"You'll stay with us until you decide," Adora said. "Won't she, mother?"

"Certainly," Mrs. Cochrane said. "As long as you like."

"She's going to stay with us for a long, long time," Adora said with a giggle. "Guy's going to see to that. Just wait until he finds out he missed you. We tried to get him to come with us, but he couldn't stand any more shopping."

"Has Guy been asking about me?"

"He talks about you all the time," Adora said. "I finally had to tell him to shut up. Where did you get that dress? It suits you perfectly."

Daisy explained that everything had been lost in the fire, that Laurel Randolph and her husband had been most generous.

"Guy will have to reimburse them," Mrs. Cochrane said. "I'm sure they are very nice people, but I can't feel comfortable being indebted to strangers.''

Daisy was on the verge of telling Mrs. Cochrane that she, not Guy, was indebted in a manner that couldn't be repaid by money, but she held her tongue. If there ever was a woman who thought money was the answer to everything, it was Belle Cochrane.

Though she disapproved of strangers who stayed in hotels, Mrs. Cochrane insisted she be introduced to the Randolphs immediately. From the moment she found out they had reserved the whole top floor, her affability was assured. Learning Daisy had been rescued by a Randolph instead of a ''prospector'' seemed to be all she needed to feel propriety had been observed. But she insisted Daisy move to their home immediately.

''I understand you have been put to some expense to replenish Daisy's wardrobe,'' Mrs. Cochrane said.

''We were glad to do it,'' Laurel replied. ''I've been enjoying her company.''

The rest of the visit passed smoothly, even though Laurel steadfastly refused any payment. Belle Cochrane spent most of the time it took them to reach their home prying as much information as possible out of Daisy about the Randolphs.

Daisy felt relieved when she was at last installed in her own room at the Cochranes', but she was sorry to have left Laurel. She liked her very much. She had wanted to be there when the baby was born. Most of all, she regretted losing this last link with Tyler. As long as she had any kind of connection with his family, she wouldn't give up hope he might come back.

Adora took her lowered spirits to mean she hadn't gotten over her father's death.

''Do you know who killed him?''

''No,'' Daisy replied. ''I was hoping your father would help me find out.''

''Papa's still in Santa Fe, but I'm sure he'll see that the

sheriff makes it his first priority. It must have been terribly frightening.''

''One of the men shot me. If Tyler hadn't found me, I'd have died.''

''He shot you!'' Adora exclaimed, her eyes wide with disbelief. ''Why didn't you tell me earlier?''

''I didn't want to upset your mother.'' Daisy pulled back her hair. ''See?''

''Golly!'' Adora exclaimed. She inspected the wound closely. ''It sure healed awfully fast.''

''It wasn't a bad wound,'' Daisy said. She had to remember the missing nine days, or she'd betray herself. ''It ruined my hair. I have to wear it in a bun.''

''It makes you look older.''

Tyler had liked it loose.

''What was he like?'' Adora asked.

''Who?''

''The man who rescued you. Was he as handsome as his brother?'' Adora sighed. ''He looked so menacing, like he could shoot you and never blink an eye.''

''Hen is really very nice. He's just worried about his wife.''

''What about the other one? Is he married?''

''No, but you should have seen the youngest brother,'' Daisy said, deciding to sacrifice Zac to Adora's insatiable curiosity. ''He's gorgeous. He stole his brother's money and ran off to become a riverboat gambler.''

''No! You're making this up.''

''You can ask if you don't believe me. You won't believe how handsome he is. He's got the longest lashes and the most beautiful eyes you've ever seen. He's just about your age.''

''Tell me everything,'' Adora gushed.

Daisy proceeded to do just that, inventing details as needed. Her conscience didn't bother her. Adora would never meet Zac, and this way she could keep Tyler all to herself.

The next morning at breakfast Adora and her mother kept up a constant flow of conversation. They seemed to be determined to do what they could to raise Daisy's spirits. The family took all their meals in this large, formal room. It was so dark and the furniture so heavy and formal it always made Daisy feel out of place.

"I'm certain you will want to observe a period of mourning," Mrs. Cochrane said, "but it's best to get past unpleasant things as quickly as possible."

Mrs. Cochrane had made it clear that *get past unpleasant things* meant marrying Guy. Daisy couldn't understand why Mrs. Cochrane was so anxious to have Guy marry her. Surely there were many other girls who would come closer to being the ideal bride for her only son.

Besides, Guy might not want to marry her once he found out about that lost week. She would have to tell him. She owed it to Guy to give him a chance to back out while he still could.

Strange, she could hardly remember what he looked like.

No, it was just that her mind was filled with Randolphs. After three of them, everybody else seemed insignificant.

"Do you know how much land you own?" Mrs. Cochrane asked.

"I have no idea," Daisy replied. "Papa seemed to think it was a lot."

"You own nearly a hundred thousand acres," Mrs. Cochrane said. "All the way from the river to the foothills."

"It wouldn't make any difference if I owned two hundred thousand. It's not worth a cent."

"It's worth quite a bit," Mrs. Cochrane said. "When it's known that it's yours, you'll find many men who wish to marry you. I hope you won't let the sudden attention turn your head. Guy's affections have been constant for several months now.''

Daisy could hardly believe what Mrs. Cochrane said was true. "But my father was never able to make a living from it.''

"Forgive me, child, but your father was hopeless at business. Properly managed, that much land will make you a rich woman.''

Daisy couldn't believe Mrs. Cochrane was right, but she remembered Tyler seemed to think the same thing. Guy's entrance interrupted her thoughts.

"You poor girl," he said after his welcome. "Mother told me last night. If we had only known. I shudder to think of you enduring so much, surrounded by no one but strangers.''

Daisy realized that though she had known them only a short time, she didn't think of the Randolphs as strangers. In fact, much to her surprise, she realized she felt as much at ease with them as with the Cochranes. She decided it must be because the Randolphs knew everything that had happened and accepted her anyway.

She didn't feel she could be as honest with the Cochranes. She would tell Adora most of what happened. She would tell Guy some, but she wouldn't tell Mr. or Mrs. Cochrane anything.

"She was very fortunate that a Randolph found her," Mrs. Cochrane informed her son. "No telling what might have happened.''

"A Randolph?" Guy asked, perplexed.

"A very wealthy family," his mother informed him. "I've made some inquiries. They seem to have a finger in everything. Henry Randolph and his wife have taken the entire upper floor of Post's Exchange Hotel for an indefinite period of time.''

"They're awaiting the birth of their child," Daisy explained. For some reason, she found it difficult to listen to Mrs. Cochrane. She'd never thought of Tyler as rich. To do so now would destroy her memories of him. They were all she had, and she wanted to keep them safe.

"You don't have to worry about depending on strangers anymore," Guy assured her. "You can leave everything to me."

"And Father," Adora added. "Daisy wants him to help her find who killed her father."

"Well, of course," Guy said. "That goes without saying. Now you must do your best to forget everything that has happened in the last few days." He took his place next to Daisy. Mr. Cochrane's chair remained unoccupied. A maid brought coffee and hot food.

Guy might as well have asked her to forget her entire existence, Daisy thought. Nothing in her life had been quite as real as the last few days. She had felt liberated. Walking into the Cochranes' home had been like walking into a cage. Guy's presence intensified the feeling.

Daisy told Guy everything she'd already told his mother and sister. However, by the time she had told it all again to Mr. Cochrane at dinner that evening, she was almost at the end of her rope. If it hadn't been necessary to enlist his aid in apprehending the killers, she didn't think she could have done it.

She told him everything she could about the men who had followed her. She thought he looked disturbed when she described the man who shot her, but his expression cleared and she guessed he didn't know of such a man.

"Leave it to me," he said. "I'll drop by the sheriff's office on my way to the bank tomorrow."

"I wanted to ambush them, but Tyler said we had to wait if we wanted to catch the man behind them."

"What makes you think there's somebody behind them?" Mr. Cochrane asked.

"Tyler says they aren't the kind of men to devise such

a plan. They're killers for hire. He said if we got them, the leader could just hire somebody else to kill me.''

"Good gracious," Belle Cochrane exclaimed. "This isn't the kind of thing a girl like you ought to be thinking about. I consider it most improper of Mr. Randolph to have discussed it with you."

"*I* discussed it with *him*," Daisy informed everybody. "After all, I was the one they were trying to kill. That's not the sort of thing you can just put out of your mind."

"I think you were terribly brave," Adora said. "I'm sure I'd have been in hysterics."

"No, you wouldn't. It's impossible to keep having hysterics for nine—" Daisy cut off the word. If she wasn't careful, she would give everything away. "—nigh on to two days, especially when you're unconscious half the time and riding a burro the rest."

"You poor girl," Guy commiserated. "I'd understand if you took to your bed and didn't get up for a month."

Daisy didn't know what to say to that. Such an absurd thought had never occurred to her.

"She can be as quiet as she likes for as long as she likes," Mrs. Cochrane assured her. "Adora and I will be only too happy to run any errands for you."

"I figure Bob Greene must be behind it," Daisy said, trying to bring the conversation back to the killers. "I have no idea why, but I can't think of anyone else."

"You can put this whole business out of your head," Mr. Cochrane said. "I disagree with Mr. Randolph. I'm sure they're just lawless drifters killing for anything they can find." He looked thoughtful for a moment. "Though your idea of Bob Greene bears looking into." He paused again. "Yes, I think it does."

"Good. I'm glad that business is behind us," Mrs. Cochrane said. "I'm sure it's a relief, dear, to know you don't have to trouble your head with it again."

Daisy started to tell Mrs. Cochrane it would never leave

hcr head until the killers and the man behind them were caught, but she realized it would be fruitless. The matter was in Mr. Cochrane's hands. Belle Cochrane wouldn't understand why there was anything more for a woman to discuss.

Daisy realized with something of a jolt that the Cochranes were just as determined to think for her as her father had been. Actually, they hoped to prevent her from thinking at all. She had expected it would be a relief to hand all her troubles over to Guy and his father, but it wasn't, not if they weren't even going to let her talk about it.

"Adora and her mother have some visits to make to-morrow morning," Mr. Cochrane said. "That will give you and Guy some time alone. You have many things to discuss." He cast his son a glance full of meaning. Guy smiled uncomfortably, but he didn't look unwilling. "Now I think you ought to get to bed. I'm sure the Randolphs took good care of you, but it's impossible to sleep properly in a hotel. With that on top of your ordeal, you must be considerably worn down."

Daisy disliked appearing so helpless, but she desperately wanted to be alone. She was relieved when she at last slipped into bed. Adora wanted to talk. Daisy pleaded fatigue, and Mrs. Cochrane marched her daughter off to her own bedroom. But it wasn't fatigue that Daisy felt when she blew out her lamp.

She was depressed at having left the Randolphs. Tyler may have been gone for days, but she had become very fond of Laurel. She didn't think she'd ever be comfortable around Hen, but his devotion to his wife was a revelation to Daisy.

She'd never seen anything like the relationship that existed between them. He was fierce in his determination to protect her, yet he yielded to her wishes whenever he thought he could. If he did something without asking—and he did from time to time—he never minded when she chastised him for it, and would reconsider. If he disagreed with her on an issue he felt strongly about, she would yield to him.

But there was something else, something almost hidden by this loving sharing of each other's lives. Daisy had the clear sense that should anything threaten his family, Hen would defend Laurel with all the ferocity of which he was capable.

Tyler gave her that same feeling. He might abuse Zac freely, but he took care of him. It must be a family trait. She remembered the time Willie had come to the cabin. Without speaking a single word, Zac and Tyler had drawn together to protect her.

That was what the Cochranes were doing, but they were doing it to keep her from behaving improperly. There was no such thing as improper behavior with the Randolphs.

Guy wanted to protect her because he thought no woman could take care of herself, but Tyler thought she was smart enough to succeed on her own. Guy said he loved her, but his feelings never once threatened to overpower him. Tyler wanted to make love to her because he couldn't help himself. She found his unruly passion much more to her liking.

She doubted Adora would appreciate such treatment. Daisy's mind boggled at anything like that happening between Mr. and Mrs. Cochrane. Yet she was certain it happened between Hen and Laurel. There was a powerful bond that existed between them, an explosive force that seemed to be on the verge of combustion. She hadn't understood at first. But now that she was back with the Cochranes, she realized she had sensed it whenever she was with Hen and Laurel.

She had felt the same thing those last days in the cabin with Tyler. It had seemed dangerous then, even undesirable, but now she regretted its absence. Everything now was calm, predictable, comforting, yet very unsatisfying.

As Daisy drifted off to sleep, she realized that nothing felt right anymore. She doubted it ever would again.

"You can't still want to marry me," Daisy said to Guy. She hadn't put her hair up this morning. She pulled at her curls. "I look a fright. I doubt any respectable woman will speak to me."

"Nonsense. Your appearance is a trifle odd just now, but once everyone knows all you've been through, they'll wear a path to the house offering to do anything they can to help. Besides, your hair will grow back."

Mr. Cochrane had gone to his office immediately after breakfast. Mrs. Cochrane had taken Adora off to visit soon after. Daisy had taken the opportunity to release Guy from his promise to marry her. She was stunned when he declared nothing would change his feelings for her.

"But I've got a scar." Daisy lifted her hair to show him.

"You can't see it."

Daisy decided she had to tell him what had happened. If he really wanted to marry her, he deserved the truth. Some of his color had faded by the time Daisy had finished her story, but he didn't falter.

"I'm positive you behaved impeccably throughout," he said. "It was wonderful of you to tell me." He took her hand and squeezed it. "But there's no need to speak of it again, even to Adora."

Daisy thought he looked a little dazed, but it probably wasn't fair to judge. He had just received a terrible shock.

"Mother says this Randolph is a gentleman," Guy said. He fidgeted nervously. "I'm sure she's right, but can you be certain he'll stick to his story?"

"He's the one who insisted I go to his brother," Daisy said. "He wouldn't have brought me to you if you'd been in town. He was determined no one should know I wasn't properly chaperoned. I'm sure he'd be angry I told you."

"Very proper," Guy said. "And the rest of them?"

"Are you worried the story would embarrass you?"

"Good God, no," Guy said, flushing. "I was concerned about you. I know it would practically kill you to have this story get out."

Oddly enough, Daisy didn't think it would.

"I know, you know, and the Randolphs know. It doesn't really matter what anybody else thinks."

"Not quite," Guy said. "I have complete faith in you, but there are many people who might not. I've asked around about the Randolphs. They're rich, but they also have a reputation for being men who take what they want. That includes women."

"You haven't met Tyler. He doesn't want anything."

"I'm glad to hear that, but this whole thing is best forgotten. I'll be relieved when the Randolphs return to their ranch."

Daisy didn't want Hen and Laurel to leave. They were her only connection with Tyler.

She told herself not to be stupid. He didn't want anything to do with her. It would be better if she could accept this, not keep hanging on to something that was over, something that had never been very much of a hope in the first place.

Guy patted her hand, a smile which seemed only slightly forced on his lips. "I know it's terribly soon after your awful ordeal. Naturally you'll want to observe a decent period of mourning for your father, but I wish you'd set a date."

"What for?"

"The wedding."

Daisy had the oddest feeling of being sad and relieved at the same time, as if something were closing in around her, choking off her air. At the same time something she feared was receding into the background. She must be losing her mind.

"I can't, not now."

"Then at least let me announce our engagement."

"No! People would want to come by and congratulate me, ask me about the wedding, about my father, all kinds of things. I can't deal with that and getting married at the same time."

"Of course." Guy smiled in a way that ought to have been endearing. "I'd like to say I want you to take as long as you like. But I really want us to get married as soon as possible. I don't want to rush you," he hastened to add. "Just know I'm anxious to make you my wife."

"I'll try. It's just that so much has happened."

"I know. You're feeling overwhelmed."

Yes, she had been overwhelmed, but not for the reason Guy believed.

Chapter Nineteen

Tyler returned to his base camp. He took care of his animals, cleaned his tools, then prepared and ate his supper. He had found more color today. He knew he was getting close to locating the source of the gold.

In the four days since he had returned from Albuquerque, the weather had turned as unseasonably mild as it had been cold the weeks before. The ground was so wet every hole he dug soon filled with water. He wished he'd packed his tarpaulin, but his cabin was 15 miles away, too far to go back. He sat on a rock, staring out over the hills as they fell away toward the Rio Grande nearly 20 miles away. Millions of stars twinkled in the clear sky, but Tyler hardly noticed.

Thoughts of Daisy filled his mind, as they had nearly every moment of the last week. He tried to go over in his mind what he planned to do the next day. But instead he found himself wondering if Daisy was still with Hen and Laurel or if the Cochranes had returned from Santa Fe.

Studying the way the water ran away from the hills, he tried to guess from the location of the bits of gold where the source might be, but he found himself wondering if Daisy was going to marry this Guy Cochrane after all. He tried to decide where to begin his digging tomorrow. Instead he wondered if she was happy.

He wasn't. He'd never been more miserable in his life.

He missed her. It wouldn't do him any good to keep denying it. It seemed ridiculous after doing everything he could to escape from her, but it was true. He found himself remembering little things he hadn't even been aware of at the time.

He liked the way the curls clustered around her face after he cut her hair. It made her look younger, more charming than she would believe. He remembered the way she wore her bandage, almost like a Turk wears his turban. It didn't bother her at all. It almost became a part of her. But he guessed his favorite recollection was of Daisy swallowed up in one of his coats. There was something about that memory that made him fiercely protective.

But most of all he worried if she was safe. She would be safe as long as she was with Hen, but what about afterward? He worried she would marry Guy Cochrane because she thought she had no other choice. He worried she wouldn't be happy no matter what happened. Not that he could help her with that.

He got up. He'd better get to sleep. He had a long day of digging ahead of him tomorrow.

But even after he went to bed, he had difficulty falling asleep. He kept remembering the times he held Daisy in his arms. That hadn't been mere lust. It wasn't a feeling he could transfer to the next female he met. The feeling was for Daisy alone, and it was still there.

It was a good thing he didn't have to go into Albuquerque for supplies for at least a month. It looked as if

255

he was going to need every minute of that time to let this feeling die. It scared him to think it might only grow stronger.

"You fool! You stupid, dim-witted fool!" Regis Cochrane shouted at Frank Storach. "I told you not to touch the girl."

"But she saw me coming out of the house," Frank protested. He was loading bales of wool from one of Cochrane's warehouses for shipment. The spring shearing would start before long.

"Did she see you kill the old man?" Regis demanded. He didn't climb down from his buggy. The yard was muddy.

"No."

"Then you could have lied, told her you stopped by for a cup of coffee and discovered the body."

Frank paused in his work. Despite the cold, he was perspiring. He wiped his forehead with his sleeve. "But she heard the shot. She was bound to figure out—"

"She couldn't prove anything. You and the fools you hired could have disappeared, and it would have blown over. Where are they now?"

"They headed for Mexico."

"Good," Regis said, as though he was thinking of something else. "You do the same thing. Go as far away as Montana if necessary, but don't come back to New Mexico. I've got to think of somebody to blame it on."

Frank stepped over to the buggy. "I could still kill the girl."

"I need her to get the land, you fool."

Frank resented being called a fool. "I still got some money coming."

"I'll give you a hundred, enough to get down the trail, but not a dime more. You botched the job. It's liable to cost me even more to fix this mess." Regis counted out the money and handed it to Frank.

"I killed the old man just like you wanted," Frank said. "You owe me that money."

"No."

"I know people who'd be interested in things I could tell."

The implacable cruelty in Regis's nature was easily visible in his eyes. "There's nobody alive who's double-crossed me. Remember that," he said, impatiently dismissing Frank's threat as though it were of no more concern to him than a gnat. "Now get out of town before I turn you over to the sheriff. Daisy Singleton has a dead accurate description of you." Regis took up the reins and drove off.

With anger in his heart, Frank counted the money before stuffing it into his pocket. He was the one who had done all the work, who'd spent a week nearly freezing looking for the girl. He knew she could identify him. It was his neck that would stretch if they ever caught him.

He went back to work, but anger against Regis Cochrane burned in his heart. He'd been cheated of money that was rightfully his. He'd been hired to kill an old man and burn down his house, 250 up front and the same when it was done. He'd been cheated of 150 dollars. It would serve Regis right if he killed the girl so he couldn't get his hands on her land.

"It's a boy," Laurel announced. "Big and blond just like his father."

Laurel was propped up in the big bed she had shared with Daisy that first evening. She looked tired but happy. Hen, who stood at her side like a proud but silent bulwark between his wife and the world, had sent Daisy a message before breakfast. Daisy had come as soon as she could get away.

"I'm sure you're proud of him," she said.

"I was secretly hoping for a girl," Laurel confessed. "I already have two boys. But I should have known better. Except for Rose, that's all anybody has in this family. Fern has four already."

"You can only blame one on me," Hen said.

"I'm sure I'll get a chance to blame you for more," Laurel said, but she didn't look the least bit unwilling. "Now you can take the boys for a ride without worrying about me. Daisy will sit with me until you return."

"I won't stir an inch," Daisy said when Hen hesitated. "If she looks the slightest bit uncomfortable, I'll go straight for the doctor."

"You're not to go near a doctor, no matter what happens," Laurel said after Hen had gone. "It's taken every bit of my persuasive powers just to get him to allow me to sit up. I told him I had Adam in the morning and cooked my own supper before nightfall." She chuckled. "It only made him more watchful."

They talked of unimportant things until they heard a cry from the bassinet. "Do you mind getting the baby?" Laurel asked. "It's time to feed him. I'd get him myself, but Hen would be sure to find out."

"I've never held a baby," Daisy said.

"It's not difficult. Just put one hand under his head and one under his bottom. He'll wiggle like jelly, but you won't drop him."

It turned out just as Laurel said. Daisy decided there was something magical about a baby. This was her first experience with one, but it gripped her instantly. She only held him a few seconds, but she was reluctant to hand him to his mother. "What's his name?"

"William Henry Harrison Randolph. I named him after his father despite Hen's objections," Laurel said as she prepared to feed her son. "I know it's a mouthful, but Hen can't have three sons and none of them named after him. He'll probably end up being called Harry, but I'm holding out for Harrison.''

The baby began to nurse with surprising aggressiveness for such a tiny creature.

''Greedy, that's what he is,'' Laurel said in a doting tone. ''Just like his brothers. He'll fit right in.''

The baby was absolutely adorable. Harrison was a real person who would someday grow up to be a man just like his father.

It was a miracle.

It required no feat of imagination for Daisy to see herself nursing her own son. Rather it required an effort not to be jealous this wasn't her child. She'd always known she wanted children. She hadn't known how much until now.

The thought that absolutely stunned her was that she imagined herself holding Tyler's son, not Guy's.

''How are things going with you?'' Laurel asked once she was certain her son had settled down to his work.

''Fine,'' Daisy said, refocusing her thoughts. ''The Cochranes couldn't be any kinder if they were my own relatives.''

''Wonderful. Have you heard from your father's family yet?''

''No.'' Daisy realized she hadn't even thought to contact them. ''I don't know their address,'' she said, realizing it would have burned up in the fire. ''I don't know how to contact them.''

''Put an announcement of his death in all the newspapers, giving your name and address. I'm sure they'll contact you.''

Daisy wasn't sure she wanted to do that. She wouldn't know what to do if her father's family did contact her.

Laurel studied Daisy closely. ''How are you feeling?''

''A little dazed. I was certain Guy wouldn't want to marry me. I told him everything that happened. He insisted it made no difference.''

''I meant how are you feeling about Tyler?''

Daisy felt heat flood her face. She hadn't had the courage to ask herself that question.

''I've put him out of my mind,'' she said. She was unable to discuss her feelings about Tyler, even with Laurel. She was too unsure of them.

''Probably very wise.''

''Guy's pressing me to set a date for the wedding. He says he's anxious to take all my worries off my shoulders.''

''That's wonderful. I'm so happy for you.''

But Daisy was well aware Laurel guarded her expression.

''I told him I wasn't ready.''

''I can understand,'' Laurel said, looking down at her son. She changed sides. ''However, it's never wise to take too long to get through a period like this. I know. I've lost my mother, father, and a husband. It'll be easier if you go on and get married. Making room in your life for a man is a big adjustment. I've done it twice, and it wasn't easy either time.''

''Not even with Hen?''

''Don't ever tell him I said this,'' Laurel confided with a smile. ''It was just a different kind of difficulty. It always is when you marry a strong man. They don't realize it, but they don't bend very easily.''

Tyler didn't bend at all as far as Daisy could tell.

''Guy and his family are doing everything they can to shield me from any unpleasantness or curiosity over my father's death. Mr. Cochrane has taken over trying to find out who killed my father. His mother will plan the wedding.''

''You're very fortunate.'' Laurel lifted her son against her shoulder. He rewarded her with an immediate burp.

''Not a very elegant way of signifying his satisfaction.''

"May I hold him?" Daisy asked.

"Sure."

Daisy took Harrison from his mother and cradled him in her arms. He didn't feel at all strange this time. He seemed awfully small, but totally wonderful.

"He looks so much like his father already."

"All the Randolph children do. I wouldn't have been able to tell Fern's boys apart if it hadn't been for their ages. I don't think Rose had anything to do with her four. They're pure Randolph."

"You don't mind?"

"I can't think of anything more wonderful than having a son who looks exactly like the man I love."

"You do love him a lot, don't you?"

"I can't tell you how much. Sometimes it frightens me."

Daisy knew she looked confused.

"Hen used to be a gunfighter. I married him knowing there would always be a chance I would lose him." Laurel smiled softly. "I hated everything I thought he stood for, but it didn't do any good. I fell in love with him anyway."

The baby fell asleep in Daisy's arms, but she hardly noticed. "You married a man you disapproved of?"

"It was either that or be miserable the rest of my life. It was the same for Iris and Fern. No sane woman wants to marry a Randolph. We just can't help ourselves. You can put Harrison to bed now. He'll sleep until he's hungry again."

Daisy laid him in his bed. Her mind was racing. Three women had married Randolph brothers even though they didn't want to. Yet it had worked out fine for all of them.

But there was a major difference, she reminded herself. Tyler didn't want to marry her. As long as that was true, nothing else mattered.

As Daisy turned, she heard the door to the sitting room open and a babble of voices enter.

"That'll be Hen and the boys," Laurel said, a smile wreathing her face. "It sounds like they had a good ride."

Daisy felt like crying. If she had to sit and watch a happy family group, she was sure she would.

"I'd better be going," she said. "Mrs. Cochrane will worry if I stay away too long. They're all convinced I am so fragile I'll crumble at the slightest thing."

"What do you think?" Laurel asked.

"I don't know what I think."

A boy of about eight burst into the room. "Ma, you should have been with us. I beat Jordy."

"He wouldn't have if that nag I was riding hadn't shied," Jordy said, disgusted. "I told you Adam and me ought to have brought our own horses."

"How did your father do?"

"Aw, he always wins," Adam complained. "Ain't no horse can beat Brimstone."

A sharp wind whipped around the rocky outcroppings. After a week warm enough to melt the last of the snow, the weather had turned cold under a clear, blue sky. Tyler continued to dig out the pieces of soft quartz with his pick. He barely noticed the thin vein of gold that laced the rock and glinted softly in the sunlight, or that it grew larger as he dug deeper into the hillside. He couldn't stop thinking about Daisy. He hadn't been able to get her out of his mind for more than a few minutes since he left Albuquerque.

He couldn't forget that last night in the cabin, the way she had felt in his arms, the taste of her kisses, the passion that warmed her body until it was as heated as his own.

But it wasn't merely that night. He missed her. He'd had plenty of time to realize no other woman had responded to him as she had. Other women didn't know what to do with him. They were careful to avoid offending him. Strange he should like the one who seemed to make a point of annoying him. He was perverse and obstinate, just like the rest of his family.

He tried to keep his mind on his work. He had thought nothing meant as much as finding gold—that was the basis on which he had made every decision for the past three years—but things had changed in less than two weeks.

The more he thought about the killer, the less confident he felt that the Cochranes could protect Daisy. He had no doubt they would have the sheriff on the killer's trail, but he doubted they would understand how dangerous this man was. Tyler doubted he would attempt to shoot Daisy in Albuquerque. He would probably wait until she visited her parents' graves.

Tyler drove his pick deep into the rock. He pulled out loose stone and attacked the vein more savagely. The click of metal on stone caused him to look up. Willie Mozel was coming over the ridge. Tyler left his digging. He had coffee on by the time Willie reached the camp.

"I came to see how you're getting along," Willie said. He accepted a cup of coffee and settled on a rock. "Did you get that gal settled in town?"

Tyler nodded.

"Don't wear your voice out talking," Willie said.

Tyler almost grinned. "I left her with my brother. Her friends should be back by now."

"You had some visitors at your cabin," Willie said, taking a noisy sip of the hot coffee. "They stayed two, three days from what I could gather."

"The three killers?"

"Don't know if they was killers, but there was three of them. Made themselves at home."

Tyler waited, knowing Willie had more to tell.

"Didn't go off together," Willie said finally. "Two of them headed south. I figure they're headed for Mexico. Money lasts longer down there."

"And the other one?"

"Big fella riding a big horse. Couldn't miss his tracks."

"Where did he go?"

"Can't tell for sure, but if I was to make a guess, I'd say he was headed to Albuquerque."

Tyler had known it was coming. He had lain awake for several nights wondering what would set him off. He didn't have to wonder any longer.

"Then I guess I'd better head for Albuquerque."

"Sort of figured you might. Want some company?"

"No need. Hen's still there. Besides, if she's with the Cochranes, there's not much I can do but warn her."

"That all you going to talk to her about?"

"What else is there?"

"That's not for me to say," Willie said with a scornful snort. "I wasn't holed up with her in a cabin alone for nearly two weeks."

"It was only nine days, and Zac was there all but one."

"Plus two more on the road."

"Nothing happened."

Willie sipped noisily. To Tyler, the noise seemed like a derisive commentary.

"Why aren't you working your own claim?" Tyler asked.

"It turned out worthless. I'm looking for another likely place."

"I'll make you a deal. You work mine while I'm gone, and I'll give you a quarter of anything you find."

"A third," Willie countered.

"Okay."

Willie didn't look excited. "A third of nothing is still nothing."

"Let's have a look," Tyler said.

Willie was a good deal less skeptical when he got a look at the rock. "You can't go off chasing killers now," he exclaimed. "This could be a big strike."

"I knew I had to go as soon as I saw you top that ridge."

"I might try to steal your claim."

"I'd hunt you down and kill you."

"I might take any gold I find and head for Mexico."

"They don't ask questions about scrawny, ugly bodies in Mexico."

Willie laughed. "Go on. I knew you was in love with that gal the minute I set eyes on the two of you."

"And you came all this way to offer to watch my claim so I could go after her."

"Something like that."

"Well, you're wrong about me being in love with her, but you're right I can't let her wander around without knowing that killer is still on her trail."

Tyler didn't even know if Daisy would want to see him. She probably felt this Guy fella was all the protection she needed. But Tyler couldn't feel comfortable with that until he got a look at Cochrane. Whether Daisy wanted him in Albuquerque or not, he was going to make sure she was all right.

"When can I expect you back?" Willie asked.

"Four or five days. It shouldn't take me long. Once I've told the Cochranes and the sheriff what they're up against, there'll be no reason for me to stay."

But as Tyler headed toward Albuquerque, he knew he had at least one more reason to prolong his stay. He had to be certain Daisy was in love with Guy Cochrane. He couldn't let her marry him if she wasn't.

Chapter Twenty

"Mama says it's time you let Guy announce your engagement," Adora said to Daisy.

Adora had come to Daisy's room to have a comfortable chat before going to bed. She nestled in the chair next to Daisy's bed to keep warm.

"I told Guy I wasn't up to facing all those people," Daisy said.

"Just an announcement, silly. You can hide in this room for the next year if you like. We'll protect you."

Daisy realized it wasn't protection she wanted. It was isolation. She wanted to be left alone until she could figure out what was going on inside her head.

And her silly, rebellious heart.

"It's not that. Things have happened too fast."

"Guy's been wanting to marry you for ages. That hasn't changed."

"Why does he want to marry me?" Daisy suddenly demanded of her friend. "There must be a dozen prettier

266

girls who'd bring him a large dowry.''

"Guy has always liked you," Adora said, clearly a little taken aback by Daisy's question. "He thinks you're
quite pretty. He doesn't care that you're not rich.''

"But does he love me?" Daisy demanded. "He doesn't
seem overwhelmed by me in the least.''

"He wants to get married right away.''

"I mean *me*! He doesn't try to find ways to steal a few
minutes alone with me. When we are alone, he doesn't
ache to touch me, to take me in his arms. He doesn't long
to do things he knows I won't let him do before the wedding.''

"Do you want him to do those things?''

"Yes.'' Daisy's confession escaped like a sigh, like a
long-held secret she had finally summoned the courage to
confess. Only it wasn't a confession as much as a discovery. Before Tyler, she would have been content with no
more than a word of love. Now she knew there was much
more. She wanted that, too.

Adora's laugh sounded guilty. "I'd want that, too," she
confessed. "I've dreamed of a man kidnapping me and
carrying me away to his mountain cabin.''

"I've been there," Daisy said. "You don't want to
go.''

"It was only a fantasy. I wouldn't want him to ravage
me, but it would be exciting to have him be so crazy about
me he couldn't control himself. It sounds to me like you
want the same thing.''

"I do. I guess I'm just ashamed to have admitted it.''

"I know Guy's not the romantic type," Adora said.
"He's too much like Papa, but he does admire you. He'll
be a good husband.''

"Why does he admire me?" Daisy wanted to know.

"I think it's your mind," Adora said. "Guy's not very
bookish. He's impressed you can read all those books and
understand what they say.''

Daisy had wanted to hear something about her eyes, her lips, even her bosom. She didn't want to hear about books.

"Would you want to marry somebody who admired you for your mind?"

"Don't be silly. I don't have a mind," Adora said.

"Yes, you do. You just don't use it."

"Men don't like women to think for themselves."

Tyler did. He had told her she could do anything she wanted.

"They want to take care of us. It's what they're supposed to do. I wouldn't want to have to make my own living. I wouldn't know where to begin."

Daisy didn't either, but she had an urge to try. She didn't want her husband to mark off a portion of his life and tell her to stay out.

"As for wanting a man to be so passionate about you he couldn't control himself, I don't think I'd really like that. A man should respect his wife, like Guy respects you. He'd never think of mistreating you. How could he look you in the face the next day?"

Hungrily. Tyler would. He'd want to do it all over again.

"I think you've just been overset by being whisked off to the mountains by a handsome man."

"How do you know he's handsome? You never saw him."

"You wouldn't have talked about him so much if he weren't," Adora said, giving her friend a hug. "Besides, if he's Hen Randolph's brother, he's got to be heavenly. Why do you go there all the time?"

"To sit with Laurel while she recovers from having her baby. She doesn't know anybody in Albuquerque."

"Sometimes I think you like her better than me."

"I'll never like anybody better than you," Daisy said, giving her friend a fierce hug. "You've been absolutely

268

wonderful to me.'' Daisy clung to her friend. ''I don't know why you like me. I'm such a complaining, ungrateful female.''

''No, you're not. You've just had a difficult time. But everything is going to be perfect from now on. You'll see. All you have to do is marry Guy.''

All she had to do was marry Guy, and everything would be perfect!

Then why was she so reluctant? Before her father's death, it had been exactly what she wanted. It didn't make sense for her to start dragging her feet now. She wasn't fooling herself. It was because of Tyler. Why couldn't she accept that he wasn't coming back?

Daisy heaved a great sigh. Their time in the cabin was over. She had experienced more than most women, certainly more than Adora, who would go to her wedding to some very proper young man without even the most innocent flirtation.

It was time for Daisy to grow up. Tyler had said she could do anything she wanted to as long as she put her mind to it. She knew marrying Guy wasn't what he'd had in mind, but it was what she ought to do. She liked Guy. She knew she didn't love him, but she might learn. Her mother had married for love, and it had killed her. Daisy had sworn she wouldn't let that happen to her. Here was her chance to have exactly the kind of life she'd always wanted.

''I'll talk to Guy tomorrow,'' Daisy said. ''I want to wait a few more days in case Daddy's family answers my ad. I don't want them to hear about his death and my wedding in the same week.''

''Are you sure?''

''Yes. Laurel told me it was always best to get over difficult ground quickly, that it would make things much easier in the end.''

''I can't wait to tell Mama.''

Daisy decided she'd feel much better once things were settled and her life had some focus, some direction. Marrying Guy would give her that direction.

She had allowed Tyler to confuse her. She supposed it happened to many young women, especially young women with no family to guide them. She was fortunate to have the Cochranes. Without them, she might have done something terribly foolish.

Daisy shaded her eyes from the sun as she and Guy approached the hotel. She wondered why the plaza was barren of trees. They would be very useful in the summer, much more so than a picket fence.

She looked forward to her visit with Laurel, but not even that could banish her sense of apprehension. She knew it was time she stopped refusing to face her future, but she dreaded facing Albuquerque society. As soon as she let Guy announce their engagement, she would be besieged by well-wishers.

Daisy wondered if all prospective brides were this nervous.

"I see Mrs. Esterhouse and her daughter, Julia Madigan, coming this way," Guy whispered. "Her husband is one of Dad's partners in the bank. Julia's husband has a wholesale business. You'll meet them all the time once we're married."

It didn't take Daisy long to realize Mrs. Esterhouse and her petite daughter disapproved of her.

"We heard about your father's death," Mrs. Esterhouse said once Guy had made the necessary introductions. "Such a shock. I know you're devastated. After what those terrible men did to you, I think it's very courageous of you to be out."

Daisy had to clench her right hand to her side to keep it from going to her head in a protective gesture. She had pulled her hair into a tight knot at the back of her head and hidden it under her hat. Mrs. Esterhouse couldn't see the bun or her scar. She had no need to mention them except to be unkind.

"It must be terrible having to stay at a hotel alone," Julia said.

"Daisy is staying with my sister," Guy offered.

Daisy had to throttle an impulse to tell Guy not to be naive. Julia was just trying to find out where she was staying.

"The Cochranes have been wonderful to me," Daisy said. She had released Guy's arm. Her fingers gripped each other tightly under the fringes of her shawl. "I'm waiting to hear from my father's family before I make up my mind what to do."

Daisy didn't know why she had said that. She'd followed Laurel's advice and put notices in all the papers in New York and Philadelphia, but she wasn't expecting to hear from either of her parents' families. She had only said it because these women looked down on her.

"I didn't know you had family," Mrs. Esterhouse said.

"Naturally I haven't seen much of them since my father came to New Mexico."

"Daisy's family is very prominent in New York and Philadelphia," Guy said. "Mama says they're bound to want her back with them. But we have to do all we can to convince her to stay right here with us, don't we?"

"Of course," Julia Madigan said, a smile pasted on her lips. "Maybe you could convince some of your cousins to move to Albuquerque. I'm so very fond of really tall men." She edged closer to Guy and looked up at him as if to emphasize her slight stature.

Daisy felt a strong desire to take her balled-up fist out of her fringe and punch Julia Madigan in the face. She was shocked by the sheer force of the anger pulsing through her. She had never felt such a violent reaction toward anyone except Tyler and Zac.

271

"I'm afraid they're all fond of tall women," Daisy retorted. She took Guy by the arm. "I'm delighted to have seen you, but I'm late for a visit with Mrs. Randolph."

"You know the Randolphs?" Mrs. Esterhouse asked. By now everyone knew of the wealthy, austere, handsome man who had hired the top floor of the hotel, practically taken over the livery stable, brought six servants to look after his wife's comfort, and tried to hire the town's best doctor for his private use.

"Daisy visits her every day," Guy said.

Both mother and daughter did a quick mental reevaluation. "Maybe you could bring her for a visit once she's ready to go out again."

"They're anxious to get back to their ranch," Daisy said. "I don't think they enjoy town very much. Now if you'll excuse me, I don't want to be late."

Mother and daughter said their good-byes and moved on. Daisy disengaged her hand from Guy's arm. "Let's go inside before something else terrible happens."

"What was terrible about that? Mrs. Esterhouse is something of a stickler, but Julia is a delightful girl. You'll love her once you get to know her."

"I'm sure I will," Daisy said, quickly repenting of her bad temper, "but I'm still not feeling up to company." She mounted the steps to the hotel. Without waiting for Guy to open the door for her, Daisy pushed through into the lobby. She stopped dead when she saw Tyler at the desk.

He had come back! Daisy felt incapable of standing still, moving forward, or acting as if she hadn't lost her mind.

He had come back!

Could it mean he loved her? Every hope, dream, and idle fancy she had struggled so hard to repress, to put out of her mind, to pretend never existed, came rushing back, making it impossible to deny for a minute longer that she was in love with Tyler Randolph or that she could ever love Guy.

She looked at Tyler's well-remembered face and found it hard to realize it had been covered with a beard for most of the time they were together. This was the face she'd been seeking from the first, the man she had known would be behind the beard.

She remembered everything she'd felt that night in his arms, when it had taken all her willpower to tell him she was engaged. She felt her body tremble and was glad she had stepped through the door before Guy. It gave her a few precious seconds to collect herself before she had to introduce the two men.

Daisy forced herself to wait until Guy reached her side. Then, making a determined effort to calm her pulse, she started forward.

Her body reverberated with shock when Guy took her arm and tucked it firmly in his. Gently, she tried to pull it back, but Guy held her hand firmly. Daisy's gaze flew to Tyler. She could see his gaze become clouded, then hooded as he withdrew within himself. She tried once more to disengage her hand, but Guy wouldn't let go.

"Hello," she said, greeting Tyler in a manner she hoped didn't betray her inner turmoil. "I didn't expect to see you back in town so soon."

Tyler rose to his feet, and Daisy felt a fluttering in her belly. She had forgotten how tall he was, how small he made her feel. She had also forgotten how his mere presence could cause her senses to go awry. She had forgotten that just looking at him could make it hard for her to draw breath, that her whole previous life seemed but a prelude to those nine days, everything since an anticlimax.

But she hadn't forgotten she loved him.

Tyler's gaze cut to Guy, then back to Daisy.

"Guy, this is Tyler Randolph, the man who found me. Tyler, this is Guy Cochrane."

The two men exchanged greetings, shook hands, took stock of each other. Tyler's eyes gave away little, his posture nothing. He simply drew back within himself. Daisy wanted to call out, to beg him not to misread the situation, but she realized it would be pointless. What could he possibly think except that she belonged to Guy just as completely as Guy seemed to think?

Guy's response wasn't the least bit difficult to interpret. He was clearly shocked and intimidated by Tyler's size. She could feel his body stiffen, see his expression become more formal. It took her only a second to realize he was feeling defensive.

"I want to thank you for taking care of Daisy for me," Guy said in his most formal manner. "I can never repay you for what you did, but I would very much like to repay you for any expenses or loss of time incurred—"

"It was no problem," Tyler replied, impervious to Guy's attempt to put distance between him and Daisy.

"My mother spoke of clothes."

"You'll have to speak to my brother about that," Tyler said.

"Did you have any success with your claim?" Daisy asked, anxious to get Guy away from the embarrassing subject of money. It angered her that Guy would try to act so proprietarily. If anybody should repay Tyler, she should be the one to do it.

"I haven't had much chance yet."

He wasn't going to help her. She could see him hiding behind his barriers, safely out of reach. She felt like crying out to him to come out, to give her a chance to explain. But she didn't. "Why?"

"I decided that before I built a hotel of my own, I'd better know how to run one. So I took your advice and got a job here."

Daisy felt as if she'd been struck in the chest by a huge

fist, a fist so powerful it could knock both breath and hope out of her at the same time.

"Is that the only reason you came back?" she managed to ask. She felt as though everything in her had dissolved, leaving her empty and cold.

"I wanted to see Laurel and Hen before they went back to the ranch. It might be years before I see them again. I also wanted to speak to Mr. Cochrane about the killers. Willie found the trail of two horses headed south, but the man on the big horse headed north. I think the killer followed you to town."

Daisy found no consolation in his concern for her safety. He hadn't come to town to see her. Couldn't he see she loved him? No, and he wouldn't admit it if he did. She doubted he knew what love felt like. He'd been impervious to it all his life.

She had to stop this senseless hoping for miracles. It was foolish to keep torturing herself with hopes that Tyler would someday, somehow come to his senses. She shouldn't let his concern for her safety mislead her into thinking he felt anything more. He'd been concerned for her in the cabin, and after nine days that was still all he felt. There was no reason to expect him to change now.

"I'll be happy to convey your message to my father," Guy said as he patted Daisy's hand in a very possessive manner. "I can assure you nothing is more important to me than the safety of my future wife."

Daisy opened her mouth to deny it. But even before she realized she couldn't, she knew it was pointless. She could see Tyler thought she had decided to marry for money and safety. By deciding against independence, she had decided against him.

That made Daisy angry. He had no right to judge anything she did. He had never done or said anything to make her believe he loved her or would welcome her love. He had walked out of her life. He couldn't expect her to sit around waiting for him to make up his mind.

"I thought you were going to try running your ranch," Tyler said.

"I'll be taking care of all my wife's business concerns," Guy told him.

Daisy got madder and madder. If Tyler didn't care about her, she wouldn't let him know she cared about him, either. Her pride wouldn't let her show him that one word was all it would have taken. It was a poor consolation, pride, but it was all she had left.

"I haven't decided what I'm going to do about the ranch," she said. "I'll probably wait until I hear from Daddy's family." She didn't know why she kept mentioning her father's family, using them as a shield between herself and something she couldn't handle just now. "Or I just may leave it up to my husband."

Guy patted her hand in such a self-congratulatory manner Daisy wanted to hit him. But she couldn't take her anger out on him. Tyler was the one she wanted to flay alive.

"Now I'll leave you men to talk about killers," Daisy said. "I'm late. Laurel will think I'm not coming."

Daisy managed to cross the lobby, but the minute she started up the stairs, she thought her legs would go out from under her. She had known Tyler didn't love her, but it hadn't been so painful until today. Now she felt physically ill. She stopped on the stairs and leaned against the wall. For a moment she thought she didn't have the strength to go on, but she had no choice. She couldn't go back down there and face Tyler.

She was also mad at Guy. He had said they were engaged to give him leverage against a bigger and more imposing man. She could understand that, but she couldn't forgive it.

Tyler Randolph had just made the biggest mistake of his life. No one could ever love him more than she did.

276

Only she couldn't even take satisfaction in knowing he'd someday discover his mistake. He probably never would figure it out.

By the time she knocked on Laurel's door, Daisy's eyes were swimming with tears. Hen answered her knock.

"We were wondering if . . . Is something wrong? Come in. What can I do to help?"

"Nobody can help me," Daisy said, allowing Hen to guide her to a chair.

So Zac had been right. Daisy was a fortune hunter. Tyler had known at a glance she didn't love Guy. She was only marrying him because he could give her all the things her mother had talked about. She'd probably have set her sights on him or Zac if she had had any notion how rich the Randolphs were.

But if there wasn't anything special between them, why the hell had he bothered to come back? To tell her about the killer? Because he wasn't happy with her engagement to Guy? He had no right to get upset over Daisy's coolness toward him. He had given her no reason to think she meant anything special to him.

But she did, and he knew it now. He had known it the moment he saw Guy tuck her arm in his. He had known it more strongly every minute he watched that man talk about Daisy as if she were something he owned, that he planned to absorb into himself until there was nothing of her left. Tyler had wanted to snatch Daisy off Guy's arm and knock his rival to the ground.

She might not be betraying him—he had to be honest and admit he'd given her no reason to think there was anything to betray—but she was most certainly betraying herself. He recognized Guy as the type of man who would expect unquestioning obedience from his wife. He was also the type to consider it his right to be unfaithful. For that Tyler wanted to hit him again.

He had been a fool to come. He should have stayed in the mountains and sent Willie instead. But he knew he couldn't have done that. No matter what came of it, he couldn't abandon Daisy now. She might not love him, she might never love him, she might not want to marry him if she did, but he would not leave Albuquerque until he was sure she was safe.

And free of Guy Cochrane.

"We found out who killed your father," Regis Cochrane announced to Daisy at dinner that evening. "Unfortunately, he has left the territory. According to the report the sheriff got, he was headed for Montana."

"Can't you send somebody after him?" Daisy asked.

"No, but we can notify the U.S. marshals up that way. They'll keep an eye out for him. Other than that, there's nothing we can do."

"So he'll get away."

"I'm afraid so. I am having the sheriff check on Bob Greene. He's always been a stiff-necked old bastard." Mr. Cochrane gave her a fatherly smile and a pat on the hand. "Now you leave all this to me and concentrate on your wedding."

Daisy was disappointed in Mr. Cochrane. She had placed her faith in him. She had been certain he would find the killer and see him hanged. Even if Bob Greene was the one behind it, the killer himself had gotten away.

If Tyler had agreed to help her, he wouldn't have given up. He would have followed that man for as long as it took. Any man who would chase after gold for three years wouldn't quibble at a few months spent going to Montana.

But Tyler hadn't wanted to help her.

Chapter Twenty-one

Daisy sat ramrod straight in the most uncomfortable chair in the Cochranes' parlor. She dreaded this interview. She had gone over what she meant to say several times, but the words never came out the way she wanted. Still, there was no going back. She had paced her room all morning. She had racked her brain for different solutions, but she knew there was no other. She loved Tyler Randolph, fool that she was, and she would never love anyone else. Wealth and all the finer things her mother had taught her to want meant nothing without him.

She was scared. She'd never attempted anything like this. Most frightening of all, she would have nobody to depend on but herself. She had told herself for years this was what she wanted, but now she wasn't sure.

Guy's entrance scattered her thoughts. She hurriedly collected them again.

"Dolores said you wanted to see me."

Daisy had asked the maid to find Guy because she

didn't want anyone in the family to know. "I need to talk to you."

Guy stopped in front of her chair, a smile on his face, his hands held out to her. "You could talk with me anytime. Dolores made it sound so serious." When she didn't put her hands in his, he dropped his hands and frowned. "What is it? You haven't fallen in love with someone else, have you?" he asked jokingly.

Daisy thought it ironic that the problem he saw as the most unlikely should be the crux of the matter.

"Not exactly."

The smile disappeared from Guy's face. "What do you mean *not exactly?*"

"Please sit down, Guy. I can't think with you towering over me."

"I think with you towering over me all the time." His effort at humor fell flat. He pulled a chair forward and sat down, perched on the edge.

"I can't marry you," Daisy said before she lost her courage. "I'm sorry. After all you and your family have done for me, I must seem very ungrateful. But I've thought about it for the last two days, and I must break our engagement."

Guy seemed to be at a loss for words. "Why?" he asked finally.

She'd known he was going to ask that. She wished she could say that was the way it was going to be and leave without an explanation, but she couldn't. She owed him that much.

"When you asked me to marry you, I liked you very much. I thought I could learn to love you. I thought that was the way things were supposed to be."

"It is."

"Then I spent nine days with Tyler Randolph, and I wasn't sure of anything anymore."

"Do you love him?"

280

"It's not a question of loving him," Daisy said, hoping to avoid answering that question. "But knowing I liked him made me question my feelings for you. Now I think maybe love should come before marriage, or it might not come at all."

"If that's all, we can wait until—"

"It's not all. I don't know how to say this without sounding even more ungrateful, but I want a chance to be on my own. You and your family have been very kind, but you want to do everything for me."

"We're only trying to help."

"I know, but I feel like I'm about to suffocate."

"Tell me what you don't like, and I'll change it."

Daisy stood up and walked a few steps before she turned to face Guy. "It's not that simple. I don't know what I want." Gripping her hands together in front of her, Daisy walked a few more steps. "When I was ten, my father gave me a book about Queen Elizabeth I of England. I loved that book so much I read it over and over again. I can even quote parts of it.

'The young princess was hemmed in on all sides, her will never her own, her life a constant struggle to please those stronger than herself. Yet no matter what she did, she was never able to please her guardians.'

"That's how my father made me feel. No matter what I did, it was never good enough. But Elizabeth became the greatest queen England ever had. They threatened her kingdom and her throne, but she never got married. She ruled a whole country by herself for forty-five years.

"I admired her and wanted to be like her, but all my life I was told I couldn't survive without a man. Tyler was the first person to believe in me, to believe I could do anything I wanted. Now the time has come for me to

281

find out if he's right. I can't find out if I allow you and your father to do everything for me."

Guy looked stunned. "What are you going to do?"

"Go back to the ranch."

"You can't. The house is gone."

"I'm going to buy a tent—"

"You'd be alone."

"—and hire Rio Mendoza to help me."

"He's an old man."

"He's just turned forty, and he's a good worker. I'll feel safe with him."

Guy leapt out of his chair. "You can't do this. What'll people say?"

"I imagine they'll say you're well out of a bad marriage."

"That's not what I mean. I'm talking about your reputation. Aren't you worried about that?"

"I don't have a reputation, at least not a good one. I thought Mrs. Esterhouse made that plain enough."

"I don't care about Mrs. Esterhouse. All I care about is you." Guy tried to take her in his arms, but Daisy twisted away.

"I don't know why you are so determined to marry me. You don't love me. You may like me, but you're not in love. I'm not pretty. I have absolutely no money. I'm taller than most men in Albuquerque."

Guy looked taken aback, but made a quick recovery. "Of course you're pretty. Everybody says—"

"They say I'm a gawk who towers over every man in sight. They've probably forgotten my freckles because of my hair and scar, but they won't forget my father and my poverty."

"That's not true. You are a striking woman. Everybody says so."

Daisy laughed. She didn't know why. She didn't feel amused, but the sound came out on its own. "Amazing, startling, staggering, shocking, or all of the above.''

Guy gripped Daisy by the shoulders. ''I'm not giving up. I'll come out every day to see how you're doing.'' He sounded desperate, even a little frightened.

''No. I want you to start looking for someone else. You deserve a wife who can love you with her whole heart. You deserve to be *in* love. Promise me you won't marry anyone you don't love.''

''You sound like *you're* in love,'' Guy said.

''I know what it's like.'' Daisy stood. ''Please don't say any more. I've made all my preparations. I'll tell Adora, but I want you to speak to your parents. After all their kindness, I don't think I can face them.''

''I don't want you to leave,'' Adora wailed. ''I want you to be my sister. Why do you want to go away?''

Daisy had left Guy, stunned and confused, to go find Adora. She wanted to tell her while she still had the courage. She had found her in her bedroom.

''I don't want to. I must.''

''That's absurd. Nobody's making you go. Just the opposite.''

''I'm making me go,'' Daisy said. ''I don't love Guy. It would be unfair to marry him.''

''You love one of those Randolph men, don't you, the young one you said was so handsome?''

''No, I don't love Zac.''

''Then it's the other one. I know it is. You haven't been the same since you got back.''

''Okay, I do love him, but I'm not going to marry him.''

''But if you love him—''

''He doesn't love me.''

Adora was silent a moment. ''How do you know?''

''He came back to Albuquerque. Guy and I met him in the hotel lobby.''

"Guy told me he came to tell Papa he thought the killer had followed you to town."

"Yes, but he didn't come back because of me."

"Maybe he's just shy."

"Tyler never had any trouble saying what he wanted to say."

"And you love him?"

"Stupid, isn't it, but I can't help it."

"Why?"

"For a lot of reasons you'll probably think very silly. He's the first man who ever made me feel petite."

"Guy said he was very tall."

"It isn't that. He simply isn't aware that there's anything different about me. He thinks I'm pretty, doesn't mind my freckles, prefers my hair short, and he was burning to make love to me."

"You didn't—"

"No, but now I wish I had. Does that shock you? It shocks me, but no one has ever kissed me like he did."

"How was that?" Adora asked, shock fading in the face of rampant curiosity.

"I had dreamed of being kissed by the man I loved, but it was nothing like this. He was out of control. It happened too fast. When he took me in his arms, I felt powerless to stop him. He pressed me to him until my entire body threatened to explode from the heat of him.

"Then he kissed me, and I could hardly believe such a powerful sensation could be produced merely by touching a man's lips. His mouth was hard and demanding. I felt as though the energy had drained out of me. I felt owned, possessed. But he kept demanding more and more until I couldn't do anything but give in to him."

"Give in to him?" Adora repeated, breathless.

"His tongue thrust its way into my mouth and fire shot all through me. I felt he had invaded me, was searching out all of me and making it his own. I felt like I had been released from a cocoon, suddenly transformed, freed to meld with him.

"Then he broke off, and I feared I would collapse. If he hadn't held on to me, I would have fallen."

Adora stared at Daisy, her eyes wide with amazement.

"A kiss like that can't happen with a man who only admires you or who will wait respectfully to make you his own," Daisy said. "Only a man who must have you despite all the rules of society, despite his own sense of honor, despite your objections can make you feel that way."

"You were never like this before."

"Don't I sound foolish? Daddy would have locked me in my room until I was over it. That's why I can't marry Guy. He would expect a quiet, dutiful wife. He'd never understand."

"What are you going to do about Tyler?"

"Nothing."

"If you love him, you must do something. You can't just let him ruin your life."

"I have no life to ruin, but I'm going to make one. I'm going to run my ranch. Tyler said I could do anything I made up my mind to do."

"And you believe him?"

"I have to. Believing him means believing in myself."

"But you'll be by yourself."

"I know."

"I could never do anything like that. I'd be too afraid."

"I'm petrified," Daisy admitted.

"You really do love him, don't you?"

Daisy nodded.

"Then he'll come back for you. If you love him that much, he can't do anything else."

But Daisy wouldn't let herself hope. She didn't think she could stand to be disappointed again.

* * *

"You told her you came back to learn how to run a hotel?" Laurel stared at Tyler as if he were a certified fool.

"What was I supposed to tell her?"

"Anything but that. I'm surprised she didn't slap you then and there."

"I warned her about the killer."

"Do you love her?"

The question startled Tyler into silence.

"Don't tell me you haven't thought about it. She has. She's in love with you, you know."

"How . . ." Tyler was unable to finish the sentence.

"I could tell by looking at her, by the way she talked about you. She was in love with you the night you brought her here."

Tyler didn't know what to say. He just stood there like a huge wooden carving.

"I don't know why men have to be so stupid about these things," Laurel complained. "It makes it so much harder on women." She gave Hen a severe look. "Randolph men seem to be particularly hardheaded."

"But we do finally learn," her husband said.

Laurel's sternness melted. "You did, but I don't know about your brother." She turned back to Tyler. "Do you love her? You've got to decide. You can't leave her wondering. She deserves to know, to be able to forget you, to make room for someone else."

This whole conversation had moved too fast for Tyler. He thought he had known why he came back, but after the encounter in the lobby, he wasn't sure. After Guy announced their engagement, there seemed no point in trying to make sure.

"It doesn't matter. Guy Cochrane said they were going to announce their engagement in a few days."

"She's still in love with you."

"Then why is she marrying Cochrane?"

''I can't answer that, but I imagine she will if you ask her.''

Because Cochrane was rich. Because it was the easy thing to do. Because she was afraid to be on her own. Because marrying someone else was the easiest way to forget him. ''She's made her decision. Nothing I do matters at this point.''

''It does if you love her.''

''I could never love a woman who would consider marrying another man.''

''Then you don't love her,'' Laurel said angrily. ''If you did, you'd go after her, beg her to change her mind, to give her one last chance. You wouldn't care about anything she did or thought of doing, only if she loved you.''

The idea of being reduced to such a cringing, groveling condition appalled Tyler. No woman—not even his hotels—was worth such a loss of pride. If this was Laurel's idea of being in love, he was glad it hadn't happened to him. He couldn't understand how it could have happened to Hen.

''It's pointless to discuss it,'' he said stiffly. ''I'll be going back tomorrow. I'm glad to see that you and the baby are well. How much longer will you be here?''

''A couple more weeks,'' Hen said. ''I want to make certain Laurel is strong enough before we begin the trip home.''

''I won't be unless you let me up for more than a few minutes at a time,'' Laurel told her husband. ''It'll take me weeks to learn to walk again.''

''I'll carry you wherever you want to go.''

Tyler quickly excused himself. He felt uncomfortable in the face of Hen's devotion to his wife. It made him feel Hen had somehow lost control. That was something Tyler feared. He couldn't control the world around him, but he could control himself. Ever since that day in the hay barn when his father found him crying, it had been the only constant in his life. He had jealously guarded it, had built a wall around it nothing could penetrate. He had clung to it all through the last years in Virginia, the move to Texas, his mother's death and his father's desertion, the terror of the years before George came home.

Now Laurel was telling him he must tear it down, become vulnerable to all the emotions that had almost destroyed him. He couldn't do that.

He'd be useless if he fell in love with Daisy the way Laurel thought he should. He wouldn't be able to work. Everybody would pity him and try to take advantage of him. Nobody would be able to depend on him because he wouldn't be in control of his own life.

But he was perilously close to that now. He had left his claim on the verge of making a strike. Even though he knew Daisy was about to marry another man, he hadn't left town. Even worse, he was considering staying still longer. He couldn't go to Daisy and plead with her not to marry Cochrane, but he couldn't leave as long as she was unmarried. Until she became Guy's wife, there was always a chance.

So he was in love, just as deeply and foolishly as Laurel could have wished. Only he didn't feel good about it. He wondered if Daisy felt any better.

Tyler cursed himself for a thousand kinds of a fool. He told himself he ought to turn around and get back to the hotel as fast as he could. He told himself he should have left for the mountains the minute Guy told him of their engagement. He told himself he was the biggest fool in New Mexico. Despite all this, he didn't slow down. Neither did he hesitate when he reached the Cochrane house.

He had heard that Regis Cochrane was the most respected man in town. And the most feared. He'd also heard Guy would do anything his father wanted. He couldn't rest easy as long as people like that had any control over Daisy. He had to know why she hadn't been to the hotel in the last two days.

No one was home but Adora. He was surprised by the petite, rather hesitant brunette who entered the parlor. She seemed an unlikely friend for Daisy. They were such opposites.

"Dolores said you were asking after Daisy." Adora's gaze was hostile.

"She hasn't visited my sister-in-law in two days. I was worried about her."

"Did your sister-in-law ask you to make this inquiry?"

Tyler felt that no matter what he answered, he would be guilty. "Naturally she's concerned. We all are."

"Then I'll be happy to send her a note explaining Daisy's absence."

"Wouldn't it be easier to tell me, since I'm already here?"

"I'm not sure Daisy would want you to know."

Tyler was perplexed. He had been prepared for unfriendliness but not animosity. "I don't understand."

"I didn't think you would. You don't seem to understand anything."

Tyler was beginning to get a little angry. He was tired of being blamed for difficulties that were not of his making.

"I might, if you would be so kind as to explain what you mean."

"I don't think you deserve an explanation."

"Daisy's the only one who can make that decision. Since she's not here, and apparently hasn't asked you to withhold the information, I think you should tell me."

Adora made a couple of passes across the end of the room, leveled a particularly angry glare at him, and started her perambulations again. She whirled. "You realize you've ruined her life as well as my brother's. She's broken her engagement and gone off to live on that ranch.''

"But she has no house to live in."

"I pointed that out, but it made no difference. It seems you told her she could do anything she wanted, and she's gone off to prove it."

"Why should she do that?"

"Because she's in love with you, you fool! Can't you see that? Though I can't see why she should prefer you to my brother. Why couldn't you have stayed in those mountains? If you had, she would have married Guy and tried to be happy. But you had to come back to Albuquerque. She hoped you had come back because you loved her. She was devastated when she found out you were as hard-hearted and unfeeling as ever."

Tyler felt as though he'd just been knocked silly by a mule kick. Common sense told him Adora couldn't be right—he was beginning to wonder why everybody in Albuquerque should know Daisy's feelings but himself—but common sense had also told him to stay in the mountains. He ignored it then, and he meant to ignore it now.

"She says I'm a dreamer, a fool chasing gold. She says I try to dominate her, that she'd rather be an old maid than marry a man like me."

"She's still in love with you."

"It doesn't make sense."

"Daisy said love didn't, that it was dangerous, but that was part of the excitement."

"Do you know what she's talking about?"

"Of course. Any woman would."

"Can you explain it to me?"

"No. Now I want you to go back to your gold mines as fast as you can. No matter what you do, don't go bothering Daisy. I'm hoping she'll soon get over you and marry Guy. My whole family misses her already."

"Does she have anybody to help her?"

"Yes, an old man who used to work for her father.

She'll be all right. Guy checks on her. Just go away. You've done enough damage already."

"Didn't she understand when I told her the killer had followed her?"

"The sheriff found out who he was, but the man has headed for Montana. She has nothing to worry about from him anymore."

But as Tyler walked back to the hotel, feeling about as well-liked as a sewer rat, he wasn't certain the man had moved on. It didn't matter. He was going to see Daisy. He couldn't rest knowing she was at that ranch alone. He had to be certain she was okay. Besides, he ought to know by now he couldn't stay away from her.

Chapter Twenty-two

"There's a lot of cows in these hills," Rio said to Daisy as he dismounted and came to the campfire, "but too many of them are unbranded."

"I don't understand," Daisy said. She handed him a cup of the strong black coffee he liked.

Jesus, the old man's nephew, rode in at a fast trot. "Rider's coming in," he said even before he dismounted.

Daisy stiffened. Mr. Cochrane said the killer had left the territory, but unknown riders still made her nervous. She picked up her rifle. She wasn't sure she could hit anything—Rio had shown her how to use it just two days ago—but she figured nobody else would know that. She felt no relief when she saw Bob Greene ride up with two of his hands.

Greene stepped down out of the saddle and approached the campfire. Daisy wanted to tell him to leave, but instead she offered him a cup of coffee. He accepted it and took a swallow.

"Sorry to hear about your father."

"Thank you."

"You planning to run this outfit by yourself?"

"Yes."

"You need a better place to stay than that," he said, pointing to the tent.

"I'll rebuild the house when I get some money."

Greene reached into his shirt pocket and brought out a roll of bills. "This ought to be enough to do it."

Daisy didn't move. "I'm not selling my land."

"This isn't for your land. It's for the cattle I sold."

Daisy felt she was understanding less minute by minute. "I don't understand."

"Each year some of your father's cattle get mixed up with mine. Rather than drive them back to his land, I brand the calves for him and sell the steers, though not as many this year as last. Manuel Cordova, your neighbor to the south, does the same thing. I'm sorry to be so late with the money, but the snow kept me busy."

Daisy's mind was in a whirl. She remembered they had always gone to stay in a hotel in the winter. Her father told them the money came from his investments.

"You ought to hire a couple more men and start branding," Greene said. "You've got a fortune's worth of cattle up there." He pointed to the hills. "You're lucky nobody's rustled the lot of them. Manuel and I tried to get your father to let us brand them for him. Hell, I even offered to round them up for free. I figured if rustlers started in on his herds, they'd be after mine next." He frowned angrily. "The old fool wouldn't let us set one foot on his land. I figured he thought we were after his gold mine."

Her father had never made any money from his gold mines or investments. Everything he got, he got from his neighbors. Daisy felt a helpless fury rise within her. All those years, doing everything he asked, treating him like a king, and he'd been lying the whole time.

"Rio and his nephew are helping me," Daisy said. "We plan to start branding tomorrow."

Greene offered the money again, and Daisy took it. He threw out the remainder of his coffee, handed her the cup, and caught up his reins. "You got some mighty big stock out there. You're going to need more than an old man and a boy. A remuda, too. I can spare a couple of hands for the next month or so. I'll throw in the horses."

Daisy wanted to refuse, but common sense told her she would be making a mistake. She couldn't believe Greene had anything to do with her father's death, not anymore. Until she got on her feet, she needed all the help she could get. "Why are you doing this?" she asked.

Greene smiled. "We've got to stick together. Ours are the only ranches Cochrane doesn't own. Maybe he's got so many cows he can stand the losses, but I can't. If it keeps up, I'll have to sell out. By helping you, I'm helping myself. I'm sure Cordova feels the same way." He turned to Rio Mendoza. "You keep a close watch on her. She's got a lot to learn."

"Why didn't you tell her you think Cochrane is behind the rustling?" one of Greene's men asked when they were out of earshot.

"She's engaged to marry his son. It's supposed to be a secret, but the Cochrane boy's been whispering it about. No sense in setting the girl against her father-in-law. It can only get her in trouble."

"Maybe she don't want to marry the boy. Maybe she wants to run this place and be her own boss."

"It doesn't matter what she wants. Cochrane will see she marries his son. He always gets what he wants."

Daisy allowed her horse to lead the cow and calf toward the area where Greene and Cordova's men where helping Rio and Jesus with the branding. She was learning to work a cutting pony. She was so sore, stiff, and tired sometimes staying in the saddle was all she could manage. It would take her a while before she felt completely comfortable on horseback, but she was proud of her progress.

"You're bringing in more cattle than anyone else," Rio observed. "You sure do learn fast."

"The horse knows enough for both of us," Daisy said. "Mr. Greene said it was one of his best."

But as Daisy headed back into the scrub growth that seemed to stretch for miles in every direction, she knew it wasn't just the horse. The cattle seemed to be finding her more than her finding them. She had hardly gone a mile when she saw another cow and calf trotting in her direction.

Daisy pulled up to see what the cow would do. It stopped and started to browse. It didn't seem the least bit concerned about Daisy's presence. Suddenly the cow threw up its head, uttered a bawling protest, and started in Daisy's direction once more.

Daisy pulled her rifle from its boot. Something in the brush had scared the cow. Being careful to keep her rifle pointed straight ahead, Daisy urged her horse forward. Following the trail the cow had taken, Daisy looked left and right, studying the vegetation.

She noticed a patch of brown in a juniper thicket that didn't match its background. She circled carefully until she was behind the concealing brush. She was determined to flush her quarry. Raising her rifle, she fired into the tangle of grass, bushes, and stunted trees.

"What the hell do you mean going around firing into bushes!" Tyler demanded as he emerged from the clump of pine and juniper.

Daisy nearly dropped her rifle when he stood up. A frisson of excitement shot through her body from toe to scalp. He hadn't gone back to the mountains. She felt all her hopes revive. There was only one reason for a man to follow a woman this way, especially a poor woman. Tyler might not know it yet, but he loved her. He was no more capable of leaving her than she was of forgetting him.

Before Daisy could recover from her shock, Tyler pulled her out of the saddle and kissed her fast and hard. Then before she could recover her breath, he lifted her into the saddle again.

For a moment, Daisy was unable to move or speak. She decided the entire world had gone crazy. Certainly Tyler had if he thought he could kiss her and everything would be forgotten. He did love her. She couldn't doubt that any longer, but it was obvious he wasn't burning to tell her. He was the same distant, unreachable man he'd always been, coming and going in her life, keeping her emotions in constant turmoil, reviving hopes he seemed to have no intentions of fulfilling.

Well she was *not* the same woman he had rescued and left twice before. She might love him, but she wasn't going to let her emotions run away with her this time.

Using every bit of self-control she could muster, Daisy tried to speak as naturally as possible.

"What are you doing here?"

"You look lovely," Tyler said. "Hard work agrees with you. I really do like your hair. Don't ever pin it up."

Accepting his compliments as just one more thing Tyler did to keep her off balance, Daisy struggled once again to talk to him as though he were nobody special. But it was hard with him looking up at her, his big brown eyes warm and shining.

"You've been driving the cows toward me!" she accused. "That's why I've been finding so many." No matter what she did, he couldn't stop trying to take care of her. But it wasn't enough anymore. Not nearly enough.

"I thought you might need some help getting started. I

didn't realize you would have half the country helping you.''

''You mean you followed me from Albuquerque so you could hide in the bushes and chase cows toward me when I wasn't looking.''

He brushed off some dry needles clinging to his clothes. ''I'm the reason you're out here by yourself. I came to make sure you're okay.''

He was as bad as Zac. He acted as if the universe revolved around him. ''Don't flatter yourself. I'm here because I couldn't marry Guy without loving him. You can head back to your mines right now.''

Tyler didn't seem the least bit disconcerted. ''I'd better get my horse.''

''I thought you only rode mules.''

''I grew up in Texas,'' Tyler called over his shoulder. ''Mules and burros are for prospecting, horses for working cows. You can't fool me there.''

Tyler had concealed his horse, a huge 17-hand gelding, behind a ridge. Mounted, he looked magnificent. Daisy swallowed, a caustic remark hovering on her tongue, forgotten. It was hard to be scathing when she'd just had the wind knocked out of her sails. It wasn't fair that his mere physical presence could render her witless. Her father had always said the mind was more powerful than the body. Before today, she'd always believed him.

''While I'm here I might as well help you drive that cow to camp.''

So he intended to talk nothing but business. That was okay. She could be just as casual as he. ''Where did you learn so much about cows?''

''I told you, I grew up in Texas. My family has a ranch there.''

''One of the ranches that generates the income you won't accept?''

''Laurel told you.''

"Somebody had to explain. You wouldn't."

Tyler started the cow and calf trotting toward the camp. "I didn't figure it was anybody's business but mine."

Daisy felt as if she'd been slapped in the face. "It isn't. It's just that people who care for you like to understand you. That's a pretty big chunk left out of the picture."

"I guess that's why I've always kept to myself."

Whatever his reason for coming back, it obviously wasn't to beg her forgiveness or anything like that. His heart was as crusted over as ever. "It saves explanations and caring. I understand now."

The cow made a break for freedom. Tyler had her back on the trail in minutes.

"What do you understand?" he asked.

"That you don't want anybody in your life. You don't want to be vulnerable, to let anybody become important to you. You've used your brothers' refusal to invest in your hotels as an excuse to drive people away. Secretly you don't think you're worthy of your good fortune. You haven't done anything to earn the money. You're keeping your hotels to yourself because when you finally get them, they'll be your justification for taking your place in the family. How did I do?"

"You talked to Laurel a lot."

"I also lived with my father for a long time. You're very much alike. I discovered he could have made a decent income from the ranch, but he was obsessed with gold."

"You think I'm like that?"

"I'm not sure it matters. It may be too late for you to become a normal human being. You may be so firmly caught in your isolation you have forgotten how to break out."

"You've done a lot of thinking."

"I've had a lot of time."

The action in camp came to a halt when they rode in.

"This is Tyler Randolph," Daisy said to Rio. "He's been chasing the cows out of the hills for me." The other men in the camp studied Tyler with appraising glances as Daisy introduced him around.

"Ready to get some more?" Tyler said when the introductions were over.

"I'm ready for you to go back to Albuquerque."

"I'm sticking. You can ride out with me or you can sit in camp. Either way, it's your decision." He put spurs to his huge gelding and started back toward the hills.

"You trust him?" Rio asked.

"Like a rattler," Daisy said as she started after him. "Come to think of it, I'd trust a rattler more." She wished it were true, but she seemed to trust him no matter how many times he left her.

"What the hell was that all about?" one of Bob Greene's men asked. "How in hell did she manage to get a Randolph to help her?"

"You know him?" Rio asked.

"Not him, but I know his family. Everybody does. They're rich as sin and mean as snakes. His brother is in Albuquerque right now. He was a gunfighter. This one's supposed to be looking for gold."

"I think he's found it," Rio said. His gaze turned to follow the pair disappearing in the distance.

Daisy and Tyler rode into camp at dusk. Tyler dismounted, helped Daisy down, then took both their horses and headed toward the remuda.

"The man knows his way around cows," Rio remarked to Daisy as they watched Tyler walk toward the rope corral.

"He grew up on a ranch in Texas. He knows cows backward and forward. He hates them."

"Doesn't show."

"Very little does." Daisy put her hands to the fire. It

was warm while the sun was up, but the temperature fell with dusk. The fire felt good. "I guess I'd better get started with dinner," she said. She stopped before she'd even picked up a pan. "Rio, go take care of the horses for Tyler. Tell him I need him to cook."

Rio looked skeptical. "You sure?"

"Just wait and see."

Thirty minutes later, it didn't take more than one bite to convince Rio Daisy had known what she was talking about. "You ever cooked chuck before?" he asked Tyler.

"All the way from Texas to Wyoming," Tyler replied. "Most of the places in between."

A grin split Rio's brown, leathery face. "Bet you've been on a lot of roundups. What do you think of this one?"

"I'd move the camp each day instead of bringing the cows into a central location. It would save time driving and upset the cows less. They don't like being taken out of their familiar territory."

Rio looked at Daisy. "What do you think?"

It sounded like a lot of unnecessary work. She wasn't going to take his advice quite so quickly, even if he did know far more about roundups than she did. She would think about it. Meanwhile she would ask Tyler a question rather than answer his. "Did you see many cattle in those hills?"

"Some big stuff two and three years old."

"I thought Daddy had you brand the calves each year," Daisy said to Rio.

"I told him I couldn't get them all by myself, but he wouldn't let me hire any help."

"And you've got rustlers," Tyler said.

Rustlers! Greene said they'd been stealing from him and Cordova. Now they were stealing from her as well.

"What do I do?"

"Stop them."

She didn't know how to do that. She needed Tyler's help even though she didn't want to admit it. That would mean putting herself in his hands once again, but somehow that wasn't as distasteful as she had expected. "How much income do you figure I'm losing?"

"Impossible to tell until we get some idea of the size of the herd, but I'd say thousands of dollars."

Daisy felt like cussing. She remembered all the years her mother had suffered because her life was so unlike what she had expected, and none of it had been necessary. Her father had allowed rustlers to take more than enough money to have made her mother comfortable, all because he was afraid somebody would find a gold mine that didn't exist!

"You know these hills pretty good?" Rio asked Tyler.

"I've been riding through them for the last three years."

"Why don't you give the orders tomorrow?"

"You'd better take that up with Miss Singleton."

Daisy would have liked to be able to spurn his offer, but Rio wouldn't have suggested it without a good reason. Besides, it was clear Greene's and Cordova's hands respected Tyler. Whether she liked to admit it or not, she felt safer with him around.

"We can try it," she said, unwilling to give in completely the first day he showed up. She was flattered he had followed her, but this was the third time he had come into her life unexpectedly. There was no reason to think he wouldn't disappear again. She loved him, but she wasn't going to let her love overwhelm her good sense.

For the first time in her life she was her own boss, and she liked the feeling. She now knew the ranch could make enough money to support her comfortably. If she could get all her cattle branded and hire a couple of dependable hands to help Rio, she would be independent. If she learned her job well, in a few years she would be free to do just about anything she wanted.

"Don't you trust me?" Tyler asked.

"I know you can cook, but I don't know whether you can organize a roundup," she replied. "I'd rather see what you can do before I make a decision."

Daisy couldn't deny the feeling of satisfaction that warmed her soul. She'd never before had the power to tell a man what to do. Until she told Guy she wouldn't marry him, she had never refused one. She actually felt like the owner of this ranch, like a boss in charge of making decisions.

It felt wonderful!

She knew she had to keep a cool head. She didn't know anything about ranches. Tyler did. But the decision was still hers. She could tell him to go or stay.

Of course he'd do what he wanted—Tyler always did—but that didn't dilute her happiness. She stood up. "I want to be in the saddle at dawn."

"You want me to cook breakfast?"

"We sure do," Rio answered for her.

"Then Jesus has got to help him," Daisy said. "You can't expect him to be cook and foreman without help."

"I don't mind," the boy replied.

"Okay with you?" she asked.

"Sure," Tyler replied.

"Good."

"Wait up a minute," Tyler called when Daisy headed toward her tent. She turned just in time for him to slip his arms around her. Before she knew what was happening, he kissed her long, tenderly, and quite thoroughly.

Daisy thought every bone in her body must have dissolved. Maybe it was fatigue, maybe it was tension, but she felt unable to stand alone. She leaned against him, the heat of his body flowing through her. Shamelessly she clung to him, her arms locked around his neck.

''I don't like to go to bed without saying good night,'' Tyler said.

She didn't know how he could talk so casually about what had just happened between them. It was like heaving ground under her feet. She would have rustled every cow between here and the Colorado border to have him kiss her good night like this for the rest of her life. By a superhuman effort, she managed to control her voice. ''I don't want you thinking it's going to earn you special treatment.''

''I wouldn't dream of it,'' Tyler said.

Daisy released her hold on Tyler and took a shaky step toward her tent. She'd been able to control her emotions all day, but she didn't know how much longer she could keep it up. It was one thing to say she was going to act as casually as Tyler. It was quite another to do it after he kissed her. It brought memories of their last night in the cabin flooding back.

Shoring up her resolve one more time, Daisy crawled inside her tent, but half an hour later she still hadn't been able to fall asleep. She might be in control of her actions, but she wasn't in control of her feelings, and her love for Tyler was just as strong as ever. It didn't help to know he couldn't forget her any more than she could forget him. As Laurel had said, Randolph men didn't come easily to love. Daisy couldn't imagine anybody coming more slowly than Tyler. She wondered if he would make it.

Daisy sat her horse, surveying the scene around the camp. She would have to find some way to repay Greene and Cordova for the use of their men. She would never have managed to brand so many cattle in three days without them. She turned away as they castrated a young bull. Tyler had said she should cull the herd, keep only the best bulls and heifers for breeding, fatten the rest to sell. It made sense, but she didn't like it.

They had ridden side by side for three days. She found it hard to believe he was the same man she'd known on the mountain. He talked. A lot. And when he wanted to, he had almost as much charm as Zac. The men would do anything he wanted. To hear them tell it, he was the best cowman in New Mexico.

She watched Tyler straighten up from branding the newly created steer. The animal got to his feet in a rage. He charged Tyler, but he simply stepped out of the steer's way. Rio cut in with his horse and drove the steer away from the camp. Tyler walked over to her. He wasn't even breathing hard.

"I don't know if anybody's told you, but you're going to have to do this again after the new calves are dropped."

"Bob Greene said not to wait, that I had too many unbranded cattle."

"He was right. I just wanted you to know. Next year you can get yourself on a regular schedule. It'll give you time to get a regular crew together."

He'd been doing that for the past three days, dropping bits of information. He was gradually educating her to what she needed to know. It irritated her, but common sense told her to keep quiet. She had to learn. Greene or Cordova might have been able to teach her just as well, but they had their own ranches to worry about.

"You won't have many steers to sell this fall, but if you sell some of the scrub cows, you ought to have enough to keep going until next year. Things will be lean until you can get a full crop. Rustlers have made some pretty good inroads into your young stuff."

"I've been thinking about the rustling," she said. "How do I stop it?"

"Most of the time just by keeping your men in the saddle checking on your cattle all the time. I imagine Greene and Cordova would be more than willing to help. No rancher wants rustlers around."

Tyler walked over to his big gelding and mounted. He rode up to Daisy. "You ready?"

"Where're we going this time?"

"A grassy canyon I discovered back in the mountains. I imagine we'll find quite a few cattle there."

Daisy turned her horse to ride off with him. As she did, she caught sight of a dust cloud in the distance. The old fear gripped at her heart. She didn't know when she would stop being afraid the next person to ride up to the ranch would be the killer. Common sense told her that even if he were still in New Mexico, he wouldn't come to the ranch with so many people about. Still, she felt the fear tug at her heart until she could make out a buggy. A few minutes later she recognized Guy and Adora.

"You go on. I can't leave now."

"Neither can I." Tyler dismounted, tied his horse to a juniper, and prepared to wait.

Chapter Twenty-three

Adora fixed an unfriendly gaze on Tyler. "I see Daisy is not by herself."

"I thought you were learning how to run hotels," Guy said.

"Or looking for lost gold mines," Adora added.

"I decided to postpone both until Daisy got settled," Tyler said, not the least bit disturbed by the undisguised hostility of brother and sister. "I don't guess that gold's going anywhere."

"Somebody might beat you to it," Adora said.

"There's always that, but I don't imagine anybody's going to find it all."

With a sniff of annoyance, Adora turned to Daisy. "We came to see how you were doing." She looked around. "I'd be afraid to stay here. There's nobody around."

"There never has been," Daisy said. "It would seem strange to have houses and people here now."

"It's not a proper situation for you," Guy said. "You

don't have a suitable place to sleep or anyone to chaperon you.''

"I have Rio."

"You can't have a man for a chaperon," Adora exclaimed. "That would scandalize half of Albuquerque."

"Especially Mrs. Esterhouse and her daughter," Daisy said.

"To hell with Mrs. Esterhouse and her daughter," Guy said.

"Amen," Daisy added, earning a rare smile from Tyler.

"I'm more concerned about you. This is no way for you to live," Guy said.

"I'm just fine. I've got my tent and enough bedding to survive a blizzard. If the weather gets really nasty, I can sleep in the shed. And Tyler's the best cook in the West."

"You cook?" Guy said, as though it were something only poor Mexicans would do.

"The best food you ever tasted," Rio said, coming up to the group. "You riding out again?" he asked Daisy.

"You go with Tyler. I'll take the next trip."

Tyler looked reluctant to leave.

"What's wrong?" Daisy asked. "You afraid you can't find any cows if I don't go along? That would be embarrassing, wouldn't it?" She was rewarded with a full-grown, honest smile.

"I'd be too ashamed to go back to Texas."

"What's he doing here?" Guy asked after Tyler and Rio rode off.

"He said he felt responsible for my being here, so he's making sure I succeed."

"I thought it was that queen who made you want to be independent.

"Both."

Guy frowned. "He doesn't look like a cowhand to me."

307

"He's huge," Adora said, impressed with Tyler's appearance in the saddle despite her antipathy. "And handsome."

"He said I needed someone to teach me the rudiments of ranching. And he's right. I can't tell you how much I've learned in the last few days."

"But you don't need to know any of it," Guy said. "If you married me, I would see to everything for you."

"But I don't want anybody to see to everything for me," Daisy said. "Not you, Tyler, or anybody else. I love being my own boss. I never realized how much until now."

"But you can't go on living like a vagabond," Adora protested. "You'll never find a decent man to marry you."

"I will," Guy said.

"I'm not sure I want to get married. At least not for a while. People like Mrs. Esterhouse will always draw attention to my size or some other part of me that's not socially acceptable. I don't want to be apologizing for myself for the rest of my life. Nor do I want my husband doing it for me," Daisy said when Guy started to voice another protest. "Besides, I like living out here. Maybe I was meant to be a rancher."

"No woman was meant to be a rancher," Guy said with conviction.

"It looks like a lot of hard work," Adora observed.

"It is, but now my muscles have gotten used to being on a horse, I don't mind it. My parents did me a great disservice by teaching me only how to live back East."

"Couldn't you run your ranch from Albuquerque?" Adora asked.

"I'd let you run it any way you wanted," Guy added.

"You'd soon start telling me what to do and expecting me to do it," Daisy said. "Men are like that."

"What about Tyler?"

"He works for me. If I don't like what he does, he doesn't do it or he leaves."

"He looks like he's here to stay," Adora said.

"He'll leave," Daisy said. She had never questioned that. The only question was whether she would go with him. Would he ask her? But she didn't mean to tell Guy or Adora that.

"Then you'll have to come back to town."

"By then I intend to have my own crew and start rebuilding my house," Daisy said. "This is my land, and I mean to live here."

"But you don't belong here."

"I'm beginning to think it's the only place I do belong."

"Then you don't mean to return to Albuquerque?"

"I don't know what I mean to do," Daisy said honestly. "I may change my mind next month or next year. But for the time being, I like where I am. I don't mean to give it up."

"And marrying me isn't good enough?" Guy asked.

"We've already been through that."

"I'm not giving up. I'll be back."

"I hope you'll always be my friend."

"I want to be more than that."

"Guy . . ." But Daisy didn't finish her sentence. Tyler rode up unexpectedly.

"The rustlers struck again last night," he said. "What do you want to do about it?"

"Follow them, of course, and get my cows back."

"Good. I'll need Rio."

"Rio can stay here. I'm coming with you. They're my cows."

"You can't," Guy exclaimed. "It would be indecent."

"You said you trusted me before," Daisy said, turning to Guy. "Can't you trust me again?"

"It's not me, it's—"

309

"I only care what my friends think. Nobody else."

Guy wiggled uncomfortably under her gaze. Tyler's was just as intense.

"I've always trusted you. You know that."

"Me, too," Adora added, "but that doesn't mean you ought to be chasing after rustlers. You could get hurt."

"I imagine they'll give up the cattle rather than risk a gun battle," Tyler said. "You can rest assured I'll have her back safe and sound before nightfall. Now if we're going, we'd better get started."

Neither Adora nor Guy appeared happy with the decision. Tyler went off, to get things ready, Daisy supposed.

"Don't worry," she told her friends. "The men compete with each other to make sure nothing happens to me, especially Rio and Tyler."

"I don't trust that man," Guy said.

"I was safe before," Daisy said, beginning to become impatient with Guy. "I'll be safe again."

"But you'll be going after rustlers this time."

"I know. My life has never been so exciting."

"I don't understand you," Guy said. "You were never like this before."

"I don't understand me myself, but then I don't know myself either."

"Be careful, and let us know if there's anything you need," Adora said. "Anything. Your feelings haven't changed, have they?"

Daisy shook her head. "Neither have his."

"There'll always be a place for you with us if you want to come back," Guy said.

"I know. I can never thank you enough for what you've done for me."

"You don't have to thank us. All you have to do is—"

"It's time to go," Adora said, patting Guy on the leg. "We can come again after Daisy catches her rustlers."

Daisy watched Guy drive away with a lingering feeling of sadness, but without regret. She actually felt relieved. She had made another step forward. Now if she could just manage to control her feelings for Tyler.

"Kill her!" Regis Cochrane shouted at Frank Storach. "She's broken her engagement." Regis had found Frank at his small adobe down one of the twisted alleys of the plaza.

"You still owe me from the first job," Frank insisted. "I'm not doing nothing till I get paid what I'm owed."

Regis Cochrane glared at Frank Storach. Now that Daisy had refused to marry Guy, killing her was the only way to get his hands on her land. Once she was dead, he could produce forged unpaid loans to her father. Nobody would question that.

His rustlers were poised to drive off Greene's and Cordova's herds if they didn't sell out soon. The small raids had just been a warning. Daisy's land was the last piece in his puzzle, and he needed it now.

Regis handed Frank the 150 dollars. "How long will it take you to hire some help?"

"I don't need nobody. I can do this on my own."

"You'd better get it right. And this time, head for Montana when it's done. I don't want to see you again."

"You sure were damned glad to see me today."

"I didn't count on that girl turning difficult. She's always done what she was told before."

"You never can tell about females," Frank said. "I stay away from them myself."

"I don't care what you do," Regis said. "Just get rid of her and get out of the country. If they catch you, I'll swear I've never seen you."

For a moment Regis was tempted to kill Frank and hire someone else himself. The man was nothing more than an ambitious bungler, but Regis was impatient to get his hands on that land. It would give him a stranglehold on those bastards who'd tried to cut him out because his mother was half Spanish and half Navajo. They were always looking down on him, trying to ignore him. What the hell were they but upstart immigrants! This was his town. He'd been born here. He'd destroy anybody who tried to ignore him.

As Daisy watched Tyler ride just ahead of her, never once losing the trail of the rustled steers, she realized she wanted him to make love to her. That was why she had insisted on coming with him. If she'd just wanted her cattle back, she'd have sent Rio. She knew that. So did Tyler. She wondered what he was thinking. He hadn't stopped talking since they found the trail of the rustled cows.

"No reason for that many cows to be together on the range," he had said, pointing to the hoofprints. "No reason for them to be heading up into the mountains. But it's the horses' hoofprints among them that's the dead giveaway."

He identified all the plants they passed, told her which grew in what season, which had medicinal value, which the cows liked best, about the grasses, range conditions, bits of information that would be indispensable to her in the coming years. She hoped she would be able to remember some of it, but she could hardly think of anything except his nearness, and the kiss he would give her tonight.

He kissed her every morning and every night. He didn't make a big production out of it. He just kissed her and went on with his work. It had thrown her completely off stride at first, but she quickly got herself under control. What had started off as a tug-of-war had turned into a Mexican standoff. He wasn't going to say anything until she admitted she needed him. She wasn't going to give in until he admitted he loved her.

She had started to feel very much on edge as each evening approached. She found herself waiting, anticipating, wanting. She could never have felt this way about Guy. She certainly would never have followed him off on a wild chase after rustlers. He wouldn't have offered. He'd have stayed home and sent someone else.

She also found Tyler's presence comforting. Despite his unrealistic dreams, he was the most capable man she'd ever met. He could cook, live alone on top of a mountain, build a cabin a professional carpenter would admire, do the work of a ranch foreman, all without missing a stride. Now he was taking out after rustlers as if it were no more than a jaunt to meet friends.

Occasionally the trail narrowed, and she found herself riding behind him. She felt safe when she had to look up into his eyes, not down. She felt secure when he picked her up as though she weighed no more than Julia Madigan. She felt very important and valuable when he didn't want to leave her with Guy. She felt desired when he looked at her with those sultry brown eyes.

"We'll soon be off your land," Tyler said. "That might make it more dangerous."

"Why?"

"If the cows are unbranded and on open land, they belong to whoever has possession. Under the law, he has as much right to them as you do."

"But they're my cows."

"You can't prove that."

"What do you plan to do?"

"I won't know until we catch up with them."

Daisy tried to imagine what might happen when they found the rustlers, but it was much more interesting to let her mind dwell on her anticipation of tonight's kiss.

The longer she rode alongside him, the more it occupied her mind. Would it be different now they were alone?

She remembered the last night in the cabin and wondered if she was prepared for the consequences of touching off the volcano of desire she knew he kept under tight control.

"We're not going to catch up with them today," Tyler said. "Maybe we ought to go back."

"That means we'll just have to cover the same ground tomorrow."

"We're getting to rough country. It could be dangerous. These men aren't going to want to give up what they've become used to taking at will."

"That's all the more reason to go on," Daisy said. "I won't tolerate any more rustling."

"And how are you going to back that up?"

"With you right now. I'll hire somebody else later."

Tyler laughed. "You've certainly got a side to you I never suspected."

"And you've got several you've kept safely tucked away. But that's beside the point. I'm not going back."

"Good. Let's find them before night. Then I can decide whether it would be better for us to confront them tonight or wait until the morning."

The rustlers might wait until the morning, but Daisy knew she couldn't.

They found the rustlers shortly after dusk. They were holding the cows in a small canyon.

"They're not even guarding them," Daisy pointed out. "Anybody could ride in, let down the poles, and drive them out."

"They probably don't see any need to post a guard."

"What are you going to do?"

"We're going to find a camp about a mile from here. I'm going to fix supper, and we're going to sleep."

"Don't treat me like I'm an idiot," Daisy said impatiently. "I may not know anything about capturing rustlers, but these are my cows and I expect you to let me know exactly what you intend to do.''

Tyler had that stubborn look. It was clear he was trying to decide just how much to withhold.

''You said I could do anything I wanted. You were the one who encouraged me to try living on my own. You can't hold back now. That would make you worse than Guy.''

They started back up the trail looking for a campsite. ''How do you figure that?''

''Guy doesn't really believe a woman can take care of herself. He might agree to any number of things to placate me, but he would never encourage me. You did.''

''Encouraging you doesn't mean I think you're ready to tackle rustlers.''

''I didn't say I wanted to tackle them. Maybe I just want to be certain you won't get hurt.''

''Is that important?''

''Of course it is. I don't want any of my employees to get hurt.''

''I'm not your employee.''

Daisy refused to fall for that. ''I may not be paying you, but you're working for me.''

''So you don't care any more about my safety than that of Bob Greene's hands.''

Now he was getting personal, digging for information. She didn't mean to give in that easily. ''Why should I? Do you care especially for my safety?''

''I'm here.''

It wasn't much of an admission, but she figured it might be the best she was going to get out of him. ''Why are you here?''

Tyler didn't answer. Daisy wondered why it was so hard for him to put his feelings into words. It was hard to imagine what could have happened to make him so insular. She'd been dominated and confined, her self-esteem destroyed, but it had only made her more anxious to find someone to love, to share her life. It seemed to have worked just the other way with him. One more reason why they weren't good for each other.

"Because I can't be anywhere else."

He fell silent. She guessed she would have to be satisfied with that.

"I liked you better the way you were back in camp."

That got him. He turned in the saddle to face her. "How's that?"

"You talked and smiled and acted like an ordinary human being. People enjoyed being around you. But I've watched you change with every mile we've traveled today. It's like you've been wearing a mask and it has been falling off bit by bit until there's nothing left but the Tyler who was back in the cabin."

"You don't like him?"

She was feeling stronger, more in control. She figured she could answer him honestly. "Not especially. He doesn't give and he doesn't share. When he talks, it's in cryptic utterances that choke off conversation rather than start it, freeze emotion rather than warm it."

She watched his back grow rigid. She wondered if his face was any more expressive.

"There is a different man inside you. The one who took care of me, cared how I felt, empathized with my suffering. I fell in love with that man, but I lost him somewhere."

There, she had said it. It had taken all her courage, but at least she had gotten the words out. And it had to come out between them.

"What if he came back?"

"He would never stay. The other you wouldn't let him."

Tyler stopped his gelding in a grove of pine and spruce that grew along a wash snowmelt had turned into a noisy stream. "This looks like a good campsite." He rode into the thicket until the trail was no longer visible.

"Suppose he did come back to stay."

"I could never marry a man like that," Daisy said. "He's not a complete person. He's a fragment, just like the sociable fragment you pulled out back at camp. I suppose you've got other fragments I haven't seen." She dismounted. "Here, give me the reins. I'll take care of the horses while you fix supper."

As Tyler watched Daisy curry the horses and picket them near some grass, he decided that the scene depicted just what was wrong with this whole relationship. It was backwards. She was taking care of the horses, and he was cooking. She was the boss, he the employee. She had control of her feelings, and he didn't. From the moment he had left Willie Mozel at his claim, he'd been operating in uncharted territory.

Why couldn't he concede that he didn't know what he was doing? It was about time he admitted his feelings of inadequacy weren't limited to his family. It was tied up with his perception of himself. He had lost control because he was trying to do something he had fought against his whole life.

He was trying to reach out to Daisy, but he was scared to death. When she said she loved him, something inside him leapt for joy. Some barrier came down, one he'd propped up for years, one he thought was impregnable. Yet Daisy with her freckles and curls had cracked it wide open with just three little words.

It didn't seem to matter that she wouldn't marry somebody like him. She loved him. For now that was more than he could handle.

He seemed to have lost his sense of pride, but that didn't mean as much as he'd expected. He'd held on to his pride all his life, and it hadn't made things any better. He had a feeling if he could just figure out how to open up to Daisy, pride wouldn't be so important.

"Tell me what you've got in mind," Daisy said when she came to the fire. "Mmm, that smells delicious. You've got to teach me how to cook like that before you leave. You've spoiled me for my own cooking."

Tyler was a little startled that she took his leaving for granted. He had never intended to stay more than a few weeks, but he had assumed he'd be dropping by periodically to see how she was doing. Apparently Daisy expected him to disappear for good.

"I thought I'd ride back to their camp sometime after midnight. Maybe I can drive off the cows without waking them up. You can be waiting here. If they follow, I can hold them off while you drive the cattle back to your land."

"Wouldn't that be dangerous alone?"

"I'm not very good with a revolver, but I can hold an army at bay with a rifle."

"You think they'll fight?"

"I don't know. They may figure it's easier to go back and rustle more. I can't figure out how you come to have so many unbranded cattle."

"My father wouldn't hire enough hands. He didn't trust anybody but Rio. He was convinced he was close to finding that mine. Maybe he thought they would try to steal it from him." Daisy poured herself a cup of coffee. She took a sip. It burned her tongue. "He wanted to find gold so he could go back and show his family he had become rich on his own. He never understood that Mother and I didn't care. How long do you think it'll take us to finish branding?"

They talked of general things while they ate, but Tyler's thoughts still revolved around the fact Daisy loved him but expected nothing of him. The more he thought about it, the more determined he was to make her change her mind.

He loved her and wanted to marry her. Fool that he was, he'd never realized that was why he'd been following her around.

Tyler's hand paused with the fork halfway to his mouth. He had fallen in love with a woman who didn't like his kind of man and wouldn't marry him on a bet. He put the food in his mouth and chewed slowly. What a hell of a mess. Somebody once told him gold was never any trouble until you found it. They should also have told him being in love was no trouble until it happened to you.

But that wasn't his most immediate problem. Daisy was only a few feet away. He didn't know how he was going to get through the night without making love to her.

Chapter Twenty-four

Daisy moved restlessly in her blankets. The ground beneath her was cold and hard, but she was hardly aware of it. Every nerve in her body seemed to be focused on the fact that Tyler lay only a few feet from her. She wanted him to make love to her so badly she almost asked him. But no matter how much her body ached for him, she wouldn't let him touch her unless he admitted he loved her.

She turned over in her bed, but she wasn't any more comfortable. It was going to be a miserable night. She almost hoped the rustlers did fight. At least it would give her something else to think about.

She lay there watching Tyler. She shouldn't have, but she couldn't help it. She felt something pulling her to him. He must have felt it as well, for he turned to face her. Their gazes met across the short distance that separated them. His eyes had always been shuttered, as though shielding him against everything outside himself. Tonight they were open, wide and luminous. He had never seemed more accessible, as though he had finally been able to set aside the barriers that separated him from her and everyone else in the world.

But there was something new in his gaze tonight, something at once warmer and more appealing. It was almost as though he were inviting her inside. She knew it couldn't be true: Tyler was incapable of truly letting anyone inside him.

"I love you."

Daisy froze. The words should have set her on fire, but they turned her mind and body to stone. She was unable to move, to answer, to think. She felt as though she had waited all her life to hear Tyler say those words, and now she was paralyzed, stupidly helpless and mute.

"Knowing what you think of me, I doubt you wanted to hear that."

He didn't know anything about it at all. But then he never had. She marveled that a man with his sensitivity could know so little about women. Even if she didn't love him, even if she never wanted to see him again, these would have been welcome words.

"I didn't want to admit it."

That didn't surprise her. He had spent his entire life convincing himself he felt nothing. It wasn't surprising it took him a long time to recognize love when it finally showed up.

"Zac knew it a long time ago. Laurel did, too. I suppose I didn't because I spent too many years refusing to feel."

"Why?"

There was a pause. Daisy thought he had lapsed into one of his long silences. She was surprised when he started to talk in a flat, measured voice.

"My father was a cruel man. Some would even say vicious. He used to make us compete against each other

321

for his praise. You've only seen Hen, but my four older brothers are just like him. I could never be as good. They were always taller and better-looking and smarter, able to ride faster and jump higher.

"When I was seven, Pa brought home a beautiful blood bay colt with black points. He said I could have him if I could prove I was good enough. He knew my brothers would let me win so I could have the horse, so he made me race against a boy I hated, Leonard Craven.

"For a week George and Madison took me over every foot of the course, advised me how to take each jump, which hills to take slowly to conserve energy, which turns were too tight to take at a full gallop. I loved that horse. I named him Cyclone because he was the fastest horse in the barn. I knew I was going to win the race.

"But Leonard was three years older. It was a matter of pride with him not to lose to me. He went out fast and blocked me when I tried to pass. He crowded me at the jumps and nearly caused me to go down. I would have won anyway, but as I started to pass him in the straight, he struck Cyclone across the head with his crop, causing him to veer off course.

"I lost by a length.

"Pa was so mad at me for losing, he gave Cyclone to Leonard. At that moment, I hated him, but I knew I couldn't show any feeling. That would only make Pa madder. So I hid in the barn. I didn't mean to cry, but when I thought of Leonard riding Cyclone, I couldn't help it.

"Pa caught me. He said men didn't cry, especially not Randolph men. He said even though I wasn't a very good Randolph, he was going to make sure I never cried again. He was going to beat me until I could take every lick without a tear. And he did."

Daisy was horrified. She couldn't believe any man could do anything so vicious, so cruel. "How did you not cry?"

"I did at first. The riding crop hurt. He would hit me, shout at me to stop crying, then hit me again."

"I don't know why you didn't cry all the harder."

"Because I hated him too much. I was going to show him he couldn't touch me, not inside where it counted. I stopped crying and stared him in the face until he quit. I only spoke to him once after that."

"What did your mother do?"

"Stood around wringing her hands and begging me not to anger my father, while one of the women in the kitchen put salve on my welts. Ma always believed Pa would be loving and kind if his sons just wouldn't make him angry."

"What was the one time you spoke to him?"

"I ran away. George brought me back, but I made up my mind to get back at Pa. I jammed a rock between the hoof and frog of his favorite hunter's left fore. When it came time for the big fall hunt, the horse came up lame, and Pa lost a big bet. I told him I did it. He nearly killed me, but I just looked at him. I told him if he ever touched me again, I'd kill him when I grew up. Soon after that we moved to Texas. Pa joined the Confederate Army and I never saw him again."

Daisy didn't know when or how it happened, but she found herself out of her own bedroll and next to Tyler, her arms around him. It reminded her of the night he held her when she cried about her father, only Tyler wasn't crying. He couldn't.

"I decided if I didn't feel anything, nothing could hurt me. I didn't feel anything when we left Virginia, when Pa and the boys left for the war, when Ma died. But now, when I want to feel something, I can't."

Daisy wondered if he had really tried. It probably scared him too much, made him feel he was losing control. She had never had control. Falling in love had actually liberated her. He had done that for her and didn't even know it.

"I didn't say this to convince you I'm any different from what you think. I'm not sure why I told you. I just thought you might like to know."

Daisy took Tyler's arm and put it around her. Her own feelings were just as tumultuous, but she was even more certain she loved him. If she could have done something for him, she would have. But by now, she'd tried everything she could think of. She could only continue to love him.

"I'm cold," she said. She hadn't meant to utter the words, but she'd been thinking them. She'd been thinking something else, too.

"I can't sleep next to you all night, then leave before dawn like I did in the cabin."

"I know."

"But you don't want to marry a dreamer, a man with a gold fever, a man who tries to boss you around."

"I love a man like you."

"I don't understand."

"Neither do I."

Tyler reached over and brushed her cheek. "I do love you. I'm not just saying that. I wouldn't want you to be sorry in the morning."

"I'll only be sorry if you don't."

"I've wanted to make love to you almost from the first moment I saw you."

It was a charming thing for him to say, but just because he said it didn't mean she had to be brainless enough to believe it. "You couldn't have, not with blood on my face and my head wrapped in bandages."

"Prospectors don't see many women. You looked good to me, even if you weren't looking your best just then."

A mixed compliment at best, but she guessed she'd take

it until something better came along. He leaned over and kissed her gently on the lips.

"I'm glad you're not petite and frail."

"And I'm glad you're not impeccably dressed with perfect manners."

"I'd still want to make love to you, even if all I had was a bed of pine needles."

Pine needles were okay as long as she shared them with Tyler. Somehow it seemed appropriate. She'd spent her whole life feeling like an outcast, first from the society that produced her parents, then from the society she would have entered as Guy's wife. She felt comfortable sleeping on pine needles next to a cowhand dressed in cotton, linen, and buckskin.

It felt as good to be in Tyler's arms as she remembered. It brought with it a level of excitement that had Daisy feeling too warm to remain under so many blankets. She didn't object when Tyler pulled her out of the bedroll. She didn't notice the cold. There was no guilt this time, no need to stop. She found it hard to believe just being held could give her so much pleasure. She liked the warmth of his nearness. She liked the comfort of his strength, the solid support of his firm, muscled body against her own.

Being in his arms just felt right.

She was aware her feet were still in the space between their two beds. She pulled them inside and shoved them deep into Tyler's bed.

"You're cold," he whispered.

"Only my feet."

He pulled her closer. He seemed to envelop her with his warmth. She wondered what could be so comforting about being in a man's arms, even a man as big as Tyler. It didn't change anything in the past. The rest of the world was exactly the same. She even doubted it would have any real effect on the future. Despite all this, everything seemed new, different, she was seeing and feeling everything for the first time.

Tyler kissed her gently, merely brushing her lips with his. It was an unexpected change from the hard, hungry kisses she had come to expect. Confounding her even more, he traced her lips with the tip of his tongue. It made shivers race back and forth over her body. He seemed to be tasting her. Her mouth opened and her tongue sought his in a series of kisses which became more and more urgent.

She could hear Tyler's breathing become a little faster. His kisses grew less gentle, more insistent. They were hot and kindled an equal heat in her.

That feeling in her belly was back. It was strange excitement, delicious and discomforting at the same time. It seemed to affect her muscles, making them difficult to control. It caused heat to flow throughout her body in a steady stream.

The feel of Tyler's hands on her body increased the heat and trembling until it was difficult for Daisy to focus her thoughts. The myriad of feelings and sensations were new, and each clamored for primacy. It wasn't long before she was overwhelmed. When Tyler slipped his hand inside her shirt and cupped her breast in his callused hand, her brain gave up trying to distinguish, differentiate, or analyze. It even stopped trying to record.

It simply experienced.

Shivers of excitement ricocheted along her ribs like shotgun pellets in a cave. The pressure of his fingertip on her nipple was like a small explosion. The friction as he gently rubbed the puckered skin drew heat from inside her. She was unable to remain still. Her body arched against his hand, bringing her stomach into contact with a hardened length low on Tyler's abdomen.

Their lips locked in a fierce kiss that mirrored their need for each other. Heat blazed through Daisy like a wind-driven forest fire through dry brush. Her own breath caught in her throat, then escaped with an explosion that caused her body to go limp. But only for a moment. The feel of Tyler's fingers as they moved down her body unbuttoning her shirt caused her muscles to bunch, her breathing to become erratic, her skin to quiver under his touch.

Tyler's tongue snaked into her mouth. Her tongue darted out to meet his. They engaged in a sinuous frolic with the grace of two dancers. They entwined in a prelude to the joining of their bodies. The feeling of urgency grew until their breathing became noisy, uneven gasps.

The feeling was even more intense when he began to unbutton her chemise. The feel of the night air on her hot, bare skin caused a shiver to race through her. Moments later Tyler's open hand covered her skin, blocking out all awareness of the crisp night air. His hand moved over her breast, cupped it, then moved down her side and to her stomach. The roughness of his hand chafed her soft skin, making the feeling still more intense.

But nothing compared to the shocks that rocked her body when Tyler leaned forward and took her breast in his mouth. Daisy thought her body would explode.

The hot moisture of his tongue scalded her skin. Her breast became so sensitive, the nipple so firm it was a mixture of agony and pleasure. At times she couldn't decide which was stronger. The feeling was only increased by Tyler's hand caressing her other breast, creating with fingertips and open palm a pleasure nearly as intense as that from his mouth.

Daisy cried out when he took her nipple between his teeth. She tried to hold it in, but the shuddering moan would not be contained. Through the blazing swirl of passion that was slowly engulfing her, she reached out with shaky fingers to unbutton Tyler's shirt. The feel of his muscles quivering under her touch was like an aphrodisiac. She could feel the power of his muscled chest, feel the strength of his broad shoulders. His body was a work of art, with the work-hardened muscles of a man who had built his body into a fine-tuned masterpiece. She buried her fingers in the soft mat of brown hair that clustered in the center of his chest and tapered to a narrowing band as it sank toward his middle.

She intended to remove Tyler's shirt, to study every inch of him until he was no longer a mystery, but she found her strength and willpower fading. Tyler had removed her shirt, slipped the chemise over her shoulders, and was in the process of slipping chemise and skirt from her body. The prospect of lying naked in his embrace made her forget everything else.

Tyler shrugged out of his own clothes. Long before she had become accustomed to her own state of undress, Tyler's naked body joined hers.

The fact that they were naked to each other stunned her. The fact that his hands wandered over her body, touching, caressing, exploring, was more than she could comprehend. Daisy felt completely at Tyler's mercy. The more intimately he touched her, the more helpless she became. Each increment of familiarity seemed more shattering than the last. She felt swept away on a tide of swirling sensations that carried her willy-nilly through one stunning experience after another.

Tyler slipped his leg between hers, and her body clamped down tight.

"Relax," he whispered. "I won't hurt you."

She hadn't thought he would, but she no longer controlled her body. She no longer controlled anything about herself. Her body reacted to him with a will of its own.

"You must relax and open for me," Tyler said.

She tried, but her body wouldn't respond to her will. With gentle pressure, Tyler moved his leg farther between hers until she felt the muscles give way.

"I promise not to hurt you any more than necessary."

It wasn't hurt she feared or felt, only surprise and unfamiliarity, anticipation of something more. Tyler put his arms around her and pulled her to him. She stiffened at the unmistakable sign of his own arousal, but he merely held her close. He talked softly, kissed her gently, caressed her hair. Held her.

The warmth from Tyler's body suffused her own and she was gradually able to relax. Even when his hand moved down her back, dipped at the small of her back, and cupped her buttocks, she was able to contain her surprise, absorb the shock waves of sensation without becoming rigid. All that changed when he slipped his hand between her legs. She gasped for breath, and her body became taut.

Daisy didn't know how she was going to feel pleasure when panic threatened to drown every other emotion. She was certain of it when Tyler's hand invaded her body. Every part of her being screamed in warning, seemed ready to rise up and fight off the intrusion.

But somewhere deep down behind the fear and the tension and the uncertainty, Daisy felt the feeling in her belly begin to grow and spread like water pooling after a summer rain. Even as her mind struggled to come to terms with what was happening to her, her body accepted it eagerly. She felt herself begin to relax, to move against Tyler, to want more instead of less. The feeling of warmth continued to grow and she felt her whole body begin to respond to his touch. Gradually her whole awareness narrowed until she thought of nothing else but the magic Tyler wrought.

She didn't know when Tyler moved over her. She only became aware when he withdrew his hand. "This may feel a little uncomfortable at first," he said.

She felt the pressure of him as he slowly entered her. But he was so gentle that in moments she was pressing

329

against him, wanting him to reach the need buried deep inside her.

"This may hurt," he warned, "but it will only last a moment."

Tyler sank all the way into her. A sharp pain caused her to cry out, but he covered her mouth with a kiss. As he began to move within her, she felt the pain recede, the aching need to grow and intensify until she felt nothing else. It seemed to reduce her body to a single white-hot kernel of such longing that she was conscious of nothing else.

She clung to Tyler, tried to envelop him, tried to absorb him so he could reach that spot deep within and satisfy the need that seemed to grow stronger with each second. Her need became urgent, then nearly frantic. Tyler didn't seem to be doing enough to end this agony which was sweet and bitter all at the same time.

Daisy's need grew until she was conscious of nothing else, cared for nothing else. Bands inside her seemed to grow tighter and tighter until she felt she would be compressed into nothingness. Only her need seemed to grow without limitation.

Then she felt the beginning of a wave that lifted her, then another, then a continuing series until she felt tossed helplessly by them. She clung to Tyler, her fingers sunk deep in his flesh, her body fighting to force him to find the soul of her need.

Waves of sensual pleasure pulsed through her, throbbed until she was certain she wouldn't be able to breathe. One last pulsating wave welled up from deep inside, and just as she thought she would die, the dam broke, and release flooded through her in waves of sobbing relief.

Only after some of the tension had ebbed from her body did she realize Tyler was now in the throes of the same need which had so recently teased and tortured her. His body was rigid, his breath came in noisy gasps, and his movement became less smooth. Moving more deeply and rapidly, he pitched himself forward until his body locked and he emptied himself into her in a series of powerful thrusts.

Finally, his energy spent, Tyler collapsed next to her.

Daisy lay still for what seemed like hours, trying to absorb the full enormity of what had just happened to her. She didn't want to talk or move. She just wanted to feel. Tyler lay with his arms around her, her body nestled protectively against his. It seemed impossible they could ever be separated after this. A bond had been forged between them that seemed more powerful than the differences between them. Everything had changed.

Yet nothing had changed.

It would take her a while to understand it all. In the meantime, she was content to remain where she was.

Tyler had never wanted to linger after being with a woman. Now he didn't want to leave. Daisy lay in the curve of his body, her warmth mingled with his. It was such an odd feeling, sharing a bed. Only it wasn't the sharing of the bed that was odd. It was the sharing of a small part of himself. Putting his arms around her, holding her to him, wanting to be near her, required that he make a small break in the ring of defenses he'd built around himself. The break made him uneasy, but it didn't make him feel bad.

It had taken every bit of his courage to admit to Daisy he loved her. That had been the first break in his armor. No, before that when he wanted to make love with her. Before that when he kissed her. Maybe even before that when he marked off the corner for her or fed her or worried about her wound.

Hell! This was no small break. His defenses were in complete disarray. They might have already collapsed, and he was such a fool he didn't even realize it. Yet somehow he couldn't summon the energy to care. He liked where he was, and he didn't want to do anything to change it.

He didn't move. He knew he had only to wake her to enjoy her again. Yet he hesitated. Things felt so good just as they were. He let his fingertips caress her skin. It was soft and warm. He'd never let himself enjoy a woman this way. He'd never wanted to before.

You never cared for any of those faceless women, only the physical release they could provide. This isn't the same thing at all.

Love was a strange thing. He didn't understand it. It started with caring about a person, wanting to be with her. But there was no end to how far it could go. He found himself thinking about far more than Daisy's body or the physical pleasure they could give each other. He thought of nights beyond tonight, days, mornings and evenings as well. In fact, there seemed to be no end to how far in the future his thoughts extended, and all of them included Daisy.

That shouldn't have surprised him. She had caused him to abandon his search for gold. He had effectively put his dreams on hold so that he could help her. He had never thought it would happen, but here he was, proof that it had.

If he was going to make sure she continued to be all right, he'd better do something about those rustlers. He knew she expected to go with him, but he'd feel better going alone. He wouldn't have to worry about anything happening to her. The rustlers probably weren't expecting trouble, but he'd never known any who weren't willing to fight for their stolen property. Daisy had adapted to her new life with remarkable quickness, but she wasn't ready for a gun battle. With a little luck, he could have the cows back before she woke.

Chapter Twenty-five

Tyler eased himself out of bed. He wanted to stay, to let the cows take care of themselves, but he couldn't.

The cold air bit into his bare skin. He dressed with more than ordinary haste and saddled his horse. Daisy did not stir. He had a momentary qualm at leaving her unprotected, but pushed it aside. She would be safer alone than with him.

The ride to the small canyon took less than ten minutes. Tyler was pleased to find half the canyon in deep shadow. If the rustlers woke, they'd have a hard time shooting at someone they couldn't see.

Tyler used his rope to lower the corral bars without dismounting. It was a simple matter to start the cattle moving toward the opening. It was even easier to start them down the trail. They were just as anxious as he to return to their familiar feeding grounds.

Tyler would have liked to take the rustlers' horses as well, but they were hobbled next to a tiny cabin. It would be virtually impossible to run them off without waking at least one rustler. As it was, one of them must have been a light sleeper. Tyler had just reached the mouth of the canyon when he heard a shout from the cabin. Seconds later a rifle shot spit into the night and a bullet smacked into a rock high on the canyon wall. Letting out a yell, Tyler drove his horse right into the cattle.

They didn't need much encouragement. They headed down the trail as fast as they could go.

Daisy jerked awake. Before she could wonder what had awakened her, a shot echoed through the night. She turned to Tyler only to find he wasn't there. Neither was his horse.

He had gone after the cows by himself. She listened intently and was able to make out the sound of pounding hooves. He must have the cows. The rustlers were after him. Daisy didn't have time to be angry at his leaving her. She had to do something.

Using all the speed of which she was capable, she threw on her clothes. It was useless to think of saddling her horse. They would be past her before she could get the saddlecloth in place. She ran to her saddle, but as she reached for her rifle, she remembered Rio telling her if it was ever absolutely essential to stop someone, she was to use her shotgun.

She snatched up the shotgun, reached in her saddlebags for some extra shells, and raced from the camp. The trail passed about a hundred yards from where they slept. She reached it just as Tyler swept by, driving the cattle before him like a drunken cowboy riding into town on a Saturday night. She knew the rustlers would be close behind.

She had never faced any kind of criminal before, but she had to stop them from catching Tyler. He had a head start, but he wouldn't be able to stay ahead of them without abandoning the cattle. She knelt to the ground just in

334

time to see the two rustlers round a bend in the trail up ahead. It was useless to attempt to warn them she was going to shoot if they didn't pull up. They wouldn't even hear her.

She raised the shotgun to her shoulder and took aim as best she could. When the rustlers were about 25 yards away, she pulled the trigger. Two things happened.

Screaming in shock and pain as the pieces of buckshot bit into their hides, the rustlers' horses came to an abrupt halt, rearing and backing into each other. The rustlers, unprepared for this surprise attack, lost control of their mounts.

The shotgun's recoil knocked Daisy flat on the ground. Only then did she remember Rio had warned her about the kick. Struggling to gather her senses, she scrambled for the shotgun and propped herself against a small pine. A second shot put a load of buckshot into the rustlers.

Before she could open the shotgun, eject the spent shells, reach into her saddlebags for the extras, and shove them into the empty chambers, a rifle shot split the air. One of the rustlers sagged in the saddle. Another shot sent the second rustler tumbling to the ground.

Tyler rode past.

Daisy scrambled to her feet. By the time she reached the fallen men, Tyler had disarmed them. One had been shot in the shoulder, the other in the leg.

"Not very good shooting," he said. "If I had been Hen, they'd both be dead."

"What are we going to do with them?"

"Take them to the sheriff in Albuquerque."

Daisy held the horses as Tyler remounted the men and tied them to their saddles. She even managed to hold her tongue while she helped him break camp. But once they were on the trail, the rustlers and the cows ahead of them, she could hold back her anger no longer.

"Why did you go off by yourself?"

335

Tyler didn't try to avoid her gaze. He expected an explosion at any moment, and from the look in her eye, he was about to get it. "I didn't want you to get hurt."

"And if they had caught you in the canyon?"

"I could shoot my way out."

"You weren't doing very well when you raced by here."

"I was heading for a narrow pass a couple of miles ahead. I could have held them off there."

"And left me back there. How was I supposed to get through?"

She wasn't going to like his answer. "You were supposed to wait until I came back for you."

She glared at him, her eyes incandescent. "And how was I supposed to know that? You didn't tell me."

"If I had, you wouldn't have stayed there."

"That's no reason." Daisy's anger burst out like water from an artesian well. "Those are my cattle. Any decision concerning what to do about them should be my decision."

"But you don't know anything about fighting rustlers. You nearly killed yourself with that shotgun."

"That's beside the point. You had no right to make my decisions for me. I'm not hurt anymore, and I'm not your patient."

Just like a woman. Let her get by one danger, and the fact that it existed wasn't important anymore. Didn't she understand he would be willing to endure anger a hundred times worse than this before he would let her risk being killed? No, because he hadn't told her. "I couldn't take the chance."

"Do you know why I decided not to marry Guy?"

She had no idea how jealous he was of Guy Cochrane. Even now Tyler felt that part of Daisy liked Guy better than she liked him. He thought once you loved somebody, you wanted to marry that person. That was how it worked for his brothers. He didn't understand why that didn't work for Daisy. That was how it worked for him. That was why he had come down off the mountain and was trying so hard to understand her.

"You don't love him," Tyler answered.

"He wanted to make all my decisions for me. He would have expected me to be a model wife at social occasions. But the rest of the time, I would have been expected to stay home, have his children, and run his household, but not be concerned with his business or what he did when he was away from home. Most important of all, he would have expected me to have no opinions."

Tyler didn't want to suffocate her mind or keep her barefoot and pregnant. What she didn't seem to understand was that rustlers wouldn't respect her property and person just because she was a woman. He'd have thought being shot at and having her house burned down would have convinced her of that.

"I don't see—"

"You never have. You think that just because you have my best interests at heart, it's different for you. But it's not. My father did that—I didn't realize how much until he was killed—but I'll never endure that again."

Tyler stopped his horse and waited until Daisy came abreast of him. The narrow trail forced them so close their knees almost rubbed against each other. "Maybe Guy, your father, and I have a lot more in common than I would like to think," he said.

"I don't see how you can say that."

"I'm not trying to defend your father or Guy, but a man just naturally thinks he's supposed to take care of a woman. It's not that he thinks she can't do it herself or that she's not smart enough. It's just his job. He wouldn't be a man if he didn't."

"Do your brothers do that?"

He laughed. "None better. You ought to hear Fern and

Laurel on the subject.'' He sobered. ''Maybe we do too much because our father did too little. My mother wanted all the care and protection you don't. She didn't get it, and it killed her. I guess that's made us overprotective.''

''I'm sorry about your mother,'' Daisy said, thrown a little off stride by his unexpected disclosure, ''but I'm not like her.''

She didn't see. She didn't understand. She was so blinded by one fear, she couldn't see anything else. Maybe the same problem affected him. ''But I know so much more about so many things than you do.''

''I know that. And I appreciate your taking the time to help me, but that doesn't mean I'm willing to turn my life over to you. Talk to me, explain things, try to convince me you're right.''

''You never listen to me.''

''Do you ever listen to me?''

He thought he did. But did he really listen, or did he just hear what he wanted to hear? According to Hen, he'd been doing that for years.

He'd better find out if he wanted Daisy to marry him. She was dead set against marrying anybody who would try to control her. Yet he couldn't just let her run loose without making sure she was safe. There had to be someplace between the two extremes. Hen and Laurel had found it. So had Iris and Monty. He could, too. If he didn't, he'd lose Daisy.

''You only remember the times I haven't listened to you,'' Daisy said. ''You forget the hundreds of times I did exactly as I was told.''

Tyler realized she was right. ''I don't do it intentionally. I'm so used to thinking things through on my own and then acting, I don't stop to think about consulting anybody else.''

''That's fine when you're living up on that mountain with your mules and that cougar, but it won't work here.''

It would be a radical departure for him. He wasn't sure he could do it, but he must.

"Go back to your prospecting," Daisy said. "The branding is about done. Now that we've caught the rustlers, there's not much Rio and I can't handle."

"You think you're ready to run this place on your own?"

"Not completely, but I've got to start sometime. As long as you're around, I'll depend on you."

"That's because I know a lot about cows."

"All the more reason to leave. I need to learn to recognize problems and think through to solutions. I won't do that with you here."

"I'll stay until the branding's over."

"See, this is just like every other time. You do what you want to do."

"That's right," Tyler said. "I love you, and I want to be with you. I want to know you're safe, that you're happy. I want to marry you."

Daisy turned her horse around. "That's something of a surprise. When did you decide gold, hotels, and solitude weren't enough?"

He didn't like the brittle edge to her voice. He had never expected telling a woman he wanted to marry her would make her angry.

"I guess I fell in love with you in the cabin. I guess that's why I didn't want you to leave. I didn't want anything to mess up my plans. I didn't want to be in love. I didn't know I wanted to marry you until a short time ago."

"What made you decide?"

"I guess not wanting to live without you."

Daisy looked at him for a long while, but she seemed to be considering her own thoughts more than his proposal. Whatever was going through her mind, it didn't make her happy. She showed none of the enthusiasm Tyler expected of a woman when a man asked her to marry him.

"There was a time when I hoped you would ask me to marry you, a time when it was just about the only thing I dreamed of."

Tyler didn't like the sound of that. Her voice was too flat, too impersonal. He didn't like the look in her eyes either. They were dull, closed, shuttered, as though she had gone away.

"Even though I didn't want to marry a man with gold fever," Daisy continued, "I probably would have accepted. I loved you so much.

"But these last weeks have changed me. You're responsible for that. You told me I could be anything I wanted, that I didn't have to depend on a man to be a person. I didn't believe you. I was too scared. I'd never been taught to think of being on my own. That's why I almost married Guy. Then you came back and forced me to consider my only other option—myself. Well, I did. But in doing so, I freed myself from the necessity of depending on any man. And that includes you."

"But you said you loved me."

"I do. I always will, but I love my freedom as well."

"But there has to be a way for us to be married without you feeling suffocated."

"Maybe, but I don't think you're ready to look for it. Besides, you're doing an awful lot of guessing for a man on the verge of making such an important change in his life. I want a man to know his own mind, not guess about what he feels. I want a husband who won't think of me as someone who messed up his plans."

"I didn't mean it that way."

"Maybe not, but until you can say it so it sounds different, you can't expect me to believe you mean anything else."

Tyler leaned out of the saddle, pulled her to him, and

kissed her hard. "Is that different enough?"

Daisy tamped down a desire to push the whole conversation aside and throw herself into Tyler's arms. "I'm not going to deny the physical attraction between us, but it's not going to change my mind. I waited too long for this chance to throw it away now."

With that, Daisy turned her horse and started back down the trail. It took Tyler a moment to recover sufficiently to follow. That was about as firm a no as a man could get. It hadn't been delivered in anger or with any other surplus of emotion. It had been stated deliberately and coherently.

She meant what she said.

Much to his surprise, Tyler found himself smiling. His brothers would give half of what they owned to have heard that conversation. But he was smiling because of Daisy. Damn, if he didn't love her even more for turning him down. It didn't make sense. He ought to be outraged, to be mad enough to leave her on the spot, but she had mistaken her man if she thought she could get rid of him that easily.

He had gone through hell falling in love, but now he liked it. It wasn't at all what he'd expected. He didn't feel even the least bit depressed. In fact, as he watched Daisy riding ahead of him, he felt more alive than at any time in his whole life.

He had always been one to pursue his goals with single-minded purpose. He wanted Daisy a lot more than the gold, more than the hotels, if it came to that. He didn't know how much he could change, but he was going to find out. He was also going to find a way to show her being cared for and protected had nothing to do with suffocation.

Daisy spurred her horse up a steep incline. She didn't panic or feel uneasy in the saddle when the sorrel scrambled for its footing on the loose gravel. She was proud of the riding skills she had acquired during the last few weeks. She was also pleased that after a day in the saddle she could dismount without having her legs give out from under her. Life wasn't all that bad even if she was the only woman in New Mexico who was six feet tall and her hair was disgracefully short.

She had almost forgotten about it. It didn't matter out here. She didn't have to worry about putting it up in a tight bun or trying to cover it with a hat. She simply ran a comb through it and put a hat on top of it. Nobody seemed to notice. Nobody cared.

She loved it.

Looking out over her land, knowing her cattle were branded, knowing the rustlers were on warning, made her feel proud. For the first time in her life, she had her own identity. She wasn't just somebody's daughter. She didn't need to be somebody's wife. She was Daisy Singleton, owner of the Noble Ranch.

She was taking a look around before heading back to Albuquerque to find a carpenter to build her house. She had intended to build down near the river as her mother had always wanted, but she also liked the view her father prized so much.

She found herself wanting to ask Tyler's advice.

She didn't know what to make of his behavior during the past two weeks. She hadn't expected him to leave when she ordered him to, but she hadn't expected him to change either.

Yet he seemed to have done exactly that. The only thing he did without asking was cook. Then half the time he asked her what she wanted. The rest of the time he acted like a regular hand. He'd answer any question Rio put to him, but he didn't volunteer any information he wasn't asked for, and he refused to do anything until Daisy had approved it.

A few times she almost laughed, watching him struggle with himself. Taking over was so natural that most of the time he didn't even realize what he was doing.

All the while her resolve not to marry him had been slipping a little each day. Tyler had volunteered to take the rustlers to Albuquerque. They didn't know who was behind the scheme, but they had told Tyler of plans to overrun Greene and Cordova. Tyler wanted to talk to his brother, but she had insisted that Rio go instead, that Tyler send a message to his brother. She should have recognized that as the first sign she didn't want him to leave, even for a short while.

She suspected she had first fallen in love with him because he saved her life, had pampered and cared for her. But she truly loved the man who had spent the last two weeks at her side. He wasn't really different from the Tyler she knew at first. He had just become a more complete person.

She had gradually come to realize it wasn't so bad to be looked after, especially when she only had to speak up if she didn't like something. That was new to her. She hadn't known it could work that way.

But Tyler had left the day before, and he hadn't said anything about coming back.

It felt strange riding without him. She kept looking for him, waiting for him to appear. She felt lonely. She had come to depend upon his companionship even more than his knowledge of ranching. The empty hills seemed emptier without him. She had been telling herself it was time for him to go, but she realized now she had been hoping he wouldn't. She was finding it painfully difficult to adjust to his absence. She didn't just love him. He had become part of her.

"I wonder what he's doing," she said aloud to her horse, a surefooted gelding Tyler had chosen for her. "I'm sure it's something I told him not to do."

But that didn't seem so bad. She smiled to herself. No one had ever caused her to have more contradictory feelings. No one had ever caused her to question everything she believed.

Daisy had to admit things didn't feel so good without Tyler. For the hundredth time, she told herself to put him out of her mind. She had urged him to go. She had told him she wouldn't marry him. Now she had to learn to live with her decision.

That made it all the more miraculous when, after having traveled barely two miles from camp, Daisy saw Tyler ride out of a small dip in the ground. She was shocked at her body's response. She felt light-headed, her heart beat faster, her breath was quick and shallow, her nerves felt strung to the breaking point. Her mind was incapable of holding on to a single thought. She knew she stared at him as if she didn't have a brain in her head.

"I thought you had gone back to your claim," she said.

"I decided to take a look around in case more rustlers had shown up."

"Why are you putting off going back? Finding gold used to be the most important thing in the world to you." Talking helped Daisy return to normal, or as close to normal as she could get this morning.

"I discovered something I hadn't known before."

"What was that?" What did she want it to be? She was afraid to ask herself that question because she wasn't sure she was ready for the answer.

"I discovered you were more important to me than the gold."

"I've already told you—"

Despite the fact that they rode different horses, Tyler grabbed her and kissed her so hard she couldn't breathe. She came up gasping like a fish out of water.

"I missed kissing you last night," Tyler said. "You know, I've been thinking about what you said. I guess

I'm a slow learner. But once I get something learned, I've got it forever.''

"And what have you learned?" she asked breathlessly.

"That I love you, and I'm going to marry you even if I have to carry you off over my saddle."

Daisy didn't know why that should strike her as funny any more than why it should suddenly make her short of breath. This was the worst kind of domination, and fool that she was she wasn't even angry at him.

"You couldn't carry me over your saddle. Your horse would break a leg."

Daisy couldn't quite figure out how he did it, but before she knew what was happening, Tyler had her out of her saddle and across his. Nightshade didn't seem to notice the extra weight. But that didn't surprise Daisy. She felt incredibly light-headed.

"Put me down," she said, holding tight to Tyler to keep from falling. Nightshade was almost a foot taller than her own horse. She felt as if she were a mile off the ground.

"I can put up with your maligning me, but I won't have you maligning my horse."

Daisy decided his mind had snapped. He'd been trying too hard to act like an ordinary human, smiling, talking, working around cows he hated. She'd have to be nice to him until she could get back on her horse and get some control of the situation. Meantime she shouldn't do anything that would upset him.

"What are you going to do with me?"

Tyler kissed her. "This, for a start."

Daisy laughed. Tyler's foolishness was beginning to infect her. She wondered if it was in the blood, if her father's mania for gold was equivalent to her infatuation with Tyler. Something had to explain how she could so blithely accept his transformation from a silent, brooding prospector to a carefree cowhand. The transition ought to have floored her.

She would have been instantly suspicious of such a change in Guy.

Her metamorphosis from a browbeaten daughter to a ranch owner had been equally stunning, and he continued to accept her never-ending string of demands. But this didn't seem to be the time to explore such an idea, no matter how intriguing. She was teetering in the saddle, fearful that any minute, despite Tyler's strength, she would find herself hurled into one of the junipers that covered the hills.

"We can't go riding around kissing like a couple of irresponsible kids."

"Why not? I've never felt irresponsible. I didn't know how much I'd been missing. I intend to make up for it now."

Daisy decided, reluctantly, that though this was fun, it must end. "Put me down," she said, pulling herself from his embrace. "If anybody saw me, my reputation would be ruined."

"Would you marry me then?"

"No."

"Why?"

"A Randolph couldn't marry a ruined woman."

"A Randolph can marry anybody he pleases."

Daisy tried another tactic. "You wouldn't want to ruin me. You're too much of a gentleman."

"Not if it would convince you to marry me."

"It wouldn't. I'd feel you were marrying me because you had to."

"Even if I'd intentionally ruined you?"

"Yes."

"But that's totally illogical."

"No, it's not. It makes perfectly good sense."

"Then if I *don't* ruin you, you'll marry me."

"You know I don't want to get married. I realize now I never did. I just thought I had to."

"Suppose I let you boss me around, make all the decisions." Daisy had to laugh. The notion of Tyler letting someone boss him around for any period of time was ludicrous. She didn't know how he'd managed to put up with it for the past two weeks.

"You'd last a week, maybe, then you'd head up into those hills as fast as Nightshade could carry you." A flash of light caught Daisy's eye. "You ought to try digging on that outcropping over there," she said, pointing to a rounded hill about 200 yards away. "I just saw the light flashing off some rocks. There ought to be plenty of—"

Insanity exploded all around her.

Chapter Twenty-six

Tyler pushed her so low in the saddle she could hardly breathe. He jerked on Nightshade's reins, causing the infuriated gelding to squeal and rear in protest. The whizzing sound of a bullet preceded the sound of a rifle shot by only a fraction of a second.

Nightshade screamed, Tyler dug his heels into the big gelding's flanks, and the horse started down the trail at a dead gallop. A second shot came uncomfortably close.

Tyler turned Nightshade off the trail, weaving an erratic path through mesquite, pine, and juniper, making it impossible for the killer to get a clear shot at them. The attacker fired half a dozen more shots, but they could have been fired in hopes of getting lucky. Tyler used the trees and terrain for cover until they dropped behind a low ridge. Keeping to low ground, Tyler kept Nightshade in a gallop until they reached the camp. Daisy's sorrel followed them in.

Daisy slid from the saddle, almost too weak to stand

on her own. She was ready to drop to the ground when she saw the bloody crease across Nightshade's chest.

"He's been shot!" she said.

"It's just a crease," Tyler told her after he had checked the wound despite Nightshade's objections. He looked up. "If Nightshade hadn't reared, that bullet would have killed you."

Daisy did sink to the ground then. "Do you think that was a rustler, maybe a friend of the men we captured?"

"No. That's the man who killed your father. I guess he didn't go to Montana."

The killer was after her again! She had been riding all over those hills without giving him a thought.

"I shouldn't have accepted Cochrane's word," Tyler said. "I should have realized there was a possibility he would come back. He could have killed you at any time."

"But how did you know he was there? All I saw was the sun reflecting off a rock."

"I've been over every square foot of those hills, and there are no rocks that can reflect the sun like that. It had to be the reflection off his rifle barrel."

So if she hadn't noticed the flash, if he hadn't made Nightshade rear, she would be dead.

Daisy was badly shaken, but she was also angry. "I've got to find out who this man is and why he's so determined to kill me."

"The answer must lie in Albuquerque. I'm taking you back. Hurry and pack. I want to reach town before dark."

"I don't want to go back."

"You were already planning to go."

"I won't run away."

"It's not running away to keep from getting yourself killed. We can't stay here, even if you sleep in the shed. He almost killed you once before while you slept. I won't chance it again."

"I'd like to know what gives you the right to think you

can order me around?'' Daisy said.

"This isn't about rights," Tyler said. "It's about keeping you alive."

"But I want to decide how to protect myself."

"Fine. Decide to go to Albuquerque."

"That's not what—"

"And decide to stay at the hotel with Hen and Laurel. I don't trust Guy to look after you."

Daisy was furious. He hadn't changed a bit. It was all a trick, a pretense. Let the first little thing happen, and he was just as bad as ever. She opened her mouth to tell him she wasn't going to run to Albuquerque like a scared rabbit when Rio came galloping into camp.

"What was the shooting about?" he asked.

"Someone shot at Miss Singleton," Tyler told him. "The killer is back."

"You must go to Albuquerque," Rio said to Daisy. "You must not come here again until the man is dead."

"That's what I told her, but she doesn't want to go."

"You want to get killed?" the little man exclaimed. "You want to break my heart, put Jesus out of a job?"

Daisy wondered why her life should have the feel of a melodrama. Nothing like this ever happened to Adora.

"You will have a job."

"Not if you die. Senor Cochrane will buy the ranch like he buys all the others. The senor does not like Jesus and me. He will not give us jobs."

"Why should Mr. Cochrane want her land?" Tyler asked. He was suddenly intent.

"He wants everybody's land," Rio said. "He got Cordova. I think he got Greene, too. Senorita Daisy is the last one."

"Well, I'm not going to die," Daisy said, "and I'm not going to sell my land. You and Jesus will have jobs as long as you want them."

"Good, then you will go to Albuquerque."

"That doesn't mean—"

"Yes, she will," Tyler said. "Why don't you help her pack. I'll see to the horses." He spoke absently, as though his thoughts were elsewhere.

"I'm not going," Daisy called after him.

"Do not be a foolish woman," Rio said. "Go with the man. He will see no one harms you."

"But I can take care of myself."

Rio looked at her with an expression she could only describe as fatherly. "What good is it to take care of yourself if you are alone?"

Daisy started to protest, then closed her mouth.

"Go with him. Let him take care of you. He will do it very well. And you can take care of him."

"He doesn't need me. He does everything better than I do."

"On the outside, yes. But on the inside he is like a child, frightened and alone. He will not let other people help. He will let you."

"Tyler isn't afraid of anything."

"He's afraid of what other people can do to him. I know. I watch him. He is like a man playing a part."

"Why should he do that?"

"Because he wants you to marry him."

"If he's changed, if he really—"

"A man like him cannot change," Rio said. "He is made one way. That's how he will stay. A woman who marries him must take him as she finds him."

"I find him overbearing and bossy. I had enough of that."

"He's bossy because he cares for you."

"Then he'd better learn to show it another way."

"You better learn how to let a good man take care of you. If not, you will end up an old woman alone."

Daisy was stunned by the vehemence of Rio's words. She was even more startled when he walked away, leaving

351

her to do her packing alone. She felt a flash of anger. Rio was supposed to be her friend. He had no right taking Tyler's side against her.

He didn't understand why she needed to be free. No man seemed to understand. They all seemed to think she ought to pick out a husband and hand her life over to him. Well, she couldn't do that. She loved Tyler. Just the thought of their night of love was enough to send a battering ram pounding against the walls of her resolution, but she would not give in. She had waited all her life for this freedom. She would not give it up.

"I thought women were good at packing."

Daisy came out of her reverie to find Tyler staring at her. He had everything ready. She had done nothing.

"I was thinking."

"You can think when we get to town."

Daisy started grabbing her things and stuffing them into her bedroll and the saddlebags Tyler handed her. "You haven't changed a bit, Tyler Randolph," she fumed. "You were just pretending, trying to fool us both. And you almost had me convinced. I guess I wanted to believe—so badly I was willing to forget everything else and—"

"And what?" Tyler asked. "Were you willing to forget everything and marry me?"

That one word had the power to stop her cold. It was bondage, slavery, subjugation. She couldn't do that.

"I don't want to marry anyone."

"But you would have been willing for me to keep on living here, helping you with the ranch, maybe even making love to you."

Daisy blushed. She hadn't gone so far as to put that into conscious thought, but she guessed that was what she'd been thinking. She did love him, she didn't want him to leave, but she was afraid to surrender to him.

"I haven't decided exactly what I want," she said.

"Things keep changing so fast."

"Things have changed pretty fast for me, too, but I know I want to marry you," Tyler said. "I want to love you for the rest of my life. I want to wake up each day knowing I'll have another twenty-four hours with you. But when I think you're in danger, I'm going to do everything I can to protect you. If I have time, I'll explain. If I don't, I'll do what I must."

"I'm not asking you to change. I love you the way you are, but I can't marry you. Please leave it at that."

"No."

"No?"

"I've spent three years looking for gold. I suppose I can spend at least three years trying to win you."

"But I've just said—"

"You've only been here a few weeks. You might decide you don't like it. Or you might decide you like me even better."

"I'm never going to give up the power to choose," Daisy declared.

"We all give it up at some time. It's just a question of when and to whom. For the moment, you've given it up to me."

"I didn't give it up. You took it."

"No, you gave it."

Daisy wanted to argue the point further, but he didn't give her a chance. He tied the saddlebags and bedroll to the saddle, gave Rio and the newly arrived Jesus a string of orders, helped her into the saddle, and they headed for Albuquerque.

All the way to town Tyler talked about the weather, the prospects for grazing for the coming summer, the number of cows she could expect to calve, the number of un-branded calves to look for in the fall, the number of years she would have to wait before she would have a full crop of steers for sale, the prices she could expect, the best markets, how to get the cattle there, the number and kind of hands she ought to hire, the traits to look for in a good foreman, the kind of house that would work best, where she ought to place some dams to control runoff and help irrigate. The topics he covered seemed as endless as the miles that rolled by.

All the while Daisy racked her mind for ways to prove to Tyler she wanted to be truly free of all men. She was still trying to come up with a solution when they reached town and dismounted in front of Post's Exchange Hotel. She had hardly stepped into the lobby when the clerk announced, ''I was just about to send somebody out to your place, Miss Singleton. Your uncle and cousin from New York are here.''

Daisy stood rooted to the floor in disbelief as Guy came to meet her, accompanied by two strange men. Without ever having seen him before, she knew the older man was her uncle. His resemblance to her father was striking. The handsome young man with him was just as clearly his son. Apparently good looks ran in at least one branch of the Singleton family.

''I was about to go out to the ranch to fetch you,'' Guy said, a wide smile plastered across his features. ''Your uncle and cousin arrived just like you said they would.''

Daisy's tongue cleaved to the roof of her mouth. She had never expected to hear from her family, much less have them come all the way to New Mexico.

''I regret it took us so long to get here,'' her uncle said. ''We didn't see the announcement. A friend told us of it.''

''We had the greatest difficulty finding you,'' her cousin added.

''Walter cut himself off from his family,'' her uncle explained. ''We hadn't heard from him in years. I'm sorry to say we didn't even know your mother had died.''

''I didn't expect you to come,'' Daisy managed to say.

She thought she must be acting like an idiot, but she was too stunned to act normally.

"Of course we came," her uncle said. "You didn't think we'd leave our only niece in a place like this, did you? Your fiance tells me you have been living on a burned-out ranch for the last month. My dear, you can't do that."

Learning Guy had told her uncle they were still engaged restored Daisy's mental powers. "I broke my engagement weeks ago," she told her uncle. "Since the ranch is the only property I own, I had no other choice. I've been trying to make up for some of Daddy's neglect. I have a crew to help me. I've come to town to see about getting someone to build me a new house."

"You don't have to live on the ranch," Guy said. "They want to take you back to New York. You're rich. Your grandfather left you his money."

"Only a part of it," her uncle corrected. His gaze settled on Tyler. "Maybe we'd better retire to a parlor, away from the ears of strangers."

"This is Tyler Randolph," Daisy said. "He's been helping me with the ranch."

Her uncle's frown disappeared. "Young Mr. Cochrane here told me you rescued my niece from the men who tried to kill her. I can't express my appreciation enough. I will see that you're suitably rewarded."

Daisy flushed with embarrassment.

"Tyler doesn't want a reward."

"It's very correct of him not to press, but I'm sure he would appreciate the money."

"Miss Singleton is right," Tyler said. "Now I'll leave you to get acquainted with your niece." He walked over to the clerk. "Is my brother in?" he asked.

"He came in with the boys a short while ago."

Tyler came back to the waiting group. "Daisy is staying with my sister-in-law. We will expect her in an hour."

"I have already made provisions for my niece's lodging."

"That was very thoughtful. You had no way of knowing it was unnecessary," Tyler said. His lips smiled but his eyes didn't.

"She is welcome to stay with us," Guy said. "It would be much more suitable than a hotel."

Daisy felt as if she were at the center of a three-ring circus. "I prefer to stay with Laurel," she said. "All my things are here." She had had everything sent to the hotel when she broke her engagement. She hadn't wanted Guy to think she might change her mind.

"My dear, should you be staying with a stranger?" her uncle asked.

"If it comes to that," Daisy said, beginning to feel irritated by the pressures all around her, "you're the strangers. Laurel and I are friends."

"But only a recent friend," Guy interjected. "You've known Adora for years. She's been hoping you'd stay with her."

"Well, I'm not," Daisy said. "Now why don't you go tell Adora I'd love to see her this evening. My uncle and I have a lot to talk about."

She could see Guy didn't want to be excluded from the conversation and was casting about for a reason to remain.

"My mother will want you all to come to dinner."

"Another night," Daisy said. "After the ride in, I'm too tired."

Giving in to the inevitable, Guy retreated.

"Now," Daisy said, turning to her uncle, "what is this about my grandfather leaving me money?"

"He said he struck gold within an hour after you left," Hen told Tyler. "He found it exactly where you told him to dig."

Tyler was having a difficult time keeping his mind on

what Hen was saying. It seemed odd his brother should think he was so interested in gold. He'd almost forgotten it. How could he think of something like that when Daisy was downstairs becoming reacquainted with her family and discovering she was an heiress? She would truly be free now. She could go back East and live in any kind of house she wanted.

He'd be miserable.

"I've already had it assayed. It's very rich. I suggest you sell it rather than try to operate it yourself. I think you can get more than enough to build your hotels."

"What?" Tyler asked, coming out of his fog.

"Haven't you been listening to anything I said? It's the biggest gold strike in the history of New Mexico."

"I told Willie I'd give him a third."

"He won't take it. He said he didn't do anything but dig out a few shovels full. He accepted a finder's fee and went off to look for a claim of his own."

"Who's at the claim?"

"It's already properly registered and guarded. In fact, I've got an offer for it already." He handed Tyler a piece of paper.

The number seemed to have too many zeros.

"I never thought you would do it," Hen said, "certainly not such a big one. Watch out. Madison will try to talk you into investing the money in railroads."

"Speaking of railroads, did Rio give you my message about Cochrane?"

"Yes, but I couldn't find out much. Many people hate him, but they all have to use his bank. Nobody will say a word against him."

"I'm convinced he ordered Daisy's father killed. It must have something to do with the railroad. I just can't figure out what. Rio said he was ready to wipe out Greene and Cordova to get their land. Why is he buying up miles of grazing land, and why is he willing to kill to get it?"

357

"The railroad will have to buy the right of way."

"He could make a whole lot more money buying land in town around the depot."

"I don't see why he wanted to kill Daisy. She was set to marry his son. He'd have had her land automatically."

"He didn't want her killed," Tyler said, suddenly remembering. "She wasn't supposed to be home. It was an accident."

"Then who's after her?"

"The killer, because she recognized him. He tried again today."

"But she's not going to marry Guy."

"So she's still in danger, from both of them now."

"But you can't prove anything."

"I know, but I will."

"Good. Now about this claim."

"Have Madison sell it to the highest bidder. He'll get a better price than I can. I've got something else to do right now."

"Does it have anything to do with Daisy?" Laurel asked. She had listened to the conversation without comment while feeding Harrison.

"Everything."

"Good," she said, smiling. "It's about time you came to your senses."

"So you're a very rich young woman," Laurel said to Daisy. They were having coffee in Laurel's sitting room. Daisy was still a little dazed from her conversation with her uncle.

"It seems my grandfather was sure Daddy would waste his money, so he left it to me instead."

"What are you going to do?"

"My uncle wants me to go back to New York. My cousin and I are his only family."

"Do you want to go?"

"I don't know. I used to think I'd give anything if I could go back East. It was a safe dream because I never thought it could come true."

"Now it has, and you're scared."

Daisy nodded. "Have you ever been to New York?"

"No. Denver was too much for me. In fact, Albuquerque's more than enough. I'll be glad to get back to the ranch." She shifted the baby, who was asleep in her arms. "Hen has finally decided we're both strong enough to make the trip. Next time I'm not going to tell him until *after* I have the baby."

"How are you . . . oh, you're joking."

"I'm not sure. It was easier having Adam in a canyon by myself than having Harrison with every doctor Hen could find standing over me. Heaven help Iris if she ever gets pregnant. The men in this family are terribly over-protective."

Daisy knew that. It was one of the reasons she wouldn't marry Tyler. Then why did she feel jealous of Laurel?

"I want to stay here and run my ranch," Daisy said, "but everybody seems to think I have to be married no matter where I go."

"What does Tyler say?"

"He wants me to marry him."

"Would your uncle approve?"

"Of course, now that he's found out how rich the Randolphs are."

"Oh."

"Yes, oh. It seems money can make everything right."

"But not for you?"

"Money has nothing to do with it. All my life I've wanted to be free. But every way I turn, there's a man telling me what to do. And that includes Tyler."

"Then if you don't want any of them, I suggest you tell them so and move out to your ranch as soon as possible.'' Laurel studied Daisy for a few moments. ''There's more, isn't there?''

''I'm not sure Tyler will leave. I tried to order him off after we caught the rustlers, but he wouldn't go. He said he was leaving yesterday, but he camped in the hills.''

''He'd go if he thought you meant it.''

''I do. I don't want him trying to change for me. Just because I won't marry him doesn't mean I don't love him, stubborn, overbearing man that he is.''

''I imagine he'll stay as long as you feel that way.''

''He wouldn't if I went to New York.''

''You'd do that to get away from him?''

''I'm not trying to get away from him. I just don't want him trying to become something he isn't because of me. It would destroy him.''

Laurel put her son to bed in the other room. ''He's like all the other Randolph men,'' she said as she closed the door to the bedroom. ''He's going to do what he wants, and there's nothing you can do to change that. It's hard for them to admit it when they fall in love. But once they get used to the idea, they don't give up easily.''

''Neither do I. If you want stubborn, just ask for a Singleton.''

But this had nothing to do with stubborn. Daisy wanted Tyler to be the one to leave, because she couldn't.

Chapter Twenty-seven

"I told you never to come to the bank," Regis said, "not even after hours."

"I came to tell you—"

"I know what you came to tell me," Regis Cochrane said, his voice an angry hiss. "You missed again!"

"I couldn't get close. That Randolph fella is always with her."

"Maybe it's just as well. She's inherited a lot of money. I can use it."

"I can still get her."

"You stay away from her," Cochrane ordered. "And stay away from me. Start for Montana, and go there this time. I don't want you to come here again. If you do, I'll say you were the one who killed her father."

"I'll tell them you hired me."

"Nobody would believe you. You'd hang, and I'd be there watching. Now get out. If I see you again, I'll have the sheriff arrest you."

Frank left in a rage. He had his pride, and he didn't like being treated like a petty killer who could be brushed off like a bug. He didn't want to leave town just yet. If he waited around, maybe he could still find a way to kill that female and collect the rest of his money. Then he'd leave for Montana.

The next morning Daisy spied Tyler across the lobby before she was halfway down the stairs. She felt a warm flush flood her cheeks. Her heart started to beat faster, and her breath seemed shallow. The same old reaction. He was twice as good-looking as anybody else in the lobby. He looked so calm, so self-possessed, she couldn't imagine why women weren't crowded around him.

Daisy took a deep breath to settle her agitation. She had made her decision. She didn't understand why she continued to question it every time she saw Tyler. Nothing had changed. She forced a look of what she hoped was calm on her face and continued down the stairs. Tyler saw her before she reached the bottom step.

He rose from his seat and came toward her. Apparently he'd been waiting for her. She dreaded this interview, but it had to come sooner or later.

"I thought you'd be gone by now," she said when he came up.

"I'll be staying in Albuquerque for a few days yet."

"You haven't given up on your hotels, have you?"

"No."

"You do intend to build them?"

"Yes."

"You won't if you don't find the gold."

"Things have changed. I—"

"I can't stand around talking," Daisy said, her agitation showing. "I'm on my way to see Adora. You can walk with me."

Tyler's eyes opened a little wider at her flash of temper,

362

but he followed her outside. It was a brilliant day. Even though it was cold, the sky was clear, the sun strong. Daisy looked at the Sandia Mountains in the distance and felt a lump in her throat. The days spent in the cabin had been the best days of her life. She even missed Zac at times, sharp-tongued rascal that he was. But most of all she missed the long, quiet days when she had nothing to do but wait for the snow to melt.

And fall in love.

Everything had seemed so simple then. All she had to do was get married and life would take care of itself. She hadn't owned a ranch capable of making her independent; she hadn't had enough money to buy and sell Mrs. Esterhouse and her precious daughter, or a rich family begging her to go back to New York, or two men promising to do anything if she would only marry them. And for most of the time she had been unaware a determined killer was on her trail.

She had no way of knowing the things that worried her most—her height, hair, and wound—would be practically forgotten so quickly. She remembered her scorn for a life spent in the mountains in such a cabin. It seemed wonderfully attractive now.

She shook her thoughts to rid them of melancholy. There was no going back.

"I suppose Laurel told you my grandfather left me some money," she said to Tyler, "and that my uncle wants me to go back to New York with him."

Tyler nodded.

"I'm going," Daisy said.

That startled Tyler. "Do you intend to sell your ranch?"

"Probably. Maybe." She didn't want to lie to him. She just wanted him to go back to his mines. She would miss him terribly. The longer he waited, the harder it was going to be. "I don't know. It doesn't make sense to keep it."

"What will you do in New York?"

"I've never been anywhere except Santa Fe. I probably won't stop going places and seeing things for years. My cousin assures me I would love London and Paris."

"You can't do all this by yourself."

"My uncle says I can easily find a dependable paid companion."

"You're turning your back on love, a family."

"No. I'm actually gaining a family."

"I meant your own family, a husband and children. Is your freedom that important to you?"

"I told you it was."

"How can I make you understand that freedom is more than having to answer to no one but yourself?"

"You can't. I've seen how men treat women."

"You haven't seen how I would treat you."

"Yes, I have. You would try your best to let me be free. But when a decision had to be made, you would make it and expect me to go along with it."

"Someone has to have the final responsibility."

"I know, and I'm not willing to give that up." They were approaching the Cochrane house. Daisy felt miserable. She wanted to end the conversation. "I promised Adora I'd be here at half past. I must go."

"This is your final word?"

"It has been my final word for weeks. You just won't believe me."

"I kept hoping . . . I guess it doesn't matter what I kept hoping. I hope you enjoy New York. I didn't like it myself, but a lot of people do."

"Do you ever visit?"

"Sometimes."

"Look me up. We can—"

"No. I want to be your husband, your lover, your friend and companion. I can't be content to be a casual acquaintance who takes you to the opera or for a yacht ride in the sound.''

Daisy held out her hand. ''Then I guess it's good-bye.''

''It'll never be good-bye between us.'' Tyler grabbed her and kissed her with ferocious energy. ''You're going to marry me yet. You're going to find out you can be much more free in my arms than you can alone in New York.''

Tyler had sounded a lot more confident than he felt. Walking back to the hotel he wondered what he could do to convince Daisy she was making the wrong decision.

''You won't do it by forcing yourself on her,'' Laurel told him a few minutes later. ''I know you thought it would bring her to her senses, but it hasn't.''

''Then what do you suggest I do?''

''Nothing.''

''Nothing?''

''You used to do it very well,'' Hen pointed out. ''Back home you could do it for hours on end.''

''This is different,'' Tyler said.

''Then I suggest you come up with a different approach,'' Hen said. ''Let her go to New York. Let her decide for herself if that's what she wants.''

''She doesn't,'' Tyler said, ''but she's convinced I won't be happy unless I'm wandering the hills dressed in buckskins and wearing a beard. She's also convinced I won't be happy unless I'm the only one giving orders.''

''I never knew a Randolph who could take orders,'' Laurel pointed out. ''Monty went all the way to Wyoming to get away from George.''

''He also married Iris, and she gives him orders all the time. What's more, he follows half of them. I love Daisy. I want to marry her. I imagine we'll have some good scraps over what to do, but I'd rather do it her way than not at all. I've told her that, but she doesn't believe me.''

"If you really love her and you're sure she really loves you, trust in love," Laurel said.

"I can't. Love's a rather stupid creature. Look what a mess it's got me into."

"I'm so glad you were able to come," Adora said as she welcomed Daisy into the Cochrane parlor. "Mama was saying just last night she wondered how you were doing."

"There seems so much to do, so many decisions to make."

Adora frowned. "I haven't forgiven you for not staying with us."

"It's best I stay at the hotel," Daisy said, wondering when she would stop feeling guilty about not fulfilling people's expectations. "I'm near my uncle. And I'm away from Guy. I know he's your brother, but I really can't marry him. He continues to think I will change my mind. I'm of two minds whether to go with him this afternoon."

"You can't back out now. It'll be his last chance to see you before you go to New York. I know he plagues you, but it's because he still loves you."

"He just thinks he does. He's gotten used to the idea and finds it comfortable. I know what love is now."

"It's still Tyler Randolph?"

Daisy nodded.

"Then why don't you marry him? Doesn't he want you to?"

"I've decided not to marry anyone."

Adora looked startled. Daisy knew Adora couldn't imagine life without a husband.

"But there'll be hundreds of men in New York who will want to marry you."

"I doubt it, even after my hair grows out. The only man who doesn't look at me like I'm a great gawk is Tyler, and that's because he's so big himself."

Adora looked at her friend with unwonted perception. "It seems to me you haven't made up your mind to go to New York as much as you've decided to run away from Tyler."

"It amounts to the same thing."

"Not at all. If you run away, you'll never get over him."

"Do you think I'll get over him by staying here?"

"No."

"So what difference does it make where I'm miserable?"

"Why are you leaving him if it makes you so miserable?"

"I don't know. I just know I can't marry him. I'm afraid."

"Afraid of what?"

"Of him. Myself. I don't know. I feel like I can't surrender myself all over again."

"Then it doesn't seem to me you really love him."

"What?" Daisy exclaimed.

"I don't think you really love him," Adora repeated.

"How can you say that! You, of all people."

"I've never been in love," Adora admitted, "but I can't imagine I would distrust my husband the way you distrust Tyler."

"I don't distrust him."

"I wouldn't hesitate to put my life and everything I possess into his keeping. I would know he would try to take better care of me than I would take of myself. Isn't that what you say his brother does for Laurel?"

"What about when he started telling you what to do, what to think?"

"He wouldn't tell me. He would advise me. If I didn't understand, he would explain until I understood as well as he."

"And if you still disagreed?"

"He would allow me my own way as long as it was possible."

"And who's to decide that?"

"He would."

"And you would accept that?"

"Of course. Once I have trusted him with my life and my possessions, it's a small thing to trust him with anything else. You trust Tyler with your life, don't you?"

"Of course. He's already saved it several times."

"Then I don't understand why—"

Guy burst into the room. "The carriage is ready. It's time to be on our way."

It was on the tip of Daisy's tongue to tell him she'd changed her mind and wouldn't go with him after all. Her feelings were in such a turmoil, she didn't think she could endure several hours of his renewed entreaties.

But his smile was so hopeful, Adora's look so pleading, Daisy decided to go with him this one last time. After all, she had asked him to look after her ranch. Spending a few hours with him was a small price to pay for all the work he would have to do.

She continued to resist her uncle's suggestion that she accept Mr. Cochrane's very generous offer to buy the ranch. She still felt overwhelmed by the sudden acquisition of wealth and family. It seemed like a dream. The ranch and Tyler represented reality. She had to hold on to it. It would give her somewhere to go if everything else fell apart.

"It really isn't necessary that we visit the ranch," Daisy said as she got to her feet. "I can tell you everything you need to know."

"I couldn't accept responsibility without your showing me exactly what you want. You could be gone for years."

So Daisy let Guy escort her from the house and help her into the closed carriage. She would have preferred a buggy. She never did like being closed in. Today it seemed to stand for the life she would have led as his wife. She had no regrets about turning him down. She could never have been happy with him. She wondered why she hadn't seen that from the first.

Probably because she had always expected to be married. She had looked upon marrying Guy as a kind of freedom, but Tyler had shown her what real freedom meant.

True, he had constantly told her what to do and had just as frequently ignored her wishes, even her direct orders, but it had always been for her safety and well-being, just as Hen did for Laurel. She accused Tyler of forgetting the times she had done exactly what he asked, but she was just as guilty of forgetting the times he'd gone out of his way to do things just for her. He had given her a corner of his cabin, unlimited hours of his time and thoughts. He had hauled and heated bathwater, taken care of her deer, captured her rustlers, given up his claim to help her with her ranch, even risked his life to protect her from the killers.

Daisy felt utterly stupid. How could she have failed to understand before now that he had already given up more than she was afraid of losing?

She felt worse than stupid. She felt frightened. She had done everything in her power to send him away. She might have succeeded at last.

"Have you decided how long you're going to stay in New York?" Guy asked. He was seated inside with her. One of the Cochrane grooms drove.

She didn't want to have to talk to Guy. She wanted time to think. She wanted to see Tyler. "My uncle thinks I ought to meet my mother's family before I decide. I might end up coming back here to escape all of my relatives."

She wasn't joking. Already her uncle was trying to plan

her life. She expected her mother's family would do the same.

She found herself thinking of Tyler as a refuge. She had a terrible feeling she would have a more difficult time being a rich young woman with many anxious relations than she had had being a poor female with no hair and a bullet wound in her head.

"I wish you would reconsider," Guy said. "New York is nothing like Albuquerque."

"If I'm not happy there, I can go somewhere else."

"Back here?"

She didn't know. Adora's words echoed in her brain. *I can't imagine I would distrust my husband the way you distrust Tyler.* Did she really trust Tyler, and if so, why couldn't she trust him with her happiness as completely as she trusted him with her life?

Without warning, Guy turned in his seat and took Daisy's hands. "Marry me," he urged. "I'll take you anywhere you want to go. We can live in New York or travel abroad. Anything you want. You have only to ask."

"Guy, I've already told you that—"

"I know what you said, but you're wrong. I do love you. And I know you'll come to love me. I'll make sure you do."

She tried to remove her hands from Guy's grasp, but he wouldn't let them go. "Don't be ridiculous, Guy. You know your father expects you to take over here. You're already doing half his work. Your friends are here. Everything you like is here. You would be miserable anywhere else."

"I wouldn't be miserable as long as I was with you."

He tried to take her in his arms, but Daisy was easily able to hold him off. She was bigger than he was, and after weeks in the saddle, she had grown stronger.

"You don't love me," she said. "You've just convinced yourself you do."

"How can you say that when I keep telling you I love you?"

"Because I know what it is to be in love," Daisy said, finally driven to tell him what she had wanted to keep from him.

"Are you referring to Tyler Randolph?"

"Yes."

"But you said you weren't going to marry him."

"I'm not, but he loves me in ways you've never dreamed of."

"How?"

Daisy hardly knew where to begin.

"I could tell you about the week he took care of me, put my needs and comfort above his or his brother's. But it wasn't until I realized he'd left his prospecting to help me get started at the ranch that I realized just how much he loved me. He put aside something that had been his burning ambition for three years to help me."

"I'm offering to change my whole life for you," Guy argued.

"He's used to making decisions without consulting anyone, but for two whole weeks, he managed to keep from telling me what to do even once."

"I haven't ever told you what to do."

"And he never touched me although he desperately wanted to make love to me."

"I would never dream of violating you."

"When he looks at me, or calls my name, it's like a caress. There's something special about his voice, his eyes, his touch. No man has ever touched me like that."

"I thought you said he never—"

"He won't take no for an answer. He says he'll wait, that one day I'll be his wife."

"I've done all that and more," Guy said.

Daisy forced herself to take her mind off Tyler. She would much rather have spent the rest of the trip thinking about him, but she couldn't do that to Guy.

"I'm sorry, Guy, but I don't love you. I wouldn't make you a good wife. I know you believe you'd do anything for me, but after we were married a little while, you'd soon begin to want to do what you had done before, to think and feel about things as you had before. I don't want you to change for me. I want you to find a woman who will love you just like you are."

Guy's grip on her hands tightened. "Why won't you believe I love you?"

"Guy, I told you—"

"You can't love Tyler Randolph more than me. Even if his family is rich, he's nothing but a mountain man. You can't have anything in common with him."

"There's no point in discussing this anymore. I shouldn't have come with you. Let's get to the ranch, see what you have to see, and get back to town."

"I don't understand why you won't marry me."

"I've tried to explain. You just refuse to understand."

"I understand perfectly well," Guy said. "You've taken leave of your senses. I can't let you do something you'll be sorry for."

"Guy, I'm not marrying Tyler. I'm going to New York."

"That's even worse. You don't belong there. Your uncle will make you marry some rich friend of his who won't understand you at all."

"Now you're being ridiculous."

Guy let go of her hand and leaned back against the cushions of the seat. All the emotion that had animated his plea disappeared. He looked almost placid. "I'm sorry to do this, but you've brought it on yourself."

"Brought what on myself? Guy, you're making no sense."

"I tried to make you see reason, but you wouldn't."

"What are you talking about?"

"We're going to the ranch, but the carriage will continue to Bernalillo, where it will pick up a padre waiting to marry us."

"You sure I'm not imposing on you with all this talk of money?" Hen said, his mouth set in a hard line. He was clearly out of temper with his brother.

Tyler's body was in Laurel's sitting room, but his mind was with Daisy and Adora Cochrane. He didn't like her being at the Cochranes. He'd only let her go because Regis Cochrane wasn't at home. He wasn't interested in how much money Madison had gotten for his gold mine. Neither did he want to hear about the cost of land in Denver and San Francisco or which parts of each city were most likely to develop into the best commercial districts. None of that mattered when Daisy was going to New York.

"You've been extremely helpful. In fact, it's not like you to go so far out of your way for me."

"I won't do it again," Hen snapped. "I can't seem to hold your attention for five minutes."

"He's worried about Daisy," Laurel explained.

"I know he's worried about Daisy. He's been worried about that woman ever since he showed up, but he doesn't do anything about it. And if I'm to take her at her word, she's fed up to the teeth with him."

"She doesn't mean it."

"Then why should she say it?"

"She's confused."

"I'm confused, but I don't go around saying things I don't mean."

"You said you wouldn't help Tyler again, and you know you will."

"I won't if he can't pull himself out of this depression."

"I'm not depressed," Tyler said. "I'm furious."

"I suppose that's an improvement?"

"I get angry over things until I figure out how to fix them. I get depressed when there's no way to fix them."

"Are you sure you can tell the difference?"

Tyler grinned. "Yeah. I probably feel like you did when you discovered Laurel had left town."

"Then God help you," Hen said, getting to his feet. "It's time I took the boys for a ride. It'll be their last. We're going home tomorrow."

"I'm sorry we're leaving you just now," Laurel said after Hen and the boys had gone, "but we've been away far too long."

"You've done too much already."

"I haven't done anything except listen to both of you."

Tyler looked up sharply.

"If it's any consolation, she's just as miserable as you are."

"Then why in heaven's name—"

"Because of the way her father treated her and her mother. She's afraid all marriages are like that. She loves you and wants to be with you, but having gotten her freedom, she's afraid to give it up."

"Doesn't she know I would never treat her like that?"

"I don't think she's sure yet. Apparently her father swore he loved her and her mother. It's certain her mother loved him. She probably thinks it's natural for men to tyrannize women."

"If she's afraid of tyranny, she'd better stay away from that uncle of hers. He's got a nice gilded cage in mind for her."

"What do you mean?"

"He means for her to marry to his advantage, social and financial."

"Daisy is too smart for that."

"Not if she's too busy looking over her shoulder to see if I'm pursuing her."

"Then give her room."

"I can't. She thinks she knows what's happening, but she doesn't."

"How do you intend to fix that?"

"Keep her from going to New York first."

"How?"

"I don't know, kidnap her if I have to."

A furious pounding at the door kept Tyler from noticing Laurel's troubled frown. He opened it to find Adora Cochrane standing there, her face white, her expression molded by fear.

"He's kidnapped Daisy. He's going to make her marry him, and it's all my fault." With that she burst into tears.

Chapter Twenty-eight

"Who's kidnapped Daisy?" Tyler asked.

"Guy."

"Where has he taken her?" Tyler demanded. "When did he leave? Tell me!" he thundered when Adora could do no more than stare up at him with tears running down her face. "I've got to go after her."

"I . . . He . . ." Adora seemed on the verge of hysterics.

"Come in and sit down," Laurel said, stepping between the frightened, distraught girl and Tyler. "You've been through a terrible ordeal." She led Adora to a small sofa, sat down next to her, and patted her hand. "Now try to calm yourself." Laurel looked straight at Tyler. "Nobody's going to rush you."

Adora hiccupped a few times. When Tyler didn't seem to be ready to growl at her, she was able to stop crying.

"Now tell us what happened," Laurel said. "Take as long as you need." A look of angry impatience stopped Tyler from interrupting.

"Daisy had asked Guy to look after her ranch. I talked her into riding out there with him. He wanted one last chance to see if he could talk her into marrying him. Naturally, I was hoping he would be successful. Daisy's been my best friend for years. I would like nothing better than for her to be my sister-in-law."

"Naturally," Laurel agreed.

"After they had gone, Papa came home. I overheard him telling Mama she was to get Daisy's room ready. When Mama asked why, Papa told her Guy was going to force Daisy to marry him. Mama said it wasn't right, but Papa shouted at her to get the room ready and shut up. That's when I came here. She loves Tyler, not Guy."

"How long ago did they leave?" Tyler asked, making every effort to keep his voice calm.

"I don't really know. I lost track of time."

"We arrived at your house at half past nine," Tyler said, exasperated with Adora's inability to remember the events of just a few hours ago. "How long did she stay?"

"Less than half an hour."

"Then they left about ten o'clock. That gives them a two-hour head start." Tyler muttered a curse. "They could be in Bernalillo by now."

"They took the carriage," Adora said. "They can hardly have reached the ranch yet."

"Are you sure Daisy said she loved me?" Tyler asked.

"She's loved you ever since you brought her down that mountain," Adora said.

Tyler headed for the door. "I'll be back tonight, and I'll have Daisy with me. Guy Cochrane will be lucky if I don't bury him alongside the road."

"Don't hurt Guy," Adora pleaded. "He's so afraid of Papa he'll do anything he wants, but he truly loves Daisy."

At least they had one thing in common, Tyler thought as he ran down the hotel stairs two at a time and headed for the livery stable. But this time he intended to convince Daisy to marry him, and Guy Cochrane, damn his cowardly soul to hell, just might have given him the means.

"Daisy, you can't leave me like this. You've got to let me up."

"Why? You intended to tie me up even more securely."

Daisy led her horse out of the corral and tied him to the rail. Guy lay on the ground at her ranch campsite, tied hand and foot like Tyler had taught Daisy to tie a calf she was about to brand.

"I can't breathe."

Daisy went back to the shed for her saddle. "You should have thought of that before you tried to compromise me." She dropped the saddle on the ground and picked up the saddle blanket. "You should have realized it was useless. I was on that mountain with Tyler for more than a week. Spending a night here with you is nothing compared to that." She smoothed the saddlecloth on the horse's back.

"But you can't leave me here. I wouldn't do that to you."

"Rio and Jesus will be in by nightfall. They'll let you go."

"You can't let them find me like this. I'll be the laughingstock of Albuquerque."

"I'm not letting you up. You'll only try to keep me here until your man gets back with that priest."

Daisy picked up the saddle and dropped it on the sorrel's back.

"I swear—"

"Save your breath. I won't ever believe another word you say." Daisy put the strap through the buckle and tightened the cinch. But rather than mount up, she turned to Guy. "Why did you want to marry me? And don't try to convince me it had anything to do with love. You'd never kidnap the woman you loved.''

''Yes, I would.''

''That's not love. That's possession. What did you want?''

''Nothing but you.''

''You're lying.''

''No, I'm not. I swear.''

But Daisy didn't hear his answer. She had heard the faint sound of a horse along the trail up from the Rio Grande. Her heartbeat skittered, then started beating at a faster rate. It could be the killer after her again! Her heartbeat jumped another notch when she recognized the huge black horse with an even larger rider coming her way at a furious gallop.

Tyler!

The surge of happiness that shot through her put to rest once and for all any idea she had about not wanting to marry Tyler. She didn't care about his gold or her freedom. At this moment she knew the most important thing in the world was that she be able to spend the rest of her life with this man. They'd have to work something out. It wouldn't be easy, but nothing could be worse than the torture she had endured these last weeks.

''You'd better be glad I let you stay right where you are,'' Daisy said to Guy. ''It's probably the only thing that'll keep you alive.''

''What do you mean?''

''Tyler Randolph is coming, and unless I miss my guess, he's mad enough to kill you.''

She tried not to be glad Guy's life was in danger, but she failed. She needed Tyler to be so furious at Guy for trying to kidnap her that he would be in a fever to kill him. She yearned for him to be so frightened he might lose her that he would forget all the foolish things she'd said in the past.

She decided the time for any show of reluctance was past. She left her horse and walked forward until she reached the point where the trail turned into the yard. There she waited, alone and immobile, her back straight, her head erect.

Tyler rode Nightshade straight at her, but Daisy never flinched. She was ready when he leapt from the saddle and swept her up in his arms. She was ready when he kissed her. She was ready when he lifted her off her feet. She wasn't ready when he gave her a swat on the behind. "That's for thinking I would ever treat you the way your father did, even if you are the most provoking woman in the territory."

For a moment Daisy didn't know what he was talking about; then she remembered what she had told Laurel. "I never did, not really."

Tyler responded by kissing her again until she felt quite unable to stand without assistance.

"Where's Cochrane?" Tyler finally asked. "I saw the carriage track turn in and turn out again. He didn't leave you here, did he?"

Daisy wrapped her arms firmly around Tyler's neck. "The driver took the carriage to Bernalillo to fetch the priest." She nodded without looking around. "Guy's over there."

Tyler looked over Daisy's shoulder. His expression changed from fury to shocked surprise. Then he broke out laughing, the first time Daisy had ever heard him do that. "Want to brand him? I think it would be appropriate. On his back, I think. Discreet but permanent."

Guy looked horrified.

"It's best to use a cinch iron. Without hair, the brand won't have to be so large."

"Let me up," Guy shouted. "Face me like a man."

"Be glad I don't let you up," Tyler said, his humor fading. "If you were on your feet, I'd kill you."

"You wouldn't," Guy protested, not at all certain of his ground. "No sane man would."

"I'm in love with Daisy. I've been insane for weeks. I'm desperate enough to do anything."

Guy swallowed, but didn't say any more.

"Are you ready to go back?" Tyler asked.

"Yes," Daisy replied.

"What about me?" Guy asked when they mounted up.

"I'm sure your carriage will be back before long," Daisy said. "You can ask the padre to say some prayers for your soul. That way his trip won't have been entirely wasted."

"Now about this trip to New York," Tyler began.

"I'm not going," Daisy said. "I've got too much to do."

"Like what?"

"Well, I've got to get my house built. I really can't go on sleeping in a tent. Then I ought to see about a bunkhouse. I don't suppose Rio and Jesus are any fonder of tents than I am."

"And after that?"

"I remember you saying something about needing to brand the new calves. Then there are dams to build, trees to plant, wells to dig—"

"Anything else?" Tyler asked, a glitter in his eye.

"It seems there was some talk of a wedding."

Hen was waiting for them at the livery stable.

"You didn't think I could bring her back by myself?" Tyler asked, a tug of irritation clouding his happiness.

"This from a man who looked over my shoulder for more than a month."

"There were dozens of Blackthornes."

"Laurel wanted me to make sure Daisy knew she could stay with us. She insists we postpone our return until you two get things settled between you. You had a long ride

381

in from the ranch,'' Hen said hopefully. ''Did you get things settled?''

Tyler looked at Daisy. He held out his hand and gave hers a squeeze. ''There might be one or two things left.''

''I wish you'd hurry up. I'm sick of this hotel, Albuquerque, and lovesick fools like you. You're wrecking my plans.''

They emerged from the stable and headed toward the hotel.

Daisy held on to Tyler's arm. It was a simple thing, walking down the street on the arm of the man she loved, yet she found it hard to believe. So much had seemed to stand between them. Their differences had seemed impossible to resolve. Yet now it all seemed so simple. She couldn't imagine why she hadn't realized it before.

She was so deep in her own dreams of the future she would have with Tyler that she almost walked right by him. But suddenly she was jerked from her daydream and pitchforked into the reality of the crowded Albuquerque street. There he was, standing not 20 feet away. The man who had shot her father.

Daisy stopped in her tracks. She turned to Tyler, but no words would come out of her mouth.

''What's wrong?'' he asked.

She pointed at the man.

Tyler looked and then turned back to her. ''Who are you pointing at? There are a dozen people in front of us.''

''That's the man who killed my father,'' Daisy finally managed to get out.

Hen grabbed for his gun, but he had allowed Laurel to talk him into putting his revolver aside while they were in Albuquerque. Tyler had his rifle with him, but he didn't want to shoot in the crowded streets. The killer didn't feel the same compunction. He grabbed his gun and fired at Daisy. Tyler brought up his rifle and returned his fire. He hit the man, but he disappeared down an alley amid screams and shouts of shocked and frightened pedestrians and vendors.

"Take care of her," Tyler said to Hen and dived into the alley after the killer.

Coming practically face-to-face with Daisy Singleton had been a terrible shock to Frank. Though he still smarted over his failure and Regis Cochrane's insulting remarks, he had decided it was time to head for Montana. He hated to admit failure, but he had decided it would be tempting fate to try to kill her again. She was too closely involved with the Randolphs. Since returning to town, he had heard plenty about their reputation, enough to convince him to make that trip north. Just his luck she should see him when he was on his way to the livery stable.

He should have turned around and disappeared into the first alley he came to, but he'd been too shocked to think clearly. He didn't know what had made him fire at Daisy. He'd missed her again, but it didn't matter. Both Randolphs knew what he looked like now.

Frank was relieved to see that Hen Randolph carried no gun—Frank would have been dead by now if he had—but he had been shocked to find out Tyler was so fast with a rifle. The bullet had entered his thigh just below his hip. He limped down the alley, frantically searching for a place of safety, a sanctuary where he could hide until he could get to a doctor. He didn't believe the wound was dangerous, but he was losing blood fast. And with it, his strength. He wouldn't be able to run much longer.

That was when he decided to go to Regis Cochrane's office. The son of a bitch had gotten him into this mess. He could hide him until the search died down. Nobody would think to look for him in the town's only bank.

"Go after him," Daisy pleaded with Hen. "You're the one who's supposed to be good with a gun."

Hen kept her moving rapidly along the street away from the buzzing spectators. He pulled back his coat to show that he wore no gun. "I can't help him unarmed."

"But you can't let him go alone."

"I don't intend to. But first I'm going to escort you to the hotel."

"I'm going with you."

"No, you're not," Hen said, and Daisy had no doubt that he meant it. "I have every intention of helping Tyler, but I won't have both our lives jeopardized by a female who doesn't know what she's doing." They reached the porch of Post's Exchange Hotel. Hen hurried her inside and upstairs. "Make certain she doesn't leave this room until I get back," he said to his startled wife. "Lock her up if necessary." He disappeared into the bedroom.

"What's happened?" Laurel asked. "Tyler didn't kill Guy Cochrane, did he?"

"No. I saw the man who tried to kill me," Daisy explained. "Tyler went after him."

Hen came out of the bedroom buckling on his guns. Laurel's face went white. "I can't leave Tyler to face that man alone, not after what he did for me in Sycamore Flats."

"I know," Laurel said, but Daisy noticed she gripped her hands so tight her knuckles turned white.

"This shouldn't take long. Tyler's already wounded him. Where are the boys?"

"I gave them permission to play in the plaza."

"Damn!" Hen swore, then kissed his wife before leaving without another word.

"Aren't you going to do anything?" Daisy asked when Laurel turned back to her.

"Yes. We're going to sit down, and you're going to tell me what happened today. And don't leave out a single word."

"But Tyler and your husband are out there. That man could kill them."

"I know. That's why you've got to talk and go on talking until they get back."

"But aren't you going to help him?"

"The best way I can help my husband is to have faith in him." She sat down, but Daisy couldn't keep still.

"But I can't sit here doing nothing."

"You can wait. Very often that's the best thing a woman can do."

Tyler wound his way through a maze of alleys that twisted between decaying adobes. Their thick walls and few windows and doors served as an effective sound barrier. Few people had even heard the shots. He couldn't find anyone who had seen a wounded man run past. He started to fear the trail had grown cold.

He kept going over the same ground, through the same alleys, knowing the killer must have traveled at least one of them, knowing there had to be a clue if he could only find it. Then he saw the spot of blood. Farther along the alley he found another one. He didn't need any more clues. He knew the killer was headed toward the bank building.

Frank managed to reach the back of the bank before his strength gave out. He leaned against the rough adobe wall, his breath coming in ragged gasps, his eyes darting right and left to see if anyone might have noticed him.

He was bleeding too much. He had to get to a doctor soon. He opened the back door and practically fell through the entrance. The bank had closed a little while earlier. At first he saw no one. Then he noticed Regis Cochrane peering out the front window, apparently trying to discover the reason for the shots.

Frank moved forward, leaning heavily on the counter

to support him. He felt his strength waning. A creaking floorboard caused Regis to turn. His complexion went ashen when he saw Frank.

"Get out!" he hissed. "I told you never to come here again."

"I've been shot. I need a doctor," Frank managed to say. He clawed at the counter to keep from falling.

"I'm not getting a doctor for you. Get out of here before somebody comes in."

"Damn you, you son of a bitch," Frank gasped. "I told you I need a doctor." Frank pulled his gun, but he had trouble lifting it. He felt terribly weak, weaker than he'd ever felt before. Everything seemed out of focus. Regis's rage-twisted face seemed to hang in space.

Regis rushed behind a counter, opened a drawer, and drew out a six-shooter. "You should have gone to Montana that first time, Frank." Regis lifted the gun and fired. The noise of the explosion rocked the small building.

The pain as the bullet buried itself in Frank's chest was like a white-hot poker being driven into his flesh. "You double-crossing bastard," he gasped as he fired one time.

Regis Cochrane's body quivered under the impact of the bullet, and slumped to the floor.

Tyler was only a short distance away when he heard the first muffled shot. He was within sight of the bank as the second shot rang out. He opened the back door of the bank to find the gunman slumped against the counter.

"The bastard tried to kill me," the gunman muttered. "He tried to kill me."

It took no more than a moment to find Regis Cochrane's body. He wasn't dead, but he was seriously wounded. Tyler turned back to the dying killer. "Who paid you to kill Miss Singleton and her father?" he asked, urgent in his need to know before the man died.

"Cochrane," the man managed to mutter in a voice that was a whisper.

"There were two other men. Who are they?" Tyler bent lower. The man's voice was a bare thread.

"Ed and Toby."

The front door opened and someone rushed in.

"Where are they?" Tyler asked. "If you want to see Cochrane pay for what he did to you, tell me where I can find them." Tyler had to put his ear almost to the man's lips to hear his answer.

"Ed and Toby Peck," the gunman said in a bare whisper. "They went to Mexico."

Tyler wanted to ask the name of the town, but it was too late. He was dead.

"Is he dead?" Hen asked.

"Yes," Tyler replied. He stood. "He told me the names of the other gunmen. All we have to do is get them to testify against Regis."

Together the brothers walked to where the banker still lay on the floor.

"If you want him around long, you'd better get a doctor in a hurry," Hen said.

"You're going on trial for murder, Cochrane," Tyler said to him. "Rustling, forgery, fraud, and I don't know how many other things."

Regis eyed him with a malevolent glare. "You have no proof, and you won't have any. Ed and Toby are dead. They were scalped by Apaches twenty miles below the border."

"Your Apaches or real Indians?" Tyler asked.

Regis shrugged.

"I'm going for the doctor," Hen said, "or he's not going to make it."

"Hand me my coat," Regis said as Hen hurried from the building. "I can't be seen without my coat."

He refused to let Tyler help him put it on. "You're just

387

as stupid as all the rest,'' he said, gasping hard for breath. ''You think you can beat me, but you can't. I don't need Daisy's ranch anymore. They let me in on the deal. I've already won.''

He struggled to get his arm in the sleeve; then his body went slack. He was dead.

Chapter Twenty-nine

Daisy was devastated. Guy had never loved her. He had only been after her ranch. But most of all she was horrified to learn that Regis Cochrane had been the man who hired the gunmen to kill her father.

"I'm glad you decided to let everyone think Frank Storach killed Mr. Cochrane when he wouldn't help him escape," Daisy said. "It would break Adora's heart to know what her father tried to do. And poor Mrs. Cochrane would never be able to hold her head up again."

"I'm just sorry Guy will get off as well," Tyler said. "I'm sure he was in on his father's plot."

"Not the part to kill Daddy," Daisy said. "I can't think well of Guy, but he would never do anything like that."

"I'm not interested in Guy or his family," Tyler said. "I'm only interested in marrying you as soon as possible."

"Soon enough for us to leave for the ranch during this calendar year?" Hen said.

"I told him we couldn't go home until after the wedding," Laurel said, explaining her husband's dark mood. "It was either that or take you back to the ranch until you're ready."

"I know you're still very upset over the Cochranes," Tyler began.

"I'm not going to put off marrying you because of it," Daisy said.

"A quiet wedding with just a few people," Laurel suggested.

"Today?" Hen asked hopefully.

"Soon," Daisy promised.

"Now I think it's time to leave them alone," Laurel said, taking her husband by the arm and propelling him toward the door.

"But they're so slow to get to the point," her husband objected.

"I think they're there."

"They'd damned well better be. At the rate they're going, you could have a second baby before the wedding."

"Not by myself."

Hen started to follow his wife, then turned back. He reached inside his coat and pulled out an envelope. "Zac sent you this."

"Is that the money he stole?" Daisy asked.

Hen nodded. "He stopped off in Santa Fe before heading to New Orleans. Apparently the pickings were good." His eyes cut toward the bedroom door. "I will expect a complete set of wedding plans when I return." He disappeared through the bedroom door.

"Well?" Tyler said, turning to Daisy.

"I want to get married as soon as you can arrange it. I'd like my uncle and cousin to attend the wedding."

Tyler settled next to Daisy. He clearly had his own plans for the next several minutes.

Daisy moved a little away from him. She needed to be

able to see his eyes. "I have a request first," she said. She could see Tyler stiffen. She hurried ahead. "You gave up your gold mines because of me. I know you planned to use that money to build your hotels, so I want you to take the money my grandfather left me."

"No." Tyler's answer was short and emphatic.

She hadn't expected him to agree, but she didn't understand the look in his eyes. It was almost defensive. "Then I guess I'll have to follow you all over those wretched mountains until you find gold. I can't say I'm looking forward to living in a cabin, but it shouldn't be too bad as long as we don't have any more blizzards."

"You would do that for me?" Tyler asked, dazed.

"The only time I've been happy is when I've been with you," Daisy confessed. "I'll follow you wherever you go."

"What about your freedom?"

"Laurel assures me she has more freedom now than ever before."

"So you're bargaining for a better position?"

"I'm asking for the only position I want, if you still want to marry me."

Tyler found a very effective way of convincing her his feelings hadn't changed.

"I have a confession to make," Tyler said a little while later. "I already found that gold."

"When? How?"

"I left Willie Mozel watching my claim. Apparently the first shovel he put in the ground hit pay dirt. Hen and Madison have already sold it for more than enough money to build my hotels."

"So you don't need my money at all."

"I need a partner," Tyler said. "Someone to share the responsibility fifty-fifty."

"What do you mean?"

"We each put up half the money. We each have an

equal vote in making the decisions.''

"And when we don't agree?''

"We'll take turns breaking the tie. I'll arm wrestle you to see who goes first.''

Leigh Greenwood is also the author of *Rose*, *Fern*, *Iris*, and *Laurel*. The proud parent of three children ranging in ages from 15 to 22, Leigh lives in Charlotte, NC, and is currently working on *Violet*, the next title in the *Seven Brides* series. You can write Leigh at P.O. Box 470761, Charlotte, NC 28226

LEIGH GREENWOOD

"Leigh Greenwood is a dynamo of a storyteller!"
—Los Angeles Times

Jefferson Randolph has never forgotten all he lost in the War Between The States—or forgiven those he has fought. Long after most of his six brothers find wedded bliss, the former Rebel soldier keeps himself buried in work, only dreaming of one day marrying a true daughter of the South. Then a run-in with a Yankee schoolteacher teaches him that he has a lot to learn about passion.

Violet Goodwin is too refined and genteel for an ornery bachelor like Jeff. Yet before he knows it, his disdain for Violet is blossoming into desire. But Jeff fears that love alone isn't enough to help him put his past behind him—or to convince a proper lady that she can find happiness as the newest bride in the rowdy Randolph clan.

_3995-8 $5.99 US/$7.99 CAN

Dorchester Publishing Co., Inc.
65 Commerce Road
Stamford, CT 06902

Please add $1.75 for shipping and handling for the first book and $.50 for each book thereafter. NY, NYC, PA and CT residents, please add appropriate sales tax. No cash, stamps, or C.O.D.s! All orders shipped within 6 weeks via postal service book rate. Canadian orders require $2.00 extra postage and must be paid in U.S. dollars through a U.S. banking facility.

Name _____

Address _____

City _____ State _____ Zip _____

I have enclosed $_____ in payment for the checked book(s). Payment <u>must</u> accompany all orders.☐ Please send a free catalog.

LEIGH GREENWOOD'S

SEVEN BRIDES
LAUREL

"Fun, exuberant, and entertaining with a special charm all its own!"   *—Romantic Times*

Although Hen Randolph is the perfect choice for a sheriff in the Arizona Territory, he is no one's idea of a model husband. The trail-weary cowboy has just broken free from his six rough-and-ready brothers, and he isn't about to start a family of his own. Then a beauty with a tarnished reputation catches his eye, and the thought of taking a wife arouses him as never before.

But Laurel Blackthorne has been hurt too often to trust any man—least of all one she considers a ruthless, coldhearted gunslinger. Not until Hen proves that drawing quickly and shooting true aren't his only assets will she give him her heart. When his pistol is at last snug in its holster, Laurel will reward the virile lawman with the rapture of her love's sweet splendor—and take her place as the newest bride to tame a Randolph's heart.

_3744-0 $5.99 US/$6.99 CAN

McCrory's Lady — Shirl Henke

"Historical romance at its best!"
—Romantic Times

Courageous and cunning, Maggie Worthington has survived alone in the rugged West, earning her keep in frontier cathouses. Once a proper, Boston-bred lady, she is more than a handful for any gunslinger with an eye for trouble. But the sharp-tongued madam finally meets her match in a rancher with the burr of a Scotsman and the body of a god.

To save his daughter's tattered reputation, Colin McCrory needs to take a wife. And even though women are scarce in the Arizona Territory, he is certain he could wed one whose past isn't as sordid as Maggie's. Yet the feisty and defiant beauty's scorching kisses fire his blood as never before, and one night in her silken embrace convinces him that he has to tame her, to possess her, to make her McCrory's lady.

_3773-4 $5.99 US/$6.99 CAN

FROST FLOWER

SONYA BIRMINGHAM

Out in the wilds of Red Oak Hollow, pretty Misty Malone has come across plenty of critters, but none surprises her more than a knocked-out, buck-naked stranger. Taught by her granny to cure ills with herbs, Misty knows a passel of cures that will heal the unknown man, yet does she dare give him the most potent remedy of all—her sweet Ozark love?

After being robbed, stripped, and left for dead, Adam Davenport awakes to a vision in buckskins who makes his heart race like white lightning. But since the Malones and the Davenports have been feuding longer than a coon's age, the St. Louis doctor's only chance to win Misty is to hide his real name—and pray that a dash of mountain magic and a heap of good loving will hold the rustic beauty down when she finds out the truth.

_3775-0 $4.99 US/$5.99 CAN

An Angel's Touch *Where angels go, love is sure to follow.*

Don't miss these unforgettable romances that combine the magic of angels and the joy of love.

Daemon's Angel by Sherrilyn Kenyon. Cast to the mortal realm by an evil sorceress, Arina has more than her share of problems. She is trapped in a temptress's body and doomed to lose any man she desires. Yet even as Arina yearns for the safety of the pearly gates, she finds paradise in the arms of a Norman mercenary. But to savor the joys of life with Daemon, she will have to battle demons and risk her very soul for love.

_52026-5 $4.99 US/$5.99 CAN

Forever Angels by Trana Mae Simmons. Thoroughly modern Tess Foster has everything, but when her boyfriend demands she sign a prenuptial agreement Tess thinks she's lost her happiness forever. Then her guardian angel sneezes and sends the woman of the nineties back to the 1890s—and into the arms of an unbelievably handsome cowboy. But before she will surrender to a marriage made in heaven, Tess has to make sure that her guardian angel won't sneeze again—and ruin her second chance at love.

_52021-4 $4.99 US/$5.99 CAN

Dorchester Publishing Co., Inc.
65 Commerce Road
Stamford, CT 06902

Please add $1.75 for shipping and handling for the first book and $.50 for each book thereafter. NY, NYC, PA and CT residents, please add appropriate sales tax. No cash, stamps, or C.O.D.s. All orders shipped within 6 weeks via postal service book rate. Canadian orders require $2.00 extra postage and must be paid in U.S. dollars through a U.S. banking facility.

Name _____

Address _____

City _____ State _____ Zip _____

I have enclosed $_____ in payment for the checked book(s).

Payment <u>must</u> accompany all orders.☐ Please send a free catalog.